The Holding

The End Time Saga
Book Five

Daniel Greene

ISBN: 978-1-7333704-1-7

For all my brothers - nobody goes it alone.
Bare is the back of a brotherless man.

ALVARADO
Outpost Barron, Minnesota

"God, it's cold."

United States Marine Corps Major Isabel Alvarado glanced up from the map she was studying.

Lieutenant Wess rubbed his gloved hands together across the table from her. The twenty-two-year-old's face was rosy. His polar fleece watch cap was pulled down past his ears, almost shading his eyes. He gave her a smile, unsure whether or not displaying some sort of weakness was appropriate. She let her eyes put that display to rest.

The wind howled outside, buffeting the tent flaps that were sealed shut to trap in what little heat their bodies manufactured.

Captain Butler's pale brown eyes shifted over to the young man in disdain and he snorted. He was an inch over average height and had an athletic build, but there was a reason she'd let Captain Heath travel south and command the northern portion of Iowa. Butler needed supervision, so she kept him close and let her reliable captain leave.

Her coffee-colored eyes considered Wess for a moment. "Move closer to the heater." With a flick of her chin, she shooed him.

A small space heater had been pilfered from the RV grocery store on the island of Barron where she had set up her outpost in the middle of the Mississippi River. The RV park had provided a perfect space to set up their outpost. Easily controlled access points, latrine facilities, and a place to dock their watercraft, most of which had been loaned to Colonel Kinnick.

The lieutenant stepped to the other side of the room, crouching down next to the heater. "Oh yeah, that's the stuff." He turned and looked at them over his shoulder. "Can finally feel my fingers again."

Alvarado ignored him and scrutinized her map. As winter took the upper Midwest by storm, her sorties into La Crosse had drastically decreased. This meant a significant increase of infected persons within the small city across the river. With the miserable blizzard engulfing their camp, she hadn't had eyes on the urban area for weeks, making her effectively combat blind with no intelligence on what the infected were doing.

She had enough experience fighting them to know all about the things they were most likely doing. Eating men alive. A horde could overrun a rifle squad in a minute. She knew. She had lost plenty of Marines. Each missing face from her command stung like the biting gales, but she held on. Someone had to fight this ugly war to the bitter end, and that kind of fight made sense to a poor girl who grew up in the equivalent of a barrio in south Los Angeles.

It was a fight for every scrap of food. A fight for every inch of space. A fight to survive the neighborhood gangs. Just like the neighborhood pit bull that was on its own. No master, no owner, only surviving by its own determined will. That kind of environment built resiliency that was compounded indefinitely by the Marine Corps.

The tent flap pushed inward. Something scraped along the material searching for a way in. Before her eyes darted for the tent entrance, her hand dipped behind her to her M4A1 carbine. Her fingers wrapped around the stock, and she placed her other hand along the magazine well. Captain Butler did the same from across the table, his movements fuzzy in her peripheral vision.

The tent unzipped fast. A man in woodland camouflage and a crystalizing frozen white beard stuck his face inside.

"Well goddamn. Hell of a welcome for the sumbitch stuck out here." The man stepped a snowy boot inside the tent. Snow fell from his pants and boots, dropping to the floor.

Wind whistled a baritone note, and the snowflakes glided past the opening at a diagonal angle, attempting to go parallel with the ground. He quickly closed the flaps, sealing them back with a zip.

Alvarado placed her M4A1 back against the tent wall, and her eyes turned to him expectantly. "Master Guns Pike, how are our Marines doing along the perimeter?"

Pike clapped his hands together and little specks of white puffed into the air. "Just about frozen stiff."

"Too bad they don't freeze stiff."

He peeled off his gloves. "That would make this business a bit easier."

She gave him a terse nod with respect. "Nothing's ever easy."

Grunting his agreement, he said, "If it was easy, they would have sent the Army." He walked over to the space heater and draped his gloves over the top. "We got the boys rotating in and out every thirty minutes."

"Captain Butler and I were discussing how to keep tabs on La Crosse without the SURCs." She didn't want to risk damaging her precious few small unit riverine craft in a temperamental river with chunks of floating ice cascading downstream.

Wrinkles creased around Pike's gray eyes. "Not much we can do without them and the bridge gone."

"I agree, but I'm not putting the SURCs into a river filled with chunks of floating ice."

A small smile touched Pike's face. "I wouldn't either."

"I need intelligence though."

Melting ice dripped off Pike's beard onto the map. He wiped the thawing hair with a hand, and the white-bearded senior non-commissioned officer grew younger before their eyes.

Pike reached out and touched the map. "I could lead a couple platoons north to the railroad tracks crossing the river, cut through French Island. It's only a hundred meters there. I'll have to see it for myself, but I'm sure we can improvise a way across. We can scale across with rope lines. That'd put us on the edge of the La Crosse."

The railroad had been blown by Lieutenant Colonel Eldridge months prior as part of the initial lockdown of Barron Island.

Alvarado didn't smile but grinned on the inside. She never let her men see her smile and didn't care if they thought she was a mad devil with a resting bitch face. Early on, she knew that's what it took to survive this debacle of a war. If anyone was going to make it out of this mess, it would be her Marines. "Improvise, adapt, overcome."

Pike lifted stiff eyebrows. "That is what we do."

Butler placed his fists on the table still considering the plan. "Create a link to the mainland that only men can cross. Then we don't have to risk our remaining SURCs. Excellent idea."

Alvarado hid another inward grin and thanked the Lord for Pike. Marines like Pike were instrumental in their success. Solid. Dependable. Cool under fire. A stellar Marine all around.

A weathered smile settled on Pike's features still thawing from the blizzard. "Can't imagine there'd be too many takers for that mission. Lieutenant, you want to join?"

The rosy cheeked lieutenant looked their way. His face said he wasn't exactly sure of his abilities, but his voice came out strong. "I can lead the recon."

Pike's gray eyes met hers. There was no doubt who the men would be looking to in the field. His eyes reassured her of success. "I'll make sure nothing happens."

She regarded Pike for a moment. "Good. Come morning, hopefully this storm will die down and Lieutenant Wess and Master Guns will lead a recon mission north." She was acutely aware that her command was only shrinking. Between the ongoing conflict and the forces she'd sent south with Kinnick she had one-hundred-and-thirty-six Marines under her command. Dependable experienced Marines weren't to be squandered.

A deep moan crawled over the outside of the tent, probing for a way inside. It melded with the swirl of restless snow and the howls of winter.

The outline of Pike's mouth tightened. The seasoned Marine had an ear for when the wind didn't sound right.

Butler followed his gaze, tilting his head to the side and narrowing his brow line at the tent entrance.

The green flap fluttered as bitter air beat the command tent. The moan grew louder now.

"Master Guns," Alvarado said, giving the entrance a stone-faced look.

Pike scooped up his carbine, warily stepping for the entrance. As he reached the flap, he crouched and unzipped the zipper with one hand while the other held his M4 pointed outward. The tent door flipped open, and the bitter cold invaded the tent.

Dropping to one knee, he twisted. He peered one way outside and then the other. "Can't see shit out there." He lowered his weapon and turned back to her. "What can we do to get those spotlights on?"

"We only have enough generator power for the ones by the interstate. Otherwise we freeze," Alvarado said, turning back to the map. *How do we fight this and win?*

Something blurred near his head.

"Ah, what the fuck?" he said. His M4 reported with resounding booms.

Pike turned around glaring at her. Blood trickled down the side of his face. He lifted his hand from a hole where his ear used to be, staring at the blood on his hands as if unsure of whose blood it was. Shoeless feet lay in front of the tent, bluish-gray from the elements.

"That sumbitch." He raised a hand to his ear feeling for the piece of him that had disappeared in the blink of an eye.

Her carbine pressed harder into her shoulder pocket.

Pike's jaw widened. "Don't . . . point those." Words stopped eking from his mouth. It worked open and closed, but now only low gurgles seeped out. He opened his mouth again as if he tried to catch his breath and then his jaw snapped closed like they'd beaten him in an argument. His head dipped forward. Tilting his head to the side, he stared at them in confusion. "Bastard . . . took . . . my ear."

"Pike, how about you prone out for me," Alvarado commanded. She removed her hand from the magazine well and pointed down at the ground with her finger. *He's gonna turn. He's gonna turn,* her mind screamed at her. *They always turn.*

Pike's face shook and his eyes blinked in rapid succession. His mouth worked as he tried to say something, but only a guttural moan came forth. "Iooooo." His eyes had shifted to the color of the snowdrift that piled higher by the second around their tent.

She didn't blink when she fired her weapon into his head. She looked him in the eyes; the man deserved that much for his service. He deserved that and a hell of a lot more he would never see. *Boom.* Pike's head shot backward and he fell to his knees and face-planted into the floor. Peering over her sights, she scanned past his body to outside the tent.

Snowflakes continued to fall, unfazed by her deadly form of mercy. Blood poured from Pike's skull, spilling on the tent floor, puddling with nowhere to go.

Her steps were soft and her mind focused as she walked forward, her carbine ready to engage any additional threats. Sidestepping Pike's body, she took an angle on the entrance.

A deep darkness blanketed the night, making it almost impossible to see. The snow had settled like an ivory mantle on the land. The wind bit at her face like it was infected. She stepped through the flaps and into the storm. The infected man Pike had shot was naked and bluish-gray, his body convulsing in its second death.

In the distance, a spotlight beamed down Interstate 14. Flurries hindered her vision as she tried to penetrate the speckled white fog. She brought a hand up to her face, trying to block icy gusts. Dark shapes sat behind the perimeter sandbags and barriers.

She glanced over her shoulder to the large warehouse that served as a barracks for a host of her Marines. Everything appeared quiet. The door burst open. Marines ran into the night. One screamed as another Marine brought him down. More Marines emerged from their insulated tents.

"How the hell did it get in? Perimeters up," Butler said behind her.

"I don't know."

Gunshots rippled from the warehouse. Marines sprinted through the snow in nothing but their undergarments, vests, and guns.

"Get formed up! We got a breach!" Butler shouted.

Calls for help rode the winds to her, distant voices, individual locations unknown. Her men fought and grappled with hostiles near the barricade.

"How are they getting in?" she said into the darkness. She spun on Lieutenant Wess.

"Get your platoon from the warehouse over to the barricade, and I want the perimeter lights on now."

The wide-eyed lieutenant nodded and ran toward the warehouse.

The report of gunfire overcame the shrill blowing air.

"Come on, Butler," Alvarado snarled.

She sprinted into the frigid landscape. It crunched as she sank almost a foot into the breakable icy crust absorbing her feet.

Headwind pummeled her and she ignored her body begging to be covered with more and more layers of thermal. Her hands had it the worst, she could almost feel the cold cracking her skin. Even with her gloves on, they were no match for extended time in the cold.

Crystals started to form inside her nose. Every inhale hardened her nostrils both inside and out. Sucking in the cold air only accelerated the process.

She neared the roofed metal barricade encased with sandbags and concrete barriers between the outpost and Interstate 14. It was slightly more effective than being in the open, keeping the elements from the Marines. She scanned the barricade. A dead body lay in a drift. The lack of uniform labeled it as a Zulu and not one of hers. Black blood soaked the snow around its head.

The sounds of men struggling caught her ear, and she ran to the machine gun emplacement. Two infected had one of her Marines pinned with his back against the concrete. The Marine held the dead away from him by their necks. She growled, her lips rising as she shot. *Clap-clap.* Any variable in her aim and she could have hit her Marine. As she let her weapon lower, the African-American Marine tossed the bodies to the ground.

He scooped his M27 automatic rifle and hugged it to his chest. His eyes were wide as he fled the barricade. "Thank you," he said, his breath fogging in rhythm.

"Where are they coming from?" she said up at him.

"I don't know, Major. They came from inside the camp."

"How's that possible, Lance Corporal?" Butler yelled at him.

"They grabbed Robinson and Hewitt. We were watching the perimeter, not the camp."

Alvarado scanned past the interstate along the naked winter trees of the island. She thought they were trees at first. Trees swaying and bending against the might of the wind, but if you stared long enough, they were there. They were short shadows stumbling in the darkness, moving painstakingly slow, but they came anyway, a flood of frozen water in dead human form.

The spotlights hummed as they warmed, shedding only a fraction of their illuminating potential.

A squad of Marines jogged up, breathing hard. Gunfire accelerated from the other end of the outpost.

"Barracks is clear, ma'am," Wess said.

She ignored her subordinate, continuing to eye the dead on her island. Wess followed her gaze, squinting. His voice eked out a quiet, "Ma'am?"

Spotlights around the base went hot, piercing the darkness and trees with light. Hundreds of the dead marched through the trees. "Jesus Christ."

She ran forward. "Help me turn this thing." Marines joined her, grunting as they turned the giant spotlight. Its base groaned over the frozen ground.

Thousands of lumens beamed off the road and ahead on the Mississippi River. The river had gone from chocolate milk to a sea of black with bits and pieces of white underneath.

The river cracked and rippled as they trod over the frozen water but held its solid state. The cold air closed her lungs, inflaming them, but it wasn't the bitterness that took her breath. It wasn't the loss of one of her best Marines although that stung like a barbed arrow to the chest. It was the thousands of dead that marched over the frozen Mississippi River.

She hopped down from the barricade. "Rally to the alternate position."

"All of us?" Wess asked.

"Everyone." And the small pit bull of a woman and her Marines ran before the dead.

AHMED
Unknown

The inside of his eyelids were a soft pinkish brown. Thick reddish veins ran like blood tributaries on a pink field. He emerged from the darkness with a soft realization that he was alive. His eyes darted from side to side beneath the thin skin as if hiding in apprehension of what lay on the other plane. He flicked them open and gasped a breath between his lips.

Blinking rapidly, he inhaled the stuffy air with a hint of must to it. He exhaled the wondrous stuff as his brain tried to comprehend the sight above him. It was a fuzzy collection of tan wooden planks. Darker knots lined the wood. *That's a ceiling.* He worked himself on his elbows and a quilted blanket fell from his bare shoulders. *I'm alive.*

Pain emanated from his chest, reminding him that he yet lived. He peered down. White bandages wrapped around his torso. He took a hand and gingerly explored his wound. It smarted beneath his fingertips. *I got shot. The Wolf Riders. Macleod murdered Ollie and Weston. Steele and Jackson's war along the river.*

Dread filled him along with the fear of not knowing where he was. His eyes bolted around the room. A weathered rocking chair rested nearby along with a vanity with a mirror. He lifted the blankets, becoming acutely aware of his nakedness under the quilt. He let his covering fall back over his body.

His voice rasped like a metal file scratching over metal. "Hello?" Searching the room for a way to escape, he located a lone window to his right. A board had been hammered over it, rusty nails ringing around the edges. No light seeped through the cracks, meaning it was dark outside.

He rolled over and placed his feet on the chilled floor that made him think he was in a freezer. Wrapping the blanket tighter around his body, he hurriedly pushed himself upright. Blood rushed to his head and his vision grew clouded. The muscles in his legs did nothing he asked them to do. He stuck out a hand to steady himself but collapsed on the floor with a thump.

Pain shot through his chest and into his back. He laid there for a moment, letting the cold air wash over him. He imagined that laying on ice was the same as the floor.

Hallway floorboards creaked outside as someone approached his room. Their footsteps struck the ground hard, like they moved in anger.

Ahmed's head swiveled as he tried to find something to fight with. He searched beneath the twin bed. A worn grungy sneaker that used to be white lay with its sole ripped open. He grabbed it, holding it close to his upper body. The footsteps stopped. Shadows of feet shifted beneath the door.

The faded brass doorknob with nicks and scratches started to rotate. It slowly ground its way around as if it resisted the hand that turned it.

The door groaned open like a lazy yawn. A man stuck his head inside. His beard and mustache were thin like a man in his late teens or early twenties. Ahmed swung the shoe with all his might on the top of his foot.

"Jeepers creepers!" The man jumped up and down on his other foot. "Little bugger got me!"

The sounds of more feet thundered down the hall. Ahmed crawled to his knees and lunged at the man. His chest screamed, but he ignored the searing pain. Lifting the man off the other foot, he took him down with a crash into the adjacent wall. He scrambled up the man's torso like a wild beast.

The man shouted. "Help me, Jesus, he's got me!" He kicked Ahmed with his free foot and knocked his head into the wall. "Help!"

Addled, Ahmed pressed a forearm into his neck. The young man's eyes widened as he struggled to breathe, fingers digging into Ahmed's flesh.

Cold steel settled on top of Ahmed's head. It was the unmistakable harsh touch of a gun barrel. "Now you listen loud and clear, boy. You let go of him nice and easy and nobody has to die today."

Flashbacks to his beatings at the hands of Puck's cronies hit Ahmed like a lightning bolt, driving him to continue to kill the man in his grasp despite certain death. He grudgingly lifted his head and released his captor.

The black hole of the metal barrel was less than an inch from his face. The man holding it had a full dark mud-colored goatee. He probably didn't need more than a week to grow it, and curled hair hung down to his shoulders. His face was thin and oval-shaped like the man in Ahmed's grip. He was older than the man beneath him, but no more than thirty. His eyes were a pale blue and pierced with the strength of hateful daggers.

He pressed the handgun painfully into Ahmed's skull. "Nice and slow, you brown bastard."

Ahmed let go of the man beneath him and sat with his back against the wall.

"Get up, Kyle," he commanded. There was a rural twang to his voice, but not a deep Southern accent, more of just a regular country boy.

The young man crawled away from Ahmed, getting to his feet. Ahmed watched at their mercy beneath the cool gaze of the man with the handgun.

"What'd I tell you about being aware of your surroundings? We pay attention to what is happening around us." The bigger man gave Kyle a shove.

"I know, Jim, but we're in our house."

"With a man we know nothing about."

Ahmed thought about snatching the pistol from him. His heart pounded in his chest. *It's got to be quick.*

The man faced Ahmed as if he read his thoughts. "What am I going to do with a feral dog like you?" Taking a step closer, he extended his arm in Ahmed's direction lining up his shot. His lip quivered with the thought of blowing Ahmed's brains into the wall behind him.

"Jim!" came a female voice. A woman shouldered past him and raced for Ahmed.

"Goddamn it, Sadie!"

She dropped to her knees by Ahmed and examined his chest. Her eyes were blue, not as pale as Jim's, but her appearance was enough like him for

Ahmed to think they were closely related.

He grimaced as she checked his bandages. Her eyes fluttered to his. Eyes that said she knew him, but he couldn't remember ever meeting her before now. Her blue eyes lingered for a moment before she whirled away, focused on her task.

"We didn't save his life just to kill him when he woke up," she said into Ahmed's chest.

Jim shook his head. "Shouldn't have taken him in. He's trouble. He attacked Kyle like one of those things out there."

"I'm not one of those things."

Sadie wrapped an arm around him, and using the wall, helped him to his feet.

"We don't know anything about him," Jim said, waving a gun in his direction. "He's fine."

"You don't think we should ask who put a bullet in him? What if they come back to finish the job? You're putting our whole family at risk."

"Don't tell me about putting the whole family at risk."

Jim's mouth snapped shut. He scratched at his goatee in anger. "You of all people know why I did that."

She looked back at Jim. "And this man needed our help." She half-carried him back into his room and sat him down on the bed. It bounced as they plopped down together, too firm and springy for his taste, but it beat the cold floor a hundred times out of a hundred. She removed his arm from around her and let him pick his feet up and place them inside the sheets.

"There we go," she said with a smile. Ahmed watched her as she busied herself with tucking his sheets around him. Her face grew a bit rosy as her hands neared his thighs. Large swooping muddy brown curls hung past her shoulders not dissimilar to Jim's, but more feminine, like care was put into them instead of a wild indifference.

She took the heavy quilt and draped it back over his body. The weight was immediately comforting.

"Who are you?"

Ignoring him, she bent back toward the end table and picked up a glass of water. She brought it to his lips and he eagerly gulped it down. The water brought a coolness to the fire in his chest, quenching the rawness of his throat.

"Not too fast. You'll get sick."

He gave her a weak smile, watching her as she set down the glass on the side table. "Where am I?"

"Missouri, honey. You obviously ain't from around here." Her face was a thin oval, same as the other men, yet she was softer. He didn't know if it was her skin or her slender eyebrows, but they were the same yet different.

"Are those your brothers?"

"Ha. Can't pick your family." Her smile lessened. "The one with the gun is my older brother Jim, and the younger one is Kyle. Me and Vicky were in the middle." Her voice grew quiet as if the mention of Vicky hurt her.

His eyes read her for a moment. "I'm sorry. I didn't mean to bring up anything."

"No." She dismissed him straightening his blanket. "We all look alike, don't we?" She wore a sad smile, and water filled her eyes, stopping at the corners.

"Yes. Your faces are all the same."

She wiped the corner of her eye and blushed. "I hope not too much."

A short smile split his chapped lips. "Not too much at all."

Her cheeks reddened and she turned away.

"I'm Ahmed."

She glanced back. "Ah-med," she said, sounding it out, the word clunky on her tongue. "That's different." Her eyes said she didn't quite believe him. "What kind of name is that?"

"Egyptian." He would not hide his identity, which a name was a part of.

"Oh." She sat quiet for a moment as if afraid she'd offended him.

"I was born here."

"Why were you out there?"

"I was scouting for my group."

Her eyes grew fearful and her throat moved as she gulped. "What group?"

He watched her, judging. He was at their mercy. The wrong answer could bring about his death even after they'd saved his. The fact remained he knew nothing about these people. They could be allied with the Wolf Riders, Jackson, or be a bunch of hillbilly assholes like Puck's band.

"I was with a group of survivors. We were trying to find a way to reach Hacklebarney, Iowa."

Her eyes lit up. "Well, I know where that is. About thirty-five miles north of here. We're near the top of Missouri."

Okay, it's not so far if I have to run. "How'd you find me?"

"Luck," she said her voice hushed. "I'm gonna let you get some rest before supper."

He was exhausted from his short excursion from the bed. "I am tired."

Her hand fell to his arm. It warmed his skin. "When we found you, you were almost dead. A bullet through the chest."

He remembered the moment. It was burned into his memory and soul. The bullet had entered his body like a stream of icy fire through his upper back, boring a hole through him. Blood sprayed from the front as it exited his body. The thought made his chest ache. Frigid air crystalized his lungs as he ran from the men riding motorcycles, each breath ragged and blistering.

"The Wolf Riders. Have you seen them?"

Her eyes narrowed in confusion. "I don't know what that is."

"They're a motorcycle gang, black wolves on their vests."

She shook her head no. "I haven't heard of them."

His heartbeat slowed down and he exhaled, relief washing over him. "They betrayed us." He adjusted his head on his pillow. He felt so weak but safer than a moment before.

"Get some rest. I'll wake you for supper. It'll be good to get some whole food in you. You've been in and out for a long time."

"Thank you, Sadie. I can't put into words what I owe you."

A smile curved on her lips. "You're welcome." She stepped softly toward the door and slipped out. The door clicked shut.

A man's voice spoke heavily in the hallway. Ahmed could only catch bits and pieces of what he said. "He's not safe." and "Them." Sadie's voice followed and the voices calmed.

Metal scraped along the doorjamb. *They are locking me in. Is that for my safety or theirs?*

He stared at the ceiling, wondering who these people were. Like a heavy quilted blanket, slumber draped over him.

JOSEPH
Cheyenne Mountain Complex, Colorado

Joseph studied a boxy screen, his arms folded beneath him. His biohazard suit crinkled as he tried to adjust his glasses from the tip of his nose back to the bridge. A thick clear plastic faceplate got in the way of his finger, and he had to press harder, indenting the plastic. He scrunched his nose trying to settle the glasses and tipped his head back until they settled into their rightful place.

"There." The needle brushed the membrane of the cell they had been searching for. "That one."

"I got it," Dr. Desai said. She pursed her lips inside her HAZMAT suit as she worked in deep concentration. The needle deflected off the side of the cell. She audibly exhaled through his headset. She tried again, this time penetrating the membrane. Hitting a button on her controls, the needle released its fluid. The cell's interior darkened.

"That's the last one." He looked at her with a short grin.

Her white teeth shone back from behind her suit and she let out an exhausted sigh. "If this works, our production will dramatically increase."

"That's some quality work, doctors," Byrnes said. The tall army doctor gave them a slight smile, his gaunt cheeks creasing. He reached out and squeezed Dr. Desai's shoulder in a friendly manner. "I'm confident that this will work, and we'll be able to produce a few hundred vials of the vaccine a day, instead of a hundred, without keeping all of us on a twenty-four hour rotation."

16

"Some regular sleep would be nice," she said.

"An end to shift work," Joseph added. He hated the odd hours and the interrupted sleep patterns. Since the successful testing of the Primus Necrovirus vaccine and the following outbreak, they'd been on shift work to ensure maximum levels of production for a grueling six weeks.

Day after day, they produced as much vaccine as they possibly could, building the government's stockpile. They lacked the pharmaceutical infrastructure to mass-produce the vaccine and had to rely on themselves for manual creation. Slowly, their stockpiles grew but only by one vaccine at a time. Dr. Desai's improvement on their process could exponentially upgrade their production.

A faint look of amusement crossed Byrnes's face, and as quick as it came, it disappeared. "No one said we would get more sleep, but we can produce more of the vaccine now."

"Why do we even bother to innovate?" Joseph said to Desai.

She shook her head. "Just so we can work more."

"Remember why we do this," Byrnes said.

"We know why we're here."

The implications of failure were well-known to the team of doctors. The remains of mankind depended on them to produce and vaccinate all that remained, giving them a fraction of a chance to survive the extinction level event. The magnitude of the event hadn't been seen in millions of years, and nothing like it might ever be seen again. One thing was for certain, there was no guarantee that Homo sapiens as a species would emerge from anywhere but the ground.

Joseph walked to the biohazard glove box. Although his suit covered his entire body, including his hands, he placed his hands inside the rubberized chamber gloves. He took the culture dish Dr. Desai had been working with and carefully took the small amount of fluid and added it to another vial.

On the far side of the chamber was an add-on glass box containing a smaller white box. Joseph opened the lid and placed the last vial in the small six-vial centrifuge. He hit the start button on the control panel, and a light humming filled the chamber. He disengaged, removing his hands, and stood.

An unknown voice scratched over the PA system. "Colonel Byrnes."

On the other side of the glass, six soldiers in black tactical gear filled the observation room of the biohazard lab. They carried black MP5s slung to the center of their chests. Their faces were covered with black balaclavas exposing only their eyes.

Byrnes went to the PA on the side of the room and depressed the button. "We're just finishing."

Desai peered at the men. "What are they doing here?"

"I don't know." The sight of guns still made Joseph's stomach nervously jump despite his limited use of them in the past. He'd never had enough time handling a weapon to acquire any sort of comfort in their presence.

The soldier nearest the glass hit his button. "Sir, we need to see you now."

"I'll be right out." Byrnes turned around and gave Joseph a quizzical look.

"What's with all the guns?" Joseph said through his mic.

"I'm sure it's just a precaution."

Byrnes studied the men for a moment. "I'm ready to get out of this suit anyway. Let's call it."

The three doctors crowded into the pressurization chamber. Their boots echoed off the metal-grated floor. Nozzles appeared from the walls and sprayed a disinfecting liquid over the doctors' biohazard suits. Then came the fog as the pressures were equalized between the two rooms.

A green light flickered on above them and the doors rolled open. They unzipped each other's protective suits and stepped out of them, hanging them on racks to be inspected by technicians for continued quality. After stripping off their scrubs, they threw them in a burn bag.

They went through another sliding door then proceeded into a locker room. Dr. Desai veered toward the other side where the female doctors changed with more privacy.

Joseph went to his locker and lifted the handle. A pair of khaki slacks, a sky-blue button-down shirt, and brown loafers were inside. Taped to the interior of his locker door was a picture of Dr. Weinroth with her plum auburn hair, sharp eyes, not the milky virus-ridden ones at the end, and pretty smile.

"She was a good doctor," Byrnes said over his locker. He buttoned his ACU jacket with both hands.

"She was a great doctor."

Byrnes nodded in agreement. "You're right. My words did not convey the magnitude of her knowledge and sacrifice." He ran a hand down his jacket and trousers, smoothing them. He grabbed his shoes and took a seat.

Joseph grabbed his pants and slipped them over his thin, pale, almost hairless legs.

The door to the locker room banged open startling him. Soldiers in all black marched in, fanning out to cover all exits. He hurriedly tugged his pants all the way up.

"Excuse me," Dr. Desai said loudly.

Byrnes glanced at the door. "Surely this is not that pressing. I'll be out in a few minutes."

The leader, a taller version of the other soldiers, shouldered his way past Joseph. He steadied himself with his locker. "What's your deal?"

"Colonel Byrnes, come with me. Now!"

"Excuse me, soldier. You do not give me orders." Byrnes stared up at the man in anger. "Who's your commanding officer?" He slipped on a shoe. "In fact, I'm going to pay him a visit right now." The colonel stood.

"Sir, I'm not sure you understand."

"I bloody well do, you insubordinate prick."

The soldier grabbed the colonel by his arm.

Byrnes knocked it away. "Don't touch me."

Two more soldiers charged past Joseph; one shoulder-checked him as he rushed by. Joseph's back hit the metal lockers with a crashing bang. It felt like a reenactment from his freshman year of high school, popular jocks manhandling him. "What the hell?"

They pounced on Colonel Byrnes, bending his arms dangerously behind his back.

"What's the meaning of this?"

They quickly forced his head down and led him out of the locker room. The other soldiers filed out after Byrnes.

"Where are you taking him?" Joseph called after them.

The door clanged closed. Joseph jogged after them, pushing past the door. The men filed out of the observation room and into the hall. "Wait!"

The soldier in the back turned around, bringing his submachine gun slightly level. "Sir. Do not move any closer."

Joseph stopped, raising his hands in the air. "Do you know how important he is to our medical team? We need him here."

"It's none of your concern. Go back about your regular business."

Joseph took a careful step closer. "We are working on a vaccine for the virus. So we can stop what's happening."

His words had zero effect on the soldier, and his weapon raised to his shoulder. "You heard me. Stand down."

Joseph held back and pointed at the lab. "We need him. Tell me where you're taking him so I can clear this up. Who's your supervisor?"

The soldier stuck out a gloved palm and fingers up. "Everything is fine." The soldier about-faced and jogged down the hall.

Joseph stepped out into the white-walled corridor, watching him jog to rejoin his comrades marching away. "You don't understand what you're doing!" But his calls fell on deaf ears.

"What was that all about?" Dr. Desai said. She wound her black curly hair into a loose bun on the back of her head.

"I don't know, but not good by the looks of it."

"Let's see if we can find Nguyen or Hollis. Maybe they know something."

The soldiers turned a corner and disappeared with Byrnes.

STEELE
Camp Forge, Iowa

His index finger tapped the hard wood of the parlor desk in distinct beats. Twisting his neck to the side, he tried to stretch his right arm while making a tight fist with his hand. It was still weak but grew stronger by the day. He suspected some sort of nerve damage, but it had healed enough to support his now dominant left hand.

A fire crackled in the fireplace. The flames snapped and popped, kicking up the chimney with tiny sparks. Any little distraction took him away from his task because he didn't want anything to do with the notebook in front of him.

He massaged his beard, rubbing the long soft whiskers as he thought. *What do I do with them?* The paper was lined with the names and units of 367 American servicemen. Rogue enemy combatants in this war but once honorable men. Now he was plagued with taking action, a decision he had delayed for too long.

Steele stood, feeling a loose pellet deep inside his leg grind as he stretched. He walked over to the parlor window. Faded wood framed the panes. It was cooler near the old farmhouse's windows, and he clasped his hands behind his back. The skin on his hand was cool clamped inside the other, his now dominant left hand engulfing his weaker right.

Where there had only been one barn when Steele first arrived at the Reynolds Farm, now there were four. Three were made of freshly cut, light tan wood and had been erected in two weeks' time with the help of the Amish.

About forty yards away from the barns, the cabins started. Thirty sizable round-log cabins sat in rows, each one holding at least twenty people. Anyone that hadn't been able to find residence in Hacklebarney ended up in a cabin. They created the framework of Camp Forge, one of the few outposts lining the western shores of the Mississippi River in an attempt to hold back the dead.

A snow flurry floated from above, finally settling on the ground. In a few moments, the chunky flake had melted into the ground. *The ground is getting colder. Soon the snow will be here to stay.*

His eyes flitted to the gray sheetrock sky. The only point of color above was the American flag at the top of a tall pole. The Stars and Stripes whipped in the brisk winter wind. It wasn't a message to their enemy—their enemy only understood death—but a symbol of hope for the people manning the base below to rally around.

Big Garrett in his Red Stripes' club colors stood near the front of a new barn smoking a cigarette, two pistols lodged in the front of his jeans. The man next to him had a mohawk running along his skull. On every corner of the building, armed men stood watching the treacherous soldiers that Steele couldn't decide what to do with.

"Mark," came a sweet voice from behind him.

He turned around and a grin formed on his lips. "Gwen."

His beautiful blonde gave him a friendly smile carrying two coffee mugs. She handed him one and he took it into his palms, warming them. He dipped his head near hers and kissed her pink lips. Shutting his eyes for a moment, he let her lips take him to better times.

He whispered, "Thank you."

She took a sip of hers. He leaned over, glancing in her cup.

"Green tea," she said, taking another sip, her eyes lighting up with excitement. "Probably the fourth time I've used the same tea bag."

"Ahh." He gazed at her rounded belly. It had grown larger over the last few months as their child grew inside her. He took a big gulp of his, letting the liquid warm his insides down to his belly. "Take a seat."

She sat down on the couch and adjusted a blanket around her shoulders. "It's getting colder out there."

She drank more of her green tea, shivering a bit beneath her blanket. "It's getting cold in here."

He laughed. "It is, but not as bad as out there."

The yellow notepad on the desk still weighed down on him. "I'm not sure what to do with the Jackson's men." He put it bluntly. She was his most trusted soundboard, and he never minded sharing his decision-making burden with her. For better or worse, she always had valuable input.

"I've kept them on the same food ration as the others, and now we're paying for the extra mouths. On top of that, they aren't equipped for the winter season. They won't survive without cold-weather gear, and I don't want to waste it on prisoners."

She took another sip of her tea. A hand fell on her belly as if she protected it from his concerns. "You should let them go."

He cringed. "These men hunted us and killed us, and you would have me let them go? They executed Kevin like a traitor, and who knows what they did to Ahmed."

Green eyes parried his words like emerald shields. "You asked my opinion. Letting them go takes them off your hands. It also prevents them from joining the ranks of the dead."

He shook his head and glanced back out the window at the barn. "I'll only have them pointing a gun back at me in a week."

She changed the subject. "I had Dr. Miller check on one of the Chosen cabins. He says it's the flu."

Steele sighed. He would much rather get in a fist fight with his old pal Jarl than handle his camp's administrative nightmare of logistical needs.

Taking a long drink of his watery black coffee, he wondered how many times they'd brewed it from the same grounds. *At least it's hot.* "We'll have to keep running water out to them. Double their carb-heavy rations and keep them away from everyone else."

"Quarantine?"

"After a fashion. Yes. We don't have any antivirals for the high risk people in the camp. Burlington and Donnellson were a bust. There's nothing we can do but try and care for the people that've gotten it. And hope it's not a bad strain." He paused a moment, weighing her disposition. "That includes you. I want you to stay away from there."

She scrutinized her tea for a moment, deciding if it was worth fighting him on. "I'll have Harriet and Joey deliver the extra supplies."

Little feet pounded down the steps and a six-year-old blonde-headed girl ran into the room. "Gwenna!" The little girl wrapped her arms around Gwen's legs and clambered onto the couch next to her. "Can I come in?"

Gwen smiled. "Of course, sweetie." She opened her arms, and the little girl let herself be embraced into the blanket's cozy warmth.

The prisoners outside drew Steele's gaze, once again preoccupying him.

"I'm going to check in with the Red Stripes and make my rounds."

"Be careful."

He gave her a short grin. "If we aren't safe here, we're not safe anywhere."

"Be careful," she repeated.

Nowhere was really safe. Everyday he strove to make their position harder. Better fortified. Safer. But nowhere would ever be safe again. Not in the pre outbreak sense. "I will."

Gwen's silver-headed grandfather poked his head inside the parlor. "I'll join ya," John Reynolds said.

Steele nodded at the man in his 80s. It was their daily time together. The old farmer liked to know what was happening on every corner of his land and Steele liked seeing the conditions and people firsthand.

He threw on his Army Combat Uniform jacket then buttoned it up. Running a hand over the center, he smoothed the captain's double-bar patch. It'd been stripped off one of Jackson's men after the battle. Steele hadn't wanted it, but his followers had offered it to him every day for weeks until he added it to his uniform. He put on an old camouflage goose-down hunting coat overtop of everything and a wool hat.

John donned his tall rubber farming boots, overalls, and down-plaid jacket. They stepped outside, the cold immediately nipping at any exposed part of their bodies.

"It's usually colder than this in December," John said.

"I'm thankful it's not."

John stuck his lips out and nodded his agreement. "Suppose we should be." He surveyed the sky. "But it's coming."

"How do you know?"

"A farmer always knows."

Steele accepted John's words as fact, and that fact would force his hand in the coming days.

They passed a corral filled with thirty-five brown, bay, black, white, and gray horses. At least ten were draft horses made for farming labor. Gwen had to bargain hard for that many.

John finished patting Patsy and Cline on their heads, and they walked around to his old barn. The doors were closed, and smoke came from a hole in the roof. Gregor stood outside with an AR-15 in his hands.

"Captain," Gregor said as they passed.

"Volunteer."

They passed the next barn all the way to the two new barns holding the prisoners where Garrett and his comrade stood.

"Anything happen overnight?"

Garrett's cheeks were red as he smoked on a cigarette. He let the smoke blow out his mouth.

"Just some jawin' about how cold they were. Told 'em we were going to set the barn on fire if they didn't shut up." He took a drag of his cigarette. "They quieted down after that."

A heavyset biker with a red bandana around his long gray hair approached them.

"Thunder." Steele smiled.

"Captain Steele. I wish I could say good morning, but it ain't good."

Steele's jaw clenched. "What's wrong?"

Thunder shook his head no. "You better come see this for yourself."

Steele let himself be led down the driveway to the small warped dock attached to the edge of John's property.

Thunder pointed across the river. "More than yesterday." He handed

Steele a pair of binoculars, the hard plastic cool to the touch.

Steele held the optics to his eyes. Lifeless trees lined the opposing shore, all manner of browns and grays. Filthy figures wandered among them. There was no clear direction or grouping, all of their movements aimless. Each and every one a lethal killer. He did quick math in his head and scanned the embankment over 400 yards away.

"Over a hundred."

"I only got to eighty yesterday." Thunder took the binoculars back and raised them to his eyes. "It's getting worse over there."

Steele watched the tiny dark figures from afar, swarming ants to his eyes. "As long as they stay over there, we shouldn't have any problems."

"That's what I'm worried about. What if they find an unmanned bridge, or shit, what if it freezes?"

"John, when was the last time the Mississippi froze in these parts?"

"Oh, let's see here." His eyes darted upward. "Must of been 'bout '38. We ran all over that jagged ice. Almost fell and broke my leg, but I didn't."

"It's been almost eighty years. I think luck's on our side."

Thunder looked unconvinced. "I'd hate to see unlucky."

The group made their way back to the camp, passing through the cabins. The cabins were constructed of round logs. Each log was roughly two feet around and notched where they lay perpendicular with other logs to lay tight atop one another, any remaining space filled with caulking. Each cabin was outfitted with a fireplace. Smoke billowed from dozens of chimneys filling the air with a permanent wood fire odor.

A beanpole of a man with a slight stoop in his neck emerged from the door of a cabin. His face was long and his hair gray. Black sleeves were rolled to his elbows.

Steele nodded to him, and the pastor was oddly silent.

As he passed the pastor spoke, "My people need medicine."

Steele turned, retracing his steps back to the man. "I know this is difficult, but there's nothing we can do. I've given instructions to double their carb ration and to help with fresh water as needed."

The pastor's eyes pierced Steele. "Not enough. There must be a way to get medicine."

"Dr. Miller's already said to let the virus run its course."

The pastor frowned, the corners of his mouth drooping like a neglected houseplant. "We need medicine, or this will spread like wildfire among us."

Steele blinked back the man's dire words. "It's the best we can do."

The pastor turned his back to Steele, his voice carrying over his shoulder, "It is not enough, Mr. Steele." He disappeared through the cabin door.

Ignoring his complaint, Steele trekked back to the Reynolds' farmhouse, the pastor's words pummeling his conscience. *Have I done enough?*

GWEN
Camp Forge, IA

"Mommy?" The voice came from the fringe. Her barely conscious mind played evil tricks, skirting around in the fogginess of the dream world.

Boy, is it you? Do you need me?

"Mommy?" the voice repeated.

The voice resonated with its familiarity. Soft and cute, that of a child. One that belonged to Haley and not her phantom boy.

Gwen's eyes shot open. She hadn't always been a light sleeper. At first, it was the dead, but now it was as if some maternal genes had activated inside her. The smallest peep in the night would send her eyes flying open.

Carefully, she shifted in the small single-person bed, an impossible feat with the caveman lying next to her. He smacked his lips and laid still. She looked over him at the bed across the room.

Haley was sitting up in bed, tugging at Becky's arm.

"What is it, baby?" Becky murmured, half-asleep.

"I don't feel good," the young girl squeaked.

"Lay back down, baby. You'll be fine in the morning."

"Come over here, sweetheart," Gwen said. Mark didn't move. He was using his manly superpower of being able to sleep through anything.

Haley's little blonde head bobbed as she climbed over Becky and softly padded over to Gwen's side of the room. She reached out the back of her hand, and Haley stretched her neck forward.

Gwen's hand met flaming skin. "Come closer."

The little girl leaned in over the side of the bed.

"What's going on?" Mark muttered, his eyes cracking open.

"I think she's sick."

Mark scooted up and picked Haley off the floor, setting her near Gwen. "Shit, she's soaked."

Gwen put the back of her hand on the girl's forehead and the other on her own.

"She's burning up." Her eyes darted toward her sister. "Becky, wake up. Haley's sick."

Haley pouted. "My throat hurts."

"I know, sweetie. You're going to be okay."

Laboriously Becky sat upright, her blonde wavy hair flying out in every direction. Her words were a detached question, not fully awake. "She's sick?"

"Yeah."

"Come here, baby." Mark handed her back to Becky.

"Oh god, she is." Becky's eyes widened. "Lay back down. We'll get you some water." The little girl crawled back into the single-person bed. Becky threw the blankets back over her, and Haley kicked them off.

"I'm hot!"

Gwen crawled out of her bed. Mark grabbed his pants. "I'll go grab Dr. Miller." He slipped his legs through and latched the belt.

"In the middle of the night?"

"It'll be light soon. I'll take one of the horses and Trent." Mark insisted on using horses every chance they had and saving the fuel for the trucks and diesel-hungry Humvees. Over twenty Humvees sat outside. Half needed some kind of repair, but the Red Stripes were working on getting them all functional.

She kept her voice quiet. "Thank you."

He kissed her lips. "No need." Softly, he closed the door and his footsteps croaked on the stairs.

Gwen went back over to Haley and knelt on the floor. She stroked the girl's face. "It'll be okay, sweetie."

Haley gave her a weak smile. "Love you, Gwenna."

The little girl's precious words brought tears to her eyes. "Love you too."

***

Dr. Miller finished checking Haley and wrapped his stethoscope around his neck. His lips flattened as he walked over to Becky and Gwen.

He sighed, his eyes pained beneath his wire-rimmed glasses. "I'm sorry, ladies. I'm afraid she has a case of strep throat."

"Not the flu?" Gwen asked.

"No, the symptoms are similar to the flu, but with those white spots on her tonsils, I would bet it's a bacterial infection over viral."

"You don't have anything?"

"I don't. I wish I did. I really do." Dr. Miller's brow furrowed as he picked up his black bag and set it on the end of the bed. With a practiced hand, he stuffed his stethoscope inside. "Anything I had we've used." His voice dropped to a whisper. "I've asked repeatedly for more. Do you think I like to stand by while people suffer?"

Becky turned away.

"I'm sorry. We're just worried." Turning to Becky, Gwen said softer. "We'll find something."

Dr. Miller's face eased. "All we can do is try and keep fluids in her and hope she fights. I'm not going to lie to you; this could be deadly."

Becky's face twisted between wanting to cry and spit at the same time. "This is too much. Why her?"

Dr. Miller shook his head. "I'm sorry. I really am. These next forty-eight hours are going to be critical." Sighing, he continued. "I'll come back tomorrow and check in on her and the others."

Gwen squeezed Becky's arm then shook Dr. Miller's hand. "Thank you, doctor. Has anyone come down with anything in town?"

"No. Thankfully, everyone's okay so far."

"Good. I appreciate you tending our people."

"I wouldn't have it any other way. Maybe another doctor or two, but I'm here to serve the community."

Dr. Miller nodded to the two women and left the room. His steps faded out of the house. Becky stood watching Haley, her arms folded over her chest.

"I need a cigarette then I'm gonna find something that will help that girl."

"You heard the doctor. There's no medicine."

"Somebody's got to have something that will help."

Gwen watched her sister, unable to console her. Becky walked over to Haley, wiped the hair from the little girl's head, and walked out. They moved to the front porch.

Becky lit a cigarette and Gwen moved upwind from her. A thin coating of snowfall covered the ground outside. Earth and dead grass struggled to stay above the collecting whiteness.

Gwen wrapped her arms around her torso. "Where do you keep getting those?"

Her sister took a quick drag. "Trade with the bikers."

"You should quit. Eventually they're gonna run out anyway."

"My daughter is lying in there sick, and you want to lecture me on smoking?" Becky shook her head in disgust.

Gwen snapped her mouth closed. She was used to looking out for her sister and always trying to correct her course in life. Sibling parenting was a by-product of divorced parents. They looked out for one another because there were no other options. It was a survival mechanism learned at a young age.

She stood for a minute taking in the Reynolds farm that had formed into a refugee campsite and militia base.

Becky spoke while inhaling. "I'll head up towards Bonaparte and hit the villages until I find some antibiotics." She blew smoke out her nose.

"No, it's dangerous."

Becky's eyes narrowed. "I'm not sitting idly by while my daughter dies before my eyes."

"I understand."

Becky blew smoke out her nose. "Do you?"

"I love Haley too, and soon, I'll have a baby." She reached for her, and Becky turned away. "I'll go." She couldn't sit by while her niece fell victim to the disease.

"Don't be silly. You're pregnant."

"I'm pregnant, but not far enough along to be bedridden. You're her mom. She needs you the most."

Becky's cig glowed a vibrant orange as she took a long and hard drag, tears welling in her eyes. "Fine."

The two women embraced for a moment.

"Let me talk to Mark."

***

He sat at her grandfather's writing table in the parlor. "I don't want you going."

She raised her chin. *Stop me.* "This is my niece. I am the mayor of Hacklebarney and responsible for the community, which includes this camp. I will be negotiating with other towns and villages. I'm the only person who should be doing this."

He regarded the papers on his desk and rearranged them. "I'm not going to lie. We need more winter clothes. I think that would mitigate some of the illnesses."

"Exactly. Who better to send than the mayor of a nearby town?"

He folded his arms over his broad chest, closing off from her. His blue eyes were darker today, a stormy sea.

"You're pregnant. Let's send Sheriff Donnellson or somebody else."

She let her eyebrows lift on her face. "You want me to send that moron to negotiate and acquire vital supplies? Prolly come back with a supply of chewing tobacco and cigars instead of meds."

Mark licked his lips, shoving his tongue into his lip at the mention of tobacco. His beard had grown even longer now. If he didn't have a mustache, she might have thought him a derelict Amish man.

He stood and made his way over to her. With a gentle hand, he took hers. His eyes searched hers for understanding. "I can't let anything happen to you. You know that."

She turned away from him before meeting his eyes. "And I won't let anything happen to that little girl upstairs."

He released her and reached for his beard and massaged it, running his hand down his mustache into his beard. He considered her as he thought.

A sparkle of amusement filled his eyes. "I'd be a fool to step in the way of your capacity for good." He waved a hand as if he didn't want a fight. "You don't need my permission, but Jackson and the dead are still out there, so you can't go alone."

She smiled. "I'm sure I'll have plenty of takers."

He laughed. "You always do."

ALVARADO

La Crescent, MN

Her Marines were a cluster of bodies huddled together in the night. The only difference between them and the dead was they breathed and would eventually tire out and succumb to the elements. If they did, the dead would fall upon them and add more unwilling recruits to their ranks.

In the freezing mass, Marines coughed and hacked as they struggled to keep going, weighed down by whatever they could carry with them, tripped up by uneven ice and snow.

She couldn't feel her feet as she half-jogged with the rest. Her hands had long since gone numb, and her chest burnt with fire from the icy air. When the wind moaned through the trees along the unplowed interstate, she would glance in anticipation at the Marines behind her.

They'd been forced to leave Marines behind. It was a tough pill to swallow. In modern war, they would not rest until the missing were recovered. But this wasn't a regular modern war with air support. Shit, they had almost no support. Only a thin line of living breathing people standing between the nation and the dead. This was a war of extinction.

She was confident that any pockets of surviving Marines would evade and fight their way back to the rally point. She'd always known that falling back was a very real possibility and planned accordingly. But she never thought they would be forced out of the outpost after such a soft fight.

The glow of flashlights reflected off the snow ahead of her. Shadows of naked trees with brittle crystalized branches loomed over the fleeing Marines. She heard a man fall behind her and she stopped. Spinning, she raised her weapon a fraction in case she needed to shoot down any dead that followed. None were close enough for concern, but they moaned in pursuit.

She grabbed the Marine by his arm and yanked him back to his feet.

"Thank you," Wess breathed.

She peered around him, taking in all their surroundings as best she could. "Keep moving."

Up ahead, she saw flashlights wavering around a short blackened building as the Marines entered their first rally point. The building lit up as they men filed into La Crescent Elementary School.

Marines spread out inside. Major Alvarado pushed Wess along ahead of her, and she was the last Marine inside the building. Bundled fresh Marines closed the doors with a bang.

Men collapsed on the tiled ground; their exhausted panting fogged the air. As quickly as they barged in, they started to spread out, manning barricaded windows.

"Major?" said a short lance corporal. He wasn't exhausted and his eyes were unsure of what was happening. *Lance Corporal Murphy?* Her mind was clogged and slow as if her brain had succumbed to the arctic elements in their retreat.

She rubbed her temple for a moment. "Yes, Lance Corporal?"

"Lance Corporal Murphy, ma'am."

The lack of blistering wind and cold air allowed her to catch her breath. It wasn't that much warmer than the outside, but the lack of wind was a divine intervention.

"The outpost's been overrun. This is our forward operating base now. Where are your backup comms?"

"Backup comms?" he said. His eyes darted around the room covered with finger paintings and posters featuring talking books.

"This facility was supposed to be outfitted with a backup radio in case we had to retreat from Barron Island. Captain?"

Butler shook his head shortly. "None were delivered, ma'am."

"Goddammit. If I had an ounce of assistance from our command, we could actually put up a coordinated effort." She sighed. "Get these doors barricaded. No one goes in or out. Everyone stays quiet."

"What about La Crescent?" Butler asked.

"They've known the drill this entire time. Elevation and silence. In the morning, we will send a unit to the homestead, and let them know that we've been overrun. Butler and Wess with me. Sergeant Riddle." Marines scrambled around the bottom floor.

A thickset sergeant made himself front and center.

"Get these Marines up to the top floor, then I need a headcount. No one fires until I give the command."

"Yes, ma'am," he said. He tapped a Marine on the shoulder and pointed him down the hall, moving the entire time.

She jogged the stairs to the top floor. A long corridor was lined with maroon lockers. Rubbing her hands together, she warmed them with her breath. Marine boots clobbered the steps as they raced behind her. Broken down into rifle squads, they quietly entered classrooms, taking firing positions at windows.

Tailing a squad, she followed them inside a classroom. Ten Marines squatted along a long dormant heating vent waist-high spanning the length of the room. The wind or the dead moaned outside; it didn't matter which. Both were deadly, one took you in an icy cradle and the other screaming piece by piece.

The dead trudged through the snowdrifts. It gave Alvarado the tiniest bit of satisfaction that the by-product of unending winter storms hindered their progress even more than her Marines. They were slower moving than in the warmer months, now marching like infectious molten lava.

She supposed it was the cold that made them slower, but they still came, populated with their new recruits of infected. Dead Marines wearing the faces of her men, the fresh dead quicker than the old.

In the night, they were hard to see as they moved like ice sculptures. The men watched over the windowsills quietly waiting for another battle to begin.

The first Zulu reached the doors and rattled the chained entrance. It was joined by another. The only glass on the thick metal door was reinforced and had been well-secured. It would hold against a small horde, but not forever. As more dead came on, they started to work their way around the building. The men sat in silence, their breaths turning to cold smoke in the dark building air.

Wess crawled across the classroom floor, his thin youthful face looking for her. "Ma'am, Captain Butler has collected your officers."

Shame boiled inside her as she followed the Marine crawling across the floor and into the hall. Once out of view of the outside, they stood and Wess led her into a windowless classroom in the interior of the school.

The square room had white concrete walls, and the front of the room had a green chalkboard. A final math assignment was scrawled across the board for homework.

Captain Butler was already inside. He pulled a lantern from a pack and placed it on the teacher's wooden desk, adjusting a small American flag to the side.

"Wait."

His hand stayed and he stared at her for confirmation. A lieutenant and three sergeants awaited her. She motioned for the last man inside the room to close the door. Gently, he shut the door, the latch clicking shut.

Butler flicked on his flashlight, letting it emit a dim red glow. Each man was enveloped by the light casting dark shadows over eye sockets. She would have killed to have any sort of night-vision equipment at their disposal.

"Sergeant Riddle."

The sergeant turned on a headlamp that let out a red beam. "We have ninety-six Marines accounted for. Corporal Dixson thinks he heard gunfire south of the outpost, but we can neither confirm or deny."

It was callous to say she didn't care if there were others alive and still fighting, but she needed to know what pieces of a command she had to work with. She did the math fast in her head. There were almost forty Marines missing in action. If the dead didn't get them, the elements would.

Forty missing Marines was the command's single largest loss since the beginning. There would be more before this war was over, but this night would haunt her. One night under her command, she'd failed to see that the river could freeze, giving the mass of dead a jagged highway to traverse unimpeded. On the other hand, she could have had her entire command overrun if she'd made them stand their ground.

"Thank you, Sergeant." She collected herself for a moment. A shiver ran down her spine as the dead wailed outside searching for a way in. *It's just the cold,* she told herself. "We won't last here. The facility is secure, but with hundreds if not thousands of the Zulus coming across unimpeded, we will fail our primary mission, and it will only be a matter of time before they find a chink in our armor."

She inspected her red-shadowed Marines. "We can't wait for spring to thaw us out. It's not an option."

Captain Butler nodded agreeably. "We could rally forces from the south and take back Barron."

He's still thinking he has the might of the American military at his back. "We would need to get word to Colonel Kinnick, and logistically, we are not prepared for a massive personnel shift. I don't think that's realistic. We must figure out a way to win this on our own." *We only have our backs.*

Butler gulped. "We don't even have a full company."

"No, we do not. What do we have?"

"We abandoned most of our supplies and ammunition at the outpost."

"How long can our Marines sustain a firefight?"

"I'd say about two days, ma'am."

"Then we must solve this problem before then."

"How?" Wess piped up. The young lieutenant's face glowered as if unnerved by the dark. His eyes shifted away from her gaze.

"How would any Marine solve a problem?" Her eyes bounced from Marine to Marine. "Improvise, adapt, and overcome with enough explosives and brawn to destroy the enemy."

Her men nodded their heads in agreement. Marines don't sulk; they would find a way.

She masked her joy of finding a way even if it promised to be a tooth-and-nail fight. "We're going to blow the ice down the river, find any misplaced

Marines, and retake Barron. Then we're going to continue south, ensuring that the river is broken up. No gaps in our line."

"Ma'am, I would love to blow up the entirety of the enemy and the river, but there must be over a thousand of them between here and there. More are coming by the second. That's 10:1 on a good day."

"Then we must move fast."

Butler nodded. "If we planted enough, I don't see why we couldn't widen the river back out."

"Who'll do it?" Riddle asked, his eyes black orbs. He knew who the hard work would fall on: the Marines in the field.

Alvarado met his eyes. "I'll go. I won't ask Marines to do something I wouldn't do myself. Only volunteers."

"I'll go with you, ma'am." It really wasn't a request but more of a declaration of duty from the sergeant.

"Collect a rifle squad of volunteers and all the explosives we have stockpiled in the school."

She turned toward Butler. "You're going to be in charge of this command while I'm in the field. If we do not succeed, there is no point in remaining here. You are to go south and link with Captain Heath and get word to Colonel Kinnick that we are overrun. Give us no more than **two days** and then you move. Take any civilians you can with you."

Butler gulped again, and his mouth settled into a pencil-like line. "They'll slow us down."

"I don't care. Make it happen. That's an order."

Butler dipped his head in respect. "Yes, ma'am."

"This can work."

Butler straightened his spine. "Yes, ma'am."

"It's a long shot, but we don't get beat, especially on our home turf."

JOSEPH
Cheyenne Mountain Complex, CO

They found Dr. Hollis in the small cafeteria for their lab section of the Cheyenne Mountain Complex that held only eight circular tables. Joseph reprimanded himself for not starting his search at the nearest food distribution center earlier.

The senior member of the Biomedical Advanced Research and Development Authority on their Mountain Integrated Medical team took a chubby finger and used it to shove the rest of a soft shell taco in his mouth.

Orange ground beef taco grease ran down the palm of his hand. He licked his fingers, savoring the grease from each one. He chewed on the double as if he were afraid someone was going to snatch it from him.

"So they came right in and took him?" he asked between chews.

"Yes, didn't say why or anything," Joseph said.

Hollis's jaw worked as he forced more food in it. His eyes darted around the room. Only a few other civilians sat at a table nearby talking quietly to one another. Loose flesh jiggled as he shook his head. "Could be anything." He inhaled between bites, sucking in air through his nose as if undecided between eating or breathing. He leaned over the table, collecting himself before he spoke in a hushed voice. "He wasn't the first to be *taken.*"

Joseph shared a glance with Desai. "What do you mean?"

Hollis set down his taco he'd been thumbing, studying the room a minute before he spoke. "I've heard of a few people who were 'walked out', and not seen again. We just figured they were transferred. I bet that's what happened. He was transferred."

"Transferred where? With no goodbyes? At gunpoint for Chrissake," Joseph said.

Hollis glanced over his shoulder. "We shouldn't be talking about this. He was transferred."

"That's what I'm worried about. What if we're next?"

Desai's eyebrows elevated. "We didn't do anything. We created a vaccine that works."

"Now that we've done it, maybe it's time to tie up the loose ends," Joseph said.

Hollis continued to anxiously eat. He leaned forward on the table, swallowing his food. "I heard from one of the warehouse clerks that there's been some dissension in the military."

Joseph's voice dropped to a whisper. "You mean like a coup?"

Hollis nodded his head affirmative. "I didn't think anything of it when he first said it. You know rumors. There's always lots of rumors. Especially when there are no good news sources."

"So you think that Colonel Byrnes was involved in a military conspiracy to overthrow the government. Treason?"

Desai frowned. "Treason? You know the colonel. Straightlaced and motivated to find a solution to this mess. Why would he commit treason?"

Hollis's eyes narrowed on his pudgy face. "I didn't say that. I. Did. Not. Say. That."

Joseph frowned. "But I thought you just said a coup?"

"A rumor." Hollis shook his head no, and used his thumb to fill his fork with more black beans and rice. "Conspiracy theories. I'm sure he'll be back by tonight."

"It looked like he was under arrest," said Desai.

"It doesn't involve us. Keep your nose clean and steer clear of whatever mess the good colonel's gotten himself into, and we'll be fine."

Joseph exchanged looks with Desai. "You want us to ignore the fact they just arrested him and took him away with no cause?"

"Listen. They don't just do that. They had to have a cause. I'm sure it's a misunderstanding, and he'll be back by tomorrow."

"Let's go find Dr. Nguyen," Joseph said, getting to his feet with Desai joining him.

Hollis shook his head. "I'm telling you, don't dig too deep on this one."

"Our friend and colleague has been taken. I'm going to find out what happened."

"You don't want to look too involved."

"Dr. Hollis, we're all involved. We're on his team. All of us."

Joseph and Desai walked out of the cafeteria. The white corridor walls were plain and generic as if a hospital and a government building had procreated the boring corridors. If Joseph hadn't lived inside them for as long as he had already, it would have been easy to get lost.

The next corridor held the doctors' offices and small dorm-like rooms. Soldiers in black stood like chess pieces near the far end of the hallway. He could sense Desai tensing next to him.

"Come on. If they wanted us, they would have grabbed us already."

Joseph bravely squared his shoulders toward the men and puffed out his thin chest. They walked forward, closing the distance on the soldiers. The one facing their direction scrutinized them with dark eyes behind his ski mask.

"That's Byrnes's office," Desai said under her breath.

"They must be searching it," Joseph said from the side of his mouth.

Walking past the soldier, Joseph deliberately slowed down when they were abreast with the open door. Papers were strewn all over the floor. Books were tossed into haphazard piles. The office was ransacked.

"Nothing to see. Move along," the soldier said, watching them.

Joseph and Desai continued down the corridor and rounded on Dr. Nguyen's office. He nervously rapped on the door. It echoed hollow like a synthetic wood.

"Who is it?" came a voice from inside.

"Dr. Jackowski and Dr. Desai."

The door opened a crack. An eye peeked through the sliver of an opening encased in round glasses. The door opened farther, and a small Asian man motioned them inside with a hasty hand. "Hurry."

Dr. Nguyen shut the door and fled to the other side of his desk. His eyes were magnified behind his thick lens. "Are they here?" He held himself with anxious hands.

"There were soldiers down in Byrnes's office. What's going on?"

Nguyen's eyes blinked beneath his glasses as if realization slapped him in the face. "I don't have time to explain." He opened his top drawer and felt around inside. He struggled with something and felt the underside of his desk.

"They took Byrnes away."

"I thought we'd have more time."

"More time for what?" Desai asked. She eyed the two men back and forth.

"To plan. I suppose this means we've failed." He tugged something from the top of his drawer and held it out like it was a rare diamond. "Take this and protect it." A plain gray flash drive rested in the center of his hand.

"What's that?" Joseph asked. He eyed it like a poison apple.

"Just take it. We don't have time."

Joseph snatched the tiny flash drive in his hand and shoved it into the bottom of his pocket, the temptation to know what it held picking at him.

A fist reverberated off the door making all three doctors jump. Desai put a hand to her chest catching her breath. A voice came from the outside cold and mean. "Dr. Nguyen. Open up."

Dr. Nguyen collected himself for a moment, his face flat and showing no emotion. He stared at the other doctors. "I tried. We tried. Trust no one."

"Open this door! Now!"

Nguyen gave himself a short nod. He fumbled around in his top drawer, removing a silver small caliber revolver.

"Dr. Nguyen, what are you doing?" Desai shrieked.

Nguyen gripped the gun, raising it in front of him.

"They're going to shoot us," Joseph said. He took a step away from the door covering Desai with a protective arm.

The tread of a boot crushed into the door. The whole door shook under the added weight. Once, it boomed then twice. The door weakened with each kick, ready to give way at any moment.

"Keep it safe," Nguyen said. "They'll kill you for it."

"What is it?" Joseph asked. The flash drive still burned inside his pocket.

Nguyen nodded, turning the revolver on himself, an inch from his temple. The leading CDC doctor, one of the best minds still alive on the planet, pulled the trigger.

An explosion bounced, rippling from wall to wall of the tiny office, and Joseph and Desai ducked. Red sprayed the walls like paint flung from a brush. Nguyen fell back into his chair, his eyes looking upward in their final death pose. The exit wound on the side of his head leaked brain tissue and dark red blood that streamed off his desk and into a pool on the floor.

"Oh my God," Desai cried. Her hands shot to her mouth hiding her fear. The door vibrated under the violent assault of the men outside. Joseph stared at the dead doctor in disbelief, the weight of the flash drive even heavier.

The door splintered. The top hinge busted off the wall and the doorframe itself burst into pieces. Black-masked soldiers forced their way inside.

STEELE
Camp Forge, IA

The small group rode away farther and farther from the farmhouse porch. Gwen sat next to Kenny Hamlin on the hayrack pulled by two towering bay-colored draft horses. A floral scarf covering her head made her look like an old-world babushka.

The hayrack was flanked on either side by Hank and Gerald Newbold in the front and Gregor and Jake Bullis in the back. Jake had a shotgun strapped over the pommel of his saddle. All of them were armed. He'd seen that they carried enough ammunition to last through just about anything.

Gregor looked highly uncomfortable atop his horse, and Jake was trying to coach him on how to steer and control the animal. He reached for Gregor's reins, trying to teach him how to hold them and the horn for an easier ride. The horse, however, had a mind of its own. Sensing the weakness of its rider, it did as it pleased, veering off to the side on the hunt for tall grass.

Jake laughed, giving his horse a bit of encouragement to get closer to Gregor. He led the unwieldy man back toward the center of the road. Gwen turned, saying something inaudible from beneath her scarf.

Steele caught glimpses of smiles among them. He had agreed without hesitation for Jake to accompany her on the journey. *Who better to watch out for her than a man that still loved her?* The man would die for her, and that was exactly why Steele hadn't protested his attendance. He trusted her and that was all that mattered in a relationship. Trust.

45

The barn housing Jackson's prisoners would take an even greater amount of trust. A trust that Steele didn't know if he was ready to accept, but he didn't have a choice.

He tucked his shemagh into his jacket. The versatile Arabic scarf provided ample protection from the chill of the day.

"Looks like this one is going to stick," John said. He eyed the sky with the experience of a farmer who knew weather determined life or death.

Steele peered at the sky. "Just in time for Christmas."

Crystalized flurries dotted the air in their earthen assault. Tiny white specks rained down with only the wind to guide them. The wind blew them any way it wanted, directing their speed and angle with careless dominance.

John wrinkled his nose. "I always liked snow for Christmas. After that, bah humbug. You can take it."

"I'd prefer that everyone was warm and not worried about freezing to death. Some additional clothes would be a bonus."

John nodded. "Aye. Gwen will find us more. Hacklebarney is stripped of almost everything, but the cabins are sturdy, fine Amish work. That will stave off most of it."

Steele put a hand on John's shoulder. "They've done a very kind thing and so have you."

John nodded fiercely. "It was the right thing."

"It's not always easy to do the right thing."

"No, it ain't, but it's easier to live with."

Steele eyed the barn. War Machines were guarding the outside today. Grinding gears made up their club colors.

"One would hope that it's easier to live with."

A familiar female voice stretched around the porch. A black-haired woman about the size of a twig, her hair slicked back, walked along the railing.

"Well, look at what we got here. The handsomest man I've seen in a hot minute."

Steele snorted a grin as Tess hopped up the porch steps.

"I meant, John." She embraced the old man and he let out a high-pitched giggle.

"You can't let Lydia hear you now. She won't be too keen on a pretty fiddle like yourself swooning around her man."

She flashed him a smile. "Runs in the family." She gave Steele a wanton look. "But I won't tell if you won't."

John shook a finger at her. "You're trouble, young lady."

"How are those defenses coming?" Steele asked.

"As much as I like digging in the frozen ground, slow. I think we'd be better off with just the sandbags and logs."

"I think you're right. Tomorrow take a cart into town and gather as many sandbags as you can. We'll get Trent's team and some of the Red Stripes to cut some logs and get started on the machine gun nests."

Steele wanted perimeter areas with a superior field of fire upgraded with machine gun nests. Their firepower had been greatly enhanced by several additions of M2 .50 caliber Browning machine guns repurposed from Jackson's destroyed Humvees as well as ungodly amounts of ammunition. Steele wasn't a fool though. He knew that at some point he would need it.

Over twenty desert-tan functioning Humvees sat empty in a long line. Two or three had bullet holes in the doors, but for the most part, these had been taken without significant structural damage. With highly inefficient gas mileage of about ten to fourteen miles to the gallon and fuel in high demand, they had been deemed too fuel dependent to use unless they were in an emergency.

On the far end of the Humvees sat the McCone airport people mover affectionately nicknamed Lunchbox.

The hulking elevated vehicle had been riddled with bullets on more occasions than Steele could count, including the time he'd taken a round off the top of his skull. Jackson had the mover outfitted with steel flaps to protect his soldiers inside from gunfire.

"Roger that, Steele. Is today the day we talked about?"

Steele made a deep sigh. "Yes." He turned and eyed the road in the direction Gwen had gone. Their forms were faint as if the snow were burying them and the woods absorbing them in a brittle embrace. He thought he saw one of them turn and wave. They disappeared into a gray-trunked forest of leafless trees, all long gone in the reckoning of winter.

"Gather the club presidents."

***

It took thirty minutes to find and gather the club presidents. They stood in an uneasy line on the porch waiting for Steele. A cigarette burned in the corner of War Child's lips, smoke wisps combining with his warm breath in the cool air. Thunder had on a red coat, making him look more like a biker Santa than ever before. The pastor hung away from them all, a slender man near the edge of the porch. Frank stood closest to Steele with an M4 carbine slung over his shoulder crossing over a silver-metal dragon, his club patch. The only president missing was Red Clare. Weeks ago, she'd been shifted with her club to Burlington to establish an outpost there.

"I don't call this meeting lightly. I call this meeting because a decision has been made about the fate of Jackson's *Legion*."

Steele nodded to Margie waiting near the Humvees with her rifle in her hands. She hopped into a Humvee and Tony scrambled into another. The taillights of the two rear Humvees fired up, letting out a red glow. The Humvees flanked either side of the barn. The War Machine guards eyed them with caution, stepping away from the entrance. Sable Pointers appeared in the turrets. One racked the bolt back on his fifty. He stared at the porch, waiting on an order to fire.

"I didn't think you had the balls to do it. Ha," War Child said in his gravelly voice. He leaned on the railing, anticipating a good show.

A slow grin took hold of the pastor's mouth. "Time to cull the Legion. Time to send them to hell."

Steele considered the barn before he continued. "Not all these men were evil or bad or whatever you want to call them. Some were following orders. Others knew no better way to survive."

"Steele, no," Frank said.

"We need the men. They'll have a choice."

The pastor's face darkened. War Child spit. Thunder's was flat. He was one of the only men who knew this was coming.

Steele ignored them and walked down the steps, followed by the lighter steps of Tess behind. He waved them forward. "Follow me."

He marched toward the new unpainted barn. The frozen snow crust crackled beneath his feet. He stopped outside the firing line of the Humvees. The biker club presidents and the pastor joined him. People emerged from their cabins and barns now.

Steele gestured at one of the War Machines. They hesitated for a moment, and he could feel War Child nodding. The two guards lifted the heavy beam off the metal hooks keeping it in place and tossed it to the side. They swung the doors outward and the barn opened up.

The soldiers inside had clustered near the entrance. They were only shadows to those on the outside. Fear and danger leaked from the barn, the men inside unknowing what fate held in store for them. The men shuffled their feet, nervous energy ebbing through their ranks. They saw their own Humvees and .50 caliber machine guns sighted in on them and knew full well what those could do to a man. Quiet murmurs rippled through them.

Steele let them embrace the thought of being gunned down in cold blood. Fear was a chilly vice-like embrace that froze their veins second after second with the realization that death loomed over them.

Tess leaned close to him whispering. "You're not thinking about gunning them down, are you?"

A vision flashed in Steele's mind of bullets cutting through the soldiers in an all-out massacre. *Then they'd be off your hands for good.* No questions of loyalty. No questions of conspiracy. Steele's hand drifted upward, and he tugged his own beard to remove the wretched thought from his head.

"Major Ludlow and Captain Ogden. You may come forward."

The soldiers inside the barn shuffled. Another tense minute passed.

"Major Ludlow," Steeled called at them. "Captain Ogden."

A short man, a hair over five feet tall exited the mass of soldiers followed by a taller man. They walked outside and shaded their eyes to the brightness of the winter day. They took hesitant steps, not wanting to be the first prisoners executed but with enough respect for themselves to continue forward. Nervous feet moved them closer.

Steele held out a hand. "That's far enough." Ludlow's bug eyes watched his every move, and Ogden's face fell into a distrusted frown like that of a confused teenage boy.

"You both have stood against the United States of America. You have killed good hardworking Americans. You have robbed, murdered, and pillaged as you saw fit under the command of a madman." Steele stopped, gathering himself. "This is your one and only chance to come back into the fold. Your chance at redemption."

The lieutenants of Jackson stared defiantly. Ogden sneered. "We're Legion. We're all that remains."

Steele's voice grew strong. "Wrong." He continued louder. "The United States government has adopted all these men as militia forces in accordance of executive order and commissioned by Colonel Kinnick, United States Air Force."

Ludlow's eyes grew larger and Ogden's narrowed.

"Impossible," Ogden called out.

Steele approached them, keenly aware that he was walking into a potential crossfire situation if the soldiers decided to rush him to escape. He stuck his hand into his breast pocket and removed a piece of paper and handed it to Ludlow.

Ludlow's eyes scanned the document, and he passed it to Ogden.

"How did you come by this?"

"Like I said, orders from Colonel Kinnick, commanding officer of Operation Homefront."

Ogden shook his head no. "Impossible. The government abandoned us. Left us to die. Why would they be giving you command?"

Steele took the paper back and shoved it in his breast pocket. "I cannot speak for their actions before, but now more than ever, we need to be united against the dead. I need your men here to help defend this part of the river."

"Ha," Ogden said. His boy-like face sneered. "Go fuck yourself."

Bug-eyed Ludlow considered Steele for a moment. "What are your terms?"

A skiff of snow settled on the tops of their heads and shoulders, little flakes of white speckling the men. The wind picked up, swirling the flurries around them. More than an inch already laid across the land and the Reynolds' farm fields.

"You have a choice. Either stay and fight or leave now, swearing to never take arms against us again."

"You're going to let us go?" Ogden asked.

"You may go, but you will be given nothing. No food. No weapons. No coats. Only what you wear on your back. Everything else will be given to the men who join and fight."

Ogden stared up at Ludlow. "You're not seriously considering this are you? We can't join this rebel scum."

Ludlow gulped, giving him the distinct appearance of a bull frog. "We will be treated fairly?"

"You will be treated fair, but know this, until we are assured of your men's loyalty, they will not have weapons, and if your men think for a second that they have free reign on these civilians like in Youngstown, my justice will be swift and harsh, and you will pay alongside your men for each infraction."

Ludlow lifted his chin. "I understand."

Ogden stuck his chest out. "I'd rather die than pay lip service to the likes of you pathetic pissants."

"Then leave." Steele turned and pointed toward the entrance. "But you have to live with the fact that your nation lived and died on these riverbanks, and you did nothing to save it." He nodded to Ludlow, whose almost unblinking eyes took in everything about Steele.

"Join or leave. You have five minutes. Talk to your men."

The two prisoner officers turned around and went back to plead their case.

After a tense five minutes, the soldiers began to trickle out of the barn. In twos and threes, the soldiers walked out of the barn and into the open. Ogden led them. The men drifted down the road like camouflaged snowflakes with no winter weather gear and no weapons. If the elements didn't catch them, the infected would.

Tess spoke from the side of her mouth. "How many do you think will stay?"

"I don't know."

More men trickled away, following the trudging feet of the man in front of them.

Frank's voice hushed into his ear. "You should kill them away from here. They'll only be trouble."

"Aye," Thunder added. "They'll either die and turn or regroup and come back. Either way we'll be fighting them again."

"The best way to destroy an enemy is to make him a friend."

Ludlow came out with a cluster of soldiers at his back. They approached Steele with respectful caution. His gut tightened. They eyed him curiously. Major Ludlow put a tight hand up to his brow in a salute. Moments later, all his men did the same.

Slowly, Steele saluted back.

"Major Ludlow, Ohio National Guard at your service, sir."

"Glad to have you on board." He let his hand drop to his side, eyes running along the soldiers. *Can you be trusted? Have I signed my death warrant? Will you even make a difference in this war to come?*

AHMED

Northern Missouri

He was already awake when the key scraped the lock and it clicked open. Sadie walked quietly inside.

"You're awake?" she said under her breath.

"Yes."

She sat on the edge of the bed and touched his arm, staring distantly at it. "We thought you were dead at first." She continued to stare away. "Like all the others."

"How did you find me?" Vague memories of farm fields and a line of timber filled his vision.

"The dogs. They sniffed you out and kept a whining." She glanced at him. "They do good warning us about the infected. Never thought they'd do good at finding the living too. Come on." With a tender hand, she placed his arm around her and sat him on the edge of the bed. She held a smile in for a moment. "You ready?"

Ahmed grunted a yes. She bobbed them up and down three times. "One, two, three." She thrust them both upright, and he let his legs take some of his own bodyweight.

"Get those legs beneath you. Nice and easy."

They took careful steps toward the door. Each footstep allowed his body to remember what it was supposed to be doing. They reached the door, and she let him lean for a moment to catch his breath.

She was slender. He wouldn't say skinny, but by no means overweight. He didn't know if that was a result of the end of the world, a genetic disposition, or a combination of the two, but he knew she was strong to be lugging him all around. "You're strong for someone so small."

"Farmer strong."

"Are we on a farm?"

She laughed a little, sounding too hearty for a girl of her stature. "My family farm. A few head of cattle."

"I've never been to this part of the country before."

She smiled. "Never too late to visit. Come on, city boy. Let's get you fed."

He had the sudden feeling that she used the same tone with the farm animals when it was feeding time.

She pulled him snugly to her side and walked with him down a hallway. The hallway opened to a kitchen with six people sitting around a rickety table. There were bench seats on either side and chairs on the ends. A fire roared in the fireplace across the next room and he could feel the heat emanating outward. Two small children played with toy cars and multi-colored building blocks on the rug nearby.

She led him to the bench and helped him take a seat. The eyes of the adults stared his way. Most were more curious than malicious, but a hint of suspicion still hid inside. All except Jim. He sat at one of the table heads. His fingers were laced over his plate with his elbows on the table. Pale blue eyes chipped away at Ahmed like ice picks.

Ahmed touched his face, aware that he probably resembled a homeless man. His black beard was snarled and much longer than he'd remembered it. His hair was longer too, a cluster of tiny black curls that puffed out every which way when they grew too long.

They all continued to stare until an older woman across the table smiled at him. "Wel-come," she said loud and broken. His eyes darted to Sadie, wondering if there was some impairment with her hearing or speech.

Sadie shot daggers at the woman and dug a long metal spoon into a black iron pot sitting in the center of the table and put a slab of roasted meat on his plate.

"He's American, Mom. He speaks English," Sadie said in irritation.

Ahmed ignored the mother-daughter spat and watched the meat fall apart on the plate, revealing a reddish inside. She scooped potatoes and drippings, letting them pour over top of the roast and settling into a gravy pool on his plate.

"It's pot roast," she said and took a seat.

"Sorry," she said. "That's my mother, Kelly."

The woman smiled at him. "It's good to have you?"

He lifted his eyes from his divine plate. "Ahmed."

Her smile didn't fade as she digested his name. She repeated him. "Ahmed."

"You know Jim and Kyle." Jim's eyes didn't waver, but Kyle's eased around the edges with friendliness. A lady sitting next to Kelly eyed him with suspicion. She shared similar chocolaty-colored hair and the same curls as the rest. "That's Barb, my aunt."

An older man with wrinkles around his hard eyes sat at the end opposite of Jim. His eyes had the same pale ice hue as Jim's. "My father's name is Brad."

The whining of dogs begging at the table turned Sadie's head. "And these are our dogs. Tank and Bear are the German Shepherds. Peanut is the coonhound. Tank and Bear are brother and sister. Tank's the girl." She grinned with a bit of embarrassment then added, "Jim named them."

"Better than something stupid like Cinderella or whatever shit you like," Jim said.

"Jimmy," Kelly scolded from the other side of the table.

"Just saying. Can't waste a good dog on a crap name." He picked up a fork, and stabbed a piece of his beef, and put it in his mouth as if the conversation was over.

Kelly smiled at Ahmed. "Interesting name. Where are you from?"

"Washington."

"The capital?"

"Yes, D.C."

"Super interesting," Jim said. He shoved a potato into his mouth and watched Ahmed as he chewed. "Long way from home, ain't ya?" he said, chewing with his mouth open.

Kelly reprimanded her son. "Jimmy, we haven't said grace."

Jim put down his fork and glared at Ahmed.

"I'm a long way from home and my friends."

"Who's you're friends?" Brad said from the other end. His voice was deeper than the others, and they all gazed down at their plates when he spoke, Jim included. His tone held the reverence of a preacher or principal, that of a man who was used to holding authority, familial or otherwise.

"It's a long story, sir." He didn't know why he added sir, but he felt like he should. It was like he spoke to his own father, a man that demanded respect through words or action or both.

Brad sucked his teeth. "Don't beat around the bush. Which group were you with?"

Ahmed took a deep breath. His words could be the end of him. "I was in a group led by a counterterrorism agent." *Hopefully that adds some clout.*

The ice-blue eyes weighed him, determining whether or not he told the truth. "Feds, huh? Don't reckon I trust them much. What's his name?"

"Mark Steele."

"Don't reckon I heard of him neither." Brad's upper lip twitched as if he had a bone to pick with them. "You know Sly Bailey?"

"No, sir. Am I supposed to?"

The icy eyes stayed on Ahmed for a moment. "Who shot you, boy?"

Ahmed took in a breath, but before he could speak, Kelly spoke. "Let's say grace; otherwise, this food will get cold."

Brad's lip twitched. "Fine, but then we get to the bottom of whatever this is." He held out his hands to either side.

Sadie held out her hand and Ahmed took it. The entire family interlocked hands.

"Bless us, oh Lord, and these thy gifts which we are about to receive from thy bounty through Christ our Lord. Amen." Ahmed fumbled along, mumbling beneath his breath. They released each other's hands, replacing flesh with metal forks.

"Say, what kind of name is Ah-med?" Jim said with a mouthful of food.

"It's Arabic," Sadie said hurriedly.

"You ain't no Christian? Can you eat beef? Isn't that sacred?"

Sadie tensed next to him.

Ahmed put his fork down. "I can eat beef, and no, I'm not a Christian, but I feel blessed to have this food as much as you." His stomach growled loudly, garnering a short smile from Kelly.

Jim frowned as if Ahmed had tricked him. "You better eat up. We don't waste nothing."

The family put their heads down and the streaks of forks and knives on plates were the only sounds in the room.

Ahmed forked a piece of beef and potato and forced as much as he could in one bite. The warm beef with the starchy potato melted in his mouth, and it was so flavorful and delicious he thought he might die.

He closed his eyes for a moment, thanking God to have let him live even if it was only to have this meal. He opened his eyes and they all were staring at him. He lowered his eyes in embarrassment.

"You were moaning," Sadie said.

He breathed a laugh. "This food is so wonderful. I felt like I haven't eaten in so long."

"You haven't," Kelly said.

Barb eyed him with continued mistrust. "You been in and out for almost a month."

"A month?"

"You were so bad when we found you. Almost white you were. Not an extra drop of blood in you. Sadie there spoon-fed you broth for weeks."

Sadie studied her plate in discomfort as if her attentive care was something that brought her shame.

Brad piped up again. "Who shot you?"

It took everything in his power to stop eating. "I was in a large group. Over a thousand people. We were trying to find a way across the Mississippi River and get north to Hacklebarney."

"Iowa? Why?"

"That was a safe point for us."

Brad narrowed his eyes. "Iowa? Idiots Out Wandering Around." He shook his head.

"Yes. We'd been driven out of Michigan by the dead." He purposely left the part about Colonel Jackson out.

"Damn son, that's bad news. Real bad."

"A group of bikers we were scouting with turned on me and killed my friends."

"They were deader than a doornail when we found 'em." Brad went back down to his food, scooping a piece of meat in his mouth. "Well, you be on the right side of the river now. Don't know nothing about your group. No sign of 'em."

Tank lifted her head and let out a muted growl. Jim scrutinized the dog. "What's it, girl?" Everyone at the table looked at the dog as if she were actually going to speak. Tank stared off toward the outside, her lip curling lazily upward. Bear turned toward the door and let out a lower growl.

Brad waved at Jim and Jim shook his head. "I swear if it's another deer," he said under his breath.

"If it's another deer, we're gonna shoot it and eat it. Save the herd."

Jim walked over to the window with a hand on his openly holstered handgun. The window was boarded up, but Jim shifted a loose board and slid it horizontally to the side. The gap gave him a small slot to peer through almost unnoticed. His eyes scanned the dimming light. "Ain't nothing there." He slid the piece of wood back into place. "Dumb dogs."

Tank's and Bear's ears drooped with the disapproval of one of their human masters. Jim retook his seat, swinging a hand at Tank as he walked past. The dog skillfully dodged the swipe and laid her head back down with a sigh.

Peanut ran for the door and paced. Brad's face turned angry. "Goddammit, Peanut. Wait a minute." The reddish-colored dog continued to pace and whine in front of the door. Truck engines rumbled from the outside. All the dogs growled and raced for the door, excited by the prospect of new people.

Brad snatched a scoped semi-auto rifle from the corner. "I thought you said there was nothin'." Jim handed a shotgun to Kyle.

"I didn't see *nothin'*."

"That don't sound like nothin'. Kelly, get those kids in the cellar. You remember the plan. Stanton's." He hesitated a moment, staring at his son. "You too, Jim."

"Dad, I'm staying with you. This is my fight."

Brad's eyes hardened in the corners. "It's our fight, but we have to let this cool down. Cellar, boy. I won't have none of it." His tone was one of no arguing.

Jim cursed and fled down the stairs.

Sadie wrapped an arm around Ahmed. "Come on." She led him toward the basement door.

"Who is it?" Ahmed asked.

"No time. I'll explain later." He let her lead them.

The family funneled into the basement. Sadie set him down next to a work bench and table for wood crafting. Tools lined the wall. One of the children cried and Barb picked her up into her arms. Sadie tiptoed up the cellar doors and watched through a crack. Ahmed weakly joined her.

"Who's there? Infected?"

Fear shown in her eyes. "The dead don't knock."

Truck headlights beamed on the front of the house from not one but three pickups.

"Jackson?" he whispered.

Sadie's brow scrunched in confusion. "Who's Jackson?"

"Don't worry," he said. "You got an extra gun?"

She shook her head no. "Dad and the boys do."

Ahmed moved his head near the crack in the cellar, ignoring the icy air seeping through.

Men were getting out of the trucks, doors slamming behind them. Their shadows filled the waning light in front of their headlights. Guns were held across their bodies; they looked like a band of deer hunters before a deer drive.

A man in a brown-and-tan uniform of a sheriff's deputy strode boldly ahead of the other armed men. The door banged on the porch and Ahmed stepped to the side to get a view of Brad. His footsteps echoed as he walked along the warped wood. Kyle stood a couple of feet behind Brad, standing taller than he would have if he were alone.

"A little late to be calling Deputy Vance, dontcha think?"

Deputy Vance wasn't a young man. Ahmed guessed he was in his late forties. A small belly poked over the lip of his belt, and his hair had enough gray in it for him not be carded at the liquor store. His facial hair was a grizzled attempt to remain professional when apparently it wasn't a thing anyone else worried about anymore.

"Now, Brad. You know as well as I do why we're here."

Brad shifted his feet. "Do I?"

Ahmed glanced at Sadie. Her face was clouded with worry that seemed to seep into the small lines of her face. Her hand covered the mouth of one of the children.

"You do."

Brad nodded as if he'd forgotten. "I know why you're here, Vance. No need to blow smoke up my ass."

Vance snorted. "We've known each other for a long time. Ain't that a fact?"

"I knew you when you were wiping your nose on your ma's apron. How is she?"

Vance glanced down at his feet. "She passed. We couldn't get her diabetes medicine, and it was only a matter of time."

"Sorry to hear that. She was a good woman even if she married a dimwit for a husband."

The deputy stiffened under the insult. "I don't appreciate that kind of tongue, Brad. My father was a damn good man."

"No, he wasn't. He was a drunk asshole."

A man a few inches over six foot tall stepped near the deputy. His hair was dark, and his nose came to a sharp point. His hands held a black shotgun. He had a handgun on his hip along with two extra magazines. "You going to let him talk to the law that way?"

Vance spoke over his shoulder. "I ain't. We're just talking." He turned back toward the porch. "Where's Jimmy?"

The dark-haired man spoke loud with venom. "We only want to talk to him, Bradley."

"Sly. You got no right bringing the deputy in on this."

Ahmed counted the men. There were at least ten armed men with Sly. He didn't doubt by their look that they knew how to use them too.

"I got every right. Your boy is a murderer."

A hand on Ahmed's shoulder pushed him to the side, and Jim eyed the crack.

"Those motherfuckers will pay." His head shook furiously. "I'm going out there."

"Jim, no." She grabbed his arm. "Dad said not to."

"He says to not do a lot of things."

Her eyes watered. "Please. If they don't think you're here, they'll leave."

He twisted his neck shaking his head. "This is crap."

The voices continued outside. "Sly. Don't bullshit me. I know why you're here, but it don't matter cause Jimmy's gone. Last I seen him was three days past. Said he was going south."

"Where south?"

"Does it matter? Won't last long out in the cold."

"Yes, it does," Deputy Vance said. "Now where'd he go?"

"He's got a cousin in Hannibal on his mother's side."

Sly leaned close to Vance, hissing, "He's lying."

Brad's finger shot out, pointing at Sly. "I don't lie, Sly Bailey. My word's good for it. Unlike your forked tongue."

Vance held up a hand. "Kyle, where's Jim?"

"Must a ran off."

"They're lying. They're all liars," Sly said.

Vance turned to Sly. "Just stay calm. We'll get to the bottom of this."

"The bastard has been lying since the day he was born. Ain't an honest bone in his body."

Brad twisted his head to the side. "Now Sly, I know you ain't calling me a liar. Those be fighting words."

"That's exactly what I'm calling you. You're a liar and your son is a murderer!" Sly said and then spit on the ground.

Brad calmly put his AR-15 to his shoulder. "Say when." Kyle followed his father's lead, aiming his shotgun at the other men.

The deputy stepped between the two parties, bringing his shotgun to his shoulder. "Whoa, Brad. Let's not get hasty here. We're only here to talk, to find out what happened." He lifted a hand off the shotgun to deter them from firing. "And I need to talk to Jim to figure it out."

"I know why you're here, Vance." Brad continued to stare down his sights, motioning with his chin. "I know why they're here. And it ain't to talk."

Vance monitored the other men in his group for ill will. "Everyone is here to talk. Ain't that right?"

Sly didn't say anything. He just stared down his gun barrel at Brad.

Vance's voice went up an octave. "Sly, put down the guns. Nobody has to get hurt here."

The tension decreased and Brad lowered his weapon. "He ain't here."

"Can I come in and take a look around?"

"As long as Sly and his redneck cousins stay outside."

The deputy held out a hand toward Sly. "He will stay outside."

Brad turned his back to the men, reaching for the door. "You really scared the hell out of Kelly, coming in here hot."

Vance took a few steps toward the door. Frigid ground crunched beneath him. A shotgun blast boomed, thundering through the night. The sound washed over them like an explosion. Ahmed jumped. Sadie squeaked in fright. Brad was pinned on the side of the house. Vance ducked low. Smoke drifted upward from Sly's barrel.

Kyle stared at his father sliding down the side of the house, his blood smearing the siding, his jaw open.

"Cease fire!" Vance screamed at him. "Jesus Christ!"

Brad rolled off the side of the house. Red streaked across the rust-colored siding, badly in need of a coat of paint, now stained in Brad's blood.

Sadie gasped and Jim's eyes went wide. "Father!"

Brad tried to shove Kyle out of the way, and brought his AR-15 to his shoulder. He started banging off shots at the other men. They opened up with a volley of shotgun blasts, rifle shots, and the rapid fire of handguns.

It was a short gunfight. Brad sank to his knees, his body riddled with bullets. Blood leaked from a dozen gunshot wounds. His body slumped. Kyle sprawled next to his father, his shotgun still in his hands.

"Is there a way out of here?" Ahmed said quickly.

Sadie nodded, her eyes blinking fear. The dogs paced in excitement, barking.

"Shut up, Bear," Jim said harshly. The dogs quieted down but continued to pace.

"What the hell was that? We came to talk!" Vance yelled at the men outside. He looked back over at Brad's body. The civilian carbine had fallen from his hand and he laid motionless on his side.

"He tried to kill us. You saw him. We just saved you more trouble."

"Jesus Christ. This is fucked six ways to Sunday." Vance shook his head. Men walked back from their pickups with red cans of gasoline.

"What are they doing?" Vance said.

Sly waved his men forward, ignoring the deputy for a moment. "What's it look like? We're going to send a message to those murdering bastards. Their kind will not be tolerated here."

The men surrounded the house, splashing gasoline as they went.

Ahmed felt a surge of panic in his gut, the kind where he didn't want to be burned alive today. "Sadie. How do we get out? They're going to torch us." He glanced back through the crack, watching them get closer.

Peanut let out a howl.

"Shit. You hear that?" Vance said.

Sly put his head back. "Dogs."

"Those fucking dogs. Let me check the house for Kelly before you light it." Vance skipped up the porch steps and around Brad. "Hello?" he shouted. "It's the police. I need everyone to come to the door. Everything's going to be okay."

Jim paced furiously, his knuckles white around his gun. The kids were crying in the arms of Barb and Kelly.

The voices of men were closing in outside the cellar doors. Liquids splashed around the cellar. Gasoline dripped through the cracks and Ahmed stepped quietly away.

"This way," Sadie said, grabbing Ahmed's arm. "Jimmy!" she yelled softly at him.

"Kelly?" The floorboards complained beneath the deputy's weight as his voice echoed above.

They didn't wait to see if the deputy came down the stairs. Jim opened another door and flicked on a flashlight. Cemented undecorated walls led them down a short corridor. He tested another door handle and that opened up to a storage room. Stockpiles of white pails of preserved food littered the shelves. Stacks of canned goods were all organized in one corner.

Jim led them to a ladder near the furthest wall. He climbed the metal rungs, his boots clicking off each one. He slid the lock on the upper hatch. He pushed with his free hand.

Anger and fear filled his every word. "It's stuck."

"Push harder. It's prolly frozen."

Ahmed knew the smell immediately but elevated his nose to be sure. "Smoke."

Flames leapt from down the hallway near the cellar. Smoke wormed along the connecting passage, a gray snake in cloud form. Sadie slammed the door closed and made it back to Ahmed. "Stay low."

The trapped people crouched to stay beneath the hot smoke. The women covered the children's mouths. Smoke flooded into the cellar beneath the door and sat heavily in the air, second by second filling the room. Sadie hacked into her arm.

"I got it!" Jim jerked the hatch up and down and threw it open.

Sadie pushed Ahmed up the ladder and Jim pulled him the rest of the way. Ahmed collapsed on the ground, the crisp air tasting sweet to his deprived lungs. They were about thirty yards from the house, surrounded by trees that blocked them from the dancing flames of the building.

"Can you use one of these?" Jim said.

"Yes."

Jim handed him the shotgun, and Ahmed crouched near a tree while Jim pulled the rest of the people from the ground. The orange-and-yellow flames engulfed the old house in a greedy siege. The men stood by the pickups, watching. Vance shook his head in disgust, but the other men laughed in delight.

Ahmed watched the flames, mesmerized by them. They took him back to another time and a former foe. Sadie touched his shoulder, startling him.

"We have a place to go."

She wrapped an arm around him, and they fled on foot deeper into the night woods.

THE PASTOR
Camp Forge, IA

The pastor dipped a rag into a bucket. The water was cold to the touch, having been chilled by the outside air. He wrung it between his hands until it was sufficiently damp. He placed the cloth over the woman's forehead, fixing a corner.

Her eyes flickered open. There wasn't much fight left in her. Fevered eyes scanned the room, searching for angels in the corners. He knew she didn't see much in her hallucinatory state. The pastor spoke softly, trying to spare her husband standing in the corner of the room chewing his fingernails one at a time.

"Go with God, sister. He awaits you with loving arms."

She closed her eyes, drifting into sleep. He stood. There were others in the early and intermediary stages of the flu. A whole row of them were lined in sweaty blankets, too weak to go outside to piss. While a fire roared in the fireplace, a few wrestled with their blankets and others shook with the chills.

"Father, is she going to be alright?" the stocky man said. His hair receded away from the front of his skull, and he had a thin mustache.

The pastor eyed him, sympathy spreading on his face. "Thomas, you are one of my finest. I would not lie to you. All we can do is pray for her. Even in despair, God is at work."

Thomas's head sank to his chest. "Yes, Father. Thank you."

"Keep your faith. We will come through this."

Thomas coughed hard into his hand. It was a wet hack of a man who was coming down with an illness.

"Take care of yourself. I don't want you falling sick."

He wiped his nose at the mention of becoming ill. "Yes, Father."

A voice came from the doorway of the cabin. "Father." The voice was confident and spoke with familiarity and reverence at the same time.

"Brother Peter," the pastor said. The curly-haired broad-shouldered man stepped inside but was hesitant as if he were afraid of the sick.

"Can we speak outside?"

"Of course."

The pastor's long strides easily took him toward the door, and he followed Peter outside.

The air was chilly and a brisk wind tugged and pulled at the pastor's clothes. He rolled his sleeves down. "What news do you have, brother?"

"He's agreed to meet," Peter said, eyes shifting.

"Excellent. Where?"

"There's an abandoned farm about a mile south of here near the battle site." Peter leaned closer. "Three men each."

"So few won't be missed. He is more clever than he looks."

Trying to make sure no one overheard, Peter whispered. "He said to meet at dusk three days from now."

"Then that is what we'll do." He put a hand on Peter's solid shoulder.

"Father, there is something else."

The pastor gave him a seasoned smile. "What troubles you?"

"There are more sick."

The pastor let his eyes close. Something as simple as the flu was ravaging his people, and that heathen warlord Steele sat in his house saying he'd done enough. They desperately needed antivirals, especially for the higher risk people, the old and the young, because it was spreading quick. His flock would be culled if action was not taken to preserve them.

"Show me."

They trudged down a sposhy path between the cabins. The snow hadn't been able to stick here, having been beaten down by hundreds of feet passing through day in and day out. Each cabin was spaced at least twenty feet from one another in ten-cabin rows. They exited the row into a lengthy opening leading to the new barns.

Men in camouflage lounged, basking in freedom they had neither earned nor deserved. These were the Romans who had persecuted his people across the ravaged remains of the United States, enemies that had been given mercy. *He gave you mercy. God's people deserve mercy. The corrupt Legion deserved to be cast back to hell.*

Soldiers stood watching him around the barn doors, arms folded over their chests. They must have recognized him from the battle. He felt his hand go to his carpenter's hammer. A wild rage boiled in his belly. It warmed him with violent fervor. A wicked smile crossed his lips like a curse.

"Father?" Peter asked, looking up at him.

The hammer was in his hand, its worn handle smooth in his palm. His vision flashed and all he saw was red as he bashed his way through them. His hammer struck out, catching men atop their skulls smiting them unto death.

"Father, are you okay?"

The pastor blinked away his daydream of violence. The men in camouflage still stood before him, watching him with curiosity. They had no weapons, and for that, the pastor was thankful. Steele's stupidity only went so far. "I am fine." He looped the hammer back through his belt, letting the head and claw keep it in place. "Take me to our afflicted brothers and sisters."

They walked down the front row of cabins. People went in and out. Some brought buckets of water. Others carried wood for their fires. He recognized some of their faces. Anthony and Buddy bowed their heads as they passed. He was plagued by the many that were missing: the blessed, Shaun and Shannon and Ian.

Peter waved him onward. "This way."

A cabin near the end of the row had its door closed. Peter knocked loudly on the wooden door.

An old woman answered, "Praise be, you're here."

"Praise be to the Lord."

She opened the door wider. "Come." She pointed toward the corner. "They're over there."

The pastor dodged through clusters of scared families. Their eyes pleaded for reprieve from the world around them. They pled for him to cure the sick, for him to stand for them, to shield them from the horrors of death. It was clear they had been abandoned in their time of need. They'd been cast to the side as meaningless mouths to feed.

Dirty blankets were draped over small forms in the corner. Tiny heads poked out from inside, making his heart sink in his chest. *More children.* He crouched down on his haunches. His knees screamed from wear and tear as bone rubbed against bone. He let one of his knees rest on the ground for support.

A little blonde girl lay in a pool of sweat, her hair matted to her forehead. He placed the back of his hand on her face. Her skin was like fire beneath his hand. He removed his hand and placed two fingers on the side of the child's neck. He adjusted his fingers, feeling for her pulse. He couldn't tell if he felt his residual heartbeat or hers. Gently he put his head near her mouth and listened. A faint rattle bubbled while she breathed, but she only breathed the tiniest amount.

He lifted his head. *God spare them this.* "And him too?" The pastor gestured at another small blanketed form.

"Yes, Father. They've all got it." The old woman's eyes pleaded with him.

"Are they all yours?"

"They've been fostered of sorts."

He inched his way upright, his old joints clicking with the effort. "You are a gracious and kind woman for what you've done. Let us pray together."

He bowed his head with the gray-haired woman for fifteen minutes, and as they prayed, the little girl passed on. He blessed her soul and waved a man from one of the other families. "Manuel, when she is done, help her take the child outside."

"Georgia, Georgia," the old woman moaned, cradling the girl's body.

Manuel's eyes shook. "I have a family."

Harsh air exited the pastor's nose. "God will protect you, but you must do this."

Manuel's eyes veered downward in shame. "Yes, Father."

"Peter, come." He stormed out of the cabin and was met by the cool fresh air the opposite of the stale corrupted air of the inside.

The pastor breathed it in, trying to calm himself. His blood boiled in anger.

"Father?"

The pastor collected himself, clenching his fists then letting them go. "Tell War Child we meet tonight. I will not take no for an answer."

"But he wanted to wait three days."

The pastor leered at his staunchest supporter, his voice unswerving. "Tonight."

JOSPEH
Cheyenne Mountain Complex, CO

Soldiers flooded into Dr. Nguyen's small office. The lead soldier drove his forearm into Joseph's neck. Joseph's feet forcibly reversed, and his back banged the wall. The soldier's meaty forearm threatened to cut off his air supply, and he pointed the short barrel of an MP5 submachine gun within an inch of Joseph's face.

The back of Joseph's head touched the wall as he tried to stay away from the end that brought death. Desai shrieked as another soldier shoved her backwards, driving her neck first to her knees. In a fraction of a second, the soldiers controlled all points of the small room.

A soldier bent down and roughly touched Nguyen's neck.

"He's dead."

The soldier scrutinized Joseph from behind his faceless mask, only his eyes readable. "What did he tell you?"

"Nothing, I swear," Joseph whined.

The soldier walked to where Joseph was held incapacitated, threatened by an expedient death at the end of a bullet. He reached an ungloved hand and squeezed Joseph's cheeks like he was trying to extract every last drop of juice from a lemon.

"Why are you here?"

Joseph blinked in painful terror. "We work together. We're doctors."

"What happened?"

"He mumbled something about not enough time and pulled a gun from his drawer and shot himself. I swear it."

The soldier's head twisted toward Dr. Desai. "Is this true?"

"Yes. Let us go. We're doctors."

The soldier's hazel eyes regarded Joseph with suspected scrutiny. "I don't give a shit who you are," he said, only his mask moving. "I'm sure we'll be talking soon."

The soldier pinning Joseph removed his forearm and took a step back.

Another soldier gestured at the door. "Get 'em out of here."

With military fervor, the doctors were escorted into the hallway. Joseph brought a hand to his neck and rubbed blood back into his flesh.

The soldiers began the process of tossing Nguyen's room with blatant disregard for the scientific material that they may be destroying or disorganizing in a fashion that would make continued research difficult.

"We need his documents for our research," Joseph called inside the room from the doorway.

"Get out of here!" A soldier pointed down the hall with his hand off his gun.

Wrapping an arm around Desai, Joseph led her away. Her eyes were unblinking, she muttered, "He . . . he shot himself."

Joseph chanced a glance down the hall. Medics rolled a stretcher toward the room. Binders were tossed into a haphazard pile in the hallway. A soldier set his laptop to the side. *They're probably looking for the flash drive.*

The flash drive seemed to burn a hole in his pocket now that he knew it was the object of such malicious pursuit.

He mumbled over his shoulder as he walked. "I know he did. Here." They stopped at his room. He grabbed the door handle. It jiggled but stood its ground. He pulled out his keys and unlocked the door. He ushered Dr. Desai inside and closed the door behind him. He twisted the lock and exhaled. "What's going on?"

She dropped down into his single chair next to his desk. "He shot himself in the head and blew his brains out," Desai said to herself.

"He'd rather die than get caught." Joseph sat on his bed across from her.

Her rich brown eyes regarded him for a moment. "What was he caught up in?" She propped her head up with her fists.

"You mean what are we caught up in?"

Her eyes turned upright with worry. "I'm scared."

"Me too," he said. "If Nguyen killed himself for it, then it must be important. He was one of us. He wanted to save people's lives." He nudged his glasses back up his nose. He carefully placed his hand in his pocket and felt the cool rectangular flash drive in his hand. His palm started to sweat as it wrapped around the object of harm. He carefully removed it from his pocket, like it was a bomb that could go off and kill them at a moment's notice.

Her brow raised. "No, Joseph. Put that away."

He extended his hand and let his fingers gradually expand, revealing the drive. She peeked away at the wall in fear and back at him. Her voice dropped low. "Those soldiers were looking for that."

"And Nguyen didn't want them to find it."

"And now we have it."

Joseph stared at the drive. Men disappeared and men died because of this tiny little portable drive sitting in his hand. His heart drummed inside his rib cage. *I should get rid of it. Smash it. Dump it in the biowaste bin and be done with it. Never happened.* His mind was ever the devil's advocate. *Dr. Nguyen's brains splattering the walls never happened? Byrnes imprisoned never happened?*

He glanced at his silver laptop sitting on his desk. The screen was black. His eyes read hers. "I could smash it and dump it in a biowaste bin. It will get incinerated. No evidence. Never happened."

Fear dripped from her, but she reeled herself in. "Don't you want to know?"

Joseph brushed his hair behind his ear. "If we know, then we are implicated in the whole thing. We're no different than Byrnes and Nguyen."

"If they did something illegal, they wouldn't have done so lightly."

"Neither would I," Joseph said. The contorted face of the bleeding-out soldier clutching his neck stared up at Joseph with wide accusing eyes. The murder he'd committed in his quest to find Patient Zero. The soldier probably wasn't innocent under Jackson's command, but Joseph had stabbed him over and over in the neck anyway, fear driving him onward. But it wasn't just fear, it was his obligation to defeat the virus.

A knock resounded off the door, and Joseph almost pissed himself. His gut did a full adrenaline dump, and he shot to his feet. His bodily systems were in total fight or flight. Desai's chair screeched along the hard floor. Her eyes widened with fright. Joseph held the guilty piece of evidence out in his hand. Her head quivered in fear. The outsider knocked again louder. *Thump, thump, thump.*

She snatched the flash drive in her hands and worked it quickly into the bun of her hair. She finished by smoothing her shirt and gave him a nervous nod.

"Who is it?" Joseph called out. He timidly walked to the door his feet fighting him on every step.

"It's Dr. Hollis. Open up."

Joseph stepped closer, listening intently for additional parties on the other side. "Is it just you?"

Hollis grunted on the other side in dissatisfaction. "Yes, of course."

He twisted the lock vertical and turned the knob, opening the door. The heavy doctor stood in the hallway, his lab coat making him look like a white tent. Joseph peered at him through the crack.

Hollis's eyes narrowed. "What are you doing? Open your door." He put a hand on the door handle.

"Why are you here?" Joseph put some weight behind the door, preparing to physically bar his entrance.

It was as if Joseph's words were a stinging glove strike to Hollis's cheek. "To talk to my colleague. Must I have any other reason? I must say you are being quite rude."

"Get in." Joseph opened the door further making room.

The wide doctor ambled inside. "Oh, Dr. Desai, I'm glad you're here. I was looking for you too."

Joseph closed the door behind him and slid the lock into place. *Click.* Hollis gave him a curious look. His eyes darted back at Dr. Desai and then to Joseph.

"What's going on here?" His eyes went back to Desai and tapered in scrutiny. "Why are you sitting in your room with the door locked?"

Desai blurted out, "It's Dr. Nguyen."

Hollis's eyes grew wider. "No. What happened?" He looked back at Joseph for confirmation.

"He's dead."

Hollis made a throaty noise like a piece of meat was caught inside. "No. Ridiculous."

"We saw him do it."

"What do you mean saw him do it?"

Joseph rubbed his forehead. "He shot himself in front of us."

"What? This . . . this is terrible." Hollis clapped his hands together and began rubbing them. "First Byrnes and now Nguyen." His eyes glanced at Joseph with beady nervous energy, a pig stuck with his head through the fence. "We could be next."

Joseph nodded. "There's more."

Hollis held up a hand. "No more. I've heard enough."

Joseph wouldn't let him escape without sharing his burden with the man. "He gave us something."

"Nope. Nope. Nope. Get out of the way, I'm leaving."

Joseph blocked the door with his body. "Can't let you leave. You're on our team. We need you."

Hollis's eyebrows raised and his jaw set in a determined manner. "Need I tell you I played prop on my prep school rugby team. With a twist of his neck, he said, "I'll smash you into oblivion if you don't remove yourself from my egress."

"Wait." She dug her hands into her hair, fishing out the flash drive. "This is it." She held it out in Hollis's direction.

He squeezed his eyes closed. "I can't unsee that."

"Nguyen gave it to us, right before he shot himself. He said we must protect whatever's on here."

Hollis round head wavered from side to side. "No. No. I don't want to be a part of this. I want to be safe and sound in a giant mountain fortress surrounded by the might of the U.S. Military, not whatever this is." He pointed a finger at it. "This . . . this thing that is killing some of the last remaining brilliant minds on the planet."

"You are one of us. You're part of MIM. Just like the other two." Desai brought it closer to him. "We owe it to them to see this through."

"Do we?" Hollis cocked his head. "I owe it to myself to forget this ever happened."

Joseph placed a hand on Hollis's shoulder. "We need you."

"For what? You both are very capable doctors. Step aside, my good sir."

"You're not even curious as to what's on it?"

"Not in the least bit."

Desai chimed in. "Dr. Nguyen died for this. We owe it to him to at least see what he died for."

Hollis growled like a dog his fat wriggling in frustration. "Fine. I'll look at it, but then I leave, and we never talk about this again."

Desai gave a timid smile and a nod. "Agreed."

Joseph grinned. "Agreed." He went to his computer and moved the mouse. The screen lit up. He scrolled to the top of the monitor. He clicked the Wi-Fi and scrolled down to the off button and clicked it. The four Wi-Fi lines disappeared and left only a pie slice outline in its place. Desai handed him the flash drive and connected it to the computer.

After a second, an ejectable drive folder popped up on his desktop. He rolled the mouse toward it.

"Do you have anything to eat?" Hollis asked worriedly behind him.

Joseph motioned blindly to a drawer. "Crackers in there."

The drawer opened and closed followed by the crinkling of a plastic bag. Joseph's cursor hovered over the folder. He looked over his shoulder to Desai. She nodded. Hollis munched food over his other shoulder.

Crumbs fell from his mouth. "Just do it. I don't know if my heart can handle the stress of waiting any longer." He finished by shoving his hand back into the bag.

Joseph double-clicked and the folder opened. A single document and video appeared inside. That was all. Men were killing themselves over this. He moved his cursor to the video, hesitant to discover the contents. His finger smashed the button, and the video started.

TESS
Camp Forge, IA

Tess rolled her neck out. She hopped on her feet and hugged herself, trying to stretch her back. The scarred skin covering her shoulders was rigid as if someone had tightened her skin into taut leather. She ran a hand over her short hair letting the unwashed grease keep it in place.

She wrinkled her nose in response to the onslaught of odor. Too many people too close together minus sufficient bathing equaled a distinctly human stench. She didn't know which was worse: the smell of piss coming from her neighbors' stall or the family of six wedged into a space no bigger than her own.

Her little corner of the barn was dark, the only light coming from the firepit built into the center. It filled the barn with a permanent smoky haze, but it was better than freezing to death.

She slipped her arms through her shoulder harness, sliding her Colt .45 1911 into its well-worn holster. Grooves and dents encased the leather along with sweat that had been ground in drop by drop over time, some of it hers, most of it from a Grand Rapids detective. She'd heard some of the survivors naming their weapons, but she'd never named hers. It was only the gun to her, an effective tool of survival passed from the lifeless hand of a detective into hers.

Its weight rested comfortably into the crease of her armpit just like it had for its previous owner. The gun carried more than its physical weight; it also carried an air of responsibility as if only the righteous could wield it. Not that she was righteous, not in the fashion that society would have shoved her into. She embodied her own form of rough righteousness, a dusky dying light fending off the darkness instead of a shining star.

She shouldered a heavy drab green winter coat. She shoved the tarp open that hardly covered her sliver of space, no more than four by six feet.

Quietly, she stepped along the wood floor. The boards groaned beneath her soft feet. She had fewer bodies to dodge as the morning sun was already making its assault upon the nighttime sky.

She kicked a lying form by accident.

"Hey," a voice came from beneath a mound of blankets.

"Sorry." Her feet weaved successfully past a few others.

Tony and Margie tended the fire in the middle of the barn. The motherly woman regarded Tess with kindness, and Tony smiled beneath black-rimmed glasses, his forehead almost too big for his receding flipped back hair.

The IT programmer in his early forties had been inseparable from Margie since Pentwater. The two did every patrol, every mundane tasking, including bedding down, together. Even with a substantial age gap, the two acted like inseparable teenage lovers.

Margie was the most relaxed Tess had seen her since Sable and outwardly showed happiness, but it was only a shroud over the stab of sorrow inside Tess's heart. Pagan's perpetually smiling face flashed before her eyes. His smile would then turn to screams and melt away into orange flames.

"Morning," Margie said. When she noticed Tess's face, her eyebrows narrowed in worry.

"Morning, Margie. Tony."

"Should have some coffee for you in a few minutes," Tony said. He knelt next to the fire and put a kettle of water on a stand over the flames. He had all the hallmarks of a man who would take his time brewing the best coffee, one of those people that hand ground their own beans. He would ensure it was all perfect, even knowing that this would be a weak cup at its finest.

"That'd be great." She squatted down atop a wooden crate.

Margie's voice dipped down. "I still can't believe he let them go."

Tess snorted. "Who? The Chosen or the Legion?"

Tony stirred the contents of the open coffeepot, studying the grounds swirling inside. "You think they'll come back?"

"I think a lot of things."

"But you know him best. What does he say?"

"He's got his reasons. But what I don't like is us doing all the fighting and dying only to let the pricks go at the end of the day."

Margie's eyebrows slanted higher making her appear even more worried. "Every day the dead gather along the river. Why add to their number when we're the ones dwindling?"

With a rag, Tony handled the coffeepot. He poured the hot liquid into a tin for Tess. She raised her mug to him in a gesture of thanks. His smile was slim.

"The Chosen fight with us after they fought against us. Now the soldiers are here. Why wouldn't they do the same?" he said, handing a cup to Margie.

The woman, edging up on her sixties, rubbed her arm while drinking her coffee. "Well, I trust the captain's leading us in the right direction. He's gotten us through tough times, and I'm not going to lie." She gave Tony a sly glance. "These last few months, while lean, have been the best since the outbreak."

"It could be a lot worse." Tess slurped her drink, eyeing a curly-headed man coming their way. He took a seat.

"Hey, Rick," Margie said.

Tony stood and handed Rick a cup of coffee over the fire. "Take this."

"Not today. I've got a prayer meeting this morning."

Tess glared at him. Rick scratched his head with a nervous finger. "See you later."

She watched him go in disgust. "Brazen motherfucker, isn't he?"

Margie turned her head to the side. "He's not a bad guy. He's fought with us all over the country."

"Yeah, and he goes and plays patty-cake with those Chosen sons of bitches." She'd never forget the looks of exultant glee on their faces as the flames engulfed Pagan's body.

Tony's voice hushed. "The Chosen have been fighting with us. You saw them."

79

Tess had seen them get gunned down by Jackson's soldiers in droves, body parts strewn about the field. She had seen the Chosen men holding their guts in while Humvees drove over their bodies and crushed their limbs. She'd seen them crawling while Jackson's Legion executed them where they lay. She would be a liar if she had told them it didn't make her happy. Fewer of them made the world better. If the earth could have opened up and taken the whole lot of them, she would have danced for joy.

She threw the rest of her coffee back. "I've got to go." She handed the cup back to Tony. "Thanks. I'll see you guys later."

Slipping through the bodies, she found her way through the barn doors. Curly-haired Rick walked through the camp toward the pastor's cabins. She spit in his general direction and drifted toward the Red Stripes' cabins. She crossed in front of the old farmhouse.

Two men stood speaking in front of Thunder's cabin. One was heavyset with a bandana around his gray hair; the other had a sturdy build and blond curly hair. She stopped and stared at the two men. Thunder gestured while he talked. When he saw Tess, his mouth clamped shut. The other man gazed over his shoulder. An evil smile crawled across his lips. He stuck out his hand and Thunder clasped it. Peter turned and walked away through the cabins.

Tess approached her old ally. "Morning, Thunder."

"Tess." A smile spread under his graying white beard.

She threw a thumb at Peter's retreating figure. "What was that about?"

"That knucklehead?" He waved a hand. "You know them. Who's digging the trenches? Who's on watch? Usual bullshit."

Her dark eyes considered him.

He cocked his head to the side. "Tess, my dear. Now don't you come in here looking at me like I robbed a panty store."

"You know I don't like my longtime bud getting all chummy with them."

Thunder placed a hand over his heart. "Scout's honor. Nothing bad going on here." He glanced over her shoulder. "It ain't them I'm worried about anyway."

Soldiers with shovels and picks walked in a gang toward the water.

"I still can't believe he let them go. Those bastards killed a lot of us."

"So did the Chosen."

Thunder scratched under his red bandana with a dirty fingernail. "Chosen weren't as good at killing."

"Don't like either of them, but if I had to pick a group to fall into a black hole first, it'd be the Chosen."

"Tess," came a voice from inside the cabin. A tall man ducked under the doorframe. She embraced his waist in a hug.

"Garrett. How are you?"

The man grinned down through a graying beard peppered with flecks of black. "I seen warmer days."

They released. "Want some chow?" Thunder asked.

"Nah, I got somebody I need to check in on."

Thunder's belly jiggled as he laughed. "All right. Suit yourself."

She cut through the cabins down a muddy beaten path. Figures formed in the distance, looking like a pack of infected. Her hand itched for her Colt 1911 .45 caliber handgun resting in its holster. She wanted to rub the rough grip and feel its coarse grains across the skin of her palm. It beckoned her with violent safety. *Make sure I'm near. You can only trust me. Not them. Never them. I am your salvation,* it seemed to whisper. Her hands begrudgingly stayed in her pockets though as she walked. The figures were too stationary to be infected, but they were deadly just the same.

Over three hundred people stood in the wintery field. Yellow stacks of grass and hay peeked out from under the snow. The people stood facing one direction. Tess shouldered into the crowd, brushing past people. People stood on tiptoes trying to get a better view.

Tess lifted her chin. A gray-haired man stood at the front, taller than the rest. She knew his long face and his lanky arms all too well. He gesticulated at the sky.

"God hath put a scourge upon us."

The people shouted, "No!"

"Yes, sadly so." He shook his head. "Many of us are not here today because they've succumbed to a disease. It is not like those who've been marked by the beast, but it kills us all the same. Our people lie in their beds suffering while those that have the power to help sit idly by."

Angry shouts erupted.

"There is medicine that could save our people. Not here. Not in Hacklebarney. But surely other places have the medicine. We needn't suffer anymore." He took a step closer to the crowd and raised his voice. "I will send Matthew to give us deliverance from this evil."

The crowd gave shouts of praise.

"My people go in peace. I only do what God commands."

"Praise be to God," howled a man.

"Praise be to the father," shouted another man.

"Thank you!" said a woman overcome with emotion.

The pastor held up a hand. "No need to thank me. A shepherd cares for his flock."

Tess formed her mouth into a tight line, speaking to herself amid the clamor. "Motherfucker. Gwen's already out gathering medicine and supplies."

"God wills it!" They turned their heads to the sky and yelled. "God wills it."

ALVARADO
La Crescent, MN

Muted sunlight filtered through classroom windows. It was a frail light from a sun obscured by wintery white clouds. The classroom walls were covered in posters of cartoon numbers that resembled people as aids to help children learn how to do simple math. Next to the posters was a chart lined with names and gold stars. She ignored the names spelled in block letters. They were probably all dead.

A couple of Marines stood near the windows looking out. There was an uneasy tension around them. Every minute more dead flooded by the school, and as more dead came, the chances they'd be discovered grew even greater. She estimated thousands had passed in the night, and every hour even more breached their defensive line.

A rifle squad rested along the wall. Heavy packs lay at their sides along with their firearms. Helmets sat on the packs and polar fleece watch caps kept their heads warm inside the unheated building.

Thickly built Sergeant Riddle stood with Major Alvarado.

"How hard did you have to push them to be here?" she asked. The last thing she wanted was men that didn't want to be there.

"Ma'am, every single Marine volunteered for this mission. Would have been easier if there were only a handful of them. Lance Corporals Odom and Rasmussen are steady Marines." She knew Odom from the night prior. Rasmussen reminded her of a young Tommy Lee Jones with bushy eyebrows

83

and a square jaw. "It's not a full squad, but they will do what needs to be done." He scratched under his winter hat. "I handpicked the rest from my old platoon. O'Bannon, Finch and Foster are tireless. Johnson is practically a horse. If it can be done, they'll find a way."

"I trust your judgment, Sergeant."

"And we trust yours, ma'am."

She ignored his compliment. It wouldn't mean much if they all died in the snow or inside the school or on the river opening the northern flank to the hordes of the dead, but it made her want to smile. A smile she wrestled deep inside. This was not a time for smiles. This was a time for a gut check. *Can we pull off the Hail Mary? Can we find an ounce of luck in our defeat?* Find an opening and never surrender.

Riddle motioned the Marines upright. Odom and O'Bannon were the tallest. Johnson was almost as tall but much wider. Rasmussen looked like his face had been carved from a square. Privates Harry and Adams appeared young enough to be freshman in high school. Despite months of fieldwork, only thin soft hair tickled their cheeks. They were Marines, every one of them. Black, white, brown, and yellow, they crossed the gambit of American humanity. And she trusted every Marine standing there. She trusted them even more in a scrap.

"I'm not going to blow smoke up your ass. We're probably going to die." Her words actually generated a smile from a few of the Marines as if she were setting up a joke that only they could know the punch line of. "You volunteered to give us a shot at closing the breach, and I wouldn't ask you to do that in my place."

"Oorah," the Marines said softly. Staying quiet was essential to surviving longer. Allowing the flood of the dead to pass was step one to their desperate plan. So far, it had worked.

"It's imperative that every single member of this squad knows what the plan is before we depart. We don't come back until the mission is complete. Understood?"

They nodded their acceptance of success or death as only Marines could with grim satisfaction that every breath went into the defeat of the enemy.

"We are going to cross north of La Crosse where there should be fewer Zulus. Then we're going to follow the river south, planting charges and blowing the ice. We will go as far as we can. This will give us some breathing room. Then we will regroup and clear the river south to Captain Heath's command."

"What if the ice refreezes?"

She shook her head. "We need to open our moat back up. It will take regular maintenance until the river can do the job for us again. Right now, we focus on regaining the initiative." She paused, eyeing her boys. "There is no shame in backing out now. We will hold no ill will toward you. This is going to be an ugly fight." She knew that peer pressure reinforced bravery, but if any single one of these men was still debating whether or not they had it in them to lay it on the line, she wasn't going to take them with her. She didn't want them if there was an ounce of hesitation in their resolve.

"Are you all in?"

The Marines wanted to yell but kept their voices at a meaningful whisper. "Oorah, Major."

She nodded. "Oorah, Marines."

She shouldered her pack and left the room. The soft tread of Marine boots on the school tile floor sounded like music to her ears. Marines never laid down. They fought off their backs and kicked and crawled their way to victory.

They passed through a lightless cafeteria full of round tables and empty blue plastic chairs for young students. Chairs and tables long left vacant by the outbreak.

Gently, she opened a wooden swinging door to the kitchen. Marines stood in the back storage room that used to hold canned goods. The Marines here were dressed warmly but not as bundled as the Marines at her back. They had rigged together metal sleds for hauling the explosives, ammunition, and supplies not carried on their person. A metal push-bar door loomed near them, danger seeping through the cracks.

Using his hand, Captain Butler silently goaded her over.

"Major, we have two big sleds here. They will need to be pulled by at least two Marines each. Maybe one once they lighten up."

"Got it." Rope was knotted in a loose sling that could be thrown over one shoulder and across the chest effectively making them sled dogs.

Butler bent down and picked up more equipment. "Lance Corporal Murphy had the foresight to acquire these snowshoes from the locals a couple weeks ago. They will keep you atop the snow and ice. They should allow you to move faster than the Zulus."

She took the two-foot-long snowshoes. She'd expected them to be braided. They were made of a lightweight alloy frame filled with a high-density polyethylene deck. A ratcheting system allowed them to be quickly put on and taken off. The fronts of the shoes curved upright to assist the wearer in natural movement whether it was walking or running. The dispersion of weight would help keep them atop the heavy snow even while weighted down by their packs. "These should make it a hell of a lot easier than getting here."

"It should, ma'am."

Butler and two other Marines handed them out to the rest of her depleted rifle squad. Nine men and herself. No, ten Marines.

"Wait until we get a bit up the road. Then you can commence."

Captain Butler's nose flared a fraction. His part of the plan had its own set of dangers, and while hers would certainly lead to death, his would be a slower kind of holdout until he was overrun. The main difference was she would probably die in the freezing cold while he would get cut down surrounded by a company of the finest Marines he'd ever met. It was a psychological difference: fighting from an elevated platform and holding out versus running and gunning in the field with zero advantages in zero-degree weather.

"We'll do it."

Her eyes read his for a moment, and she cleared her throat. "Once we get the river cleared between us and La Crosse, you can begin the cleanup of the area but focus on retaking our comms from Barron. The colonel must know what's happened here."

She purposely left out the last part about the movement south. Butler knew what the odds were that she would succeed. Almost zero, but there was a chance they could reopen their protective river moat, and if there was a shot, by God, she would take it.

The reality of the situation was that Captain Butler would have to decide when to break free of their impromptu base and make a dire run south to Captain Heath's command. She had ordered him to give her time, but once she pushed the barred door open, he was effectively in charge. He would do what he was told, but when push came to shove, he would operate as if she were already dead. He was a good Marine, albeit a bit unsteady on his own, but he would attempt to fall back and regroup.

Butler stuck out his hand and brought it sharply to his forehead.

Alvarado was surprised by this. They did not salute in the field for many reasons, and the situation did not call for such formalities. The other Marines in the room did the same. Equipment creaked in their silent salute.

Her voice lowered. "Captain, no need."

The captain shook his head no. "Every need, ma'am. Thank you. It's been an honor." His lips tightened as if he were controlling his emotions. She could have easily ordered himself or Wess or anyone else to go on this mission, but that wasn't her style. Her style was to do the dirty work herself and show them that at the end of the day, she was no different. A motivated leader who would fight and get the job done. No questions asked. But her captain and the other Marines saluting meant that she had earned something that so many men and women strived for but never got, and that was respect. Respect of these men was worth more than their weight in gold. More than that, it was priceless.

She placed a hand to her forehead in return. "I trust you Marines will give the enemy hell. We will return when the mission is complete."

"Oorah, Major!" Their voices echoed in the kitchen. Didn't matter if they were loud now. A desperate fight was coming no matter what their actions were.

"Oorah, Marines." She let her hand fall crisply to her side and rested back down on her weapon. She pulled her balaclava up over her nose and mouth and secured her hat over top. One could leak all their heat from their head and die before they knew they were freezing to death.

She put a gloved hand on the push-bar door. Softly she depressed the bar and the metal doorjamb clacked. She didn't need to signal the Marines; she knew they would follow right behind her.

The door opened just a crack, no more than an inch. White light poured inside the lightless kitchen. Wind whipped up flurries that snuck through the opening. Weight pressed back from the other side. She stuck a foot into the door and placed her shoulder into it.

Twelve inches of snow weighed in from the outside. The door ground as both snow and ice resisted her. She hefted her M4A1 to her shoulder and stepped out into a drift. Her feet sank deep into the cold whiteness step after step. She covered their way but going hot so close to the school would put them in a dire spot early.

A mound of snow-covered dumpsters lay unmolested nearby. She scanned the alley entrance while her men set up sleds and secured their snowshoes with their hardened metal crampons that would give them traction on the icy terrain.

A Zulu wailed as it slowly marched by. She felt her gut tighten and kept her sights trained on it. All her Marines stood silent, stopping everything they were doing. The grayish almost black-skinned creature swayed as it trudged past the alley opening behind the school.

Her breath came out in a forceful push. Marines bounded past her and covered her while she put on her snowshoes. She tossed the shoes atop the snow and ratcheted her boot into the center of the shoe. Unsteadily, she did the same with her other foot.

She took a step and was able to stay atop the white winter quicksand. The snowshoes were awkward at first, but it was infinitely easier than sinking into the drifts, your energy being zapped with every step. *Crunch. Crunch.* She joined the rearmost Marine.

She patted the Marine in front of her, skipping by them one by one until she took her place near Sergeant Riddle. She rested a quick hand on his shoulder. He gave her a terse nod.

They moved on the double from the alley to the street. Looking east, she saw hundreds if not thousands of dead marching in their direction and she shuddered. She felt fear, by God, how could anyone not feel fear? But she kept moving north. Step by step they advanced despite the fear. There was no time for fear.

GWEN
Near Shimek State Forest, IA

The dampened clops of horse hooves echoed off the snow-covered road surface complemented by the jingle of the hayrack's harnesses. They had made a quick stopover in the town of Donnellson, Sheriff Donnellson's ancestral contribution to the local region. The thought of that man sharing lineage with the founders of a town made Gwen shake her head. They knew the medical center had been stripped down already. But they did a quick search of it anyway, unable to find anything. They carried on mile by mile toward Farmington.

The group closed in on dense naked timber. Jake pulled his horse to a halt in front of a brown wooden sign in the shape of Iowa. Yellow engraved writing on it read Shimek State Forest. He drew his heavy denim overcoat tighter around his body, his shotgun barrel sticking out the side. He wore a heavy felt cowboy hat and a thick scarf over his face and neck making him look like a bandit.

His voice was muffled beneath the scarf. "We should take shelter in that house over there."

Gwen tightened the scarf over her head and readjusted the blankets around her body. She eyed the ranch-style house sitting on the edge of the forest. "No, we should keep going."

Jake studied her warily. "Gwen, it's mighty cold out here, and there ain't no guarantee we'll have shelter in the woods, and we sure as hell ain't making it through by nightfall."

"That's fine. We ride until we get to Farmington."

Jake removed his scarf so she could see the angst on his face. "It's too cold for that. Once the sun goes down, we are looking at the temperature dropping into the teens. It ain't good for the horses or us."

Gerald chimed in. "I agree. It's cold and we could use a break." His jaw was just as broad as his father's, and when it settled, his look impersonated a stubborn bulldog. He pushed his lips up under his nose with a willful nod of his head. He wore quilt-lined black coveralls and a black stocking hat.

She shared an eye with Gregor. She knew he would go along with whatever decision she made; he was loyal like that. Hank sat on his horse, his teeth chattering and his rifle slung diagonally across his puffy-coated back. He appeared to have had enough of the cold for a lifetime.

She shook her head no. "We go on. Every minute counts. The longer we're gone, the more that will die."

"You're pregnant. You need rest," Jake said.

Gwen pulled her scarf down her face. The cold wind bit and nipped like a pack of wolves at her skin. "We keep moving."

Jake pulled his scarf back up over his face, muttering something about Reynolds and mules and asses. He clicked his tongue forcing his red mare onward.

Flicking his reins on the backs of the two larger draft horses, Kenny said, "Get on now." They picked back up at a slow walk. "Get on now," he repeated louder. The two horses pulled a bit quicker.

They passed the Shimek State Forest sign and entered the woods. They made it about a mile in before the light faded and the temperature dropped. She could see the men around her hunker down on their animals against the biting wind. Hats were pulled lower, coats drawn tighter, and heads dipped to deflect the freezing onslaught.

The animals and group slowed as the hours ticked by. Gwen grew tired and she felt frozen to the seat and the rock of the wagon. Her eyes dipped and she shook herself back awake. Jake led them forward using a flashlight to spot-check their route in the layer of white snow guided by the thick unmolested timber of the Iowa state forest on either side.

The forest gave way to a clearing and a cluster of buildings. The group slowed down and Jake led them to a silver-sided barn. The wagon slowed to a halt. "Why are we stopping?" she mumbled. Jake hopped off his horse and stiffly made his way toward her. He took her in his arms and lifted her off the wagon. "Stop."

"Now, I see there's a few of ya, but just move along." A man pumped a shotgun, the international signal to make haste in your departure. Three men stood near the road guns in aimed at them.

Jake stopped with Gwen in his arms and glimpsed in their direction like he was escorting her to their wedding suite.

"What you doing with that one?" the voice shouted.

Raising his voice over the howls of the wind, Jake said, "We're freezing. We need shelter."

"Don't take too kindly to strangers making demands."

Jake made himself bigger, puffing out his chest. "Where's Bart?"

"Who's asking?"

"Tell him Jake Bullis's come looking for his payment."

"You tell Jake to get the hell on out of here before he takes a slug to the chest."

Frosted air exited Jake's nose. "You tell that dirty no good scoundrel Bart that he better pay before I get the sheriff involved."

The man laughed. "Sheriff Donnellson? That old goober? He'd rather march around town and shake hands than uphold the law."

"I guess we'll have to fight it out then."

Hank and Gregor leveled their weapons at the rival men.

Jake waved them down. "I'll handle this, guys."

The men marched within a few feet of Jake.

They stared at one another for a moment. The other man sucked in his cheeks, staring up at Jake, and then lowered his gun and shook his head.

"Coming in here like a bunch of cattle rustlers. Jeez, man. I almost shot you." His eyes narrowed. "And I ain't paying nothing."

Jake shook his head. "I ain't asking for payment. Just a place to stay."

Bart nodded. "Boys, go clear out some stalls for their horses." Then turning back to the newcomers. "Get on inside."

The entire group marched down a snowy driveway and the young men took their horses.

Deer carcasses hung in the trees near the house. The deer were stretched longer than normal, their insides removed leaving them hollow. The frigid outside acted as refrigeration for the animals. Four-wheelers and snow mobiles sat on the front lawn if it could be called that, along with another dilapidated shed and a camping trailer.

Heat blasted them as they entered the home, stinging their cheeks. A black iron wood stove pumped out heat in the corner, and along the wall, a fireplace danced with orange flames.

"Make yourselves comfortable, I'll put on a kettle," Bart said and disappeared.

Gwen plopped down on a beige couch and sat for ten minutes before she removed her hands from her swaddling of blankets and clothes. She faced them toward the fire, enjoying the heat that reddened her skin. The warmth took its turn thawing her frozen limbs.

Bart returned with metal cups in his hands which he distributed to the group. Gwen took a cup, scalding her hands, and she didn't care one bit. He stood near the door watching them for a moment.

"Can't say I know these boys, Jake. Where'd they come from?" He took a sip.

Jake's cheeks were red from their reintroduction to heat and he cupped his mug in his hands. "That's Gregor and Hank." The men nodded. "From Michigan."

"Well ain't you a long ways from home."

"We are," Hank said. He stood as close to the fire as he could.

Bart peered at the men, expecting a longer answer, and when he didn't get one, took another sip of his hot drink. "And I don't believe we've met."

"I'm Gwen Reynolds, Mayor of Hacklebarney."

"Now, that don't sound right." Bart's face crinkled in puzzlement. "I thought George Dobson was the mayor of Hacklebarney."

Gwen let the cup painfully heat her hands. "He was." She eyed him.

He pursed his lips and nodded. "As you can see, we don't get too many travelers in Shimek, and I don't hear too much about what's going on out there. Everything I hear on the radio sounds like madness. When I heard anything. Damn thing's quit working."

"Things are bad," she said. "We got a war on our hands."

"With who?" he asked, his brow furrowing. "Ain't the Ruskies, is it?"

"No, it's the dead."

"Dead? Shouldn't be too bad if they already dead."

Her lips formed a thin grim smile. "The sickness you heard about raises the dead back to life as monsters."

"Jesus." He rubbed his neck. "You can understand my misgivings, but that sounds crazy."

"Worse than crazy. My grandparents' farm is now a militia training base. The military's got us trying to hold the river against the dead."

"Jesus. I just can't believe this."

"Believe it. The dead are coming."

Bart breathed a sigh. "What brings you out here?"

"There's an illness in our camp. We need medicine and we welcome anyone who wants to fight."

Bart shook his head no. "I'm sorry. You're welcome to look at our first-aid kits, but I don't think you are going to find what you're looking for." He took a sip as he thought. "Did you try the medical center in Donnellson?"

"We did. They've been emptied."

Bart scratched a gray and black stubbly cheek. "That's a shame. Farmington might have something."

"We're headed that direction."

She eyed him expectantly.

"My boys and I are doing fine here. We can handle whatever comes our way."

Gwen nodded. "If we get overrun on the river, the dead will march through here and consume everything. Your horses, you, and your boys. The battle is on the river."

"You'll have to forgive me. We're a cautious lot." His head bobbed slowly as he chewed her words like a gristly steak. "I'll think on it."

She eyed him.

Bart raised his tin cup in salute. "I'll leave you be then for the night."

"We'll be off early.

"I'll see that Patrick and Pete make sure your horses are well-watered and fed during the night. They dehydrate fast in the winter."

"Thanks, Bart," Jake said, shaking hands with the man. Gerald and Kenny did the same.

The men bedded on the floor with Gwen on the couch. She sat with her phantom boy, watching the flames of the fire die down into glowing coals before sleep took her.

JOSEPH
Cheyenne Mountain Complex, CO

A video window opened on Joseph's screen. The long face and slender shoulders of Colonel Byrnes appeared. He sat at his desk in his small office filming himself on his computer. He folded his hands in front of his body, resting them on his desktop, and cleared his throat. His gray eyes pierced the camera.

"If you're viewing this, I'm gone, taken, imprisoned, and most likely dead." His words cut into Joseph. They were the words of a man acknowledging his own death with cool complacency.

Hollis chomped in apprehension behind Joseph.

Colonel Byrnes's face settled into his natural glower while he stared at the screen. "I'm not sure how we got here. I can't tell you how much it pains me to see our nation ravaged by the scourge of Primus Necrovirus. We've all sacrificed so much to ensure our survival, yet our government is failing the people it has sworn to protect. As a man of science and the military, I never would have imagined a failure of this magnitude. I would never have imagined myself in this position."

Joseph studied him unblinking, his eyes drying, not wanting to miss a word or phrase the colonel said. Everything felt surreal. He waited for Byrnes to tell the camera that it was all a joke, but he knew he wouldn't. Desai reached over and took his hand, squeezing it for support.

"We've made a miracle vaccine in record time. More testing is still needed

95

as well as mainstream production, but this truly is a gift from God. As a man of science, I have always been skeptical of the existence of such a deity, but this discovery is nothing short of a divine intervention on man's behalf. My team has worked a miracle and deserves complete and utter recognition, especially those that have perished at its hand."

Joseph stared down at his hands for a moment. The death of his team member, Dr. Weinroth, rubbed salt in the raw wound that was his heart.

"Our success is but dry ash in the mouth of a nation that deserves better. When you are done, read the attached document. Our government has no plans to distribute the vaccine to anyone outside the Golden Triangle. It's meant to be a tool of control rather than a chance at life. It is meant to bring the remainders of humanity to their knees as loyal slaves rather than free them from certain death. This is not why we developed the vaccine. We developed the vaccine to save people. To continue mankind's existence, not control them."

Byrnes's eyes flashed to his door and then he leaned closer to the camera. "We aren't the only ones. Even now, we've started sneaking the vaccine to safe houses within the Golden Triangle, but it will only be enough for a fraction of the people. We must ensure the people get the vaccine." He glanced at his door again. "Others are willing to go even further, but I need not mention what that may entail." He took a deep breath, sucking in air through his mouth and exhaling. "Many things will be said about me. Let this be a record of my actions and the reasons I have taken such risks with my own life and others. We will find a way. It's our duty as Americans to stand for the weak and see that justice is done. We are the Sons and Daughters of Liberty." He reached forward and turned off his camera.

Joseph leaned back in his chair and the other two doctors were quiet as they contemplated the colonel's words. Hollis rammed his hand back into his bag of crackers, rummaging for more food.

"So Nguyen was a member too?" Desai said.

"Must have been. "

Hollis munched thin crisps between his teeth.

"We have to know what set them down this path." Joseph moved the cursor to the PDF document and double tapped the mouse.

It opened an official US government document marked TOP SECRET. He read it word for word. And each and every one slipped off the page like poisoned food falling from his mouth as he whispered them in silence.

"Operation Homefront: Phase II. Non-Distribution order of the Primus Necrovirus vaccine. Centralized control of all vaccine production. Neutralization of dissidents. Disarming of surviving populations. Fortified labor camps. Food and personnel levies in exchange for vaccine." Each bullet point of the government's contingency plan made Joseph cringe. "Are you reading this?"

Desai nodded her head, her brow wrinkled as she read. Hollis wiped crumbs off his shirt. "I wish I didn't know this."

"Vaccine for loyalty. Neutralization of dissidents. Sounds more like execution of dissidents." Joseph looked back at him. "Forced labor camps for food production. All control coming from the Triangle." He jabbed his finger at the screen. "Signed by the vice president. This is their plan for the future of America." He shook his head in disgust.

"Looks like a roadmap for tyranny," Desai said.

"Or guaranteed survival of the government," Hollis said.

Joseph folded his arms over his chest. "There has to be a better way than this. We can't sit by while people are exposed to the deadliest virus known to man with nothing to protect them from its exposure. This vaccine was meant to save lives, not hold them hostage."

Hollis's jowls shook with his head. "We created this vaccine for the government. It's not ours to decide how and when it's distributed."

"No. This isn't right. People need this vaccine. We have no right to keep it from them. For God's sake, people are getting butchered out there. You saw the models. We only have a seven percent survival rate with mass application of the vaccine," Desai said.

Joseph cut her off. "They want to keep it for themselves even if others will surely die. We are doctors. We created that vaccine for benefit of all. This is not who we are." Joseph rose to his feet and stuck his chest out. "MIM was a collaborated effort between all those that were left. And we did it. I'll be damned if I sit by while our government fails to save its own people." He eyed the other doctors. "We take a stand right here just like Nguyen and Byrnes. I say we join the Sons and Daughters of Liberty." He stuck out his hand. "Who's with me?"

Hesitantly, Desai stood, joining Joseph by his side. "I agree. It's our duty."

Joseph smiled at her. "If you're in, put your hand on top of mine."

She draped her hand over his. He could feel the heat coming from her skin. They eyeballed Hollis, expecting a response.

Hollis snorted in irritation like a bull they'd been poking with sticks. "This is ridiculous. Do you know what happens to men like me outside of here? I can't run and I can't handle a weapon. My survival is dependent upon this place and you want me to betray it." His voice dropped to a whisper. "And the government while I'm at it."

Joseph pointed back at the computer still showing the second phase of Operation Homefront. "Look at that." Hollis glanced over at the monitor. "That is not why we're here. That isn't what a government that's run by the people for the people does. Those are the actions of a dictator, not a president."

"You two are like the goddamn Hardy Boys." He sighed, shaking his head. "I'll do it, but I'm telling you. I'm not running anywhere, and if you expect me to leave this mountain, I won't do it." He tepidly put his hand over top the others. "I can't believe we are putting our hands in the middle like a bunch of teenagers making a pact."

"Even better. Thank you, doctor." Joseph nodded. "We make a pact. We find and free Byrnes and aid the Sons and Daughters in their cause." Joseph eyed Desai first and then Hollis. "For MIM, for Byrnes, Nguyen, and Weinroth."

Desai followed suit. "For MIM, Byrnes, Nguyen, and Weinroth."

"Hollis?"

He rolled his eyes. "For MIM, Byrnes, Nguyen, and Weinroth."

STEELE
Camp Forge, IA

The fire sizzled and sparked in the parlor fireplace. Fieldstone surrounded the fireplace's arch, leading upward to a thick wooden mantle beam. An old worn musket with a rusted-out barrel rested there, a bayonet folded backward running along the bottom.

"When's the colonel supposed to reach out?" Thunder asked. He leaned forward, elbows on his knees.

Steele sat at John Reynolds's writing desk, his fingers interlocked in front of him. The polished wood was in bad need of being refurbished. "Six o'clock."

Thunder's eyes glanced at the rustic gold-rimmed timepiece on the far end of the mantle. "He's late." It read three minutes after six.

He's never late. "He'll call."

The green rectangle sitting on the writing desk glowed with power, but no voices came through. The crypto-capable high-frequency radio resembled an old ammo box turned on its side. Each commander holding the Mississippi had one. It had better function with an antenna, and Steele's wire antenna ran the height of the old farmhouse.

The high-frequency radio lit up. Steele snatched the black-corded telephone receiver. "This is Steele."

"Captain Steele, this is Captain Heath, United States Marine Corps."

"Captain Heath, it's good to hear your voice. Any word from Colonel Kinnick yet?"

"No, sir. I haven't heard from Major Alvarado either."

Steele pressed the receiver to his ear. "Neither of them?"

"No."

"How are things north of here?"

"We've had some success. My force has expanded as we've recruited farmers from inland, but things could be better. It's getting colder and our outreach has stalled due to the weather."

"It's getting cold here too."

The radio crackled. "Gentleman. This is Kinnick."

Steele grinned and partially relaxed at the sound of his voice. "Sir, Steele here."

"And Heath."

"Glad to hear from you two. I'll begin."

Captain Heath's voice sounded off. "Sir, what about Major Alvarado?"

There was a pause for a moment. Steele glared at Thunder and the man's mouth tightened beneath his bushy gray beard. Silence was hardly ever a good thing.

"There's no easy way to put this. We lost comms with Outpost Barron three days ago."

"Sir?"

Steele kept silent. Kinnick was a fine commander. He would relay the information they needed, but why would he wait?

"I was giving them time to fix the issue before we took action. At this point, we can only assume the worst."

"Sir, there were over two-hundred Marines in a fortified base in the middle of a river. If they've been overrun, our chances are worse than I thought," Heath said.

"I understand that, Captain. Any way you slice it, this puts us in a tight spot. If the threat is north, then we must meet it."

"What would you have us do?" Steele asked.

"We're going to have to shift units to the north. If it's the dead, I'd reestablish the outpost. I'm going to need Captain Heath to shift two companies north to investigate and reestablish the outpost, if needed. Captain

Steele you will move two companies of your militia north to support Heath. Do you understand?"

Roughly two hundred fewer fighters for our defense. This is a thin line we are forming, he thought. "Yes, sir." His words were echoed by Heath.

Steele waited a moment before he spoke, the weight of the situation bearing down on him. "Sir, I've had a disease run through my forces centered in Hacklebarney. About ten percent of my force is incapacitated."

"Understood. I assume this won't be a problem?"

"No, sir. We'll make it happen."

"Good. Captain Heath, as soon as you've made contact at Outpost Barron, I need a situation report. Captain Steele, ensure your units are on their way as soon as possible."

"Wilco."

Heath followed. "Wilco."

"Reconvene, same time, same place next week."

"Yes, sir."

"Oh, and gentleman, I almost forgot. We're getting close to the holiday. Merry Christmas."

Despite the situation unfolding, Steele smiled. "Merry Christmas, sir." He put down the receiver and clicked the radio off.

Thunder raised his eyebrows. "What'd he say?"

"We've got to move two companies of militia north to support Heath while he investigates what happened at Outpost Barron."

"Red Stripes can do it."

"Nah, I'd rather keep you guys close to my chest. I was thinking about off-loading a portion of Jackson's men with the War Machines to watch over them."

"War Child will make sure they stay in line, but I'd hate to lose his gang if things go south here."

"We will miss him, but I want to break Major Ludlow's men up and spread them out. If they want to fight the dead, we would be stupid to stop them."

Thunder leaned forward. "Not sure how I feel about giving them guns.

You should have shoved them into the river and been done with it."

"Would you rather have me send two companies of my loyal fighters and have them all bunched up down here? No, we utilize the ones willing to fight."

"You think I like the idea of putting down servicemen? I am a fucking Marine for God's sake."

Steele drifted back to his desk. "No more than I do."

Thunder found his feet. "Send the bastards north, but remember who's had your back. Trust is all you got in this world, and I don't trust them."

"Thank you, Thunder."

Steele's staunch ally left. He knew Thunder spoke the truth. How could you have people you didn't trust watching your back? Bullets in the back, teeth to the front. No options were good options, but he had to drum up something if they wanted to survive long-term which included acquiring the government's vaccine. *If they have a vaccine? They do. Kinnick wouldn't lie. What if they lied to him?*

He sighed, looking at the radio. *I'll send the War Machines and a full platoon of Ludlow's men, but I need my own eyes and ears on the ground. Tess? Margie? Larry? Ahmed would have been perfect, and now he's gone along with Macleod.*

A knock came from the doorway leading to the foyer. A slender woman stood there in her bulky green coat, her hair slicked back. She leaned on the frame, her arms crossed as if she expected an answer to a question. She eyeballed Thunder's back.

"Whatcha doing?"

"Figuring out who to send north. We've lost contact with Outpost Barron."

"Ouch." Her ebony eyes awaited his response. "Who're you going to send?"

"Thunder volunteered, but I want to keep him close here. I'm going to send the War Machines and a platoon of Ludlow's men."

"Getting some of the Legion out of here?"

"Yes." He glanced at his map. "The next question is who we have as *our* eyes and ears on the ground?"

She moved inside the parlor and made her way to the fire. She rubbed her hands between one another and held them in front of the fireplace. "I'd send myself or Margie. We'll make sure the job gets done. Not to mention we're *loyal*."

"What are you trying to say?"

She gave him a side eye. "I'm trying to tell you everyone isn't what they seem."

Steele furrowed his brow. "Tess. Don't skirt around. What are you saying?"

She left the fire and plopped down on the couch. "I saw a few things yesterday that didn't sit right with me."

He waited, watching her make herself comfortable.

"The pastor is out there hemming and hawing about how you aren't helping the sick."

Steele stretched his neck and stood. He moved near the window. "We don't have any medicine. It's gone. Gwen went to get what she can."

"He sent people out too."

Steele sighed. "He shouldn't have done that." He inspected the soldiers returning from trench duty around the camp. It was a thankless job in hard ground, but someday it would pay off and they couldn't afford to wait until spring.

"You aren't going to do anything?"

"What would you have me do? Punish a man who is trying to help?"

"He could ruin the negotiations that Gwen is conducting."

"He could. I'll speak to him."

"There's more."

"More?" He turned around to face her.

Her features took on a foreign seriousness. "I saw Thunder getting all chummy with Peter earlier."

He felt anger bubble in the pit of his gut. "What do you mean?"

"They were talking close together and shaking hands. Not something that I'd expect out of the big Thunder Cat."

"They're allowed to talk."

"I dunno. I just got this inkling that something wasn't right. Like they were hiding something. When I asked Thunder about it, he said they were planning their patrols."

"Something I would expect them to coordinate."

Tess gave him a skeptical look. "You and me both know I love Thunder, but he wasn't acting right. Listen." She scooted closer to him. "I know that man. He's hiding something. He hates the Chosen just as much as me. He might not be as vocal, but there isn't any reason for him to be chest-butting and patty-caking with Peter even if they were coordinating patrols."

Everything she said was valid. Since the Battle of Little Sable Point, there was bad blood between the bikers and the Chosen. The Sable Pointers hated the Chosen too, but they followed Steele's lead and reluctantly accepted them. That wasn't even taking into consideration the fact that Tess had attempted to assassinate the pastor while he slept, furthering the divide between his followers.

He took a hand and ran it over the scar traversing the top of his skull, a wound he'd taken in the hills of West Virginia. "I appreciate you telling me this."

She clapped her hands together softly. "What're you going to do?"

"I'm not going to do anything. Thunder's my ally. One of my best allies. I can't believe there is any guilt in this." His brow creased tighter, tugging at his hardened scar tissue.

"And why would Thunder meet with Peter? Garrett plans the patrols."

Steele held up his strong hand. "I won't hear any more of it. Keep track of the pastor, but please drop the stuff about Thunder. If I can't keep him on my side, who can I trust?"

She raised her eyebrows. "Me."

He stepped closer to his desk, speaking over his shoulder, "I can't survive with just one ally." He jotted a name down on a piece of paper. "Which is why I need you here. I won't hear anything more about Thunder." He faced her. "Nothing."

"But."

"I will not hear conspiracy theories. I don't care what you think you have." His eyes hardened signaling an end to discussion. "I'm going to send Margie north with the War Machines and Major Ludlow's men." Steele studied his units and their deployment over the southern portion of Iowa on his map. *Everything just got a little slimmer.*

THE PASTOR
South of Camp Forge, IA

He floated far above orange-and-yellow flames that danced a scalding ballet. Unable to control himself, he hurtled toward the inferno. His body was nonexistent, only a level of consciousness making him acutely aware of his own existence.

The ball of fire exploded, enveloping him with heat. Blinded, he closed his eyes. Even as he tried to turn away, he couldn't. The blaze leapt before him and encircled him on all sides.

Then the voice came to him. It was so deep he almost couldn't understand the words. "Open your eyes."

The voice brought upon him an unknown dread. A fear beyond anything imaginable made him want to scream. The inferno was a wave of holocaust surrounding him. *The fire will burn me. My eyes will melt and turn liquid and run down the curve of my face. The flames will lap my tongue, searing it, and lick my skin, boiling it.* Yet he couldn't emit a sound despite the terror that filled him.

The voice came again, dominating the roar of the flames. "Open your eyes. See."

He chanced to open his mouth instead, and his words dribbled out pathetic and weak. "The fire."

"Only the guilty feel my righteousness."

His voice was frail. Soft. Insignificant. It quivered as he spoke, a mere infant in the eyes of such power. "Yes, Lord."

"You have fallen behind the false and blind." The words washed over him like a tidal wave, drowning his very essence.

The pastor's voice was weak and frail before the omniscient holy being, a form he could never begin to understand. "I am your humble servant."

"Your enemies will burn before your eyes. Their idols will be shattered and their cries will fill your ears."

He didn't dare open his eyes. He feared it would be his last act. "Yes, Lord."

"A champion comes. Look for him."

"Yes, Lord," he cried out. The fire roared in response like he was responsible for detonating in a massive explosion. He couldn't hide from the inferno. He had to embrace it. He cracked open his eyes, and the flames crawled into his empty sockets and the gaping hole that was once his mouth.

He blinked, coming back to this world. His chest heaved. Light clouds covered a full moon in the night. The blazing tempest was gone. His breath fogged in front of his face like a cool mist. The temperature was bone-chillingly cold, cutting through his layers of clothes. He almost yearned for the flames again.

"Are you okay?" Peter breathed next to him. He held an AK-47 in his hands, a strap keeping it close to his body.

"Yes, Peter." His respiration leveled out. His vision was so vivid and real he could still feel the heat on his skin.

The barn ahead of them was a rickety old thing. Boards were missing along the sides and shingles vacant from the roof.

"Do you see our comrades?"

"No, Father."

"Come, Peter. The omens are good." Their feet crunched in the soft powder turned frosty and frozen in the nighttime air. Near the doors, the men stopped and listened. Peter dipped inside the barn, checking the corners of the unlit structure. The pastor hesitantly followed his man.

A tense silence held the dark hostage. The quiet hid the presence of others undisclosed. *Shhick. Shhick.* A tiny flame lit up the barn. It drifted toward an old wrinkled face and glowed against the tip of a cigarette. The faint odor of cigarette smoke wafted in the air. The man sucked in and an ember gleamed with life.

The man's voice sounded like feet stepping through gravel. "Pastor." With a creak of worn leather, the burning ember leapt back for his face.

"War Child. Your attendance is comforting."

Peter stared into the corners of the barn, his AK-47 held in unrelaxed hands.

War Child snorted in the blackness at his words. "Mammoth. Iron. Tiny. You can stand down."

Leather-clad men emerged from the shadows, faint war gears on their patches. Both men were burly, hairy, and heavily armed with M4A1 carbines with optics. Weapons stolen from the soldiers they'd defeated. The wood groaned above the pastor, and he let his eyes follow the sound. Booted feet skipped down a ladder. War Child was cautious and clearly didn't trust the Chosen.

"Go outside," War Child said. The bikers stepped around the pastor and Peter. The largest stared the pastor directly in the eyes with a nasty grin on his hair-cloaked lips.

He could feel Peter tense at his side. The other biker chomped his teeth in Peter's face, and Peter went rigid like a two-by-four.

The pastor placed a long-fingered hand on his disciple's shoulder. The man was solid but not terrifying like the bikers, more stout than violent. "You may stand watch outside, my son."

"But Father, these men." His voice dipped quieter. "They cannot be trusted."

"Have faith. While they may be uncouth, all men have their use to the Lord."

"Hehehe," War Child laughed. It came out like a dusty wheeze. "Your altar boy can stay if you'd like. Makes no difference to me."

Peter bowed his head in deference. "Yes, Father." He turned away, leaving them.

"Your people are loyal," War Child said.

The pastor took a step forward. "So are yours."

The two men admired one another from across the barn.

"It seems we have something in common that our captain does not."

A faint grin formed on War Child's lips. "It seems we do." He dropped his cigarette on the floor and ground his boot into it. "You know nothing personal on the lakeshore. Just business."

The pastor felt his face shudder. He licked his lips, feeling the dry chill of the night. "I understand your business." War Child and his men were heathen mercenaries that could be turned to God's will with the right divine hand guiding them.

"Then you understand why I'm here."

The pastor spoke with the articulate reservation of a politician. "Our current leadership isn't meeting my expectations."

"Is that so?"

The pastor gulped. *This man wouldn't be here unless he was willing to make a deal.* His mind wracked itself with doubt. He knew this man was a treacherous scoundrel, and he could be attempting to entrap the pastor on Steele's behalf. He knew his foundation with Steele was weak despite the shaming he'd given Tess when God held her hand from taking his life.

Shhick. Shhick. War Child lit up another cigarette. An evil sneer sat on his leathery face. His snowy beard was still trimmed although not too close. He blew smoke out his mouth. "The boy's been lucky to still have his balls sewn on straight. He shouldn't have let all those soldiers go. I'm afraid we'll wake up tomorrow and be staring at the same dumbasses down the barrel that we were before." He took another drag off his cigarette. "We can't afford those kind of mistakes."

The pastor lifted his chin a fraction. "We need a man in charge who can order the harshest of actions done to ensure the survival of his people."

"Aye. A man who is comfortable with his sins."

A small smile crept on the pastor's face. "Or a man absolved of his sins in the name of the Lord."

War Child took a few steps forward. "I think we share the same vision. What did you have in mind?" He breathed out smoke.

"God came to me."

A crooked grin carved onto War Child's lips. "Did he? What'd the bastard say?"

The pastor ignored the man's blasphemy as such men had their vices and, more importantly, their uses. "An angel came to me and he brought with him the fiery wrath of the Lord."

"Did he? He's vengeful, ain't he?"

"He's righteous and shows us the way."

War Child twisted his head. "Meant no offense." He placed a hand on his breast. "I'm a God-fearing man myself."

The pastor eyed the biker to see if he was mocking his faith. "We should all fear him for he holds the power to make men great and to lay men low. What is your name?"

"You know my name."

"No, your real name. The name given to you at birth."

War Child took another step forward, his boot thumping the barn floor. He was within a few feet of the pastor now. Close enough to strike him if he wanted. His white beard was brighter now as if he were transforming into a ghost.

"My real name is Paul. Paul Burnett."

It was the pastor's turn to smile. "Paul the apostle. Once the persecutor then the champion."

War Child wheezed a laugh, slapping his thigh. "Now ain't that something." He gave the pastor a rough whoop and laugh. "Never thought of it that way." He pointed at him. "What does God have in store for us? Is he going to cut us down or raise us up?"

The pastor's mouth curled in a smile. "He will raise his prophet and his champion to the heavens."

Their hands met like a thunderclap in the silent barn.

AHMED
Northern Missouri

They neared a small home with no lights on. The siding was a pale gray, and the reflection of snow made it seem even lighter in the darkness. Trees surrounded the home that pressed upon on the edge of a field no larger than an acre. In the distance, a sizable barn stood on the border of a tree line. It was only the third house they'd come across as they'd trekked while shivering from the elements.

Jim stopped them near a tree with sweeping branches devoid of all leaves. He scrutinized the building for a moment from behind the oak.

"Why you waiting, Jimmy?" Kelly asked.

"Sly knows we's got cousins in these parts. Why wouldn't he come looking here too?"

"He's prolly forgotten that Lee's my mother's cousin. Hell, I had to remind Brad half the time." Her words trailed off as if her mind had finally caught up with what she was saying, reminding her that he was gone. She glanced downward at the white crusted ground. Flurries trickled through naked branches in the cold night like frozen tears.

"I'm gonna go check it out," Jim said. He trudged ahead, and the rest trooped through the snow like they were stalking deer in the night.

They reached the porch, and Jim hammered the door with a fist. "Lee," he called out.

The porch light flicked on, illuminating the front steps in an eerie yellow glow. The door eked open and the black barrel of a rifle emerged in its place.

"Who's askin'?" came a voice.

"It's me, Uncle Lee. Jimmy."

The door swung open, revealing a man in an open blue robe and boxers. He resembled a mad scientist on the verge of a breakthrough, his gray hair sticking out every which way.

"You crazy, boy? Coming out here in the night. What in hell's the matter with you?" He shook his head. "Never mind. Don't answer that. Whatcha doing here?"

"We got run out."

"Run out of what?" Lee stared out into the night and squinted over the porch light toward the other people. "Kelly?"

She walked forward, feet crushing brittle brush. "Hi, Lee."

He shaded his eyes from the glaring light. "Are those kids?" He gave Jimmy an evil look. "Why didn't you say you got kids with you? You got a block for a head like your father?"

Jim stared at the ground for a moment. "He's dead."

Lee's mouth stayed closed, and he judged the young man for a moment. "Get these poor folks in here then you can tell me." He motioned them on. "Come in."

In a few minutes, they were all inside, huddled around a small wood-burning stove trying to thaw the winter from their limbs. Ahmed felt each step of their trek through the woods inside every muscle fiber of his legs.

Lee brought in a handful of blankets and passed them to the chilled people. He handed one to Ahmed and stared at him for a minute.

"Well, you ain't one of Kelly and Brad's. Sure don't think you're Barb's neither." He raised his eyebrows. "Unless one of the migrant workers slipped one over on Kelly."

"I'm not from here."

His bushy eyebrows worked up and down. "Clearly. You don't sound funny though."

"D.C."

"From the swamp. Figures. I won't hold it against you." He turned back to his distant relatives. "What's happened?"

Jim studied the floor, his jaw clenching. "They killed Dad and Kyle."

Lee took a seat on a worn-out sofa and draped his robe over himself. "Who and why?" He didn't sound as surprised as Ahmed thought he should.

"You know who. It was Sly and his henchman Vance." Jim stared at him.

Lee sucked in some air through his nose, shaking his head. "After all this time, you're still fighting the same battles. It was only a matter of time before somebody really got hurt."

"Those are your battles too," Kelly chided Lee.

Lee rolled his eyes. "That was a long time ago and nobody died," he emphasized the word died at the end.

"They shot Brad in the back and gunned down Kyle in cold blood."

"Suppose notifying the authorities is out. Vance is married to a cousin of Sly's. Not that they're doing much now."

"They never did much anyway," Kelly said, looking away.

"Why'd they come now?"

The room grew silent like someone had sucked the sound right out of it. Ahmed eyed Jim and then Sadie. A secret stifled the room, one that he didn't know.

Jim peered at Lee, his words coming as if he were reaffirming to himself what he'd done. "I killed Rog a week ago."

"Why'd you go and do that? You know we got issues with them."

"It was an accident. He came sniffing around. I got hot." He threw a hand toward Sadie. "I was looking out for my sister."

"Let him sniff all he wants. The girl's got a mind of her own. Let her decide."

Jim's mouth tightened and his icy eyes gored Lee. "She said she didn't want him coming around."

Lee nodded and sighed. "And now they come and kill Brad and Kyle. This is ugly business, Jimmy. You should have thrashed him and let him be on his way."

"They killed my boy and my man and burnt our home down," Kelly said. "Ain't right."

"No, it ain't. Suppose Jimmy wants help in getting vengeance."

"It's only a matter of time before they make it this way and burn us out again."

"I suppose it is." Lee leaned forward and clasped his hands in front of his body. "Tomorrow I'll get the horses saddled up, and we'll make sure they know they've done wrong." His eyes glared at Jimmy. "By talking."

Jimmy stayed silent.

"I'm going to try to get back to sleep." Lee stood and eyed them all. "We don't have much space, so you'll all be out here."

"Thank you, Lee," Kelly said. Her words were echoed by Barb.

The refugees took places along the floor. Jim made sure Ahmed knew he wasn't pleased with him bedding down next to Sadie but didn't say anything. Ahmed let an arm settle over Sadie's waist like a seatbelt. She snuggled in closer, and in moments, drifted into sleep.

***

He awoke with the dawn of the day and the sound of soft voices. He found himself alone and chilled on the floor. Sadie gave him a soft smile.

"Been waiting for you."

He sat up and she handed him watery coffee. "I was exhausted."

"We all are." Her eyes worried.

The door banged open, and Lee came in with a googly-eyed young man that looked just like him but with brown hair instead of gray sticking out every which way.

"Andy and I got the horses saddled. Harry Bailey don't live too far from here. He's got a square head on his shoulders. Maybe we can talk this out. Get some kind of truce."

"You know we ain't talking this out," Jim said.

Lee stomped his boots on a mat, snow dropping in clumps. "Maybe you ain't, but I am. You want us backing you? We talk."

Jim licked his lips. "You don't tell us Singletons what to do."

"Then you can find another place."

Lee's wife, Gina, was a short woman with big hips and a robust chest. She balked at him. "Where would they go? They're family."

"If there's shooting, I'm not going. I'm not getting killed for something stupid." Lee crossed his arms over his upper body.

"This ain't stupid. Stay then." Jim weighed Ahmed as if to determine any sort of value. "Brown guy. You want to ride with us?"

Ahmed had been called so much worse throughout his life. The term *brown* didn't bother him. His skin tone was more brown than white he supposed, or more brown than pink in most people's cases. The fact that the man knew his name and refused to call him by it is what really bothered him.

"My name is Ahmed."

"Whatever. You want to ride with us? We could use the help." His angry ice-cold eyes told Ahmed he didn't really care at all. He felt Sadie's gaze upon him as well.

"Be nice to him," Sadie scolded.

"Thank you," Ahmed said softly to her.

She blushed at his words.

"Jesus, Sadie, you been swooning over this guy for weeks. Try to keep it in your pants. Your father and brother were killed yesterday. They deserve justice."

Ahmed stretched his chest. There was pain, but he could fight. The real question in his mind was a matter of if he should. These people were being persecuted by another group. He'd witnessed the slaying of two in cold blood. He'd seen what the authorities had done. There was no hope of succor from them. The Singletons had cared for him while he lingered on the precipice of life and death but embroiling himself in the middle of a violent family feud wasn't going to get him back to his people. He hesitated, weighing all the information as fast as he could.

He could feel Sadie's light blue eyes on him. They lit something in him that he didn't understand. He nodded. Something kicked in his chest and simmered in his gut. He couldn't place this excitement of being with someone he really cared about, and the thought scared him at the same time. He was doing things for someone he'd only really known for a few days, and because he couldn't say why, it perplexed him deep inside. "I'll go with you."

Sadie exhaled and a smile spread on her lips. "Thank you."

Jim's eyes fell to Andy's, testing his manhood. His younger cousin held a reverence for the older, one that yearned to be seen as a man in the eyes of the elder males. Jim pushed him further. "You comin'?"

The young man quickly nodded.

"I knew you'd man up. Not back down from this fight."

Lee gawked at the ceiling in consultation with the Lord. "I thought I raised you better than this."

"This is how you raised me, Dad. It's blood. There's nothing thicker. If we don't have their backs, who will?"

"I should have stayed in bed last night."

Kelly gave Lee a nasty glare. "We don't want to impose. We just thought you'd be one for helping family in need."

He waved his cousin off. "No. No. We could never put you out. But I don't want this fight. Nothing good can come from it."

"We didn't neither, but this is what we got."

Lee took a moment to judge Jim in silence. "I'll go with 'em. Try to keep this somewhat civil."

Jim grabbed a shotgun from the corner and handed it to Ahmed. "Come on, brownie."

Ahmed held the gun for a second, watching the man walk outside. *Asshole.* He followed him anyway, keeping his word if only for Sadie.

A fraction of snow had covered the cold ground in the night. Sticks and dead leaves stuck out here and there as if they defied their frozen white blanket. Jim, Lee, Andy, and Ahmed marched out to the horses and mounted up.

Lee looked at the young men. "This ain't much of a posse."

"This all we got. We could go up north and grab Dennis and Ethan or the Foxworth boys."

"Nah, we got enough to make 'em talk."

Jim snorted and kicked his horse down the dirt driveway, tossing dirt and snow alike. Ahmed climbed on his horse with a grunt and urged it forward with his hips.

The land was dead or in the process of seasonal dying. The country roads melded into one long tunnel of wilderness, indistinguishable from each other. Ahmed knew he would never make it back to Lee's without help.

"It'll be Christmas soon," Lee said.

The thought was in the back of Ahmed's mind, but the realization had slipped him. Without the constant barrage of Christmas advertisements on television, he'd hadn't remembered. Then there was the whole end-of-the-world thing that had gotten in the way of him recollecting holidays, months, or days for that matter. "I'd almost forgotten."

"Don't celebrate?"

"Took the free holidays."

Lee eyed him, waiting for more. "Far from home."

"It feels that way."

They rode in silence for a moment before Ahmed spoke. "Home is where you find those you love. Otherwise, I might never have a home."

"Thoughtful words for a young man."

Talking about his religion with strangers sometimes felt odd, especially when he knew his reception might be less than cordial. "I'm Muslim, but most of my friends weren't, so I kind of celebrated, I guess with them." That seemed like a lifetime ago when things were normal and America still hummed with life.

Lee smiled. "Ahhh. As-salamu alaykum, friend.

This caused Ahmed to smile as he was immediately reminded of his family. "Wa 'alaykumu s-salām."

Ahmed stared at the wild-haired man with a grin. "How do you know that greeting?"

"I used to be in the military. A long time ago. You go, they teach you a bunch of things, forget most, but you remember a few." He finished with a smile. "Or you select a few to remember."

They turned down a road that appeared to be a long driveway in silence. Pines and maples gave way to rusted-out cars and other random junk in a yard. Long expired off-white refrigerators. An oven. Corroded brown fencing worthlessly tossed in a pile. A faded blue swing set with no swings, only rusted chains hanging.

A pickup sat in front of a dilapidated house. A man unloaded boxes from the pickup's bed. The exterior wood siding of the home was rotted. A window was covered with plastic. The storm door was bent to the side, unable to latch back in place. He didn't look up until they were close enough to shout.

He squinted at the riders. Jim kicked his horse into a gallop, riding hard for him. The man dropped the box he was holding. Using the truck bed to propel him, he scrambled for the back seat.

"Christ!" Lee cursed. He spurred his horse after Jim with Andy and Ahmed close behind.

Pickup windows shattered, spraying shards of glass, as Jim fired his shotgun at a gallop, an almost impossible task. Bullets banged out of the cab as the man crouched behind his truck.

Ahmed pulled the reins hard on his horse, half-stumbling, half-falling on the icy ground. He let the horse trot away and dropped his knee into the cold earth. Gunfire came from the house with muffled pops. Even while muffled it made him jump. Dirty snow erupted off the ground and his heart pounded even faster. His fellow riders drifted toward the edge of the house trying to avoid the gunfire, circling back in front.

Rapidly, Ahmed dropped from kneeling to prone. Now he could see the man behind the pickup. His only thought was to win. He could make out the man's jeans-clad thigh, calf, and tan-booted foot. He let his trigger go, and a slug sailed into the man's meaty leg.

When the slug hit, it was like someone had removed his femur with a wicked giant's punch. He tipped over on his shoulder, screaming in pain. A man ran from the house and began dragging him toward the door. The wounded man fought him, trying to put pressure on his wound.

Pumping his shotgun, the spent shell ejected. He fired again. This time, the slug took the other man in the foot. The boot with the foot inside separated from his body leaving a bloody streak in its place. He went down wailing next to his friend.

All the while, Lee screamed in the background for everyone to stop, but it was too late. Jim and Andy steered their horses toward the wounded men, peppering them with bullets. Ahmed bounded forward for concealment, keeping a constant gaze on one of the windows. The shades moved, and he sent another slug through. Cries came from the inside of the house.

Jim dismounted with his shotgun. He sprinted and kicked in the door. Andy trailed behind him, and they disappeared. Ahmed reached the bodies of the two men. The only part of them still moving were bloody pink trails of leaking insides pooling into the layer of crispy white ground.

Jim dragged a woman out of the house by her hair. She kicked at him, her legs splaying wildly.

Lee reached in his direction. "Jimmy, stop!"

Raising a hand, Ahmed said, "Jim." The fighting was done. There was no more need for bloodshed.

Blue eyes flared at him. Jim put a Smith and Wesson .40 caliber handgun to her head. She quit kicking and sobbed, snot running from her nostrils onto her lips.

"Fuck you!" she screamed. When she caught the sight of the two dead men, she screeched, her mouth vibrating with her wails. "You bastards!"

Lee gestured at her. "She's a woman. Stop this."

"You think that they give a shit about women?" Jim kicked at her rear with his boot sending her onto her hands. "You think they gave a shit about the kids? They burnt down our home after shooting Dad and Kyle in the back. That's the good faith a Bailey will give you. Guarantee of a bullet."

The woman caught her breath, her lips snarling. "He'll find you." Her chest heaved. "And he'll kill you. He will."

Jim snarled, pressing his pistol into her head. "Shut the fuck up, you slut."

Her anger took over. "You're all fucked anyway. You may as well kill me too."

Jim shoved her with the gun. "Don't tempt me, bitch."

"Does she deserve this?" Ahmed said.

Jim spit. "Don't she? She's with them." He pointed at the bodies. "Those two pieces of shit were there. They gunned them down." Ahmed vaguely remembered their shadowed faces near the pickups, but he couldn't be sure.

"Was she there?"

"She'll run to Sly and prolly breed a bunch more just like 'em."

Ahmed took a step closer. "She didn't commit the crime. She wasn't there. No more than Sadie and Kelly are here. Don't condemn her for something she didn't do."

"Sly'll kill you," she said. Her eyes were far away in a distant place.

Ahmed trained a finger on her. "She's not guilty by association."

Jim's eyes lit up. "That's exactly what she is." He squeezed the trigger, the barrel against her head. The gun recoiled, metal sliding fluidly over metal. Fire erupted from the end and her head flew to the side and straight into the ground. She laid motionless, her mouth open a crack.

Ahmed's jaw dropped like the woman's.

"Dear God, Jimmy!" Lee turned away disgusted.

The woman bled from her head wound, blood seeping out like she was a tipped over bottle of chocolate syrup. Ahmed blinked in the carnage. *What have I done? Am I on the right side of this?*

"If it's a war they want, it's total war." Jim spit on the woman. He gathered his horse's reins in one hand and used the pommel to pull himself into the saddle.

The other men stared at Jim. His horse nervously stamped the ground.

"What?" he spat. He forcefully holstered his handgun.

Lee's face twisted in disgust. "If we're going to kill somebody, let's at least see if there is anything of value."

They went inside the filthy house. They threw food, ammunition, and guns into bags. Another young man lay dying on dirty carpet, bittersweet fluids from his side seeping into the floor.

"Who are these people?" Ahmed asked Lee.

Lee bent down slowly next to the young man. He picked up the shotgun next to him and placed it atop his shoulder, anger settling in his eyes. "Does it matter?" He glared down at the teenager bleeding out in disgust. The young man's skin was visibly paling by the second as his lifeblood drained from his body.

"I'd like to think we did the right thing."

"Killing is the right thing?"

Ahmed shook his head, taking in the poor surroundings. "In this case, the

Singletons were being murdered. They shouldn't have to sit back while they are killed."

"And now we've murdered their brethren." Lee cocked his head. "So is it their turn to murder us?"

"The Singletons deserve justice as much as the next man. I saw those men execute Brad and Kyle." His sense of justice was being shaken. Who was right and who was wrong?

"These people ain't Sly."

"Why didn't you stop Jim?" Ahmed stepped closer to Lee.

"Why didn't you?"

Ahmed opened his mouth for a moment then closed it. "I don't know him. I'm not from here. I'm not a part of this."

Lee smirked. "But you are now."

TESS
Camp Forge, IA

Two long pontoon boats had arrived in the night from Burlington. They were basic water beasts, each one no more than a long flat platform overtop two large pontoons. They'd been used for Mississippi River tours before the outbreak.

The top of each craft was open air, clearly made with summer sightseeing adventures in mind. The sides were made from a thick canvas and windows made of heavy clear plastic that could be rolled up or down as needed. Either way the trip would be freezing up the river and would only get worse the farther north they traveled.

Twelve Sable Point Volunteers stood clustered together with filled backpacks and their assortment of firearms, but instead of looking like a fierce fighting team, they resembled a group of friends that were going on a ski trip. An additional small pontoon would carry them north, freeing up the two larger pontoons for the War Machines and Lieutenant Gunther's full platoon of soldiers.

Tess stuck her hands deeper into the pockets of her winter coat. The Sable Point Volunteers were handing their packs along a human chain and stacking their gear evenly on the small pontoon.

Margie stood next to her. She wore a black trapper hat with gray rabbit fur insulation. The hat rose in the back where her hair bun poked out. Her breath fogged in front of her rosy cheeks.

"It's going to be even colder on the river," Tess said.

Margie eyed the pontoon then her eyes shifted across to the far bank. More dead lined the edge, waiting for any opportunity to cross. Faint moans carried over the water like ripples of a skipped rock.

"I know."

Tess inspected their work. "You know why Steele is sending you in particular?"

Margie's eyes didn't leave the other shore. "To make sure the soldiers don't get out of hand."

"That's why he's sending the War Machines. He's sending you because you have proven yourself to have sound judgment and you're loyal. It's not just the soldiers you're going to be watching."

Her brown eyes searched Tess for an answer, and her voice dipped lower. "What do you mean?"

Tess licked her dry cracked lips. She would have done anything for some lip balm. Her tongue scraped along the rough skin. This winter still wasn't as bad as it would have been in Michigan. "I don't mean anything." She tongued her lips again, trying to scrub away the dry skin. "If you see anything weird, you have to get word back to me."

"How?"

Snowflakes trickled down from the sky at a leisurely pace. Tess watched two War Machines carry an M2 Browning .50 caliber machine gun aboard the largest of the pontoons. War Child stood nearby watching his club load up.

"Find a way. Get word to Heath. Send someone you trust and don't be afraid to put one of these sons of bitches down. You're going to be arming those soldiers."

"You're telling me to watch the soldiers and watch the War Machines while we are supposed to be fighting the infected?" Margie shook her head in a worried manner.

"Yes. I'm asking you to do all those things and something else."

Margie faced her full-on, her eyes irritated, but in a manner that made her look too worried to be taken seriously. "What?"

"Stay alive. We've lost too many people. We need you and your team to come back."

A grim smile found its way onto Margie's lips. "I'll do my best."

Tess smiled back. "Stay alive."

The two women embraced, their coats scratching as they hugged. Tess squeezed her tight before releasing her.

Tony approached, a hand-knitted woolen scarf wrapped around his neck and face. His glasses were fogged on top of his pink nose. He tugged the scarf off his face and below his chin. "We're loaded up. Got enough extra fuel, bullets, and food to last us for a least a week until we reach Clinton."

With clear affection, Margie said, "Thank you. Hopefully we won't need all of it. The other outposts should have something to spare."

He shrugged his shoulders. "Can't hurt to be prepared."

The general love and care between the two struck Tess like a flash of lightning. It warmed her insides for a moment, but the brief emotion faded to an aching pain. She'd had something like that once with Pagan. Now only bitterness filled her.

A younger army officer spoke with War Child now. He wore ACUs and cupped his hands to stay warm.

"I'm going to meet with them," Margie said.

"If you don't mind, I'd like to tag along."

The three Sable Pointers walked over to the largest pontoon crawling with bikers.

War Child's arms were folded over his leather-clad chest. "Why, Tess, it's good to see you." His voice sounded like someone pouring gravel from a bucket onto the ground.

She gave him a slight nod. "War Child. Now you take good care of my people."

He smiled beneath his white beard. "You know I will." War Child pointed a finger at the lieutenant. "Let me introduce you to Lieutenant Gunther."

"Ma'am," Gunther said with a nod. He was a little over average height and wasn't a day older than twenty-five. His face was thin, and he had a dimple on his chin. "We're anxious to get back into the fight. This is my platoon sergeant, Sergeant First Class Wade."

Wade didn't look pleased to be there. The African-American man was older than his assigned lieutenant, and his mouth was tight like he was ready to spit at a moment's notice. "Ma'am."

"I'm Margie and this is Tony. We are the militia group that will be attached to your unit."

Gunther nodded and War Child grinned. "We're gonna stop off at each of the outposts set up by Colonel Kinnick for supplies as we travel north to Clinton," War Child said, his voice grating. "Should take about a week, give or take. First pit stop is Burlington. Get to see how our old gal Red Clare is doing."

"When can we expect to get our firearms?" Gunther asked. Clearly he was concerned about defending himself and his men, but could they really trust him and his platoon? He looked trustworthy enough. She turned her gaze to Wade. His eyes were dark. Something troubled him that she bet he never spoke about.

Margie piped up; it was clear she was still a little nervous about asserting herself in front of the other commanders. "Not until we reach Clinton. Captain Heath has assured us that the Marine squad there has enough weapons to outfit hundreds of soldiers."

"If I may be frank, what if we need to fight before we get there?" Wade interjected.

Margie held her ground. "The War Machines and the Volunteers should be able to handle anything along the river."

Wade's mouth tightened even more.

"I think that's a mistake. We joined Captain Steele. We deserve to protect ourselves," Gunther said.

"And those were his orders," Margie said.

War Child spread his arms. "Fellas, I understand. Being an ex-military man myself, I get feeling naked out here." He slapped Gunther on the shoulder, jostling the man. "My crew is carrying plenty of extra guns and ammunition. If we get in a scrap, I'll make sure each and every one of your soldiers gets a gun."

"We'll be sitting ducks out there," Gunther said.

War Child reached out and clapped the lieutenant on the back again. "I'll take care of you. You have my word."

"I don't like it." Gunther eyed Wade for confirmation of his assessment.

"Beats manual labor," Wade said.

Gunther nodded his head in affirmation. "You can understand why we don't want to be out in the open unarmed." His eyes were honest. "But we'll wait until Clinton."

War Child canvassed the sky and the falling snow. "Best get this show on the road before it gets too cold." He wheezed a laugh and patted his jacket for his pack of cigarettes.

"Sergeant First Class Wade, can you get 1st Platoon on board?" Gunther asked.

"Yes, sir."

"Ladies," Gunther said and walked back to his pontoon.

War Child gave them a grin as he threw a cigarette into his mouth, flicking his lighter. "Should be fun." He boarded the waiting pontoon.

Tess squeezed Margie's shoulder. "You're going to do well." It almost felt awkward to be comforting a woman almost twice her age.

"Thank you." Margie made her way to her tiny pontoon boat. Men unraveled mooring ropes, and people settled aboard the boats, huddling down in an attempt to cut the wind.

Motors fired up with a chug-chug-chug. The unwieldy long watercraft reversed and slugged up the river. Tess wiped her almost frozen nose. She twitched her it, trying to get sensation back into her numb appendage, and flared her nostrils, attempting to break apart crystalizing snot.

She walked away from the docks back to the fortified homestead. Stacked logs had begun to be erected around the farmhouse, cabins, and barns in an attempt to harden their base. She traversed through an unfinished part, rubbing her shoulders as she tried to keep warm.

The faint sound of men chopping wood reached her ears. Far across the farm fields and into the timber was where most of the healthy men would be. Every day, they chopped a little farther into the forest. Nearby women carried buckets of water from the hand-pump well and tended fires inside the cabins and barns.

The two cabins closest to the Reynolds's farmhouse contained the Red Stripes motorcycle club. *I wonder what they've been up to?* She wiped her nose again as the wind picked up. The bulkiness of her coat blocked most of the freezing air, but some still managed to get up and under her clothes, making her slender frame shiver.

She crossed the center of the camp. The ground here was trampled into a brown soupy mush from the hundreds of feet that traveled through on a daily basis. She sauntered up to the doorway and rapped the recently cut tan door.

"Anybody home?" she called out.

Testing the doorknob, it spun and she stepped inside cautiously. "Half-Barrel? Thunder?"

The cabin was a sizable single room with a wider than average fireplace and chimney on the far side. It could easily fit over twenty people or even more, depending on how personal people wanted to be with one another.

Sleeping bags and blankets dominated the floor. Beer cans and wrappers were strewn about carelessly, giving the appearance that they'd been ransacked in the night. The fireplace emitted a weak warmth. The Red Stripes had been gone long enough that their fire was only a few hot coals. She rubbed her hands together and blew on them.

"Anybody home?"

She kicked a can with her foot, and it rattled across the floor before resting at the foot of a sleeping bag. Her boots clopped on the floorboards. She peered around their mess of a cabin. She spied a green hiking backpack in the corner.

Squatting down, she flipped open the top. She peeked inside, angling the bag for better light. She rummaged through pulling out porno magazines: *Sexxxy Time, Grandma's Cookies,* and a *Bush Chaser.* She shook her head. "Animals." She tossed them to the side, digging deeper into the pack. The bottom was lined with boxes of bullets. Some were spilt and the loose brass tinkled together. She shoved the bag back into the corner and stood.

She found bags of food and a few guns, nothing incriminating, and nothing that furthered any suspicion of a connection between the Chosen and the Red Stripes. She held her thawing nose for a moment, trying to think if she missed anything.

"I know I ain't crazy." Her footsteps echoed as she cut through the makeshift beds of the bikers. *Maybe I'm wrong about them.* She walked past the fireplace, each step sounding out. Her left foot struck a board, stopping her.

"Hmm." Her footstep sounded funny. Tilting her head to the side, she listened. Her foot creaked over the floorboard. Shifting her weight to another board, she listened. The sound was damp and dull with a solid feeling to it. She lifted her foot, resting it upon the suspect board, a hollow sound echoing forth. Gazing downward, she examined the wood. It was the same color as the rest of the floorboards, roughly hewn and hardly sanded cedar.

Pulling her knife from her waist, she threaded it through the cracks around the edges. She pried the piece of wood up until she could get her fingers beneath it. She rolled the floorboard to the side, revealing a gaping black hole. Dropping to her knees, she flipped up a few more nearby floorboards.

"What do we have here? Hiding something?" Placing her head closer to the hole, she found it difficult to make anything out. She thrust her arm into the open space and felt around. Her hand grasped a hard plastic handle, and she hefted it. It was heavy with her arm extended, weighing over thirty pounds. She grunted as she used her back and shoulders to hoist the bag upward.

The black bag rattled like she'd dropped a thousand marbles as she threw it on the floor. "Secrets, secrets are no fun." She crawled over to the duffel bag and unzipped it down the middle.

Varying sizes of see-through orange bottles with white childproof tops layered the bag. She knew right away. Twisting one in her hands, she inspected it. "Take one a day for ten days even if no flu symptoms are present." She shook the pill bottle and tossed it back into the bag. Antibiotics, antivirals, pain killers. Each container rattled its illness treating contents. She flung a bottle back inside and sat back on her heels.

"Motherfuckers been hoarding the meds." She shook her head. "I can't believe this shit." She peered at the door. "All while that son of bitch pastor's been preaching how there's no medicine." She gritted her teeth and picked up a bottle, shoving it in her pocket. "Motherfuckers are setting us up."

JOSEPH
Cheyenne Mountain Complex, CO

A frown had settled on Dr. Desai's face. "How does one go about finding a secret group of conspirators?"

"Do we put out a signal or something to let them know we want to meet?" Joseph asked.

Hollis grimaced like he wanted to choke on his crackers. "Heavens no, we wait for them to contact us."

Both Joseph and Desai blinked at the heavyset doctor. "How do you know?"

"How do they know we joined?"

Hollis's fat jiggled. "Have you ever seen a movie? Secret rebel groups always find new people to recruit. I know one thing for sure: if we start asking around, we're going to end up in one of those cells along with Byrnes if in fact he's still alive."

Joseph prodded his glasses back up his nose. "I think you're right. We can't be too forward or somebody we don't want catching wind will find out, but what do we do in the meantime?"

"Amateurs." Hollis snorted a laugh. "We go about our normal business. I will start by seeing how much of the vaccine I can misplace for safe houses in the Golden Triangle. You two must go about your normal routine. Get to the lab and create more of the vaccine."

"You're right." Joseph stood. "Let's get back to the lab."

Desai rose, inhaling a deep breath. "I'm ready."

Hollis shook his head. "We can't all leave at once. Let me go first. Wait five minutes then you can go back to the lab." He exhaled heavily. "We're going to get caught. Try and act normal out there." He eyed them. "Like you aren't waging a coup against the government." Placing a hand on the door, he turned. "I'll talk to you later." He whipped open the door and left.

"How is he good at this?"

Joseph smiled at her. "I don't know, but he's right. We have to keep it cool. Real smooth like. Paul Newman in *Cool Hand Luke*." He nodded at the thought of himself emulating the handsome, suave, and resilient prisoner.

"What's a Cool Hand Luke?" Desai asked.

"What is *Cool Hand Luke*?" He shook his head. "What we have here is a failure to communicate."

She stared, unknowing of his movie reference.

"You'll have to watch it."

"Okay, Joseph. I will."

"Promise me?"

She laughed, her nerves a little less strained. "I promise."

Joseph checked his watch. "It's been about five minutes. Let's go."

He stepped into the hallway with Desai on his tail. Two figures in all-black military gear patrolled in their direction. He felt his glute muscles involuntarily tighten at the sight of them. *Act normal.* His hands fumbled with his keys, but he managed to get it locked. He gave Desai a nervous glance. "Shall we?"

"Yes," she uttered.

The doctors paced forward and crossed paths with the ammunition- and gun-clad soldiers. They both eyed Joseph and Desai, and the soldier on the far left nodded to them as they passed.

After a few feet, Joseph glanced back at the retreating men. Neither soldier considered them again. He let out a heavy breath.

"Did you see the one on the left?" he asked quietly.

"Yes, what do you think it meant?"

"I don't know. Do you think he's part of the Sons and Daughters?"

"I don't know."

They reached the lab and passed the observation room, entering the locker room. Desai went to the women's side and Joseph to the other. A normal shift for the doctors minus two members of their team. He lifted the handle while unbuttoning his shirt with the other.

The metal clanged as the locker slid open. A small envelope was taped inside the door. Instantly, his heart sped up. He looked around the empty locker room to see if anyone noticed. *Could this be a trap?* Unsticking the envelope from the door, he ripped it open. He unfolded the letter and read the words carefully.

If you want to know what happened to Byrnes, you must go to where the first one fell at 2200. - Sons and Daughters of Liberty

"The first one fell?" he said to himself. He tucked the paper into his pocket. His heart pounded his rib cage without mercy. "First one fell?"

"Are you ready?" Desai said from on down the row of lockers.

"Jesus," Joseph said. He ran a hand through his hair.

She wore light blue scrubs with a blue cap covering her head. She frowned at him. "What is it?"

He took a step closer. "This was in my locker." He handed her the letter.

She gulped and took it. "Who's the first one?"

"I dunno."

"Patient Zero? He's the first one."

"Could be? Wouldn't that just be in the other lab?"

"Yeah, where he succumbed to his illness."

Her coal-dark eyes read him. "What if they meant Weinroth?"

Joseph stared back. "Weinroth?" The name stung him. She was his match across the board: intellectual, beautiful, and driven. She had been taken by the virus like so many others. His voice eked out a whisper. "Weinroth?"

"Her room?"

"Nobody's been moved in there."

"Could be." He breathed hard. He hadn't even looked inside since they had gunned her down like an animal in the hallway. "I'll go there."

Desai reached for him. "I'll go with you."

He smiled at her. "Thank you."

"Together, remember?"

He nodded. "Together."

***

Desai and Joseph sat in his room watching the clock. The clock face glowed a red 9:53 p.m. He rubbed his hands together in anticipation.

"What if it's a trap?" he said looking at her.

"Then we made a mistake and MIM is out of doctors."

"If we pick the wrong side, mankind loses."

"We haven't picked the wrong side."

Joseph breathed hard. "What if we're wrong?"

"Then we did it in good faith, and we pay the price."

"Then we pay the price." Joseph nodded. Her confidence calmed the waves of nervousness crashing in his gut. "Are you ready?"

"Yes."

They walked down the hallway toward Dr. Rebecca Weinroth's old room. Turning a corner, they continued on. They stopped at a sign near the side of the door.

"This is it." It was a plain door. Nothing conspicuous about it. Nothing to indicate the woman that resided here and her death.

Joseph twisted the knob and the door opened. It was dark inside. There were no windows in the deep mountain compound, something that unsettled Joseph's nerves when he thought about it too much. Made him wonder if the outside still existed or if they were in some sort of controlled experiment like mere rats in a maze.

With an air like he was deciding his fate, he walked through the door followed by Desai. The door gently closed behind them. His fingers fumbled for the light switch.

"Leave it off," came a man's voice.

Joseph's heart leapt in his chest, and his hand hovered near the switch, the temptation to flip it and reveal his co-conspirator egging him on. His voice cracked, "Why?"

"Light switches set off sensors in the security system. They'll know someone was in here when they weren't supposed to be."

"Who are you?" It was uncomfortable speaking to a man he didn't know in the dark. It was odd addressing a general area.

"We don't do names although I know who you are. Byrnes spoke of you with high praise and you as well, Dr. Desai."

"Thank you," she said softly.

"We do not meet in person unless it's absolutely necessary."

A small flashlight flicked on, illuminating a man with close-cropped reddish hair. He wore a light blue Air Force uniform with the gold oak leaves of a major on his shoulders.

"There were many of us, but someone got scared and flipped. Now they're rounding us up one by one. I fear it's only a matter of time before my name is brought under suspicion and I disappear as well." His words weighed the air. "You read Phase II of Operation Homefront?"

"We did."

"You and who else?"

"Dr. Desai and I," Joseph said quickly. If they were in a trap, best to avoid implicating Hollis. She glanced over at him and he ignored her.

"Let me see your ID card," the airman asked.

Joseph unclipped it and handed it to him.

The major pulled out a laptop and stuck the card inside. "Byrnes is in grave danger. We have to get him out and soon." He hammered away at the keys on this laptop. "I'm updating the certificates on here for access to level - 4."

"I thought Cheyenne only went down to -3?"

"No, there are more layers inside this complex that I don't even know about, but level -4 is where Byrnes and the others are being held."

"What are we supposed to do?"

The man glared at them, irritated. "Get them out. I can't. It's too hot where I am."

"How are we supposed to do that?"

The major's eye twitched like he'd been under too much stress for weeks. "I figured you were more resolute." Running a hand over his face, he stared back at his screen. "I have no reason to go down to that level. I'm merely glorified admin." His fingers clicked on the keyboard. "However, you have the perfect excuse to go down there."

Joseph gulped trying to soothe his drying throat. "What's that?"

"You're a doctor. You have plausible deniability. You know what's at stake here?"

"I do."

"Let me refresh your memory. These people will be executed if we don't get them out. If we lose Byrnes, the movement will collapse."

He handed Joseph his ID card back and took Desai's. "You should have access now to the level. The rest is up to you."

Keys tapped away. "This is the best I can do. Good luck. We've dallied too long already." He slammed his laptop closed and slipped it back into a bag. "I have to get out of here before someone notices I've been gone for too long." He flicked off the flashlight, slipping into the hall without a word.

They stood quiet in the darkness. Only the sound of their breathing in the air.

"He wants us to break them out," Desai said.

"How the heck are we going to do that? I'm a doctor not a covert operative."

"We'll think of something."

They felt their way to the door and opened it. Joseph peered out either way. No one in sight. They left Weinroth's room, walking in silence as Joseph tried to create some sort of plan in his mind. "What's the first step of any prison escape?"

"What's that?" Desai asked.

"I was hoping you would know."

Their footsteps were soft but echoed down the empty hall.

"We're scientists. We don't have big brains for nothing. Where do we start?"

"Scientific method. We know the question. How do we break them out?"

"Yes." Joseph smiled. "Then we do our background research." He held out his ID card. "We find out where they're being held."

STEELE
Camp Forge, IA

Steele swung hard into a maple tree wide enough that he couldn't wrap his arms all the way around. He reset his feet, his breath fogging like cold smoke. He nestled his chin inside his green-and-black shemagh he was using as a scarf. Breathing in the warm air, his lungs thanked him for the blast of warmth in the cold.

A thin layer of snow dotted the forest. The trees were leafless and dormant. Steele's men, armed with axes, slew them by the dozens on a daily basis. At first, he had felt guilty cutting into the Reynolds's forest, but now it was commonplace. They needed wood for fires to keep people warm and to build the fortifications higher.

He adjusted his grip on the wood axe and cut deep into the tree's trunk, revealing its almost white interior. He swung again harder, his left arm doing a disproportionate amount of the work. His right arm grew stronger by the day, but his hand still didn't function like it should. He wondered if a doctor could have fixed that in the old world. Best not to think too much about the old world. The thudding of axes and the grating of saws echoed in the forest around him.

Big Garrett stopped nearby as he caught his breath. He was over six-and-a-half-feet tall with the look of a man who used to be muscular in his twenties and thirties but now in his forties was just big. *Can't teach size.* "Looks like you need some help," Garrett said through his more salt than pepper beard.

136

Steele wiped his forehead. "Ha. A little more than that. At this rate, I'd be out here all day."

"Let's speed that up." They took turns, slamming axes into the tree like a strongman competition. After what seemed like the entirety of the day, the towering maple started to teeter on itself.

"Timber!" they shouted.

Together the men gave the tree a shove and ran to the sides. The big tree crashed through the smaller saplings and thumped the ground.

Steele's breath steamed in the brisk winter air. "Time for a break. I'm going to check on John."

"Eh, I don't need your help anyway," Garrett said with a grin.

"Anyone ever tell you you look like Paul Bunyan?"

Garrett's smile twisted nasty. "You want to be Babe?"

Chuckling to himself, Steele navigated his way through a field of stumps and broken branches. Every day, the men from Camp Forge cut farther and farther into the timber, and the walk got a bit longer.

His feet cracked the brittle undergrowth battered by the feet of many men. Van Fogerty, one of the neighboring farmers, hitched two powerful draft horses to a felled tree. Steele gave him a nod as he passed. Earth and snow alike had been churned up here as trunk after trunk was dragged toward the homestead.

They'd labored almost continuously night and day to harden their position. The wall grew taller around the homestead, encompassing the cabins and barns. Where two walls met, an elevated tower was erected and sandbagged to form a fortified machine gun nest.

John was directing Larry and a few other men from Sable Point in stripping the wood for use. Steele made his way to them. The logs were set up between shorter upright logs in a V-shape so they wouldn't roll while they were prepped for building. Shavings fell to the ground as they chiseled away at the wood although those would not be wasted. They would be used as kindling for the camp.

The elder farmer directed the novice carpenters and engineers at their work like an old-time foreman. He gestured at Larry and adjusted his grip on the curved drawshave.

"You have to pull back like this." The old man took the double-handled tool with a rounded sharpened piece of metal in the middle. "And angle it down. It will shave the wood better."

"How's it coming?"

The old man wrinkled his rosy nose at Steele. "Well, it's colder than the dickens out here, but these tenderfoots are picking it up pretty quick." He smiled broadly. "Got an extra bark spud over there if you want to help."

"I have to speak to Thunder, but I will come back later and lend a hand."

"Sounds good, son. I know you're busy planning your military actions, but we can always use an extra hand."

"I know you can."

A few of the men dragged a log over to the fortification wall. Thunder and his group would load the log atop the others.

"Thunder."

"Steele." The heavyset biker with a long gray beard grinned at him. Eight men heaved the log and placed it atop the one beneath it. Then they would lash it down. Spaced out every ten yards was a thick post supporting the structure. The biker panted as he joined Steele.

"The wall is coming along."

"It is. Another couple weeks and it'll be tall enough."

"Then maybe we can relax for Christmas."

Thunder, who already doubled as a biker Santa in his workshop, scratched his red bandana. "Damn, it is the season, isn't it? Kind of lost track of time."

"Everything seems like a lifetime ago."

"May as well be a different planet."

Steele motioned toward the wall. "Show me the progress."

"Sure." The two men dipped down through a trench and walked near the wall.

Thunder inspected the interior. The other side of the log wall was filled with sand and dirt that stretched four feet to another log wall. "This should prevent any bullets from penetrating."

"You sure?"

"It worked for the pastor's men along the hills, except we are putting an extra foot of earth between the walls. Here."

"Look."

Thunder gestured between the logs. "You see? If a bullet penetrates the wood, it'll have to get through another four feet of packed soil then another log before it has access to anyone inside."

"God, that's great. It's like our very own HESCO bastion they use in military bases."

"It is. Not quite as uniform, but it will definitely do the job."

Steele studied the elevated machine gun nest. "Is that fortified enough?"

Thunder scratched his beard. "Should be. We have layers of sandbags inside up to chest level for protection."

"That should do." The Reynolds Farm was transforming into an apocalyptic fortress with enough protection to ward off the living or the dead. He surveyed the trench and knew the two-foot drop was not enough. Flashes of the dead crawling over the wall at Quarantine Base Cobra stung his memory. He pointed at them. "I want these deeper."

Thunder cocked his head to the side. "Not sure about that, the earth is freezing. Hard to dig when it's cold."

"Then we need to go faster. I'll grab some of Ludlow's men."

"All right. They can work the areas we've already done so we don't need to traverse as big of a trench."

Steele nodded to the biker. *How could this man be up to no good? Tess can't be right.* He jumped down into the hard-soiled trench. He bounded the entrenchment and cut through the hole in the unfinished wall. Inside the homestead, the heavy smell of burning wood cloaked the camp.

He passed through the cabins and made for one of the new barns that held the soldiers. A few stood outside the barn in soiled Army Combat Uniforms, easy to tell them from the other members of Camp Forge. Between their disheveled appearance and violent desperate gazes, it was clear they were men grasping to their last thread of humanity. He hoped he could give them something to fight for again, something that kept them from gunning him down instead of the infected.

A short Latino private inspected Steele up and down. "Steele."

Steele eyed his name tag. "Private First Class Campos. Can you find Major Ludlow for me?"

Campos stared at him for a moment, his jaw working a piece of chewing gum. "It's Sergeant Campos."

The markings on his uniform indicated otherwise.

"Sergeant Campos?"

The soldier's jaw continued to work the gum. "Promotions come quick nowadays." He spit on the ground with disrespect in his eyes. "I'll get him." He dipped back inside the barn. A minute later, he returned with Major Ludlow.

"Captain, you needed to see me?"

Steele judged the major for a moment. *Can I trust you?* "I wanted to thank you for the fortification recommendations. The walls are coming along nicely."

A thin beard masked Ludlow's face. Steele didn't know if he grew it in an attempt to stay warm or out of laziness. "I want to be protected from the dead as much as the next man."

"We need more help deepening the trenches."

Ludlow glanced over his shoulder. "We already have almost a hundred men either chopping wood or digging."

"We need everyone. Those trenches have to get deeper. I was at the quarantine base when we were almost overrun."

Ludlow's far apart eyes blinked registering what he said. It must confirm at least some of what Jackson had told Ludlow about Steele. He wondered if Jackson had told his subordinates about Operation Anaconda, the blowing of the bridges in Pittsburgh that Steele had conducted or if it was only the Battle for Steel City when his command barely escaped.

"The dead piled atop one another and the walls became insufficient to hold them until Jackson turned his artillery around." He paused the name stinging his tongue. "We had to take drastic measures. We have to expect that we may be facing even more infected here, maybe even the living."

"Jackson told me about the base."

"So you understand. The ground is freezing, and if we don't finish this soon, we won't be prepared for the long winter."

"I will get everyone that isn't sick or injured to help dig."

"Thank you, Major. We need to stand together on this."

"We do. My men and I are happy to be back in the fold."

Steele nodded. *Are they?* "We're happy to stand with you."

"I'll gather the men and see what we can do."

"Carry on."

Ludlow disappeared into the barn, and soldiers emerged slowly from its interior with shovels and picks.

Steele watched them leave and go into the trenches. Something tickled the back of his neck. It was a feeling, but one that he knew was perceived and not actually there.

He turned.

The pastor stood outside a cabin watching him. The man's long face was emotionless, and dour lines ran along his mouth. The pastor ducked back into a cabin. Steele studied the door for a moment as if he expected an answer. *What are you up to, old man?*

ALVARADO
La Crescent, MN

The blowing wind was a blessed curse. The howls of the wind masked the scrunch of snowshoes on the top layer of the snowpack. The elements were a neutral player in the contest between the living and dead, beating both sides with indifferent consistency. It was felt more by the living, cutting through layers of clothes with ease, but hindered the dead by bogging them down to a crawl.

From the bitter sting of the frozen air, she knew it must be in the single digits. Her eyes had a deep chill inside them as if they were freezing all the way back into her brain.

Snowdrifts dominated the small town, sweeping on buildings and gusting over entire city streets unmolested by man. Despite the snowshoes that kept the Marines mostly above the drifts, the trek proved hard going, and their progress was slow.

When they had traveled a few blocks away from the school, Butler kicked off his part of the mission. The diversion. Gunfire barked away behind them, popping off like a fireworks display. The dead veered in the direction of the rapid small-arms fire and away from her squad.

It took her squad almost an hour to go over a mile between hiding, killing, or evading the dead. They took turns hauling the sleds, wrapping the rope over their shoulders and torso. They didn't pull long like human sled dogs, ten minutes tops before the sled haulers were exhausted and ready to trade out.

Sergeant Riddle's boxy frame led in front. He took them toward a warehouse and drew them to a halt with a closed fist. He pointed at a long cut in the terrain of a dead forest leading east toward La Crosse.

The sprinkle of gunfire hammered away faintly in the distance.

Alvarado snowshoed closer to Riddle. He dipped his head around the corner. Steam fogged from behind his balaclava.

"These look like where the railroad tracks should be." He aimed a finger for Alvarado. "Once we go down these tracks, it won't matter about Butler. They'll be able to spot us out in the open." Alvarado did the same as Riddle, quickly peering around the corner. He was right. The tracks were surrounded by a thin perimeter of trees and open frozen lakes before they reached the river. Easy line of sight even for the dead.

"Catch your breath. In five, we go fast." The thought of moving in view of the enemy made her heart rate drum harder than it already was under the exertion of her pack in the freezing cold. Her balaclava and gear hid any fraction of worry she could have shown her men. She knelt, taking a rest, doubling up on her time to say a silent prayer to God. *God give us the strength to overcome this. If you are there, pick us over them. We are your Marines.*

The five minutes passed with a swirling dust of flurries. She wasn't sure if it helped to be sitting for so long, but Riddle led the squad on the tracks at a quick jog. The trees on either side of the rail did nothing to impede the dead. Hundreds of dead, lifeless eyes turned their way as the rifle squad ran against the tide.

They awkwardly ran through the snow, the white heaps sucking the energy from them with every footstep. The Marines manning the sleds fell behind. The speed they needed to survive was not an option with the equipment involved. Alvarado turned, running back.

"Go hot," she commanded. She placed her M4A1 to her shoulder and unleashed a controlled burst of fire.

In response, gunfire rippled from her Marines. Nothing crazy, not one wasting ammunition that was a premium in the field. Steady, premeditated, and efficient, taking only shots that were high percentage.

She made it back to one of the sleds and took the rope harness from one of the Marines. He collapsed into the snow, panting.

"Come on!"

He pushed himself upright and awkwardly jogged in his snowshoes.

Dead closed in from either side of the tracks as they moved like a slowly tightening vice.

The rope cut into her body as she tugged and pulled, trying to gain both momentum and leverage at the same time. She was small and the sled was heavy, the weight of it sinking it into the snow. They made it to the first railroad track bridge and crossed a frozen section of river. The dead beneath them flowed seamlessly, a river themselves.

"Cease fire!" she called forward, breathing heavily. As the tracks elevated, the infected were squeezed into the narrow funnel, stalling their attack and removing angles of pursuit.

There were four railroad bridges that traversed the Mississippi River, and Lieutenant Colonel Eldridge had only blown the bridge closest to La Crosse before he'd been killed. The Marines trudged forward with the smallest bit of breathing room, snowshoeing above the hordes.

They crossed two more railroad bridges until they reached the center of the last bridge. The metal of the tracks was splintered and twisted, a gaping hole ranging almost forty feet where intact track used to be.

Eldridge had picked the juncture nearest La Crosse because the dead would be funneled to French Island just off the shore of La Crosse, effectively trapping them for easy bombardment. No air support ever came, and now, those dead roamed free across the ice. Eldridge's prudent move blocked the Marines safe access into La Crosse unless they wanted to run the gauntlet below, which would be the same as running through the ocean and not getting wet.

The river of ice rasped beneath the feet of the dead while the few dead that had followed them, struggled their way down the elevated tracks. Some would slip and fall from the sides, falling before crushing the dead below. They weren't lucky enough for them all to meet this fate, and the determined dead doggedly marched upon the trapped Marines.

Alvarado knew this was an obstacle they'd have to traverse. Her Marines took firing positions, aiming their guns backward and forward.

Riddle's voice grunted behind her. "Major."

She turned. "One-rope bridge!"

"Someone has to make the run," Riddle said. His eyes scanned his Marines, choosing which of his men would face certain death.

Odom raised his hand. "I'll do it."

Riddle nodded, the relief clear around his eyes that his man went willingly instead of being ordered. "It's got to be fast. Once those dead get close, we are going to have to go hot. Then the gig is up."

"I can do it." The tall Marine slipped off his pack and placed them on one of the sleds.

"Two hundred yards," said another Marine, facing the dead on the tracks.

"Fast," Alvarado said. "That carbine is just extra weight." She stuck out her hand. Odom didn't question her but handed over his primary means of survival.

Riddle secured a knotted rope to a steel girder of the bridge and handed the other end to Odom. He slipped it around his body. Three Marines took hold of the rope to lower him down.

"Fast." She gazed at the young man, knowing the peril he placed himself in was guaranteed.

"Yes, ma'am." He peered downward for a moment at the dead and ice. Horrid moans were a decibel softer than a roar as they marched for Butler's base.

She joined her Marines and wrapped her hands around the rope hoisting Odom. Foot by foot, they lowered him down like they were going to go fishing for the dead with the Marine as bait. The rope swayed in the wind, and the three Marines struggled beneath the onslaught whipping their fellow Marine.

After seconds of trying to keep the rope steady, they flew backward as all the weight disappeared. Alvarado forced herself to stand then ran over to the jagged edge of concrete, wood, and metal that made up the blown train tracks. Leaning dangerously off the side of the tracks, she stared down. The rope went taut and unraveled as Odom ran.

Odom had released his harness early rather than be lowered into the ranks of the dead. He wrapped the rope around his arm as he sprinted. The dead nearby turned as he scampered past. The woodland-camouflaged Marine weaved through the Zulus with the agility of a running back making his way to the end zone through hundreds of defenders.

He forearmed one into the ice and spun as another grabbed at his arm with bony fingers. The cluster of dead drifted in the direction of the fresh bait.

A Marine spoke loud behind her. "A hundred yards, Major. Requesting to open fire."

She turned around, the dead on the tracks behind them had made determined progress.

"Open it up!"

M4s banged as they fired behind her. She was less worried about the dead to the rear and more worried about her Marine dodging across the icy river. If he didn't make it, they would have to fight their way off the elevated tracks and backtrack or lower themselves down one by one into the waiting frostbitten hands of the dead.

Odom stumbled on the ice, falling hard on his hands.

Get up. Get up.

The dead closed ranks around him. She joined Riddle and the other Marines, firing her M4A1 into the mass of dead around him. The Marine fought with fury, forcibly separating himself from the dead. He leapt over the fallen dead and scrambled up the other side of the railroad tracks.

She took aim down her sights. The wind and the dead howled fiercely together in her ears. It wasn't that Odom couldn't outrun the dead; it was that he had to stop along the tracks and tie the rope so the rest of them could get across. She depressed her trigger like she'd done more times than she could count, each shot a little easier than the last. Her M4A1 carbine's extractor pinged with relief of releasing its projectile. She pressed the trigger in a fluid motion again and again. Sounds of gunshots surrounded her but played second fiddle in her mind, like white noise from a war zone with her gunshots the only accents. Her sole thought was to keep the infected gaping mouths off Odom's back.

Destroyed Zulus collapsed on the slopes of the frozen river embankment. Falling dead plunged into the others, turning them into a tangle of arms and legs. When she missed, another Marine would take down the infected at a frantic pace.

Odom haphazardly tied the rope to a buttress on the other side. He heaved as he yanked slack out of the one-rope bridge.

The dead surged on the tracks behind him. She couldn't take a shot without risking putting a round through Odom. He went hand-to-hand with the Zulus, striking and kicking.

Riddle growled. "Fuck!"

Watching Odom struggle, Alvarado stared in disbelief for too long. She fleetingly glanced behind. More dead had found their way along the bridges toward the trapped Marines. Time was against them. The infected would eventually reach them. They would run out of ammunition then it would get sticky as they went hand-to-hand, but the jaws of death would take them one by one. Someone else had to finish what Odom had started.

"Hey! Hey!" a voice shouted from afar.

She turned back. Odom slid down on his back into the frozen river. He waved his hands at the dead. They slipped and fell after him. He gave one a kick to the skull as he flagged them down. The dead followed. He turned and jogged north of the river only fast enough to keep them interested. *Christ, bless that Marine.*

It would mean something; it just had to. She ignored the fact that Odom ran to his brave death. His sacrifice had to count even if it was just to kill more of the ugly bastards.

She tugged down hard on the line. It had little give under her hand. They must do their part and quick, or everything was a waste of good Marines.

"Get those sleds rigged up. Riddle, you and Harry first."

Riddle hooked himself to the rope along with Harry.

"Quiet on the other side if you can."

He nodded quick and jumped up, wrapping his thick arms over the line. He grunted as he swung both legs around the rope. With quick movements, he moved his hands one over the other as he pulled himself over the frozen river and dead alike. Harry latched on and went close behind him. The rope sagged under their combined weight.

When they reached the other side of the blown bridge, four Marines hastily attached the sleds to the rope. O'Bannon hopped out in front and dragged the sleds behind him, tugging the sleds with jerking movements.

Everyone operated with such fast self-preserving haste that she almost forgot the Marines watching their backs.

Corporal Johnson shouted over his shoulder. "Two mags left!"

As more and more Marines filed along the singular rope bridge, the dead had made headway on the tracks. Their heads bobbed in a mass of incoming death. She studied them for a moment. Their disgusting existence made her want to puke and then systematically destroy each and every one of them.

"Grenade them," she ordered.

Johnson looked back at her. "Ma'am, this bridge is fucked up, could take us all down."

She marched to the rear of her rifle squad and ripped an M67 fragmentation grenade off her vest. It was roughly the size of a green baseball with a safety lever running from the top along the side. Holding it firmly in her throwing hand, she looped a finger through the pin and tugged it free. She rolled it forward like she was trying to bowl, keeping it on the railroad bridge. It skipped and bounced into the air then was trampled under dozens of feet. Marines took cover. She ducked down, covering her head. Two more seconds passed. It all depended on if the fuse was put in on a Friday or not.

The grenade burst in the center of the infected mass. The sound was deafening even with her ears covered. Bodies and limbs in the immediate area were thrown into the air with indiscriminate violence. The dead flew from the tracks, plummeting into a bloody mess on the river ice. Guts and chunks rained on the dead below.

She stood before the rest of her Marines, taking a moment to scan the river. The Zulus within earshot of the grenade blast turned in her direction. *Bought a bit of time.*

"Get on that line." She pointed at the single rope.

The thick Marine grimaced and stood. "Major, more are coming."

"A lot more," she said. "Now get on that line."

The rear two Marines charged past her, linking themselves on the line. Her grenade had put a gaping hole into the dead that was beginning to fill again, like a festering wound with pus.

She put her carbine to her shoulder and fired ten shots in methodical precision.

The last two Marines scaled over the to the other side, suspended on ropes above the river.

Her feet grated churned snow as she made her way to the line. The rope had been tied higher than she'd remembered. Behind her, the dead gave a victory moan. She chanced a glance back. They closed in. No time for a harness. Fight or flight. She growled and jumped up, clutching the line, her M4A1 dangling to the side. Wrapping both legs around the rope, her numb fingers clutched with exhausted urgency. She scooted out into the expanse, her unwieldy snowshoes clanking together as she hurried.

A few feet from her, the Zulus reached the edge of the remaining tracks. The Zulus were always faster than she thought they should be. Fingers grasped her snowshoe. She kicked at its dead weather-beaten face, and it fell from the edge, unable to reason that it was ever in any danger. It smacked the ice with a sickening thud. The dead in the back drove the ones in front spiraling to the jaggedness below. In twos and threes, they tumbled off the edge. Limbs splintered, heads exploded, and bodies were impaled on the chunks of solid river just as hard as concrete.

She switched her grip so her elbow was locked around the line and hauled her way across. With no fresh distractions, the dead beneath her marched for Butler's last stand, all except the ones on the tracks behind her who committed suicide trying to reach her before plummeting to their deaths.

The rope swayed. She bent her neck backward and stared upside down. The Marines were setting up their sleds and dealing with any interested Zulus with quiet surprise. *Why is my line swaying? Every Marine knows how to tie those knots.* Her mind shot to Odom. He'd disappeared down the ice, a couple hundred of the staggering Zulus close behind him.

She worked her feet across, propelling herself. The rope dipped a few feet and she gasped in surprise, clutching her wrist even harder. Riddle and the other Marines had noticed.

Riddle yelled with a cupped mouth. "Bridge is going!"

Squinting, she searched for the line issue, trying to gauge how much time she had left. The girder bent forward, and she dropped another few feet, causing the line to sag. Her stomach pitched inside her gut.

Her fingers dug even farther into the flesh and bone of her wrist. She spied down at the Zulus that were much closer than they were a second prior. Only twenty feet separated her from certain death.

They shuffled beneath her, oblivious to her presence suspended right above them. They shifted and swarmed below, driven like an infectious sea of maggots. Her men couldn't do a thing. If they pulled the line back toward them, the girder would break and she'd fall into the horde, a tumbling meatball from the sky into their waiting mouths.

She dug her boots into the line and heaved herself upward over and over. Her arm shook and quivered with her effort. The wind blew her, her body swaying with each frigid gust. Her fingers were beyond feeling. More like numb clumps of flesh attached to her hands. Her back and shoulders screamed in pain, pain she forced deep inside. Pain she refused to accept.

"Come on, Marine," she said to herself. Clenching her legs, she propelled herself upward. Hands grasped her shoulders and waist yanking her. Her heart leapt.

Riddle's face leaned over and a smile enveloped the corners of his eyes. "Just like the O-course on Parris."

She shook her arms, relieving the tension in her blood-filled muscles. "A bit slower than I would have liked."

"Ain't that a bitch." Riddle glanced at the sleds.

"Yes, it is." She swung her carbine off her back and into her fatigued icy pins-and-needles hands. "Let's heat that ice up."

TESS
Camp Forge, IA

Her most trusted Sable Pointers stood around the firepit built in the center of the barn turned dormitory. Larry added scraps of wood shavings into the flames as they rippled higher. The fire greedily digested the wood fuel.

Tess picked up a few Meal, Ready-to-Eat tan bags and shoved them into her pack. It was black and only suitable for a day hike. She clipped two water bottles to either side. She tapped the handle of her Colt .45 1911, reached across her body, and touched the baseplates of two magazines that strapped into her shoulder harness. A box of fifty rounds lay in the bottom of her pack, but she was banking on not needing the extra firepower. She could sense their eyes watching her every move.

Her dark eyes moved to Trent. His goateed mouth pursed, searching for some missing chewing tobacco. His camouflage ball cap sat a little tilted on his forehead. His hunting rifle rested between his legs. She shifted to the man next to him. Larry ran a hand over a completely bald head. No hair had even remotely grown on his head, not even his sideburns since she'd known him. Nathan sat next to him, his collared formerly white shirt saturated with sweat and grime. He wore a tan overcoat, making him almost look like an old-time detective. His face was unamused.

"What?" she said.

"You shouldn't go by yourself," Nathan said.

Trent jumped in. "Nate's right. Between the infected and Jackson and god

151

knows what else, it's too dangerous. No place for a lady to be alone."

"Give me a break. You're all acting like I'm some sort of Susie homemaker." She slapped her chest. "It's me, Tess. I been through plenty of shit."

Worried eyes stared back at her. Harriet gulped, squeezing a small boy closer to her body. Her auburn curls shook. "Nobody should be by themselves out there. Not even the Red Stripes go alone. Always in pairs."

"I told you. I'm going and alone."

"I'll go." Trent gave her a half-smile. "I got plenty of wilderness experience."

Tess touched the center of her chest. "Your lack of confidence is disturbing. No, Trent. They may be looking for you for timber duty, but not me."

"Steele will look for you."

"Nah, that knuckle dragger is tired of hearing from me." He'd practically chewed her head off when she even hinted that Thunder might be involved in treachery. *I must go. That idiot Steele won't listen, so I'll get the only person he'll listen to: Gwen.* "He won't come looking, and you can't tell him I left. Nor anybody else. If they ask, tell 'em I'm sick and not to be disturbed." She peered over her shoulder at the other tarps and stalls in the room.

Her voice hushed. "Tell no one I'm gone."

A confused look engulfed Larry's face. "You mean no Sable Pointers?"

Tess tilted her head for a moment in anger at the man's stupidity. "You're lucky we keep you around for your good looks." The bald man who closely resembled a primate ancestor looked at the others around the fire.

"Nobody not here right now," she hissed. "Especially Rick."

The small group exchanged glances with one another. "What did Rick do?" Harriet asked.

Tess shook her head. "Just don't tell him shit. He's not to be trusted by any means."

Nathan nodded. "Okay, Tess. We got it, but what are we supposed to do while you're gone?"

Tess leaned her head back. "What you normally do." She sighed. "Larry, did you get the horse saddled?"

His bald head bobbed. "Yes, ma'am. He's waiting."

She slung her pack over her shoulders. Pulling hard on the straps, she tightened them so the it rested snuggly on her back.

"If I wait too much longer, it'll be daylight." She put on her gloves and secured a knit hat over top her short-haired head. "Trent, you made sure the guards are ours?"

The hunter scratched at his goatee. "Mason and Emmet know you're coming."

"All right, you did good." She nodded to them. "You look out for Steele. I can't say what, but something ain't right in this camp."

Her people stared at her with concerned eyes. In the end, all they had was each other, and they were closer than any family she ever had. Survival has that effect on people. It binds them. "We will," Harriet said.

Tess turned and Nathan shoved open the barn door as quietly as he could. Frigid air swept inside and Larry led her to the horse corral.

The beasts—some standing, some lying on the ground—slept with blankets wrapped around their bodies.

Larry clicked his tongue. A gray horse leisurely stood. It was the only one saddled. He patted the horse's snout.

"His name is Willie." He stroked the horse's nose repetitively with a gentle hand. "He's old and we don't use him often. Mostly for short jaunts."

"All right, Willie." She'd never ridden a horse or been so close to such a large animal. She tentatively reached a hand for him.

The shadowed gelding jerked his head to the side and let out a loud snort, smacking fleshy lips. Tess pulled her hand away as if the animal had tried to bite her. "What the heck?"

"Shhhh," Larry said, petting Willie's neck.

"They bite?" she asked.

Larry gave a short laugh. "Yeah, they can and it hurts." He led the horse out of the corral and next to Tess.

"Maybe, I'll just walk."

He ran a hand over Willie. "You said this is important. If you walk, it'll be cold and long. You can't take Rhonda. Steele would know."

Tess sighed. He was right. "How do you steer these things?"

"Well, let's get you up there, and I'll teach ya." He gestured at the horse's stirrup. "Get your foot into there."

She fumbled but got her foot slipped through the metal stirrup.

"Now pull yourself up with the pommel." She gripped the leather knob-like pommel and pulled herself into the saddle. "Get your foot in the other stirrup."

She wrapped her legs around Willie; he was wider than he appeared from the ground. Swiping her foot back and forth, she finally tucked it through the other stirrup. The horse stamped a hoof into the soft snow.

"Now, you give him a little kick with your heel to go, and you pull those reins to make him stop."

Larry grabbed Willie's bit and she practiced a kick. The gelding stamped his foot again. "He won't go."

"Don't be mean but let him know you're the boss."

She dug a heel into the horse's side, and he tossed his head in the air with irritation but started to walk.

"There you go," he led the horse forward.

"He's doing it," she whispered excitedly. They crossed the enclosure, the horse's hooves crunching the ground beneath them along with Larry's booted feet.

"'Course he is," Larry muttered. "He knows what to do."

She scowled in his direction. They passed windowless cabins with smoke eking out into the nighttime sky. The half-finished walls rose about five feet, and two dark forms stood guard near the wall.

"Larry," a shadow grunted. A short thickly muscled African-American man emerged in the darkness, his black beard curling off his chin almost to his chest.

"Emmett."

They had found the two men south of Gary, Indiana, during their flight from Michigan south and west. They had joined the caravan in silence and had picked up the slack when needed and not asked questions.

A man stepped up from the other side, his beard the color of a penny. He was taller than Emmett and almost as wide.

"Mason," Larry said.

"Larry."

"All right, Willie, take care of her," Larry said and patted the horse's flank. He admired her from below. "Take care of yourself, Ms. Tess."

"You too. I'll be back in a few days and remember what I said."

"We will."

Tess gave Willie a heel kick and the horse begrudgingly walked forward. The smell of burning wood from the fires entered her nose along with the cool night air. She eyed the camp over her shoulder. The wall rose, a dark mass in the night, farther behind it the roofs of cabins and the far white farmhouse.

"The things you do for love." She spurred the horse onward. "Come on, Willie."

MARGIE
Mississippi River, IA

Her vision was hazy as if she were staring into car headlights everything unfocused. She used a wooden spoon to shift around a mound of scrambled eggs in her cast iron skillet, cooking them to a soft scramble on low heat. The smells of the onions and green peppers mixed in made saliva pool under her tongue.

Brian walked through the kitchen to the coffee machine, pouring himself a mug of the black liquid. A newspaper was tucked under his arm.

"Kids are making all sorts of racket down the street. Hollering their heads off."

She didn't look up. "Kids are just being kids. It's the weekend. Let them play."

Her husband sat down in his seat, and she could hear him slurping his coffee.

The crinkle of paper folding and unfolding made her look over her shoulder. "How'd the Tigers do last night?"

Brian bent the newspaper in half and peered down through his reading glasses.

"How would I know? This is yesterday's paper. That damn kid can't even deliver the paper. See if he'll get a tip for Christmas this year."

"He's just a kid."

"The news said the Tigers cancelled again."

"Again?" She lifted the skillet and took it over to Brian, spooning scrambled eggs on his plate and went back to the oven to pull out the bacon.

Brian shook his head. "Yeah, it's that flu getting everyone spun up. Gerry said the plant should be open next week, but I dunno. All this news has got me worried."

Putting on a checkered oven mitt, she bent over, pulling out the thick center-cut meat. "I wonder about Katy and Kevin. I hope they don't come down with anything." She used tongs to place the bacon on a plate lined with paper towels.

"They'll be fine. Weird season for the flu. I'm more worried about how we're gonna pay for their school if the plant stays closed."

She sat down next to him, setting the bacon in the middle of the table. "I could go back to work to help."

His walnut-colored eyes regarded her over his glasses. They were the same eyes that she had fallen in love with over twenty-five years ago. It was only the rest of him that had changed. She hadn't known while it was happening because aging is a slow process. But one day she looked at him, really looked at him, and he had changed. They both had changed. More weight had appeared along his chin and cheeks. Wrinkles had formed around his eyes. She used to think it was the stress from work, but it was time. His belly sagged with additional weight. His hair had faded atop his head, but his eyes were the same. "You could, but I don't want you to have to do that."

She munched a piece of bacon, its salty and savory flavor tasting delicious in her mouth. It made her feel something, an ounce of pleasure in the routine. She wiped her lips with a napkin. "Nonsense, honey. Now that the kids are out of the house, I figured it would be a good time for me to think about making some extra money before you retire."

He nodded his head. "I just didn't want you to have to do that." He smiled at her apologetically. "Good eggs."

"Thank you."

They sat in silence for a minute, each eating and not speaking as people that had been married for a long time did. Brian had never wanted her to work even if she wanted to. She found so much gratification raising their children she never really complained, but as they got older and began creating distance, her purpose seemed to diminish with each passing day. It would be nice to get back on her feet, find something to fulfill her again.

"Should be nice this week. Mid-seventies every day."

"I suppose we should enjoy it before it gets too cold."

The weather. Brian's favorite past time. One might have said he was obsessed, but then again, it was the only changing thing in the stale structured world their marriage existed in.

"That'll be lovely."

"Maybe I'll get out to cut the grass."

She smiled and picked up her fork. The kitchen door thudded, and she jumped in her seat. Brian glanced from his newspaper.

"What the hell? Goddamned kids and their stupid basketball." Something thumped the door again. Brian shook his head in anger. "Those little punks. This isn't some sort of gymnasium." He threw his paper on the table and marched out of the kitchen. His voice rose in the next room. "I'm calling your father!"

The thumping continued. Each thump more violent and louder than the last. Margie carried her plate to the kitchen sink. She sprayed the plate with the hose-attached nozzle.

Brian's voice rose in anger from the next room. "Get the hell out of here."

Sounds of struggle and grunting came out of the doorway.

Margie stopped spraying her plate, looking over her shoulder.

"What is wrong with you?" Brian screamed.

Margie dropped her plate and dashed for the front door. Brian wrestled with a dirty man on the floor. They rolled back and forth.

"Call the police," Brian yelled at her. His assailant growled as they fought, biting into his arm.

"You, you, psycho!"

Margie ran for her phone in the kitchen. Her hands shook as she tapped 911. *Boo-R-Eee.* "I'm sorry, your call cannot be completed as dialed. Please hang up and try again."

She slammed her finger into the phone again, rushing back into the living room. *Boo-R-Eee.* The phone uttered its mocking tone of disconnection. She lowered the phone, her hand visibly vibrating. The woman's voice was muffled as the prerecording repeated itself.

Brian had gained the advantage on the other man, rolling atop of him. Another form staggered into the doorway. His chin dropped and he emitted a deep ominous moan.

"What in the hell?" Brian shouted.

Margie dropped her phone.

"Get the gun!" Brian's glasses were on the ground. His eyes were wide. She sprinted the carpeted stairs, her feet pounding each step with fear. She ran into their bedroom and to his waist-high cedar chest with gold handles. Ripping open his underwear drawer, her hand stabbed into his white and gray boxers, feeling for the revolver she knew he kept in there. She hated having that thing in the house. It was like he was hiding a viper in his underwear drawer that could rear its ugly head at any moment. Just knowing it was there made her cringe.

Her fingernails scratched the bottom of the drawer until her fingers wrapped around the cool handle of his two-inch barrel Smith and Wesson .38 special revolver. It was heavier than she expected. Her hands shook under its violent weight.

"Ahh," Brian screamed from below.

She dug around his drawer for a small rectangular box of ammunition. Rounds clattered on the dresser top. They rolled in small semicircles of freedom. Fumbling, she tried to slip a cartridge into the revolver.

The soft sound of tearing, like someone gently tore a shirt in two but wetter, traveled the stairs. She stopped holding her breath, tears running down her cheeks. Her breathing came in sharp pangs as she picked up her phone. As quietly as she could, she typed in 911. The phone rang. "Oh my god, yes," she uttered.

"Nine. One. One. What is your emergency?"

"Men have broken into my house and attacked my husband."

"I'm sorry, but we are going to have to put you on hold. All units are currently engaged."

"Men are in my home," she said louder. *Please God don't let them hear me.*

"Remain calm and please stay on the line." The dispatcher's line went blank. No sound came from the receiver, only dead air.

"Hello? We need help." Silence answered her. She could hear the footsteps of a person below. She set the phone down and raised the small pistol. *Maybe I can scare them away.* Trying to get enough air into her lungs, she breathed in and walked without a sound, her entire body shaking, for her bedroom door. She quietly pushed the it open.

"Brian?" Her voice echoed down the stairwell and crashed into a wall of tension. There was silence then the sound of feet. But no response. Knowing that someone was there and not making a noise raked over her with spikes of fear.

A man appeared. He stared up the stairwell with eyes like the freshest white snow. Crimson blood ran from the corners of his mouth, dribbling down his chin and to his shirt. He opened his mouth wide, showing bloodstained teeth and let out a low-pitched moan. "OOOOooo." He charged up the steps.

She took a step back into her room and slammed the door. The man's body crashed into the barrier at her back. "No," she cried at it. The body thumped again, and the door trembled. She put her back against the door and sobbed, holding the empty gun in her hand.

The 911 dispatcher never came back on the line. The police never showed. The dead outside her door didn't leave for six hours until she was too exhausted to cry any more. When she went back down the stairs, Brian's body was gone. Only pools of darkened blood were left in his place.

***

She shuddered in the freezing cold, watching the bleak dark brown water flow by her pontoon boat. Dead trees lined the banks of the river in forests of gray with floors of white. They followed the large charter flat-topped boats filled with soldiers and bikers.

Tony put his arm around her from above, squeezing her tightly into his body. "I think we're getting close." His breath misted in the chilled air. His black-rimmed glasses fogged on his face. He took them off and rubbed them with the soft underside of his coat and placed them back on.

She studied her paper map. "Another mile or two. I'm hoping we can get out of this open cold for a little while before we have to move on." Her team of eleven Sable Pointers stared back at her from beneath layers and layers of clothing they had put on in an attempt to stave off the cold.

The dead had lined the shores of the river for miles. They would follow for a time before they would find something else to follow. There always seemed to be more of them than before, and it gave her a fraction of a percentage point of hope that they might succeed in staying alive.

"I'd do anything for a hot chocolate," Tony said. His eyes crinkled on the edges. Not so different from Brian, but different.

"That would be glorious." She shared his smile, which was more than she shared with Brian before the outbreak. Her marital life had been lacking as much as her childless home. She had found comfort in the younger man, but she was so much different than she was before the outbreak. She couldn't help but wonder what her life would have been like had Brian survived or the outbreak had never happened.

Same routine. Day in and day out until one of them croaked. She'd be sitting at home doing a crossword, bored out of her mind waiting for Brian to get home from the plant. She'd hand him his paper and they'd sit down to a fried pork chop or spaghetti or something they'd both had a thousand times. It was just easier to make what you already knew. They'd talk about the weather or the Tigers or the yard work that needed done, and everything would be normal and routine, easy and boring.

The outbreak was her ugly, nasty, fresh start on a new life as a new person. A new person that had fallen for this younger man. She felt little guilt about her new relationship. Her other life was a million years in the past, and each day was its own lifetime when every minute could be your last.

Buildings on the outskirts of Burlington were dim and unlit. As they got closer to the downtown area, they drifted the boats to a metal dock. The long pontoons holding bikers and soldiers lined either side of the dock, and Margie had Berry take her pontoon to another shorter nearby slip. Tony jumped up on the dock and wrapped a rope around a pillar.

With stiff limbs, the Sable Pointers offloaded their packs and they disembarked. The War Machines were making their way to a big warehouse ahead of them followed by Lieutenant Gunther and his platoon of soldiers.

Margie shouldered her pack and led her group toward the steel-sided and metal-roofed warehouse. Margie didn't expect much warmth and comfort in its interior.

The Sable Pointers entered a side door. A female biker with a heavy jawline and striking chin smiled at her when she walked past. Margie removed her scarf, unwinding it from around her neck.

"Is Red Clare here?"

The woman grinned. "Over with War Child."

"Thank you." She turned to Tony. "Can you make sure the pontoon is refueled and anything we need is ready?"

"I will." He grabbed Will and they walked away toward fuel tanks housed inside the warehouse. The Seven Sisters sat congregated near the center of the building. A contained fire blazed in the middle. Temporary heaters blew hot air, all directed toward a cluster of people.

She approached War Child and Red Clare. They both shared a cigarette. Red Clare was probably the same age as Margie, but the effects of smoking had pruned her mouth and wrinkled her cheeks, making her appear much older. Her coarse red hair ran unkempt down her shoulders and back.

"Can't say I remember you," she said. Her voice sounded froggy like she needed a glass of water.

"Margie, Sable Point Volunteers."

Red Clare nodded. "One of those by the lake. War Child was just filling me in on the plan."

"We're headed north to help Captain Heath hold his line while he investigates Major Alvarado's missing Marines."

Red Clare smiled, her wrinkles around her eyes deepening. "I know."

"Dana," Red Clare waved over a lean and strong-looking woman with well-defined cheeks. "Let's find a good spot for the Volunteers near the fire."

Margie did not want to be brushed to the side. "Pleasure to see you again."

"We'll see each other again soon enough." Red Clare smiled wide, showing her yellowing teeth.

"Tomorrow morning, early, we'll head back out," War Child said. He regarded her for a moment, blowing smoke out of his nose. "Good night." He dismissed her like she was but a fly buzzing around his head. He turned back to Red Clare.

Margie followed the tough-looking biker, waving the Volunteers behind her.

They were led to a section of ground near the fire.

"This should do," Dana said, gesturing at the ground.

"Thanks."

Tony tossed down his pack, peeled off his gloves, and unraveled his scarf. "Colder than heck out there." He wiped his nose and leaned over the fire like it was a long-lost friend.

"Is the boat fueled up?"

He glanced at her through his glasses. "Topped off and ready to go."

"Good," she said, nodding. Stripping off her pack, she set it near his along with her rifle. She ran a hand over her knife on her hip. Soon she found herself leaning over the fire, embracing its warmth. The soldiers placed themselves near the far end of the building, bedding down in neater rows but still not exactly as uniform as she expected.

Her eyes kept returning to Red Clare and War Child. "I wonder what those two are talking about?"

Tony looked up, breathing on his hands between bouts of shoving them near the flames. "Red Clare and War Child?"

"Yeah." She cupped her hands together. "They are pretty chummy for rival gangs."

"Haven't they known each other forever? Besides, they're on our side."

"I guess you're right."

He put an arm around her. "Not everyone is out to get us. There are still good people left out here."

She rested her head on his shoulder. "Sometimes it doesn't feel like it anymore."

He breathed into her hair. "You got me, don't you?"

"Yeah." The flames danced a midnight fury.

JOSEPH
Cheyenne Mountain Complex, CO

The elevator slid closed behind him with a loud metallic clang, making him almost visibly jump. His steps echoed from wall to wall through the narrow passage. Recessed lighting hung from the ceiling along with a myriad of piping and exposed electrical wires bracketed in place.

The corridor was lined with four doors on either side. Small windows, four-inches round, were at eye-level on each door so an outside observer could look in on the detained person. Every cell was dark. He was only three floors deeper into the complex. That was as far as the elevator would take him.

A solid white door met him at the end of the hall. Near the doorframe was a boxy keypad and scanner. A rectangular security camera angled down on the doorway, getting a clear view of anyone going in or out.

Joseph put his ID card next to it. No beeps, dings, or dongs rang out. He whispered under his breath, trying not to look guilty. "Goddammit." He rearranged the card over the face of the proximity card scanner hoping a new angle might grant him access. Tugging on the door handle, he was still denied.

Did our mysterious major screw me? He nervously adjusted his glasses on his nose and fixed his lab coat.

The red-lighted camera continued to peer down upon him, continuously watching and recording his every move. The weight of being on camera drew him in, and he gave the security camera above the door a furtive glance. He adjusted the card to the upper right corner of the scanner and let it rest there.

Come on. It made the ba-da-beep sound, and the door lock disengaged.

Joseph speedily grabbed the door handle opening it. Metal-grated steps led down to a cave tunnel. *Have I reached the end of the facility?* He hesitantly stepped through. The tunnel was smaller than the ones near the surface that could handle cars and trucks. This one was meant for people. He stopped at the end of the steps.

The modular building complex rested atop giant springs. He assumed it was for earthquakes or nuclear strikes to give the buildings within the mountain flexibility to absorb such events and ensure the facility's survival.

The carved rock walkways were wet here, and he was reminded that he was essentially in a giant mountain cave with caverns and that the only real end to the complex was decided by how far man wanted to dig into the bowels of the earth.

There was a slight downward decline as he walked, following the dripping walls of metal piping and the open hanging lights above. The tunnel bent and turned as he walked even farther into the mountainous depths. Even the air seemed tighter than inside the modular complex as if they hadn't extended the ventilation system this deep and every bit of oxygen was being used.

The shapes of two men standing in front of a rust-ridden door graced him through the shadowy lights. His heart sped up in his chest as he closed on the two armed soldiers. Their guns were slung downward. Their faces were uncovered, revealing young men.

"What are you doing down here?" said the shorter soldier.

"I. Um."

The shorter soldier squinted at him and raised his gun a few inches. "I don't know how you got down here but go on back to the facility." He waved him in the other direction.

"You can't be here," said the other guard, shooing Joseph with his gun.

"No, I'm supposed to be here. There's a sick prisoner." *Oh God, please be the right place.*

There was recognition in the guards' eyes. They understood what he was talking about.

"I didn't know any of them were sick," said the short guard.

The taller guard frowned. "Yeah, I heard the old buzzard was down-and-out."

The shorter guard shook his head in disgust. "This fucking duty." He waved Joseph toward him. "Scan your card." He stepped to the side revealing another card reader.

"You aren't supposed to just let me in?"

"Come on, doc. You know the rules. You can't gain access to this point unless you have a clearance and a need to know. Scan your card like everyone else."

Joseph gave a shaky nod. "Of course." He took out his ID card and placed it over the scanner. Pushing it hard on the reader, he waited and moved it over to the other side trying to find the sweet spot. Meanwhile the guards complained as if he weren't there.

"This duty is the worst man. So boring," said the shorter guard.

"Just another four hours to go."

"Are you kidding me?"

"Beats being outside."

Joseph shifted the card to the other side. *Work, you stupid thing.*

"Does it? What I'd give for some fresh air, instead of this stinking recycled bullshit. Makes me claustrophobic, ya know? Like I'm in a coffin."

"I'm telling you man, I started on the outside months ago. When civilians started showing up, it got nasty."

"You have to go hot?"

"Yeah man, it was rough. Only once, but that was enough. I'd rather be down here on some forgotten guard duty than up there manning the fence."

"I guess." The shorter guard turned to look at Joseph. "Can't you figure that out?" Snatching Joseph's card, he inspected it. "Hmm, you don't have level-four access. Should say it right here." He jabbed a finger on the card in the area where the missing number should have been. "You sure you're supposed to be here?"

Joseph's throat jumped. "It was a last-minute thing. I don't know. They told me that a prisoner needed treatment and pointed me in this direction."

The guard shook his head. "Here, let me try." He put the card in the top

THE HOLDING

right corner of the reader. The door clicked. "Damn thing doesn't like to read unless the card is in the magic spot. I guess that's what you get when you only update things every twenty-five to thirty years." He smiled at Joseph and handed him his card back.

Joseph clipped it on his belt. "Thanks." He stepped inside a wide cave with a shallow ceiling. The door shut behind him.

Two guards in all black sat at a small table with MP5 submachine guns strewn on the tabletop. One read a nudie magazine with the words *Sexxxxy Time* scrawled along the top, and the other played solitaire with a deck of cards. The one looking at the porno peered over the magazine at Joseph.

"Why are you here?"

"One of them is sick."

The guard tossed his magazine down. His name tag became clear as he moved closer. *Greer.* "All I ever hear is a bunch of bitching and moaning out of these two-timers." His eyes glared at Joseph expectantly. "You know where they are?"

"No," Joseph said timidly.

The soldier stood and snatched his MP5. "All right, come on." He lazily draped the submachine gun's sling over his shoulders and waved for Joseph to follow. They walked to the far end of the cavern. Only a jagged rock wall stood before them. The soldier stopped.

"There," Greer said with his chin. A square hole in the rocky ground emitted only blackness. The soldier flicked on his flashlight and grabbed a metal ladder. He grunted as he lowered it into the earth. When it hit the ground, he locked it into two metal bolts near the opening. Cruel eyes laid upon Joseph.

"Holler if they get frisky, but I ain't going down this ladder for you, so you're on your own. Which one of them's sick anyway?"

"No one said."

The guard shook his head and snorted. "So secretive. Where they gonna go? Outside the Triangle? Death sentence. Either way, I guess they're sentenced to death." The guard laughed. He hacked a loogie and spit down the hole. "Fucking traitors."

Joseph gave a short smile. "Yes, I assure you, we aren't going anywhere."

"You sure aren't." With no urgency, Greer walked back to his table. Joseph gripped the ladder and clambered down rung after rung into the dark mountain cave. His foot crunched over loose rock.

"Byrnes?" Joseph said quietly. The stench of open sewage and unwashed bodies stung his nose. It was potent and sour and the air seemed even tighter here. A single light hung from the ceiling.

The sound of people getting to their feet ground out. Grimy and beaten people stared at him, not knowing what to make of this newcomer. Their eyes spoke volumes of mistrust and betrayal. Camouflaged uniforms. Dress uniforms. Civilian clothes. Others continued to sit desperately exhausted and defeated. The only way out was through the hole in the ceiling.

A short young man with a single bar on the chest of his stained ACUs perceived Joseph. He could have been Joseph's nephew. He wasn't very big, his shoulders were slumped, and his eyes were a light mocha color that held intelligence. "Who are you?"

"Dr. Jackowski. Is there a Colonel Byrnes being held here?"

The soldier's eyes didn't leave Joseph. "Why are you here?"

Joseph shoved his glasses up his nose. "To see Byrnes. Is he here?"

A slender man walked between the others. "It's okay, Elwood."

Colonel Byrnes stepped into the dim light. "You came."

TESS
Southern Iowa

Willie's shod hooves puffed snow into the air as he walked. When the wind picked up, it caused the fresh flakes to swirl and blow away only to drift into a new place. Tess kept her head low, avoiding the frigid dust. She'd kept on the road to Farmington through the early morning darkness. Often she would turn and make sure she wasn't being followed. Only bare trees, bent yellow cornstalks, and harsh winds trailed behind.

After avoiding Donnellson, she continued along Interstate 2 until she could no longer feel her fingers, and her face was completely numb. She was sure that she had little bearing on what or where the horse went. He walked and she stayed on top. Every now and then they would have a battle of wills as he bent his head down, trying to munch browning grass from the side of the roadway. She would struggle with the reins and Willie would pull back, stretching his neck in an attempt to get enough slack to reach food.

A road sign engraved with the outline of Iowa read Shimek State Forest. Denser timber surrounded the interstate going forward. A brown ranch-style house sat on the outside of the forest like a sentinel.

"Better stop while we can," she said to the horse. Willie stood resilient. She tugged on the reins. "Come on, boy." Willie's ear twitched, but the horse stayed in place on the road.

She stared over at the house, wondering if the horse knew something she didn't. Did Willie have some sort of animal sixth sense? The kind of intuition that let them know an earthquake was coming and to run.

The brown home was layered in snow, and the windows were lightless. No smoke rose from the chimney. Two cars rested in the driveway, but they looked abandoned as snow had drifted around the tires. "Willie, let's go."

She could feel the horse breathing beneath her, his sides flaring in and out in rhythm.

"Mush or whatever," she said at him.

Willie tossed his head in response. She gave him a heel and yanked on his reins. He resistantly turned his head in the direction she led him.

"Come on. Why are you such a dick?"

He didn't respond. His hooves crushed the frozen gravel-covered ground as he walked.

Nearing the house, she reached in her coat and slowly unsnapped her Colt .45 1911 from its holster. Her fingers were numb, and they felt useless in such a technical task. Near the heat of her body, her fingers never wanted to leave the warmth of her jacket. She freed her gun and brought her hand outside back into the cold. The handgun felt more like a clunky weight. She switched the reins between her hands and held the Colt near Willie's flank.

The horse led her around the back of the house. The cars were coated in a chalky layer of white. A single step led to a back door and there were no footprints lining the ground. A weak snowdrift had built up about six inches to the bottom step.

"Looks perfect for me." She unhooked her foot from the stirrup and swung off Willie's back. Pins and needles of numbness shot through her toes as her foot touched the ground. She hopped as she tried to get her other foot free.

Willie turned to watch her struggle. "What you looking at?" She escaped the stirrup then jumped up and down for a moment as she regained the sensation in her rigid frozen feet. She led Willie over to one of the cars and wrapped his reins around a side mirror. "Stay."

Shoving a hand in her pocket, she walked for the house. A white-framed storm door barred her way, and she pulled on it. It didn't budge, so she threw her back into it. The door rattled as it sprung free from the ice locking it into place. She glanced over her shoulder at the only being present for her struggle.

170

The horse stared in her direction.

"Not a word." She tried the doorknob, and to her surprise it twisted one-hundred-and-eighty degrees. The hinges groaned as it opened.

In silence, she walked inside a kitchen. The smell hit almost immediately. It was sickly nauseating, and she knew what it was right away. The inherently revolting scent of death. She covered her mouth with a thick sleeve of her jacket. She lifted her weapon level with her eyes, scanning for threats. A small white kitchen table was set with two place mats, cream-colored plates and silver utensils.

A skillet rested on the stovetop, and blackened food encrusted the center. Maggots had long since come and gone through the rotting food. She checked her corner and walked into the den. Black stains caked the carpet. They streaked out of the room and down a hallway. The sight of the dried blood made her heart leap in her chest. No matter how many infected she'd seen or killed, it was an innate part of the human experience to have a physiological response to the sight of blood, even old dried blood of violence past.

Down the dark hall, she could see the form. It was a humanoid shape sitting on the ground. She pointed her pistol at the figure, and it didn't move. *Prolly dead.*

She holstered her firearm and drew her knife. Step after step, she moved down the hallway. The carpet squeaked beneath her feet. The form grew larger. It had the broader shoulders of a man but was thinly clad in flesh as if he'd starved to death.

Stooping down near the dead man, she thought maybe he was just regular old fashioned dead. He had a cold putrid smell to him. Her heart bounced when its head tilted up. A hand reached for her, and she reacted by ramming her knife into its temple with a dry crunch.

"Jesus, you slow fuck." She shoved the body to the floor. It slid on its shoulder and lay motionless. She put a foot into its neck, and bent over, and yanked her knife free.

The door behind him vibrated scaring her. "God damn." She sighed getting herself under control. The infected slapped the door almost methodically. It let out a groan muffled by the barrier.

"Shut up," she said at it. She rested her head near the door for a moment. "Just shut up," she whispered. It slapped the door. "Just shut up." She leveled her head and exhaled, gripping her knife as she psyched herself up for her next close encounter.

"That horse looks like good eatin'," a voice said from behind her. She spun around. A camouflaged man stood in the center of the hall holding a common woodcutter's axe in both hands. She didn't hesitate. Her knife thudded on the carpet.

The man charged down the hallway at her. Her fingers grasped the skin around her armpit inside her coat. He bounded like a wild animal with long strides. Her fingers found the rough handle of her weapon. As he neared, the axe rose over his shoulder for a downward strike. She ripped the Colt 1911 from her harness and ran for an open doorway. She backpedaled into the room and tripped, her back hitting the wall as her bottom hit the carpet. He yelled as he rounded the corner.

She sighted the handgun on him, and his eyes went wide as he recognized his immediate fatal danger. He halted himself, and a look of calm washed over his stubble-covered face.

"Back the fuck up," she ordered.

A perverted grin split his face. "Sure, babe. You do you." He let go of his axe, held it with one hand and took a step back. "Don't get hasty. Just wanted to talk."

"Drop the axe, you piece of shit."

He squatted and set it on the ground. "Sure thing."

She used a twin-size bed to help herself, keeping her gun trained on him with a single hand. The thumping of the infected in the other room increased. She eyed the man standing with his hands held up in the air. His camouflage was dirty. The name tag on his breast read Low. His stubbly cheeks were gaunt, his cheekbones pointed beneath his eyes.

"Keep backing up," she ordered.

The man backed down the hallway. She followed him and stepped over the body of the infected.

He stopped in the living room. His hands wavered in the air.

"No funny business," she yelled at him.

The infected continued to pound the bedroom door with fists.

The soldier still smiled at her.

"What the hell are you smiling at?"

He shook his head lightly. "Nothin'."

The sound of a window breaking forced her to turn. Her eyes flashed to the bedroom, and Low bolted for the kitchen.

"Goddammit," she swore. She sprinted down the hallway and turned the corner. The door banged as it swung back and forth. The wind keeping the storm door open.

The soldier's footprints dented the snow as he sprinted for the line of nearby timber. Following him to the door, she watched him run into the woods.

"Yeah, that's right. Run, you prick." She shook her head as he disappeared.

She glanced at her gray horse. Willie stared at her with big black eyes. His off-gray color made him seem like an offset outline in the snow. "Could have said something." The horse stared at her and stamped his foot. She shook her head at him. "You got a lot of attitude. You know that, Willie?"

The audible click of a gun hammer was a bass drum in her ears. She gulped, but her throat was dry.

"Drop the gun, girlfriend." Her Colt 1911 clattered on the kitchen floor. She slowly raised her hands. The barrel of his gun dug into the back of her skull, and she gritted her teeth at the hard metal. The thought of a bullet screaming into her brain made her grimace.

She turned around and a scraggly-bearded man sneered down at her. A necklace of gray-and-black fingers was draped over his chest as if they wanted to play his chest like a piano. Some of the fingers were stacked atop the others. He grabbed her by her jacket and drove her up into the kitchen cabinets with such ferocity her eyes bugged out of her head.

Twisting her face to the side with grime-stained fingers, he sneered. "What do we have here? A nice little piece of ass." His sneer became an all-out smile filled with yellow-filmed teeth. "Ripe for the takin'."

GWEN
Shimek State Forest, IA

The evening sun filtered through the dormant forest. It was warmer than yesterday, but when the wind kicked up, it still nipped at any exposed skin.

"Not so bad today is it, Kenny?" she said. The older farmer next to her laughed a short laugh.

"Could still lose a finger or toe if you ain't careful."

"I know you could."

He flicked the horses harnessed to the hayrack. "Get goin' you two."

"Opening ahead," Gregor grunted. He gestured with his chin forward.

The trees dissipated to snow-concealed farmland, and when she squinted, houses.

The group kept onward, and Gwen held herself in check from forcing them into a trot. Time was lives and there was a little girl in particular she didn't feel like losing anytime soon.

Wasted corn lay on its side, trampled beneath weather, animals, and rot. Their horses marched through the unplowed roads, and the houses grew larger. They passed the first few simple ranch-style homes. Interstate 2 became the main road through the town of Farmington. People walked around one of the homes.

Jake brought his shotgun to his hip. "That don't look right."

"Way too many people out for this kind a weather," Gerald said.

Kenny confirmed with a nod. "Aye, they should be inside."

Gwen gulped. "I agree. Be ready for anything." Within her blankets, she removed her hand from her belly and released her Glock 43 9mm from its holster. The men of her group unslung their weapons. Gregor struggled and almost toppled off his horse but managed to move his AR-15 to his front.

Her party continued walking, getting closer to the home. A cluster of people had formed at the front doors and windows. Gwen steadied herself. She knew they were infected. Their skin was a deep shade of gray as if they had frozen and rotted at the same time. They weren't clothed for any kind of weather.

"Should we drive on past?" Jake asked.

"No, there could be people inside. Nothing risky but take them down."

Jake and Gerald kicked at their horses, followed a few seconds later by Gregor and Hank. Kenny flicked his wrists and the team hurried after.

Gunshots penetrated the winter air, dominating the crispy silence. Jake point-blanked an infected woman with a boom as she turned around to face the newcomers. A third of her head disappeared. Gregor's AR-15 banged into an echo that washed over the houses like a thunderstorm.

"Stop the wagon," she commanded.

"Whoa," Kenny said with a shout. His team drew to a halt.

She lined up her sights on the skeletal face of a man with a gaping jaw. He had lived a long life before he turned, and now he still moved slowly. Her grandfather flashed through her mind, but she knew that it wasn't him. He was safe at Camp Forge. She squeezed the trigger. *Pop.* The infected went down like a bag of bones.

"Gwen," Jake yelled. She turned toward him. He pointed his gun near her and kicked his horse forward. Infected struggled along the edges of the wagon.

"Ah shit," Kenny cursed. "Giddy up!" he yelled at the horses. The wagon lurched and she braced herself. She twisted her body and fired multiple times. *Pop-pop-pop.* Jake drove his horse into the others, forcing them back. He swung his shotgun like a club and unleashed a slug into the head of another, a raw fierceness taking him over.

Another emerged from the side of the house. Its shoulders swayed hard as it walked. It raised a bony hand for them. Stringy limp hair hung from its head down its back like ragged weeds.

Gerald drew a brush hook from his saddle, a twelve-inch hooked blade with a three-foot shaft on it. He brought his horse to a trot, and as he rode by, cleaved his tool downward and to the side. It caught the infected in the neck and cut deep through artery and bone alike. The force from the impact whipped the infected around, and its head slipped to the side and the body collapsed. The dead lay strewn about in the snow.

Gerald turned his horse back toward the group and sat looking pleased with himself. "We use them for trimming trees. Thought it might be a tool against these things."

"I'll be damned. It is," Jake said with a laugh.

The farmer slid the brush hook back into his saddle.

"We should check on whoever's inside," Gwen said.

With a curt nod, Gerald rode to the house.

A small group walked down the road toward them.

Kenny squinted. "More infected?"

Gwen studied them. They all held guns. Their gaits were controlled and calculated. "No, they look normal, but that doesn't mean they're friends."

"Ha, my eyes just ain't what they used to be."

She touched his shoulder. The strain on the elder farmer must be trying. But like all old farmers, he was sturdy and used to the hard work. "You're doing fine, Kenny."

"Happy to help, Ms. Gwen."

She draped her blanket over her pistol. The four men stopped near them and fanned out in a line. The man in the center wore a black 5.11 winter coat, tan trousers, and a brown campaign hat of the Iowa State Patrol. He held a police-issued AR-15. The other men were dressed in hunting coveralls and jackets with shotguns.

"Who are you?" the trooper said.

"We come from Hacklebarney." Jake turned toward Gwen. "This is Mayor Reynolds."

"Trooper Linden, Iowa State Patrol." He scanned the still dead bodies strewn about, pieces of human meat. "Must have slipped across the Des Moines in the night. Why are you here?"

"We need medical help."

Linden eyed them for a moment, judging them truthful. "Follow me."

They trailed behind the trooper along the town street. He steered them to a single-story red-bricked town administrative building. He pushed open a glass door, and a woman stood, waiting for them inside. She had gray hair drifting toward a snowy white.

Linden nodded at the woman. "Mayor Tibbets, these people come from Hacklebarney."

"Please sit down," she said, holding her hands in front of her body like a kindly grandmother.

Gwen took an uncomfortable seat on a stiff lobby couch. "I apologize for coming in unannounced." She grasped her hands together. "I come on behalf of the town of Hacklebarney and Captain Steele, commander of U.S. forces in southern Iowa."

Tibbets took a seat across from Gwen. "Are you warm enough, sweetie?"

"I'm okay, thank you."

Tibbets glanced at her. "Linden. Get her that blanket. Can't you see she's pregnant?"

The trooper handed her a bulky down blanket and Gwen wrapped it around her body with a tiny shake.

The mayor smiled, a thoughtful look settling upon her. "Do I know you?"

Gwen snuggled further into the blanket. "I don't think we've met."

"Hmm. You look like somebody I know. What'd you say your name was again?"

"Gwen Reynolds, ma'am."

The older woman's smile deepened. "I didn't know John and Lydia had any daughters?"

"They didn't."

Tibbets raised her eyebrows. "Oh?"

"I'm their granddaughter."

Mayor Tibbets nodded her head. "I knew you had their look." She wagged a finger at Gwen like a teacher. "I know John and Lydia from a long time ago. Must've been over ten years since I've seen them. How are they?"

"Holding on."

Her smile saddened. "I suppose that's all we can do in times like this. How can I help you?"

"I'm afraid my task is urgent. Hacklebarney has been hosting the U.S. military forces at Camp Forge. We're holding the Mississippi against the dead.

"Camp Forge?" Linden interjected.

"Yes, Officer. Named after Valley Forge. It's a training base for militia defending the river."

"I didn't think much was left on that front, but I'm happy to hear that some are fighting."

Gwen turned back to Tibbets. "But we have a problem. There's been an influenza outbreak, and now, a strep outbreak through the base. It's rendering the forces ineffective. We've had multiple deaths already."

"I'm sorry to hear that."

"It's severely weakening our ability to defend Iowa against the dead." She made sure to stress the word Iowa. "If you have any medicine, antivirals, antibiotics, any spare clothes and blankets, we would be forever indebted to you." Gwen leaned forward toward the mayor. "My niece has come down with a bad case of strep. We don't have much time."

Tibbets pressed her hands together. "This is an unfortunate effect of terrible times. I'm so sorry." She tilted her head to the side. "My dear, have you been to Farmington before?"

"I have." Gwen nodded.

She gave her a tepid smile. "Then you know we are only six hundred people here." She glanced at the trooper. "We didn't even have an official law enforcement presence until Trooper Linden showed up in the night. We only have a single doctor. No pharmacy. I'm not sure how much we can help."

"Please, we will take anything."

"We'll do our best to find something. Us Iowans, we look out for each other."

"We do and thank you." Gwen relaxed. "I must ask."

"Yes, dear?"

"Captain Steele requests all willing and able men and women who wish to fight to come to Camp Forge for training."

"You have our deepest thanks for helping us today, but as you can see, we have our hands full here defending our town. I think you would put us at risk if you took away what few folks we have that are capable of fighting."

"I understand, mayor, but the battle isn't here. It's on the Mississippi. If we don't hold there then the nation will be overrun. This town won't last more than a few minutes against the masses of the dead."

Mayor Tibbets face paled. "We've heard." She stopped for a moment. "Rumors mostly. There's no real information. Trooper Linden has dealt with most that have wandered in from Missouri, but what you speak of is unimaginable."

"Ma'am. It's real. Tens if not hundreds of thousands. Here. We need anyone you can spare."

"What do you know about Captain Steele?"

"He's a militia captain commissioned by the United States government to lead the southern Iowa area of operations and my partner."

Tibbets gave a short smile. "Quite a mouthful."

"That it is." Gwen gave a small grin.

The women sat in silence for roughly thirty seconds. Tibbets's eyes were a pale hazel, and her mouth stayed flat.

"I just don't know if we can spare the men, but I'll say that I'm not an expert in security and defer to Trooper Linden."

Linden's face was thin like a triathlete with a righteous look about him as if he embodied every aspect of upholding the law. She could tell he'd at one point had a flat-top that had now grown out. His eyes were the color of rich fertile earth. His AR-15 was slung down the center of his chest.

"Ma'am, we can spare it. If what she says is true, then we can't afford to stay out of this fight."

Massaging her hands, she frowned as if the whole idea made her a bit sick to her stomach. "I trust you. How many?"

"I'd say I can take five men."

Tibbets nodded her affirmation. "You'll go with Mayor Reynolds and report back your findings. If this is as bad as she says, we will send anyone able."

"Thank you, ma'am. I know I only come with asks, but this is important. Can you spread the word to the villages of Van Buren? We need any and all people's help. Tell them to come to Camp Forge as quickly as they can."

"I will send word."

A moment passed before Gwen spoke. "But I also come with a give."

"What's that?"

"If we can hold the line long enough, the government has a vaccine. Anyone who fights will be the first to receive it."

Tibbets put a hand on her chest. "Oh, my Lord." She shook her head in shock. "That's unbelievable news."

"But it's the flu and strep that are crippling us. We have nothing left."

"I'll send for Doctor McKee in the morning." Tibbets stood, smoothing her heavy wool shirt over her jeans.

Gwen shook her head. "In the morning, ma'am?"

"He lives over ten miles out, and I will not risk my people's lives getting him in the night. Between the snow, the cold, and the infected, it's not worth the risk."

"We will get him."

Tibbets's jaw settled as she dug her heels in. "Trooper Linden will go in the morning. You can bed down in the McFarlen place overnight."

"Please, mayor, we need his help now."

The older mayor grew stern. "I will not risk his life or yours. You are pregnant, aren't you?" She didn't wait for an answer. "Tomorrow will be just fine. For now, I suggest you get some rest."

Gwen gritted her teeth. "Thank you, ma'am."

AHMED
Northern Missouri

He threw on his jacket and stared at himself in the mirror. His entire form was a dreary shadow. The mirror was aging with dark spots along the edges and gaudy large round unlit bulbs lined the top.

His face was paler than he remembered it. Gaunt cheeks like someone had sucked the extra weight from beneath his skin. Not that he had much to begin with. He rubbed a hand over his jet-black beard. The girth of his beard was extensive and made his narrow cheeks look thinner and the bottom part of his face round.

A whisper leaked from his mouth. "I can't be here. This is not my fight."

A soft knock came at the door. He glanced over. The chipped brass handle twisted. "What?" he said quietly.

Sadie's voice, muffled by the door, came through. "Can we talk?"

He glowered at himself in the mirror. The man there seemed to be fading as if the shadows would overtake him, owning him. "Give me a second." He collected the shotgun from the corner and twisted the knob, popping the lock.

Sadie waited on the other side. Her oval curls hung around her shoulders loosely and her slender arms were folded over her chest. "Are you okay?"

His mouth clamped shut before he gave her a terse answer. "I'm fine."

"You haven't said a word since you got back."

Ahmed reached out and grabbed her by the elbow, pulling her toward him. He spoke in hushed tones. "Sadie. We killed people today." He turned away. "I'm not sure we did the right thing. It didn't feel right." He shook his

181

head, his eyes reading hers for a moment. "I don't belong here."

"Please stay." She interlocked her hand with his arm. Her eyes were a doe's and she pled like a child.

It made his gut perform circus acrobatics. *Why did she make him feel like this?* "You've done so much for me, but my fight isn't here. My people are north." The words didn't sound as true as he knew they were. Doubt clouded over him. "I think anyway." *Gwen was north although nothing is certain.* Nothing could displace his loyalty to Gwen but this woman in front of him. Her aura sucked him in. Her presence shrouded him at all times. Loyalty pulled him another way, but she yanked him the other. *Is it attraction or a sense of duty to pay back the woman and people that saved my life? My debt is paid. I helped them get vengeance on the murderers.* His mind continued to torment him with the truth. *And became one yourself.*

His mouth worked before his mind had thought anything through. "Come with me. I have friends in Iowa. Leave all of this. This feud. Being here will only bring us more suffering."

Tiny crow's feet formed around her eyes in pain, her head shaking short nos. "I. I can't leave them now. It's been so bad. We've already lost so much. It would break them."

Ahmed bobbed his head, using their grip on one another to pull her closer. He leaned his head to connect with hers and they stood in silence for a moment, taking in the physical touch of another person not hell bent on causing the other harm. After a moment, she raised her head, her lips pursing. He needed no goading. Their attraction was clear. They touched. Her lips were soft even in the dry air. Their connection shattered in a fraction of a second, her very presence disappearing away. The yearning willed him to do anything to get it back.

She composed herself. "Let me see your wound before you go."

He gulped his desire and gave her a curt nod, stripping off his jacket and shirt. She unraveled his bandages. Round and round they went, and he lifted his arm so she would have an easier time. She stuck a fingernail under the sticky bandage and peeled it back, bringing a few stray pieces of bristly chest hair with it.

"Ow," he said softly.

Her eyes darted up at him for a moment and a small smile crept to her lips. "You get shot, but you complain about the bandage."

Getting shot was a fraction of a second in his mind. Like a wounded deer, fear and adrenaline had forced him onward until he dropped behind a log. A searing poker jammed through his chest before he blacked out.

"I don't even remember it."

"They were bad men like the Baileys?"

"Worse than the Baileys."

With a finger, she prodded around the wound, staring at the surrounding tissue as if she searched for something.

"How do you know about this?"

"About what?" she continued prodding.

"Wounds and medicine."

Taking an antibiotic cream, she rubbed some over top and around the healing hole in his chest. "I have an associates in veterinary medicine from the community college."

Ahmed laughed a bit. "You're a vet?"

"Vet tech. You're my biggest animal yet." A small grin embraced her lips.

He stared down at his chest where the wound had sealed up into a painful itchy scab. The area around the wound wasn't red and infected but relatively smooth, fresh skin.

"No sign of infection. That was the hard part. Keeping your strength up to fight off any infections. With no oral antibiotics, you would've struggled."

"What about the bullet?" It still struck him as crazy that a projectile could be inside his body.

"It went clean through you. I'm not sure I could have fixed a bullet fragmentation inside your body." She ran a hand across the bandage pressing it hard back on his chest.

"I guess I'm lucky you didn't decide to put me down."

Her smile grew as she circled the dressing, still stained with dried blood, around his body. "You should be more appreciative. That idea was discussed."

"Jimmy's idea?" He threw his shirt and jacket back on.

She put loose bandages back into a white first-aid kit. "I won't say."

They stood in silence for a moment. "Do you think Lee will let me borrow a horse?"

She gazed at the kit and closed it with apprehension. "You mean give you a horse? Cause we both know if you leave, you ain't coming back."

He reached for her, and she let his hand fall to hers. "I have people that need me."

"A girl?"

"No." After a moment, he continued. "Not like that."

She sighed. "Lee'll give you a horse, but you have to promise me one thing."

"What's that?"

"You'll come back."

Should you make a promise you can't keep? Between the infected and everybody else still left, there's no way I can make it back here. "I'll come back after I find them and make sure they're all right." He stopped for a moment. "I have to see them through. We've been . . . "He paused. "We've been through a lot."

"I'll wait for you." She nodded.

He wanted to tell her the reality of the situation. It wasn't to wait. Not for him. She shouldn't hold out for anyone. She should live every day like it was her last because in this world, it very likely could be. Instead, more lies slipped off his tongue like poisonous honey. "Then I won't make you wait long."

"Don't," she said softly. She left him standing in the bathroom a shamble of emotions, some good, most bad.

He hefted his shotgun and walked for the door.

Jim sat at the table with his handgun resting in front of him. "Where you goin'?"

Ahmed stopped. He expected some sort of determent, but Sadie's was the only one that held any clout for him. "I'm sorry, but the time has come for me to leave. Thank you for helping me. I won't forget it."

"No you ain't." Jim's eyes laughed at him with icicles.

"I have people I must see after. They need me."

"You ain't leaving us." Jim started to twirl his gun in a circle on the table, spinning it with his fingers like he was about to play a game of handgun spin the bottle. The gun rattled in circles on the table. Round and round it spun.

Is he going to shoot me? The gun continued to spin. "I have to. I have responsibilities to people just like you."

"You got a responsibility to us. You're a part of this now." His index finger kept the gun going. The gun skipped over the table round and round.

"A part of what? Your blood feud?"

With his palm, Jim stopped the gun, laying a hand on the handle. He stared at it as if he contemplated its fate. "Sly will be back." He glanced back at Ahmed. "You gonna leave Sadie to that fate?"

Sadie peered down at her feet. Ahmed wished to God that those words hadn't affected him like they did, but the mention of her name tugged each and every one of his heartstrings. Logic wrestled his heart, throwing it on its back for a three-count.

"She has you and Lee to protect her. You'll be fine." His words felt thin like he knew better. He knew that when he walked out that door, he'd be condemning her to death.

"We'll fight, but we'll lose without your gun." Jim gripped the handgun. "Your hands ain't clean. They as bloody as mine. Sly will come, and when he does, he will crucify what's left of this family. You want that blood on your hands too?" He gave direction with his firearm. "Walk out that door. Put us to death."

Every single person's eyes were upon Ahmed.

"No one told you to charge in guns blazing. We could have talked to them."

A disgusted snort snuck from Jim's throat. "They'd stall so they could get in position to gun us down. You and me both know nobody was gonna do no talking. We went for vengeance and we got it. There may still be time for talking, but it wasn't yesterday. Not until the scales were righted."

The man was delusional. Ahmed shook his head. "You killed that woman."

Jim snarled, pointing his weapon haphazardly at Ahmed. "Nobody's clean in this!"

"You're right, but I'm going."

"We need you for one more night."

The words rolled quick off his tongue. "I'm gone."

Jim's eyes softened just a fraction. "Lee set up a meeting tonight. We are gonna talk this out, but if I show with three guns to Sly's ten." He shook his head. "Sly will end us there. I sent Andy over to Foxworth's. There's another three boys there, but it's still lopsided. There won't be any point in making a deal. We need him to make a deal."

The guilt of leaving them weighed heavily on Ahmed's conscience. "I won't do it."

"I only need you to stand there ready to fight looking all mean and scary." Jim gave him a flat-lipped grin.

"Then I am gone." Ahmed couldn't believe that he uttered those words.

Jim bowed in mock deference. "Carry on your merry way, my brown friend."

"I'm not doing this for you."

"Don't care who you do it for as long as you do it."

Ahmed glanced at Sadie. *She is the reason.*

She smiled and mouthed, "Thank you."

Jim holstered his sidearm. "The Old Grossman Farm. Tonight."

TESS
Outskirts of Shimek State Forest, IA

The soldier smacked his lips as he chewed with his mouth open. He sucked his teeth and ran his tongue across the front. He shoved his gold plastic spoon back into the brownish MRE pouch and stared at her. "You sure are lucky you had these little meals, or we would've eaten that stupid horse of yours." He leaned forward on a horrible pastel-colored floral-decorated couch holding his MRE in a hand. Her gun rested on the table in front of him along with her harness he'd ripped from her body, leaving her shuddering in the cold.

In the unheated house, her body shook without her heavy coat. Her hands were tightly bound with some kind of rope behind her back. She sat upright on the floor and glared at him. Her teeth clinked against one another in a desperate plea to stay warm. "Fuck you."

Jarvis stopped chewing and eyed his comrade. "Can you believe the mouth on her?"

Low licked his lips. "Yeah, I can. She's one of them from Steele's camp. I seen her before." Clearly the subordinate follower of Jarvis, Low was the smaller of the two.

"Is that right? You one of Steele's play toys?" Jarvis wore a disgusting set of gray fingers dangling from his neck. Tess could tell right away that the man had gone feral and would kill at the drop of a hat. His eyes were empty, lacking the empathy a man should hold, but still gleaming with a wild glint said he enjoyed the act of killing.

Her eyes narrowed. "No."

"You're lying, girl." An evil grin split Jarvis's lips as he rose striding to her. He bent down near her. "You are, ain't ya? You got a thing with him. You love him." He reached a dirty finger out and stroked her cheek. Trying to turn away, he forced it back upward. "It's true." He let her look away. "What are you doing so far from home?" He stared down at her.

"I was looking for somebody."

"All by your lonesome? Well, that ain't too smart is it? But don't worry, me and Low will take care of ya. Ain't that right, buddy?"

"Sure will." Low's stubble-clad cheeks raised in mirth. His eyes went distant as if he imagined his dastardly deeds in real time.

The infected still pounded the door in the back bedroom.

Jarvis jerked his head in its direction and forcibly exhaled. "Low, I thought I told you to take care of that."

The other soldier looked hurt. "I was hungry, man. It ain't going anywhere."

"I'll fucking do it. Axe."

Low scooped up his axe and tossed it to Jarvis who caught it out of the air. Tess's stomach flopped as he dragged the axe along the wall as he walked. His voice came out mocking. "Lucy, I home."

With a quick glance at his disappearing ally, Low stood, his blanket flaring out behind him.

Jarvis knocked back on the door, tormenting the dead behind it. "I'm right here. Come on and get it."

Low stepped closer to Tess, chest rising and falling rapidly. He crouched down with a quick glance back down the hall. "I can help you."

She nodded yes.

"But I need you to help me."

His eyes shrouded with menace. He fiddled beneath his blanket.

"What are you doing?" she asked.

"Shhh. We don't want him getting upset."

"Fuck you, man," she said loudly.

His eyes grew gaping and he grabbed her cheeks. "I said shut up. Do as you're told and I'll get you out of here." He released her and his hands went beneath his blanket again.

"Help!"

His hand cracked her cheek with fire, and she tipped over against the ugly blue carpet. She'd had worse. "You hit like a bitch."

"You—"

Jarvis's voice echoed. "What the fuck?" He stood in the entrance to the hallway, blood-covered axe in hand.

In fear, Low retreated a step. "I was teaching her a lesson for talking back."

Jarvis glared down at her and back at him. "You were trying to squeeze one out quick while I did the fucking dirty work."

"No." He gave her a sharp glance. "I wouldn't."

Hands squeezed the axe tighter, forcing Jarvis's knuckles white. "You know I get them first. I'm of higher rank."

"I know the rules." Low cast his eyes downward.

Cocking his head to the side, Jarvis sneered. "Do you? I'm thinking you need to be taught a lesson."

Low took a step back. "Come on, man. I wasn't."

"Yes, he was," Tess piped up.

Jarvis's eyes went wide. He lifted a hand off his axe and pointed an angry finger at her. "You be quiet. I'll deal with you in a second." He faced his comrade.

Low had inched his way toward his rifle and now he lunged for it, diving on the ground. The glass living room table tipped and shattered, sending guns, gear, food and glass shards everywhere.

The M16A4 tipped on its side as he fumbled for it. Jarvis ran for him, taking big steps and swinging his axe over his shoulder like an experienced lumberjack. Low got a hand on his rifle, pulling it in tight. The axe blurred through the air and gunshots exploded in the room.

Tess's ears were assaulted by high-pitched ringing. She rolled to her shoulder, sitting upright. Piteous screams came from Low's mouth. "My fucking hand!"

She scooted her hands beneath her and kicked her legs while pulling her arms out from underneath. Her slender body and flexible frame proved enough to get her hands to her front.

Low's screams cut off as Jarvis choked the man with both hands. Low fought him with his single hand pushing Jarvis's face, bleeding on him with his stump. Blood soaked both the men, staining their soiled uniforms. Jarvis growled as he strangled his friend, his eyes growing wider with rage.

As the men struggled, Tess crawled over the broken glass, looking for anything to fight with. The MRE package lay tipped on its side. The canvas plastic package crinkled as she crushed it with both hands and found the golden-brown plastic spoon. Her greedy fingers wrapped around it. She yanked it free from its package-like sheath. Bits of rice and beans still clung to the end.

Both men were slick with blood as Low's hand slipped off Jarvis's face. He slammed Low's head into the floor repeatedly. "Die, you fucking coward."

She was almost silent. Her boots were soft on the carpet with only the occasional piece of glass crunching, and Jarvis paid her no heed in his violent rage. Low's legs kicked frantically.

Crunch! Her boot ground a shard of glass. Jarvis turned in her direction, face twisting in surprise.

With both hands, she swung with all her might. The spoon snapped on impact, but the handle punctured the soft tissue of Jarvis's eyeball, sinking into his skull. His hands leapt to his face. "You fucking bitch!" Squeezing his eye socket, he tried to hold the pieces of his eye together. A mess of reddish fluids seeped between his fingers and ran down, saturating his face. His other hand felt on his hip for his axe handle.

Tess stumbled for the door and ripped it open. Bullets punched through it, revealing its hollow insides. She kicked the storm door, and the bitter cold night bit at her as she ran.

Willie jerked his head up as she bolted into the cold. Using both hands, she unraveled the horse's reins as quickly as she could. The windshield of the car imploded. The snow and glass sunk inward.

Yanking Willie's head to the side, she led him toward the forest. She tried to slip her foot into the stirrup again and again as they hobbled along.

"Get back here!"

His boots crushed the snow beneath them. He shot more bullets in her direction, all of them missing their mark. She used the pommel to hoist herself atop the beast and rode into the forest. She turned back as the nasty cold air whipped her, and she could see the soldier running out of the house in a mad dash, rifle on his back and axe in hand.

Willie moved into a gallop and she leaned in abreast of his mane.

Jarvis's voice trailed behind them. "Get back here, you bitch!"

ALVARADO
Northern Mississippi River

Marines were spread along the stretch of river ice in two teams. Each team had a sled and took turns bounding over one another as they planted blocks of C-4 and ran detonation cord between them.

Any kind of air support would have changed the game. Even with civilian helicopters, they could hover above and drop amounts of C-4 explosives at intervals and fly away, making it a four-man job tops. They could even ignore the dead staring mindlessly up at them in the process. They could even enjoy the mutual destruction of the dead and ice from a safe distance. But on the ground, everything was different.

The river hadn't frozen all at once leaving the ice in a smooth surface like a small lake or pond, something that she would imagine local kids skating on. No, the river was composed of rough irregular ice chunks pressed together and jutting into the air like rebellious tectonic plates.

The Marines slipped often and found traction difficult even with the sharp crampons attached to the snowshoes. They'd been forced to shoulder their snowshoes and carefully make their way along the center of the frozen river. They hustled along the ice, dealing with any single Zulus with knives and entrenching tools.

Running the cord between the blocks was a nightmare, and both planting teams made slow progress as they stuffed the nylon cord, really a compressed explosive, in nooks and crannies to avoid a negligent Zulus from tripping over it.

The other problem they were facing was getting far enough away and on land when the explosives went off. If they detonated as they went along, the dead would be drawn in by the explosions making forward progress impossible. They would have to clear a sizable section of river to make a dent in the horde of Zulus, starting with the river front near Outpost Barron.

Alvarado knelt to the ice. She attached the open end of a blasting cap to the detonation cord then gently pushed the explosive edge into the brick of C4.

Standing, she evaluated her sister team led by Riddle. They should have bounded past her by now. The landscape was a dreary bleak off-white, difficult to make out anything in particular. Her men and the dead were black oblong shapes struggling along it.

Triple gunshots penetrated the air, echoing like someone had dropped a pallet on a cement floor in an empty warehouse. The sound rippled down the river's frozen surface, nothing to impede the acoustic wave.

Her eyes instinctually went in the direction of the booms. The clouded sun still managed to blind them off the jagged whiteness and she was forced to shade her eyes. Only three Marines were standing. More gunshots blasted from their weapons. The order had been explicit: only use firearms in the most dire of situations.

She turned and looked the other way. Dead trickled in from the Wisconsin side of the river, adjusting their almost seamless course. She peered back at the besieged Marines. A pack closed in around them. The fourth Marine now stood. His form was shaking, his head jerked from side to side as the virus began attacking his nervous system. He lunged with the agility of a fresh Zulu, his mouth biting the neck of the Marine next to him. He ripped his head backward, taking clothing and flesh away from their owner. His victim's hands leapt to his throat as he collapsed to his back.

She forced air from her nose to steady herself. "You two with me." She eyeballed Lance Corporal Rasmussen. "If we go down, blow it."

His eyes expanded beneath his heavy brow and bushy eyebrows. "Ma'am?"

"No questions. Just detonate everything."

"We aren't getting far without the other sled."

"Set 'em and run. That's an order."

Rasmussen glanced at Finch and O'Bannon. "Yes, ma'am."

An M27 thundered in the distance. *Powpowpow. Powpowpow.* Zulus jostled and went down as bullets sprayed gore like they'd hit a wall of denser than normal flesh, larger bits flying.

She took off running toward Riddle's team. At least to her it was running. She was slow over the ice, each uneven chunk taking its turn to step up and trip her. Nothing could be done as another Marine went down while others engaged in frantic hand-to-hand combat. Only the lone Marine near the sled fired his weapon. He spun in a circle, firing a burst in one direction and then the other, taking down the nearest Zulus.

Slowing, she steadied her firing platform. An infected closed on the Marine from the rear. There was no order to their assault, just assault. She shot her weapon, and its head jerked to the right, partially spinning its body. Not bothering to make sure it was still, she closed on the besieged men, air biting her lungs like infected.

A Marine turned and faced her, blood drenching his lips. She thought it was Adams. Crimson spread over his face like he'd been drunk while applying make-up. She shot him in the head, and he rolled on his side. O'Bannon and Finch covered her flanks, firing like mad into the dead.

Riddle spun with his gun pressed against a meaty shoulder and aimed at her. He blinked recognition. "Jesus."

She glared past him. "Let's move, Marine."

He patted on his leg. "Leg's twisted. Leave me."

"We ain't leaving any Marines."

Riddle's face twisted in anger. "Blow those charges!"

"Major, more are coming!" shouted O'Bannon.

She bent down and removed a detonator from her cargo pocket and attached it to the det cord. She flipped a switch on the detonator. A thirty-second timer powered on, ticking down with every quick second.

"Good on you, Mad Isabel. Finish the mission. I'm nothing but dead weight." He rotated to the side and rattled off a few rounds with his M27.

His eyes widened in surprise as she wrapped an arm around his broad back, gripping his belt on the other side. She heaved and grunted with exertion. "Move, Marine." O'Bannon grabbed his other side and they stumbled toward the shore.

"What about the sled?" screamed Finch.

"Leave that shit!"

Finch covered their backs as they moved. "Our explosives?"

"Leave it."

She glanced down river at the Marines ahead of them setting charges. They ran for the shore, scrambling over the uneven terrain. "This way."

They were almost to the icy riverbank when a roar ripped the landscape, riding its frozen surface like the earth was cracking in half. They were boosted into the air and thrown like tiny ants on an exploding ant pile. As a group, they were launched into hard ice layered with accumulating snow. The impact took her breath away, forcing her eyes closed.

As much as she wanted to hold her stomach, she covered her head for the secondary effect of an explosion, the debris.

Chunks of ice rained from the sky in a hailstorm of death. It was a shower of frozen shards like the heavens were falling to the earth. The sound was as deafening as the explosion itself, the crackling of ice on ice prevailing over everything else.

As it lessened, she moved to her knees and crawled over to Riddle and O'Bannon. She placed Riddle's limp arm over hers and she tugged. He hoisted upward a few inches.

"Wake up!" The ringing in her ears was fierce like her head itself was the bell.

Hands gripped her jacket from behind. She chopped rearward with a forearm that turned into a shove. She fell back on top of Riddle, fighting to get her carbine from her side.

Muffled yells pierced the bells in her ears. "Major!"

She blinked away her fury. Living, breathing, fighting Marines stood in front of her. Uninfected by the virus. Not the dead.

They helped her to her feet, gesturing toward some sort of waterfront warehouse. They hauled Riddle and O'Bannon upright and dragged them to the building. Rasmussen waved her forward and inside followed by the others. The warehouse doors rolled closed behind them, and they stood for a moment, weapons trained on the door. Tense seconds fled in half-time with her heartbeat. No dead followed them.

She bent down on her knees, catching her breath, letting herself relax. She forced herself upright after her momentary display of weakness. There was no shame by being overcome by a close call with survival, but she knew she didn't have the luxury of digesting that scrape with death.

Private Finch's voice was muffled like he spoke underwater, and she couldn't understand him.

"What?"

He motioned at her and rotated his thumb up and down mouthing, "You okay?"

"Fine," she yelled.

He held a single finger over his lips. The Marines spread out into teams, clearing the insecure warehouse. Stacks of wooden pallets were piled high throughout, towering almost to the ceiling. Alvarado placed her weapon back to her shoulder and scanned for threats, following her Marines. They passed stack after stack of wooden pallets. Nothing appeared touched by the living or the dead since the outbreak. She'd figured the people that worked here just stopped going to work or were killed early on. The stacks gave way to an office that doubled as a break room.

They helped the wounded Marines to the floor and closed the door, sealing them off from the rest of the warehouse. Not ideal for keeping an eye on their surroundings, but they needed to take stock of their wounded, and layers between them and the dead made a difference both in physical security and psychological wellness.

She stretched her jaw, trying to gain a level of hearing back by unclogging her ears.

Rasmussen smiled at her. "Close call."

She nodded her head, opening her mouth wide and rotating her jaw.

"How are we going to get back across?"

She opened her mouth again, trying to adjust the fluids inside. "We aren't done."

"The area in front of Barron is clear."

"Not enough of it." She unslung her M4A1 and set it on a table. "We need to take the river south of Barron as well. From my estimate, we only made it about halfway to our priority. There's still plenty of work to do."

"How are we going to do that?" Rasmussen said. He glanced around and added, "With all due respect, Major." He temporarily lowered his eyes in deference. He'd seen her fight for her men on countless occasions to know that she treated all her Marines the same and would die for them if need be. "The sleds are gone."

"How much do we have left?"

A thick pack was thrown on the table. Foster dug through its contents, laying out bricks. "I'd say another mile tops. Maybe a bit farther if we stretch it out. Hope that the weight of the Zulus will break up anything still solid."

"We blew that cord on our sled," Riddle said. He sat with his back against the wall. "You're going to have to set timers from here on out." His leg lay limp.

"How's the leg?"

"The bone is pushing on the top of my boot."

"Keep that boot on tight. It should keep swelling down."

"I'm not worried about my leg. It's setting those timers. We'll risk getting blown on every charge. If there's any delay, we're screwed."

She eyed the Marines. They'd lost two more since Odom. Her party shrank by the hour. "I understand that, but I won't go back until it's done."

"But we rang the dinner bell too early. Now we got every Zulu in the county headed our way," Rasmussen said.

"Then we're going to have to move fast out there."

A slight frown took his lips. "It's suicide, ma'am."

"Since when wasn't this a suicide mission, Marine? We cleared a section of the river and that was good, but we need another mile to make a difference, more if we can stretch it. We reclaim Barron and get word to the other outposts to clear their river before it freezes."

"What if they've already frozen?" asked Finch.

She shook her head. "Pray to God they haven't."

TESS
Shimek State Forest, IA

Within a minute of hitting a gallop, Willie slowed to a trot and then down to a walk. Tess glanced back over her shoulder into the night. The faint unintelligible calls of Jarvis still echoed out, ricocheting from tree to tree. She heeled Willie's side.

"Come on, boy," she urged.

Willie tossed his head, his mane flaring. She gave him a hard heel. "Willie, we have to move." He flapped his lips together and exhaled forcefully, his flanks quivering. She pleaded harder. "Come on, boy."

The horse picked up to a trot for thirty seconds before he slowed back down to a walk. "What is wrong with this thing?" Her voice was absorbed by the night.

Willie stopped. She leaned close to his twitching ear. "Willie!" She half-heartedly punched his neck in frustration. "What's wrong with you? Go!" She glanced back over her shoulder. Jarvis's calls were softer, but barely. Her breath fogged, and her whole body shook. Crimson blood spotted the ground, trailing alongside their tracks.

With numb hands, she patted her own body down. Nothing. Everything was in place. She climbed down from Willie's back. Her feet sank into the forest snowdrift untouched by humans. Willie knelt. She patted him until her hand felt a warm wetness on his hindquarters. He complained with a high-pitched neigh. She moved up toward his head, petting him. "Shhh. It's okay."

She ran both her hands down the flat of his nose to his nostrils. They were wet too despite the cold. He calmed beneath her touch. "I'm sorry, buddy. I have to go."

The roar of Jarvis continued to echo through the frozen woods. Willie panted as his breathing became more labored. The cracking of branches and yelling grew closer. She kissed the horse's snout and stood.

Like an animal, Jarvis's voice roared. "Somebody's not doing so hot."

Tess took off into the timber. She jumped a log, using both hands to vault over it. She trailblazed through the snow and forest alike. The puffy layer absorbed her steps like quicksand, and she struggled to gain ground. She knew if she stopped she would freeze to death. Her face, hands, and feet were beyond numb. Her warm parts were frozen, and her body shook violently now. Her breath came out in quick bursts of icy mist.

Visibility rapidly diminished in the fading light. The forest was as dark as she could remember, stealing whatever light remained. Each direction was more trees—oak, hickory, and maple—all naked and gray except for the pines with their thin tiny evergreen needles.

She stomped around in a circle, running one way into the forest and then backtracking. Hopping down near the uprooted end of an ancient maple, she took cover. Snuggling close to the ground, she tried to keep her teeth from audibly chattering. From underneath the trunk, she watched and waited.

His form weaved through the forest. His labored breathing audible in pursuit. He reached the clearing, following her tracks.

"Don't slow down," he shouted into the trees. "Saw your little friend back there bleeding out. I'll eat him later."

She spied him through the timber. The spoon still stuck out of his eye socket. He was a nightmare in living form. His face was painted in blood. His gray, brown, and green standard issue combat uniform was varying shades of dark red. As he marched closer to her fallen tree, the wet fingers of his necklace tapped his damp chest as if they impatiently waited for his next kill.

Stopping, he held his axe in one hand. She spied on him. He dipped his skull, straining to see the ground more clearly with his single eye. He studied the tracks for a moment and followed her decoy trail.

She audibly exhaled, her teeth clanking together. She squeezed her elbows closer to hold in her fading body heat. *I have to get my hands free and get warm.* Her mind briefly flashed the thought of using Willie as a horseflesh sleeping bag. *No, not Willie, but that prick Jarvis would be fine.*

The unsteady scrape of boots on uneven terrain came closer. She sucked in air and held her breath. *This stupid asshole doesn't know when to die.* He wavered as he walked back into the clearing. He coughed, letting her know he was close.

"You thought you could trick me," he said, spitting blood on the ground. "I know you're here. Why don't you come on out and we'll have a little party?"

Her breathing came out more forced as she tried to keep from shivering to death.

His footsteps sounded as he walked the perimeter. "Just you and me, babe." He leaned around a tree, looking at the ground not more than twenty feet from her. He let his axe drag along the rough trunk of her fallen maple. The metal on the wood clinked and clanged as the axe skipped over the bark's rivets and divots.

Tess closed her eyes for a moment, attempting to calm herself. The footsteps got closer and closer to her hiding place. Her heart thundered in her chest, trying to both keep her alive and give her away. She opened her eyes again.

Two tan combat boots splattered in blood and snow stood in front of her. "Why can't we just have a nice little date? You and me." A hand grabbed her shoulder, pulling her upright. He moved the axe blade toward her neck. She shook, struggling to not collapse. Fresh pink fingers lined his necklace.

Leaning closer, he said, "I'm going to add a few more tonight." Blood still dripped from his eye socket's mess of flesh. He punched out with his axe into her nose. The blow sent a shockwave of pain into her skull, and her world spun.

In a daze, he stretched her along the fallen trunk with her hands hanging off the other side. "You don't need these? Do ya?" he spat into her face.

She blinked, trying to gain something to fight him away with. "No."

"Now hold still. If I miss, we might take off a bit more than we'd like."

"Prick."

"Or how about an eye for an eye? Eye for your hands. What's the difference?" He brought the axe over his head like a medieval executioner. The only solace she had was knowing that after he was done, she would bleed out fast never having to know the rest of her body's fate.

A jingling drifted in the air. Jarvis turned his head to the side. "What the hell?"

A four-legged form galloped through the trees. The shadowy beast ran into the clearing.

"Motherfucker?" He turned and took a step toward Willie as he charged. Tess threw a bony shoulder into his back. The axe swung too far to the right. Willie let out a high-pitched neigh and trampled Jarvis beneath his hooves into the ground.

Jarvis let out a groan from the ground. His leg was bent backward, and his eye rolled into his skull. Willie slowly walked up to Tess. He bowed his head and brought it near hers. She put a shaking hand on his nose and leaned forward, resting her head on his. The horse's breath fogged the air and night crept upon them. Willie's head dropped and he lowered himself, rolling on his side. Tess watched him as his chest stopped. His last effort having saved her from Jarvis's wrath.

She crawled down next to her mount. "Thank you," she whispered into his warm neck. She stroked his neck. A loud moan brought her shivering body to attention.

Jarvis pushed himself up with a single hand. His other draped around the axe, using it as a crutch off the ground. He spit warm blood, and it sank into the snow. "You stupid fucks."

Tess stood shakily. A nasty snarl curled on her lips. "You killed my horse."

"That's just the first thing I'm going to do to you."

She ran at him, throwing all her weight at the battered man. They burst into the powder on the ground. She crawled atop him, hitting him with her joined fists. He laughed at first. The second strike, he grunted as she struck him on the spoon handle. He jerked when she slammed her palms into the handle. The third blow she connected, he started to shake and spasm. Again and again, she pounded the spoon handle until it disappeared beneath her hands and into the recess of his skull.

She screamed in his face. "Raarh! You killed my horse." She sat back on his stomach breathing hard, the heat of her rage the only thing keeping her alive. She looked around the clearing. "Son of a *bitch*."

Darkness overtook what little light remained. Exhausted, she let her chin fall to her chest, the adrenaline in her body subsiding gradually. The cold would kill her quickly. She shoved at Jarvis's body. "Bitch."

A voice startled her. "Don't move or we'll shoot ya."

She faced the man's voice. A shotgun was trained on her. Three men had spread out behind her guns aimed in her direction.

"If you ain't sick, say something now or die."

She looked down at the dead soldier then back at the twilight sky and sighed.

"I won't ask again," the man said gruffly.

She stared him in the eyes. "He killed my horse."

The hunter lifted his shotgun skyward. "Jesus Christ." He jogged to her, feet crunching through the frigid underbrush. The other men closed in from the sides. When he got close, she prepared to strike him. He must have seen the look on her face because he stopped short. "We're not going to hurt you."

"Holy shit, she killed that army guy."

She gave him an exasperated look and the man took a step back.

"Don't you forget it." She tipped over into the snow and felt herself become weightless to the faint sound of voices.

STEELE
Camp Forge, IA

The line of men and women were spaced out evenly with over four feet between each person. Their ages ranged from as young as sixteen to as old as seventy, and they all faced the same way. They held their mixture of long guns toward the ground in a safe position. A sergeant walked behind them.

"When I say the line is hot, you may begin to engage your targets. We are focusing on accuracy not speed. Anybody can shoot fast, but it don't mean shit if you can't hit 'em in the head."

Most of the people that had come to Camp Forge for training were farmers. They were not foreign to firearms, most having handled them from a young age, and learned well under the instruction of the soldiers.

Thunder stroked his beard as they observed. The civilians came to the camp on a rotating basis for training, giving them split time between farm maintenance and military instruction.

"The squad structure seems to be working well with them," Thunder said.

Steele nodded, watching. The men and women displayed their weapons, planting them into their shoulders. "Ludlow's men are a great asset." He rested a hand on his tomahawk head.

"Fire!" the sergeant yelled. Gunfire kicked off as they sighted small circle targets at the end of the field. The two men stopped talking and inspected the civilians. The firing line died down.

"Is the line clear?" the sergeant yelled.

The other instructors confirmed. "The line is clear. You may stand back. Next squad."

Thunder and Steele walked away from the firing line and toward the next group training. Two additional squads worked in tandem with one another. One group simulated laying down covering fire while the other moved. They shouted as they ran. "Moving!" The trainees went prone and took aim at fictional enemies in the trees.

"Suppress fire," yelled a sergeant at a trainee. He stood behind the man lying prone. "Get that SAW up." The trainee struggled with the bipod of his SAW light machine gun. "Cover your squad!"

A team leader shouted from the other squad. "Left side, move!" They bounded out of the snow and ran in a flanking maneuver.

"They're learning," Steele said.

"But are they learning fast enough?" Thunder asked.

Steele watched a man trip and fall, dousing himself in white. "As fast as we can train them." He rubbed the top of his scarred scalp. *It has to be enough.*

"Come, Thunder. I need your advice inside." Steele ushered the big biker forward, and they trudged through the dirty snow back to the Reynolds' white farmhouse that served as Steele's headquarters.

They kicked off snow from their boots as they entered the foyer. Thunder plopped on a bench. John and Lydia Reynolds sat next to Becky at the kitchen table. Lydia rested a hand on Becky's shoulder, attempting to comfort her.

"How is she?" he asked them.

Becky looked up, tears in her bloodshot eyes. She rubbed a hand over them. "She's okay. Same as yesterday."

"I'll check in on her later." He watched her for a moment, not knowing the exact words to comfort her.

Becky gave him a faint smile and tilted her head to the side. Her voice croaked. "It's my baby."

Steele had to exhale before he became emotional himself. Haley was an extension of Gwen and therefore an important part of his life. "Gwen will come through."

Becky gulped her throat quivering. "She's always been the hero."

A sad smile crossed his lips. "I know." He turned to John. "Can you join us in the other room?"

The wrinkles around the eighty-five-year-old man's eyes deepened. "Of course."

He took his leave and joined Thunder at the parlor table. A map was laid out with circles over broad swathes of areas.

"War Child's command has arrived in Burlington, which is good, but I'm worried about Keokuk. We don't have a good presence down south yet."

Thunder's chocolate-colored eyes reminded Steele of a twinkling Hersey bar. "With some help, my club can stand up an outpost down there."

Steele shook his head. "No, I want you here." His voice dipped. "I still don't trust the pastor and I need you close."

Thunder silently gave a short nod. "I understand that concern."

"What I'd like to do is get some of this militia in the fight. We have about four hundred additional militia from the surrounding areas on a rotating basis. I'd like to move a company of our most highly trained with a squad of military advisors down to Keokuk. Set up an outpost. Then as the other groups get trained, we can rotate them out."

"I don't see why that wouldn't work."

"The others I'd like to get some trigger time on the infected. I'm thinking we should start two squad patrols between here and Keokuk and Burlington."

Thunder stared. "What about water routes?"

"When we need extra speed, but I want these roads safe from infected or otherwise."

"You think Jackson'll show his ugly face again?"

"He may." The idea of the rogue colonel roaming free in his rear was unsettling, but he didn't have the resources to scour the countryside and bring him to justice. "I don't want him harassing the people here while their sons and daughters are off fighting."

"Agreed."

He faced John. "Where is a good base to set up an outpost? Not all the way in town, but recognizable enough for people to find."

John wrinkled his nose as he thought. "Well. Let me see here. Hmm." He exhaled forcefully. "There's a plant down there."

"Where?"

With a gnarled finger, John tapped the map. "'Bout here." His fingered touched the outside of town. "Yup, they make steel castings. Right off US 218 there."

"That should work. Now, who to lead this militia company?"

John rubbed his chin.

Thunder's gray caterpillar like eyebrows closed in on one another before he spoke. "Garrett would do it. I don't want to lose him, but he has prior military experience."

Steele nodded. "I trust him to get the job done." He put a hand under his chin as he thought. "John, do you know of anyone local that could do the job? Somebody that everyone trusts?"

"Well, let's see." He leveled his chin as he thought. "Van Fogerty was in the army. They like him down at the American Legion. He could probably do it."

"Let's get Van in here."

***

Hours later, Van and Major Ludlow stood in the parlor. Steele sat behind his desk and leaned back in his chair. Major Ludlow's arms were folded across his chest. His bug eyes observed Van with interest.

"I just don't know Captain Steele." Van sighed. Crow's-feet wrinkled around his eyes, and his formerly blond hair had retreated before the onslaught of gray. He had cold blue eyes. "I don't want to leave my family."

"We need men like you to lead in our militia. John recommended you, and that means he trusts you. Your résumé is good. You acted as a drill instructor at Fort Benning. You served in Persian Gulf."

"Everything you say is true." He set his jaw. "But I'm not leaving my family no matter how bad you need me. Not in a time like this." His mouth formed a flat line of resistance.

Steele scratched at his beard. "I have no objections to you taking them with you."

With a strong shake of his head, Van said, "I won't force them into an area that isn't secure and a place that ain't home."

"Well, what about here at Camp Forge? I can promise them a place to stay. It's secure. The walls are up. We got plenty of fighters. We need you. Your country needs you to serve again. This is our one and only line of defense. Your farm will disappear beneath the feet of the dead if it doesn't hold."

Van let out a deep sigh. He understood the request. They were asking a lot of him. But like all good men, he knew when to stand. "I'll bring them in, but you have to promise me their safety."

"As safe as my own."

Steele shook hands with the man. "I'll expect you in the morning to depart south." He addressed Major Ludlow. "I'd like to send a squad of your men with him." A look of relief settled on Van's face.

"I have a sergeant willing to go. Sergeant Campos. I'll make sure his squad is ready in the morning."

"Thank you, Major."

Ludlow dipped his chin and left the room.

"We are sending our best with you. Plenty of ex-military in that company. We're going to have you set up in a steel factory north of town. John says it's a good spot. It's gated, fenced, strong concrete walls."

"Victory Steel Castings. I know it."

"Collect everyone still alive there. You're call sign is Outpost Victory. I want you clearing out Keokuk, collecting survivors, and setting us up for success in the region. In three months, we will rotate a new company down south, and your militia will go on call as needed."

"We'll do our best." Van nodded.

"We can do this."

"You're asking a lot."

"I'd ask more if I could."

Van stood in silence for a moment. "All right."

"I'll see you in the morning."

"See you in the morning, Captain."

Van left the room, and Steele stretched. He spread the fingers in his right hand as far as they could go and then clenched them in a fist. He glanced at the fieldstone fireplace for a moment. The fire skipped and danced in the stone enclosure. He stepped out of the parlor, eyes running up the chipped and dinged wooden stairs.

Each step groaned beneath him, complaining his entire way to the top. The first door on the right was closed. He stood next to it. His hand hovered over the door handle. His hand formed a fist and rapped his knuckles on the wood. A deadened sound resounded.

"Becky?" he said softly.

He tested the doorknob, letting it twist and swing inward. John knelt by the side of Haley's single bed, his hands clasped in front of his body folded over the girl.

"I'm sorry, John," Steele said. He started to close the door.

The grandfather kept his head down and his voice wavered. "Wait."

Steele stopped, poking his head back in. "Yeah?"

"Come in."

Steele walked inside the room and stood near the single bed. Extra blankets were thrown over the little girl. Her cherubic face, small and precious, stuck out from underneath them.

John slowly got up from the ground. He stared at her from above. His voice came out slow and tired. "I pray every day for her. Every hour really." He gulped. "She never leaves my mind."

"I know."

John went to say something and stopped, tears forming in his eyes. "I ask God why her? Why not me?" A faint smile filled his lips. "I've seen love and experienced pain and lived a life worth living, and I'm near the end. I'm ready." He sucked his lip trying to cover his emotions. "But this girl. She's only just beginning. She doesn't know these things. She won't for many years. Yet here she lies, so young and full of life, and here I stand, old and worn. It just don't make sense."

"No, it doesn't."

John licked his lips. "Why not me?" His eyes searched the ceiling for an answer. "Why her, Lord? Take me instead." He stared for a moment, awaiting a response from the heavens.

"She will hold on."

"Will she? She's going to die. Dr. Miller said it's in her lungs. She barely breathes now." He frowned.

How do I console a man speaking the miserable truth? A man who's whole world is sinking. Steele moved closer to John and put an arm on his shoulder. It was bony beneath his shirt, a frame lacking sufficient siding. "Have faith. Things will be all right."

John shook his head, looking at the pale girl. "To watch your little ones die before your eyes is hell. It's unimaginable."

"It is. I'm here for you."

The two men stood in silence for a minute watching the girl hang on to life, her tiny chest struggling to rise and fall. John exhaled audibly.

"I'm not sure I'll ever understand this." His eyes were worried, seeking assurance. "You'll look after them, right?"

Steele cocked his head. "I do look after them."

John gave a terse shake of his head. "After I'm gone."

"Don't talk like that."

Dry seriousness settled on John's features. "We all dance to death's tune." His eyes darted to Haley. "Some sooner, some later than others."

Steele guided him out of the room. "Some later," he whispered.

GWEN
Farmington, IA

Dr. McKee's office was a single room doctor's office with a full window peering into the lobby. The senior doctor's mittened hand shook as he unlocked the front door, the key jingling softly. "People've mostly been coming to see me at my house." He glanced at them with a soft smile on his pink lips. "They don't get much unless they're really sick. I don't have any diabetes medicine left." His Adam's apple bounced beneath his scarf. "There's not much that can be done for them."

"Thank you," Gwen said, nodding. The doctor had the decency to arrive by mid-morning.

He opened the door. Gwen, Jake, Gregor, and Linden followed him in. The hunched doctor walked to the next door and tested a gold doorknob and it opened. They passed a single evaluation room, cupboards, and a sink. A heart monitor machine rested off in the corner on rollers, lifeless without power.

Doctor McKee removed his mittens before opening the cabinets. "Now, let's see what we got left." He adjusted small white packages to where he could read them. "Normally, we would send people to the pharmacy, but we still carry some medicine on hand for patients in immediate need."

Moving the medicines one by one, he held them up in the air, inspecting the sides. He glanced over his shoulder. "You say the flu, right?"

"The flu and strep."

"Strep is pretty darn tough to tell without testing at a lab."

Her voice hardened. "We need antibiotics and antivirals."

Dr. McKee nodded his head thoroughly. "All righty. He scooped up four boxes and set them on the counter. "There we have it. I got four antivirals and two antibiotic treatments."

Gwen's heart sank in her chest. "That's it?"

He gave her a sad smile. "'Fraid it's all we got. I hope we don't catch a glimpse of that here this winter. Plenty of old folks." He eyed her for a moment with an experienced eye. "You know you need to take better care of yourself, young lady. Both illnesses can be deadly for mother and child."

Gwen entertained him. "Thank you, doctor. I'll remember that."

He handed her the packages and she clutched them to her chest. Medicine was one of the most precious objects of an apocalyptic world, a finite resource that dwindled daily. Jake could see the pain in her eyes.

"We will find more," he said.

He brought her in for a hug and she let herself be comforted. He held her for a moment before letting go.

"There's not enough. Not even close. There must be almost a hundred people sick at Camp Forge. We have enough for four people."

"Bonaparte isn't too far and Dr. Farmer in Keosaqua has already helped with the injured after the battle. I'm sure he will help again," Jake said.

"We don't have time to waste. Every day means something. The more time we spend finding medicine, the more people that will die."

"I'm sorry. Wish we had more," Dr. McKee said.

"Thank you, doctor."

They followed his short hallway and back through the sitting area. Gregor waited there.

"Did you get enough?"

"No." *But I have enough for Haley.*

They went back outside. The wind picked up and howled across the road. The scrapes and grinds of shoveling met her ears. A truck rumbled by with a plow. The doctor gave a short wave. "We're on fuel rations, but he clears out the street once a week. Helps people move around a bit."

The small town's main street consisted of only a couple businesses, a restaurant, and an administrative office that doubled as a post office.

"I have to go check on Mr. Simmons. Bad leg." The doctor waved as he peeled off down a side street.

Everyone else congregated in the administrative building. Mayor Tibbets paced inside. "I'm worried, Trooper. What if they come in force? What will we do?"

Trooper Linden's appearance was almost relaxed. "I'll have Greg plow snow on the bridge. Ficke and Martin should be able to handle any in ones and twos."

"There were at least ten that surrounded the Anderson's house. 'Bout gave Mrs. Anderson a heart attack."

With a curt nod, Linden eyed Gwen. "If you don't want me to go, I will abide by your direction, but I think we would do well to see Camp Forge for ourselves."

Mayor Tibbets bobbed her head in agreement. "You're right. You're right. These people need our help." She faced Gwen. "Did you find everything you needed?"

"Unfortunately, no. We were only able to find enough for a few people."

Tibbets wrung her hands in front of her. "I'm sorry. I know Dr. McKee would help you as much as he could."

Gwen sighed. "You've all been so helpful. Thank you. But we must move on."

Linden checked his magazines and his sidearm. "Me and my men are ready."

His stoic demeanor and handling of firearms tipped her off as to someone that was more than just a gun and a badge. "Trooper, were you prior military?"

"Yes, ma'am. Did two tours in Afghanistan with the 10th Mountain Division." His men, decorated with a dusting of flurries and their miscellaneous winter gear—coveralls, overalls, and down flannel jackets—crowded inside the building. "Gents."

"Thank you, Mayor Tibbets. We will keep up communications with

Farmington by person or radio."

The older woman steadied herself. "We'll be here."

They stepped into the street. A line of horses stood in the snow along with the hay wagon. Kenny helped himself up and offered her a hand.

"Bonaparte's about nine miles if we stay on this side of the Des Moines River," Kenny said.

"It's longer, but let's try to make it by nightfall."

"We will be just fine."

"Wait," came a voice echoing through the town like a creeping avalanche. Two men and a smaller form came trotting down the street on horseback.

The smaller woman waved her hand in the air. "Wait!" Its voice was feminine and familiar. Gwen squinted.

The woman kicked the horse into a trot and pulled it along the wagon.

"Tess?" Gwen uttered, confused. She eyed what became the Westerling sons, Patrick and Pete. "What are you doing here?" Her heart leapt in her chest. "What's wrong?"

Tess breathed hard. "Gwen." Her nose was swollen and round where it had once been small and petite, the woman's slender features now robust and purpling, the shade of a summer sky.

"Oh my God, what happened to your nose?"

"I was attacked." She shook her head, holding a hand in the air. "Not why I'm here. We don't have time for that story."

Gwen inspected her mounted men. "We were just leaving for Bonaparte. We still don't have enough medicine to return to Camp Forge."

"We have enough at Forge."

Gwen narrowed her eyes. "What do you mean?"

Small worried seams formed on Tess's brow. "Steele's being betrayed by Thunder. He's got plenty of meds hidden under the floor of his cabin."

Gwen digested the words, her mouth settling into a nasty scowl. "Thunder has medicine?"

"Enough to treat everyone in camp."

"People've been dying, and he's holding out on us?" Gwen turned to the side in disgust. *How can this be?*

Tess's mouth twisted. "I. I don't get it, but it's true." She removed a pill bottle from her jacket pocket and tossed it in the air.

Gwen caught it with a rattle. The prescription antiviral medication was scrawled on the side.

"You're sure there's enough? Antibiotics too?"

"A duffel bag full."

They had a chance if the right medications were there. Haley had a chance. The medicine had been there the whole time. Her stomach roiled with anger. "We go back."

JOSEPH
Cheyenne Mountain Complex, CO

Joseph didn't think it was possible for Colonel Byrnes to be more gaunt than he had already been, but he was wrong. The lines creasing his cheeks were deeper, and his skin stuck tight to his narrow, almost emaciated face.

"Over here," Byrnes said. He led Joseph to the corner of the open cave cell, giving him a thin-lipped smile. "I knew you would come."

"This place is awful."

"There's a spigot in the wall over there, so we have plenty of water. A little short in the food department. Like we're an afterthought."

"How are we going to get you out of here?"

"They've rounded up so many of us. I'm not even sure who's still out there." Byrnes looked down. "I'm not sure who flipped, but the true traitor is still out there."

"Me neither. I'm new to this whole thing."

"You did good getting down here."

"The challenge is getting you out. We'd have to get you past all those guards, cameras, up the elevators past who knows how many more soldiers. You're in an impregnable mountain."

Byrnes's chin sunk as he thought. "There are more of us outside the complex. We must get word to them." He coughed heavily and gave Joseph a weak smile. "Wet down here. We must move sooner than later. We don't have time."

"What do you mean move?"

"This is bigger than a few disgruntled officers. We have loyal units throughout the military, but they won't move without an assurance we can succeed."

"Loyal units? This is madness. This is the United States government."

"The government that is twisted in its own hunt for survival. You read the document?"

"Yes."

"Then you know what their plan is. Executions. Camps. Forced Labor. Vaccine for loyalty. State control of everything."

"I know."

"This is not only the fight for survival of our people but for our nation and beliefs." He gripped Joseph's shoulder with a bony hand. "We cannot let this government execute our people and withhold a life-saving vaccine," he hissed. "They only want to hold on to power. Not for any other reason. You know this. We must stand against this."

Joseph edged closer. "Look at where you are? I'm not some kind of ninja. I can't get you out of here."

Byrnes gave a soft shake of his head. "I don't give us long. The vice president doesn't seem like he's going to leave loose ends hanging around. We've already been condemned. A couple days and they'll line us up and put bullets through us."

"I can't believe this is happening." He glanced up at Byrnes. The colonel's eyes were filled with sorrow, but a glint of fight still lingered in them. "I'll think of something. I just don't know what."

The guard's voice echoed through the hole. "Everything all right down there, doc?"

Joseph gave a worried glance at the opening. "Just finishing up!"

Byrnes squeezed his shoulder. "You're our only hope."

Drifting through the prisoners, he left his friend and colleague in the darkness of a cave prison cell. He gripped the ladder. The soldier's shadowed face stared down from above.

"Wondering if they ate ya," he said as he laughed.

The metal rungs clanged and the guard helped him out of the hole.

"You get too many people in a cave. Turns them into monsters." The guard pulled up the ladder. "Which one of them is sick?"

"The tall man. I'm not sure his name. No names here, right?"

The guard nodded and grinned. "That's what they say."

He gave him a doctor's glower. "They will all catch the same illness if they are not fed more and regularly."

"Don't matter too much. A few are scheduled for their sentencing in a couple days. Why waste the food on a bunch of traitors that are going to be put down like the dogs they are."

"I see."

"Frankly, I'm surprised they sent someone all the way down here to look at them."

They walked back to the door.

"What's your name again?"

Joseph gulped trying to hide his fear. "Dr. Jackowski."

The guard glanced at his badge as if verifying the information.

"I'll be back tomorrow to check on the sick prisoner again. Scheduled for death or not, they deserve to be treated humanely."

The guard snorted. "Fucking bleeding hearts. You'd think this disaster would have gotten rid of all of them."

Joseph spun on the man. "Have you seen what the spread of an airborne disease does on a contained ventilation loop?"

The guard stood taken aback. "No?"

"Let me tell you what happens." He pointed at the hole. "If those people down there catch an airborne illness, guess who's going to be the first to contract the disease. You. Then that spreads through the complex's population like wildfire. If we don't have enough medicine to treat everyone, then people will start to die, but all while only some of the air is being recycled which means that disease gets stuck down here. So you might want to treat them a bit better, or this whole place could go under."

His head nodded dumbly. "Okay. We'll get them some extra food tonight."

"I'll be back tomorrow."

AHMED
Northern Missouri

The Old Grossman Farm was more of a field and less of a farm. Tufts of straw-colored grass stuck through the light dusting in dense clumps. Trees outlined the grassland like natural fencing. The land had been cleared at some point but had overgrown with neglect as nature took its liberty.

Ahmed scanned the area. "Where's the farmhouse?"

Jim hopped down from his horse. "Used to be over there." He pointed near the outline of a dirt road. Only empty space remained. "Fell down about twenty years ago."

The Singleton group followed their de facto leader Jim, dismounting from their saddles. Jim's other distant relations, the Foxworths, had made the trip north to join them. The three men, one no more than a teenager, looked like aged clones of one another.

"So it's not a farm anymore?"

Jim gave him an irritated look. "Somebody still farms it."

"The Grossmans?"

"No, we go off who owned it the longest, and that was the Grossmans, so we call it the Grossman Farm."

"But they don't own it?"

"No, that's what it used to be so that's how we know it."

"I see, so it's not the Grossman Farm."

"Technically, no." Anger bubbled behind Jim's ice-like eyes. "Drop it,

218

brownie. You're making me regret bringing you."

Ahmed removed his shotgun from his saddle. "You and me both. You think it's wise to be out in the middle of a field?"

Jim patted his horse's flank. "The Grossman Farm is a no man's land. Neutral zone for us. No harm and no foul out here. It's off-limits."

"Why?" If he was going to be embroiled in this conflict, he wanted to try and understand the roots of it.

Green pines were the only ones with anything left on their branches. All the maple, elm, and oak were barren of life. Jim stared, watching them all equally. "I dunno. Just is."

Lee cleared his throat. His hair was billowing in the wind like a field of gray wheat. "Marv Grossman married Tillie Singleton. Grossman was a cousin of the Baileys a hundred years back. This became a neutral site when the two clans needed fair ground to discuss terms on. Roughly halfway between the old Bailey and Singleton homesteads. Now that I think of it, it may have been part of the Bailey lands at some point." He reflected, rolling his eyes upward. "Anyway, no one was shown no preferential treatment nor ill here. Over time, it became a customary meeting spot."

"This has been going on for a hundred years?"

Jim shook his head and spit. "Longer. Theodore Bailey stole a cow from Rod Singleton in 1829." He waved in a direction. "Prolly six miles that way. We been feuding ever since."

"Wait. This is all over a cow?"

Jim gave Ahmed a baleful gaze. "No, it ain't over a cow." He straightened his jacket. "It's just how it started."

"Christ Almighty," Ahmed said. *How can this be happening in a modern society?*

A frown clouded Jim's face. "Hey. I don't want to hear any of that coming out of your mouth. It ain't natural."

A chuckle formed in Ahmed's throat for the first time he could remember. "You know we have him as one of our prophets too."

Jim's eyes expanded with shock as if Ahmed had slapped him. "I won't be hearing any of that tricky jumbo. Isn't beef sacred to you guys?"

"Those are Hindus. Muslims are supposed to refrain from pork."

"I pity your poor soul." He shook his head. "Fried tenderloin sandwiches, roasts, ham, bacon. Dear God, man, please say bacon is not on the list?"

"Bacon is on the list. At least from pigs. Beef and turkey are okay."

A mean sneer took place beneath Jim's goatee. "Turkey bacon. You can go to hell."

"Trying to avoid that."

"Now that ain't right. You're missing out on one of the few joys that man can experience."

"Don't. It's a choice." No use in getting Jim all riled up before they were about to enter peace talks with their rival. *No shootouts for this guy. A civil little talk then I'll be on my way.*

Pickup trucks with yellow-beaming headlights drove down the country road nearby. They dipped over the ditch, rocking, and into the field, driving toward them. Four truckloads of men.

Ahmed stopped counting at sixteen. There were more than before, despite the loss of several members. They more than doubled Jim's crew.

The trucks stopped roughly twenty yards from where they stood with their horses. Men stepped out, guns in hands. Ahmed's heartbeat increased. Sly's men would win a shootout for sure. Many had military M4s or AR-15s; it was difficult for him to tell at the distance. Ball caps and hunting vests, full-length deer hunting suits, along with jean jackets and warm farming coats.

The man in front had wavy black hair and a light blue jean jacket on. He stood for a moment, staring at Jim and his men. He was counting the adversaries and deemed them not a threat.

Holding his long gun in the air, Sly waited a moment before setting it on the hood of his pickup. Jim did the same, shoving it in his saddle. Each man made big overt gestures of putting their firearms away, but Jim tucked a handgun into the small of his back.

The two groups marched forward toward one another like two rival street gangs preparing for a melee with knives and bats, a reality that could break bad at any moment. In that case, the Singleton gang would again surely be overcome by numbers.

The leaders met in a stare down. Their gangs sized each other up. The man directly across from Ahmed sneered at him beneath a single eye then spit black juice into the blanket of ground snow.

A mocking smile slid onto Sly's lips. "Lee had good sense to call this meeting. Finally put that big brain of yours to use." All of Sly's words brimmed with venom.

"He called it on my behalf," Jim said.

"Did he? Surprising considering your most recent actions."

Sticking his tongue into the side of his lip, Jim spoke. "We only made right what you done to Brad and Kyle."

Sly's smile didn't fade. "We were making good on what you did to my youngest brother."

"He's my *brother*," One Eye said across from Ahmed.

"Our brother, yes."

"Enough slaying's been done," Lee said.

"I would agree, but your leader seems to think killing women is an acceptable action in our *feud*."

Jim thrust a finger at Sly. "She was guilty just like the others." He twisted his head to the side. "You would have burned my mother alive if we hadn't escaped."

"I believe our local officer of the law checked the premises before we burnt down that treacherous nest a vipers." Sly shrugged his shoulders. "It's neither here nor there. I come for peace. No more hostilities. Keep the past where it belongs. In the past."

Jim's jaw dropped. "You're lyin'."

Wavering his head back and forth, Sly kept his face steady. "I'd love to end this here and now, stick a knife in your gut, but it ain't my decision."

Jim furrowed his brow. "Try it."

"You've always been a hothead, Jimmy, but there's somebody that wants to meet you."

Turning around, Sly waved an arm wide over his head. Lights flicked on and a rumble of motorcycle engines fired up. The sound made Ahmed's heart jump.

His eyes grew large as a cluster of motorcycles cruised down the road, taking the ditch in stride, shocks absorbing the rough patch. Ahmed's stomach roiled as they got closer, making him want to puke with anger. They rolled straight to the gathering. They were covered in leather, heavy coats, and masks. He recognized their patches right away. Black wolves with gold eyes.

The eight bikers dismounted. They passed through the mass of Baileys. The lead man swaggered his way to the front and took a place next to Sly. His black goatee was streaked with gray and ran down his chest like a snake, ribbed with rubber bands in intervals. His hair hung to his shoulders and his eyes were fierce with a wild glint. *Macleod.*

Macleod slapped Sly on the back. "So these are the hooligans disrupting our operation?"

"They are," Sly said with downcast eyes.

Macleod licked his lips, forming a dry smile. "Who's the boss?" He ran his eyes over the Singleton men. "Which one of you *fine* men should I speak too."

"I am," Jim said. He stood tall, not afraid of the bikers or too stupid to show it.

Disbelief enveloped Macleod's eyes. They stared at one another, unblinking, and Ahmed tried to fade into the background. Macleod surely had some unfinished business that he would love to take out on him. "Sly does some good work for me, and I don't want that interrupted, so I can't have you guys fighting." He put a hand on his hip. Every man there tensed, thinking he was going to draw down on them. "How can we bring this to a close? How do we call a truce?" He opened his arms. "Ideas?" Fiery eyes scrutinized the Singleton party and he sighed. "I suppose I could kill you all right here. That would fix it."

"Try it," Jim said. His confidence was not shared by his outnumbered party. A Foxworth took a step back.

Sighing, cold smoke misted in front of Macleod. "You're either brave or really stupid, but I don't want myself or Sly all shot up. What do you want *Jim?*" His eyes narrowed, trying to figure Jim out.

Blinking, Jim studied the ground for a few seconds. It had been the first time that someone had actually forced the man to think about why he was doing what he was doing. "What I want is Sly to admit he's wrong, admit he's guilty for what he done."

"Seems easy enough." He turned to Sly. "Apologize to Jimmy for what you've done."

The Bailey patriarch's mouth fell open before he forced it closed. Dipping his chin to the ground, Macleod waited for the apology like a drunken parent disciplining two fighting kids.

"I ain't admitting I was wrong. I was right for what I done. It was justice."

"No, no, Sly." His chin rose and his dark eyes fell upon Ahmed. Macleod blinked, trying to place him.

Ahmed didn't turn away. He kept his face devoid of all emotion, facing the man who'd shot him, killed his friends, and betrayed him in a time of need.

Gradually, Macleod released Sly's shoulder. He took a few steps closer, chuckling to himself as he walked. "No, no, no. I killed you." He paced a few more steps forward between the groups. "We killed you." Squinting his eyes, he swept his jacket back revealing a handgun. "Can't be." He got within a few feet and sucked his own cheeks, weighing him the entire time. "AH-med?"

Ahmed's heart thumped inside his body wanting to escape. Macleod was the only armed man in the group aside from Jim. "It's me."

Breathing a wicked laugh, Macleod looked at the clouds for an answer. "Not that it could have been anyone else. I mean, come on? How many Arabs do you think live in butt-fuck Missouri? One, two, not unless they got some ISIS training camp they're all hiding in." An evil smile spread on his lips. "How you been?" He took a step closer, pressing his face near Ahmed's, his breath a rancid mix of whiskey and beef jerky. "Been hindered by the going-away present we left you?"

"I'm fine."

Macleod turned back toward his bikers, raising his hands in the air. "He's fine." His gang laughed cruel hard tones like they'd already put another bullet into his body. "I been jabbering for minutes on end and he says he's fine. Ha. Now I know why Steele kept you around for so long. You're quite the conversationalist. How is our noble agent and fearless leader by the way?"

"I don't know."

"Well, I can tell you this, he sure ain't alive. Jackson's men were coming in from the north, south, east and the river was west so you can imagine how that ended up. Better to jump ship early and often in this world." Boldly he walked back to his men, leaving himself exposed without fear.

He could feel Jim's eyes upon him. "You know these guys?"

"They're the ones who killed my men."

Macleod strolled back to Sly's group again without a care in the world. "All right, bumpkins. This is what we'll do." He wagged a finger at Sly. "My boy Sly here is going to apologize for all wrongdoings on his knees like a good little boy."

"By God I will not!"

Twisting his neck to the side, Macleod's tone hardened. "You will do as you're told, or I'll make your wife watch as I cut your balls off and feed them to you." He raised an eyebrow at his insubordinate partner. "Fair trade?"

The Bailey leader visibly paled, his face taking on the shade of the ashen ground he stood on. He shook his head. Kicking the back of his knees, Macleod forced him to the ground with a *thwack!* Not one of the Bailey men intervened.

Running a hand through Sly's wavy hair, he massaged his scalp with his fingertips as if he were comforting the man one moment then going to take his scalp the next. "How do you get your hair so luxurious?" Macleod stopped massaging Sly's head. "Never mind. I don't want to know. I like you, Sly. I really do, but let's let bygones be bygones. Shall we?" His tone became annoyingly patronizing. "Say you're sorry to Jim Bob over there."

Sly stared forward, fear clouding his eyes, but his hatred for Jim was so much greater. His mouth remained closed. Macleod laughed at him. "You're stupid. Roody tell Pork to bring up his wife. Pride is a damnable offense."

"Wait." Sly's brown eyes peered at Jim. "I'll say it."

Macleod bent down next to his ear. "You're slightly smarter than you look. Slightly." He turned his palm up like a circus ringmaster. "You may continue."

Collecting himself with a sigh, Sly stared at Jim. "I apologize for killing your father and brother."

"Not good enough," Jim spat.

Macleod cocked his head. "A better apology?" He kicked at Sly. "Make sure to add in it will never happen again. I suppose it couldn't 'cause you only get one dad, but you could have more brothers. Do you have more brothers, Jimmy?" Macleod eyed the men around him. "That one there looks like you a bit."

"I don't have no more brothers," Jimmy growled.

"Too bad. All right Sly, lay it on us. Make me feel it in my soul." He bent down close to the man's face. "We're waiting."

"I'm sorry for the troubles my family has caused yours for generations. It's our fault this happened."

Macleod nudged him with his knee, shielding his mouth from Jim's group, he said harshly, "And brother and father."

Clenching his jaw, Sly gritted his teeth as if each word pained him. "I'm sorry for killing your father and brother."

Jim snarled. "You murdered them!"

"And what about Grayson? You murdered him, his two sons, and his wife."

"Boys, boys. No need to shout. Remember what we're doing? Sly, you were apologizing for the murders." He locked eyes with Jimmy. "Some people."

The words came forced. "I'm sorry for murdering them."

Macleod raised a single eyebrow with his arms folded over his chest. "That seemed pretty sincere."

"It was okay."

Macleod nudged Sly again with his knee. "Stand up." He searched the sky for divine inspiration. "I am healing this torn divided nation. I'm like Abraham fucking Lincoln." He took a step toward Jim. "Now I've done you a great service and given you what you wanted. Let me tell you what you can do for me." He raised his eyebrows to the top of his skull. "Seems fair, no?"

"What do you want from us?"

"I want you all to get along, and you to fall under my club's protection. That's all. Easy enough."

"We don't need protection."

"Ah, but you do. But you do." He paused and his tone hardened. "You do. There are so many bad people out there. Not to mention the infected. Tons of them across the river there. Ugly fucks each and every one. But they provide a bit of fun, don't they, Ahmed?"

Ahmed had no words for the man. This man, no bastard, killed Ollie and Weston and betrayed them. He had nothing to say to such a traitor.

"Come on, buddy? We were friends once. No need for the silent treatment."

"Go to hell."

Macleod gave him a toothy grin. "That's better. That's why I've always liked you. Quiet and noble. You are a true *hero*." He pointed over at Ahmed. "You got what I want, Jimmy. You give me Ahmed, Sly will keep the peace, you will keep the peace. You will be protected from all the boogeymen out there and everybody wins."

All eyes fell on Ahmed. Jim's eyes read him, chewing on the corrupted words that Macleod spewed forth. Slowly shaking his head, Ahmed said. "No."

"Jimmy, I upheld my part. I got you what you wanted. Now give me what I want. You clearly have no love for the Arab."

Jim continued to weigh Ahmed. He had no delusion how this would go if Jim agreed to Macleod's terms. Macleod would draw his handgun and put a bullet in his head like he did to Ollie and Weston, and that was if he was in a merciful mood. If he wasn't feeling sympathetic at the present time, he would take him back to wherever he was holed up and torture him before sawing off his head or something diabolical that men could only fathom in nightmares.

A fight would be over quick. Ahmed would try to knock his teeth in before being subdued by the bikers and Baileys. Maybe he could land a few hits on them, but nothing substantial, nothing that any of these men hadn't experienced before. Bruises and broken noses that would disappear in a few days while Ahmed's corpse rotted on top of the frozen earth, the coyotes tearing at his carcass followed by the mouths of the dead. He'd take the coyotes over the dead.

Jim broke eye contact, his icy eyes flitting back to his rivals. "Mr. Macleod, you've done me great service today."

A proud smile spread on Macleod's face.

"You've gotten more out of this deceitful rat of a man than my family has in generations."

"I've always been a great mediator." He mouthed *Abraham Lincoln* to Ahmed.

Jim put a hand over his heart. "Thank you."

"So you accept?"

Jim regarded the ground as if he were judging its worth for planting. "Well, you see. I have a problem with handing Ahmed over. He's one of us now, and I don't turn my people over to some jerk-off." He paused as if he almost forgot. "And while I wasn't surprised to see Sly on his knees, I didn't buy a lick of his apologies."

Macleod's lips tightened into a sneer. "You're more stupid than Sly here." His hand rested on his pistol.

Jim's hand latched on the handgun in the small of his back. "Yeah, I been called stupid but never disloyal. Ahmed's one of us. Remember that."

A hearty laugh came from the back of Macleod's throat. He slowly stopped, mirth lining his cruel eyes. "Jimmy, my boy. You and your whole family are going to pay for this."

"We'll see."

"I'll be seeing you later." Macleod aimed a finger at him like his hand was a gun. "Pew."

Jim stood there, his outward appearance giving an air of being generally unimpressed. Macleod walked back to his motorcycle, and Sly and his men to their trucks. The Wolf Riders fired up engines and rolled back over the bumpy field, the Bailey men behind them in pickup trucks.

The Singleton group stood for a moment watching them go. Ahmed moved closer to Jim. "You should have given me over."

Jim turned toward him, face steely. "To the likes of that? Nah. Wouldn't've been right."

Ahmed's face broke into a grin followed by Jim. "You still thinking about leaving us?"

His body responded before him. "No."

"Really?"

Ahmed's smile widened. "Wouldn't be right."

GWEN
Camp Forge, IA

The walls around Camp Forge had grown since she'd been gone, reminding her of a toy log fort. The hooves of ten horses trampled the snowy earth. On the corners of the structure, sandbagged platforms sat elevated. Tiny little heads poked out from behind the protective barriers.

They walked their mounts along the road, the hayrack's wheels groaning as they churned. Men watched them from the timber, axes in hand. She knew they were hers. They'd seen tracks of other men on their return from Farmington. A few bodies of frozen dead soldiers stripped naked of all clothing. Prisoners that Steele had let go. Feral men that'd been released on the countryside.

Facing west was a large metal gate that could be hoisted up with a chain. It bore resemblance to a volunteer firefighters' warehouse garage door. Slender metal slats were layered and would bend under force but not break. It'd been welded and supported by the thick stripped tree trunks turned fortifications. A man on the wall peered down at her.

"It's Gwen!"

The head disappeared and muffled yells echoed out of the camp. The gate cranked upward from the inside.

Nathan walked through the entrance holding an AR-15. A big smile spread on his lips. "It's damn sure good to see you, Gwen."

"Nathan," she said, returning his friendliness.

"Did you find the medicine?"

Gwen exchanged a look with Tess. "Yes."

"I won't hold you longer then."

Her group entered the fortifications. She scrambled down from the hayrack and hurried straight to her grandparents' house. Steele stood on the porch. He embraced her tight.

He whispered in her ear. "I was worried."

"Me too."

"Did you find the medicine?"

"Yes."

He let her go. "Hurry, the infection's moved to her lungs."

She didn't say a word. She burst through the door and bounded up the steps. Not bothering to knock, she went into the bedroom.

Becky glanced at the door, tears in her eyes that softened in relief. "Oh, Gwen."

Gwen raced to her side. Setting down her pack, she said hushed, "She's not?"

A shaky breath escaped from her sister's lips. "Barely."

Ripping open her bag, she removed a package of antibiotics. She scooped the bottle out and twisted off the cap, shaking pills into her hand. Leaning close to Haley, she whispered, "Open up, sweetie."

Haley's eyelids opened the tiniest crack, causing Gwen's heart to break. She smiled at her, tears forming in her eyes. "Open up, sweetie."

They adjusted Haley so she was laying more upright. Placing the pills in her mouth, she followed it with the bottled water. "Down it goes."

Haley coughed, her chest rattling, and swallowed the medicine. Gwen exhaled forcefully as they let Haley back down. Becky went about tucking the blankets around her child neatly as if she were playing house with a doll.

Gwen's little phantom boy stood near the edge of the bed. He wore a little knit red hat with tassels that hung past his shoulders. He watched his cousin with grave concern as if he couldn't fathom why she couldn't play.

"I came as fast as I could."

Becky didn't acknowledge Gwen but stroked the hair off Haley's forehead.

She bent over and dunked a washcloth in a shallow washbasin and placed the cloth back on the tiny girl's head. "You've always been there for us." She paused as she stared at her little girl lying on the edge of death. "But there are others."

Like hard candy she'd swallowed whole, Gwen had to digest her decision to trust Tess and abandon her search for medicine. She had chosen the option that got her back the fastest. It was a decision others would die for if she was wrong. It was a decision she would have to live with.

She stroked the little girl's hand for a moment. "We have more medicine." She stood with authority and anger, wanting to yell. *It's been here all along!* But she held her tongue, not wanting to cause Becky even more stress than she already was under.

Gwen left the room, and Steele followed her like a shadow down the steps. People had begun to congregate outside the house, mostly the Chosen but many others. They knew her mission, and word quickly spread of her return.

"There's something that I need to tell you."

Steele muttered behind her, "I don't like surprises."

Stopping in the foyer, she took a deep breath. "I don't like this either." She shook her head unknowing a better way to say it. "Thunder's been hoarding medicine. I don't know why, but he has."

Steele's eyes turned stormy. "What are you talking about?"

"Tess told me. She said you wouldn't listen to her."

His lips twisted a bit in irritation. "What do you mean Tess told you?"

"She found me in Farmington and told me about Thunder's treachery."

"She was gone?" Steele looked back into the parlor. "Where is she?"

Tess's voice called out, "I'm here." She emerged from the parlor. Her battered face visibly shook him.

"Jesus, what happened?"

"Ran into some of Jackson's finest on the road." She brought a finger to her nose. "Don't suppose Dr. Miller can set it? Otherwise, it'll be crooked forever."

Steele rubbed the scar atop his head. "Of course he will. What is this business with Thunder?"

"I tried to tell you, but you wouldn't hear it. He's been pulling one over on us like I said. Got medicine and plenty of it. Been hoarding it underneath a floorboard in his cabin."

"No." He rested a hand on his tomahawk. "I already told you once. Drop it." His eyes avoided Tess and peered at Gwen.

Her green eyes watered, and her jaw set in resistance. Everything depended on Tess being right. If she wasn't, a lot more people would die. "I believe her. She wouldn't have risked our lives and that of all these people to reach me."

He regarded Tess as if he could sniff deceit. The twig-like woman stared back unafraid.

"Do you realize what this will do to us?" He shook his head in disgust, his beard scratching across his uniform. "He's our greatest ally. If I accuse him and I'm wrong, we could have a war and lose them. People will die."

"I'm not wrong. I had it in my hands, I opened the bag and saw all its contents."

Steele gritted his teeth and stretched his neck. "By God, you better be sure." His temple tensed. "You're sure?"

Her voice took on a snarky tone, "No, I just made it all up for some attention. Of course, I'm sure."

"Dammit. I never thought it would be him."

Reaching for him, Gwen rested a hand over his. "I know."

"He's been with me the longest," Tess said.

His eyes darted toward the door as he formed a plan. "On the sly, grab a bunch of the Sable Pointers. Get somebody on one of the .50s but don't fire up the Humvee until we confront them. Be quick and quiet." He turned toward Gwen. "How many men do you have here?"

"I have five plus the men from Farmington."

"You trust those men?"

"I do."

"All right. This has to be a surprise. Let no one you don't trust know. I won't have a shootout but be ready for one. Ten minutes."

Gwen gulped and he pierced her with his dark ocean-blue eyes.

"We move."

MARGIE
Burlington, IA

Red Clare's lips curled into a crinkly smile. The corners of her mouth held creases, and her teeth were a faded brownish-yellow. She wore a black leather jacket with her club colors, seven ghost women holding swords. Her reddish hair was in a tangled mess on her shoulders. "We'll be here if you need us."

"Thank you," Margie said, glancing at the pontoon boats. "Hopefully, we'll be back soon." She unraveled the rope, tying her pontoon boat to the dock. They would travel the rest of the day north and link up with the Special Forces detachment on the outskirts of Davenport. After that, they would finish the journey to Clinton, joining Captain Heath's command.

Margie wasn't familiar with military structure, but she knew enough to do what she was told and accomplish her task. At least she kept telling herself that. An inferiority complex wasn't going to help her or her team. She felt overmatched by the other leaders, especially War Child, like they were supposed to be there and she wasn't. She had to remind herself that Steele had chosen her for a reason and to do her job.

A dense fog hovered over the river like a cold smoke. She waved at Berry, who fired up the motor, and they slowly pulled out into the open.

"What's with the fog?" Tony asked, eyeing it suspiciously, knowing it could hold all sorts of evil.

"I dunno. The air freezing. Brian talked about ice fogs, river fogs, and valley fogs when we were married." She looked down after she spoke and back at Tony. "I know, super interesting." She didn't like remembering him. "Sometimes in marriage, the only thing that changes is the weather."

Tony smiled in response. "No shame in reminiscing."

She didn't like remembering that day or any of the days after as she starved alone in her bedroom, waiting for someone to find her. The frantic phone calls to her children unanswered. The crying, the hiding, the running, all formed into a distant nightmare.

Scratches echoed off the pontoons. Tony leaned over the bow and studied the water. "It's still water here, but what is that?" He gestured out. "It looks like a slushy."

Karen glanced over too. She'd been a middle-school science teacher. "It's frazil. It forms when the river is in the first stages of freezing. The water movement interrupts crystal growth, and the crystals don't join together to form a sheet of ice."

The water continued to flow even in its congested state of solidifying into lumps of white. "How do you know that?"

"Weather and climate curriculum. "

"You were teaching kids about frazil?" Tony smirked. "Kids nowadays. Smarter and smarter."

"You wouldn't believe it," Karen said, her eyes grinning over her scarf.

"Can a river like this freeze?" Margie asked. Arguably, the Mississippi was a large river, and if this frazil stuff was forming, surely it could cluster enough to freeze. Those in her crew shrugged. They weren't from this area. They didn't know the answer.

Karen said, "Not sure. Maybe it's possible if the temperature drops enough for long enough."

"Keep an eye on it."

Margie hunkered down, keeping her body compact to stay warm. She waited for anything, her wood-stocked deer hunting 30-06 rifle resting across her body.

The rumble of pontoon motors and the repetitive lap of propellers drowned out the hollow moans of the dead that tracked them unseen on the misty banks. They motored along the river for roughly thirty minutes.

"They're slowing down ahead," Berry said from the captain's chair.

"Must be the lock," she said. They knew they would have to traverse locks on their way north. Many locks were on the Illinois side which meant contact with the infected and it was either get the locks working or find another way.

She stood, letting the cold wind bite at her face. The dim shape of Lieutenant Gunther's long pontoon was getting closer.

"Cut it back," Margie said to Berry. He eased off the throttle and steered the pontoon with enough space to pull alongside the other boat. The boat rocked as they drifted closer. Camouflaged men stood along the railings.

Margie cupped her mouth. "What's going on?"

She recognized Sergeant First Class Wade's face among the cluster of men. "War Child's bringing us to a stop. Said engine problem."

"We'll check it out."

"All right," he called back.

Margie glanced over her shoulder. "Pull us up to War Child." *Damn. Nothing is smooth.*

Berry edged the engine carefully forward. They drifted along the flat motorized platform. A knot of War Machines moved on board their pontoon.

"Hey!" She rested her hands on the port side of her small pontoon. "What's wrong?"

The bikers ignored her, continuing to gather. She could see the white-haired biker talking to his sergeant-in-arms. Margie waved in his direction, arm above her head. "War Child!"

He made his way to the railing and grinned at her. "We're having engine trouble. I'm thinking maybe Gunther's boat can tug us. It'll be slow, but I don't see another way."

"Shit," Margie swore. *Nothing is ever easy.* This miserable journey was about to stretch a lot longer. *Just make do.* "I'll wave them up. If we don't freeze to death first."

War Child lit a cigarette, the beady little ember going to his lips. "I wouldn't worry about that."

Her brow crossed in confusion. "Ha. Okay." She gave him another quizzical glance and walked to the other end of the pontoon.

"Berry, take us back to Gunther's boat."

"Got it." He made a wide arc with the pontoon to turn them around.

They had by far the most mobile of the three watercrafts. Picking up speed for a few seconds, he cut it when Gunther's pontoon emerged from the foggy river. Soldiers hung over the railings waiting for more information.

God, my hands are cold. Make this quick. Margie cupped her mouth. "War Child's motor's out. We're going to have to tug them."

Gunther's youthful face stared back. "Really?"

"That's what he says. He wants you to go on ahead and lash the two boats together."

"All right." At a sluggish pace, Gunther motored forward in the mist.

"Stay close behind them," Margie said back at Berry. "We want to be close enough to help out if they need it."

"On it." Berry followed Gunther's boat close enough to shout at one another but far enough to not cause any issues, giving the longer more cumbersome pontoons extra space to maneuver.

She watched them as they pulled abreast the drifting watercraft. The War Machines lined the railings.

"Here's a rope," a man yelled.

A rope unraveled, lashing the two boats. It was almost silent for a moment. Only Gunther's motor idled, churning semisolid water.

The fiery thunder of a .50 caliber machine gun made her jump. Her adrenaline spiked as fire erupted from War Child's boat like a broadside of cannons between two man-of-war ships.

"What the hell is happening?!" Margie screamed.

Automatic weapons raged, clapping her ears. Realization forced her eyes wide. The tarp-lined sides of Gunther's ship went flapping as they were shredded from the onslaught of lead. Bodies splashed into the water as the men fell overboard. Screams of the dying raked her eardrums. The Sable Pointers stood rigid, watching the massacre in awe.

War Machines pivoted in their direction. Bullets screamed for them now. They dinged off metal pontoons and cracked into the sides sending plastic flying. Berry took a round through the jaw, bursting out his neck. He toppled out of the captain's chair.

Margie dove to the ground, but it was more of a fall atop her rifle. She clutched it in her frozen hands as the bullets sailed over her. A string of rounds took Karen in the chest, and she collapsed along a bench seat. Tony plunged over top of Margie covering her with his lean body.

The bullets continued to pound their small boat with a fury that was unstoppable. Tony's arms wrapped around her body. She stared into his fearful eyes behind his glasses. The bullets stopped searching for them, and a quiet hum filled the air. She breathed for what felt like the first time in minutes, her breath coming in shaky spurts. The rise and fall of men yelling reached her ears.

His name leaked from her lips between labored breaths. "Tony."

He stared at her eyes still wide. Unblinking. She shook him. "Tony?"

She disengaged from his arms and rolled him over. White feathers puffed out from his coat. She sat up and ran her hands along his back. "Wake up, baby."

He was silent, letting her hands search with no objections. Her hands found the indentations in his back and she raised her eyes to the sky as her heart plummeted to the hell of loss. She shook his lifeless body. "Get up." His head jostled from side to side. Warm liquid dribbled over her hands as if his own blood were reluctant to tell her he was gone. "Please, God." She let him rest, staring at the sticky fluid coating her palms.

The pontoon rocked in the river. She wiped her hands into her face hard as if trying to figure out if she was still alive. The fallen Sable Pointers lay strewn where the bullets had brought them down with violent effectiveness.

She crawled to Berry, his eyes already glazed over where he had collapsed. Her hands stuck to the floor as she reached for Karen. Margie tugged her down from her seat. The woman's head thudded off the ground, her body lifeless.

Random gunshots kicked off as the War Machines boarded Gunther's boat. "They're coming for us next," she whispered to herself.

Karen's mouth hung open as if she had something to add. Crimson fluids dripped from the corner of her lips, but no words came from her mouth.

"They're coming."

Hand over hand, she scrambled to the driver's chair. Ripping the steering wheel to the side, the boat changed course. The craft angled for the Iowan shore. Gunfire banged out in quick succession from War Child's boat. Bullets pounded the deck of her pontoon again, and she dropped down, staying low to the rear. Without a second thought, she muscled over Karen's body and launched herself into the icy waters.

The water was an immediate shock to her system. She had no time to consider that a bullet could have been mercy. The air in her chest seized, squeezing any oxygen from her body. Frigid water penetrated her clothes, enveloping her skin and making every moment a struggle. Beating the water with her gloved hands, she ignored her instinct to shed clothing.

Her head burst through the surface. She sucked in as much air as she could but couldn't ingest enough. The water made her heavy, beckoning her downward. The shore was close, so close she could see the rocks and dead grass around it. Her hands formed into frozen cups, and she kicked and squirmed and fought against the water. Her pontoon crashed into the shore nearby, scraping over rocks into an icy shore. It found a final resting place, leaning to the right with its motor metal grinding away at the frozen land. More bullets pinged off the metal pontoons.

She beat the water furiously and went under. The freezing water stung her skin, and her face went numb. Brian's face flashed before her eyes. She wasn't sure of the last time she'd taken a breath. Tony's lifeless face appeared before her. Her mind faded as the cold took her deep into its bowels. As Margie blinked, the men disappeared into the river depths. Her body didn't feel anything anymore, only a general numbness inside. Maybe it was better to be numb than to ever have to feel again. *No,* her mind whispered.

She burst from the water, sucking in air. Slapping the surface, her feet sank into the mud beneath the surface. She struggled to the shore. Her jaw shook. "Must get dry." In a haze, she gripped her torso and stumbled for the trees.

STEELE
Camp Forge, IA

He ran a hand over the length of his beard, smoothing it with his fingers. With a furtive eye, he watched Tess and the Sable Pointers start to assemble near the front of their barn seemingly nonchalantly. A few gazed wide-eyed near the Red Stripes cabins, guns on backs or held loosely in hands. *Don't give us away.*

"You'll stay here," he said to Gwen.

She shook her head no. "I will not." Her green eyes smoldered like witching flames. "If he held out on us, he could have killed Haley." Her voice became softer. "He may still have."

He clenched his jaw. Any man would protect his woman and unborn child, but she didn't want protection. She wanted to be right there next to him in the thick of it. His fight was her fight. "I can't say no to you." *Is she too hot to bring to a confrontation when cooler heads may prevail? Hell, she might put a bullet in me if I don't let her go.* He slipped his tomahawk in his belt and touched the handle of his M9 Beretta 9mm. If things went south, and it could quickly, he'd need to cover Gwen's escape.

He took a long overcoat off a hook in the foyer and threw it on over his ACUs. Pulling down hard on his collar, he left it unzipped for easy access to his firearm.

John stood in the kitchen with worried eyes, his quilted flannel coat on, ready for the elements. "I overheard."

239

"Stay inside, John."

"Not with my granddaughter in harm's way."

Steele sucked in air through his nose. These people were nothing if not stubborn. He nodded at the old man and opened the door. Wintery coldness flooded inside, and he stepped on the porch.

Jake and Gerald regarded them with cool eyes. Steele gestured with his chin. Hank stared at Steele, rubbing his hands together. Gregor's hair floated in the wind even with his knit wool hat on. The men from Farmington all appeared nervous, like a skittish herd aside from the state trooper whose demeanor was as frosty as the winter air.

"Trooper Linden," the dour-looking state trooper said.

"Captain Steele, former counterterrorism agent."

"I've seen plenty of men with that look on your face, Captain." His eyes regarded him with a certain wariness.

Steele glanced over to the Sable Pointers by the barn. The group started to walk for the cabins at an almost casual pace but with more urgency than normal. Walking slowly, he eyed the Red Stripes cabins. *Just out for my daily stroll.* The men followed him.

"That look means violence, Agent Steele," Linden said, striding next to him.

"I don't have time to tell you everything, but those men have betrayed us. Are you with us?"

Linden's cold brown eyes scrutinized the cabins. "I trust your wife, and by proxy, I trust you."

Steele nodded to him. "And I you." He turned his back on Linden and started his walk. His boots cracked through the hard layer of snow.

"Who are the traitors?" Linden said behind him.

"Red Stripes motorcycle gang." He could practically hear Linden stiffening behind him, tension building, ice speeding up in his veins.

"Perhaps we need more men."

"I always need more men. I'm hoping that this is a big mistake."

"I'm hoping no mistakes are made."

The walk was short to the large cabin. Smoke churned out the chimney into the frosty air. The snow was packed down and dirty near the entrance. The door was simple wood both clean and tan. Sturdy Amish work.

He collected himself before giving the people behind him a glance over his shoulder. At least fifty people watched in the cold. Others from Major Ludlow's barns and the Chosen cabins stood outside. *Always get more with honey.* Placing himself slightly off center from the doorway, he made sure Gwen was far to the side of any immediate gunfire.

Steadily he exhaled and rapped his knuckles hard on the door with the force of authority. After a moment, the door opened, and a tall broad man filled the doorframe with two pistols shoved in his belt. His smile faded.

"What's wrong? We under attack?" He ducked, his eyes searching the walls.

Steele peered up at the man. "We need to talk to Thunder."

Garrett turned his head, scanning the mass of armed people. The rumble of an engine perforated the air along with the crunch of a Humvee rolling to a halt.

"I'll get him," Garrett said, turning to close the door.

With a firm hand, Steele stopped the door. "Let's leave it open."

Garrett eyed him with misunderstood concern and turned inside.

A few moments later, Thunder appeared. His jovial manner disappeared upon seeing the armed people gathered outside his door.

"What the hell is going on?"

"We have word that you've been hoarding medicine. Medicine we need and I'm here to get answers."

"Who the fuck said that?" His brow creased with contention. "We don't have shit."

"It doesn't matter who. I don't want this to be a bigger issue than it is." He dropped his voice. "This is serious."

Tess shouted from behind Steele. "I fucking found it, you no-good two-faced son of a bitch."

Thunder's bushy eyebrows coalesced in hurt, and his voice rose in anger. "What the hell are you talking about?" He faced Steele. "Now I know this must be a joke." He snorted a laugh until saw the Humvee with the M2

Browning .50 caliber machine gun aimed in his direction. The clamoring of Red Stripes grew louder in the cabin. Steele was sure they were arming themselves for a fight.

"Thunder."

The grizzled biker looked like the angriest Santa of all time. Angry enough to sentence them all to an eternity on the naughty list.

"Let me look around, and we can put this behind us."

Thunder's wide eyes turned into malice. "Do you realize what you are doing? Accusing us of betrayal is against everything we stand for. This is unforgivable, boy."

Steele peered back at Tess. "Let's put this to bed. Can I come in without a problem?"

Sidestepping in the doorway, Thunder waved him in. "Why of course."

"I'm not stupid. Let's get your club out here, and we can do this a lot easier. No weapons."

Thunder studied the floor and cocked his head to the side in disgust. "You've got to be kidding me with this shit." He gestured at his men. "Garrett, get the boys outside."

Red Stripes filed through the door. The men were angry and resilient. They lined up against the cabin wall like they were going to be booked and sent to jail.

"Follow me," Tess said, leading the way brazenly inside.

The place was a disorganized disaster of sleeping bags and trash. Guns lay strewn about. Gwen and her followers filed in behind them.

"You ain't gonna find nothing," Thunder said, folding his arms over his meaty chest. "What's wrong with you girl? You mad cause I didn't help you kill the pastor?"

Tess stepped intently on the floor, letting her heel roll over each floorboard. She moved to another board and repeated the process. "No, I'm mad because you fucking betrayed us. People died because of you."

Thunder's lip curled. "I didn't betray nobody. I swear it on my club's colors."

Tess stalked over the floor listening until she stopped near the fireplace.

She rolled her heel over a floorboard. She sidestepped to another then rolled it on the suspect board again. "This is it."

"What's it?" Thunder bellowed.

"This is the hideaway." Tess released a knife from her belt and squatted down on her haunches. She forced the knife into the cracks between the floorboards and dug into the wood using her fingers to pry the piece out. After the first one, the others flipped over on the floor revealing a hole. Her arm disappeared into the ground, and she pulled out a black duffel and tossed it at Steele.

He glanced at Gwen and then Thunder.

Tess lifted her chin. "Check it out."

"I don't know where that came from."

Steele crouched low. Grabbing the zipper, he opened the bag. Bottles and pills rattled as he stuck his hand inside. He removed a bottle, eyeing the medicine.

"Pills. Antibiotics. Antivirals." He shook his head at Thunder and stood. "I don't understand why."

"I told you," Tess said.

"She must have planted it," Thunder said.

Gwen jabbed a finger at Thunder. "You monster. Our kids were dying, and you held on to this? What's wrong with you?"

Thunder threw a hand back at her. "How'd she know where to look? It's a plant. We're being set up."

"I could tell your Red Stripes were up to no good meeting with the pastor."

"Meeting the pastor? Ha, I hate the bastards."

"How do you explain this?" Steele said.

His bushy eyebrows pinched together. "Well, I can't, but I didn't do it and neither did my club."

Steele could feel Gwen shaking with rage next to him. "Let's take a walk outside." He picked up the bag, holding it in his less than compliant right hand.

Thunder eyed him for a moment before nodding. They all walked outside. A crowd had formed, encircling the armed Sable Pointers and the Humvee with its turret gunner trained on the cabin. Frank elbowed his way through the crowd. "What the hell is going on?"

Thunder bellowed at him. "Trumped-up charges on medicine."

Steele pushed his people into the open. The pastor stood with Peter and Luke, watching from the edge with interest. Major Ludlow and a contingent of soldiers were easily discernible with their camouflaged ACUs.

Placing a hand in the air, Steele spoke. "I need everyone's attention." The crowd quieted to a stifled murmur. "It has been discovered that Thunder and the Red Stripes have been holding out on stores of medicine."

All parties roared in anger.

"False!" Garrett yelled.

"Not true," Thunder said.

Keeping his hand in the air, he waited for the anger to subside to a boil. "I didn't believe it myself, but we found this bag hidden in their cabin." He lifted the black duffel into the air for all to see. He then bent down and unzipped it, holding it open with both hands. Shaking the bag, they all could hear the guilty rattle of the pill bottles. Audible gasps could be heard.

Thunder growled at them. "It was a plant."

The pastor worked his way through the people until he stood inside the circle. "Children have died." He pointed a long finger at Thunder. "All of this suffering because of your greed."

"And fuck you too, Pastor," Thunder said.

The pastor turned his eyes to the sky. "God has given us reprieve from our torment. Praise be to God." He turned his eyes back to Thunder. "May you suffer for this evil you've brought upon these God-fearing people. What say you, Steele? Will justice be served?" His voice held the religious fervor of the pulpit.

"We cannot stand for this injustice." Steele handed the bag to the pastor. "Please put this to good use."

The pastor lowered his head in deference. "I would be honored to give life where only death presided."

Collecting himself for a moment, Steele took a step in front of Gwen before he spoke. "Thunder and the Red Stripes, I place you under arrest for conspiracy to commit harm to Camp Forge and the people within." Quick on his handgun, he drew it, sighting it on Thunder's forehead.

JOSEPH
Cheyenne Mountain Complex, CO

He clicked the lock on his door and turned around, facing his co-conspirators. "We have two days."

"Two days?" Hollis exclaimed.

"Byrnes said they're about as far into the earth as you can go without popping out in China."

Hollis's face reddened and the veins in his neck expanded, threatening to blow any second. "How the hell are we supposed to break them out so quick?"

Joseph sat on the edge of his bed. "I was hoping you would have an answer for that."

Staring at Joseph, Hollis shook his head. "We shouldn't have opened that dumb flash drive. I knew it. I told you not to!"

"They're going to execute him for treason. We're their only hope for survival."

"We're going to get killed in the process." Hollis put his head down into his hands. "Oh, God. Oh, God."

"Think. We're smart. We have to be able to come up with something."

They sat in silence for a minute. Joseph went first. "I already planted the seed that the prisoner might be sick. What if we fake a life-threatening illness? Then we can cart out the person."

"How many can we liberate before they catch on? Then where do we take them? That doesn't free them from the mountain itself," Dr. Desai said.

Pushing his glasses back to their rightful place on his nose, Joseph tried again. "We could drug the guards? There's four of them. Two outside the door to the cell. Two inside the cell room entrance."

Hollis humphed, sounding like an irritated cow. "What? Are you going to force them to take a pill and wait for them to fall asleep?"

Joseph raised his eyebrows. "We could inject them? Random vaccination."

"Then what? We still don't have a way out of this facility crawling with soldiers. Besides, are we going to vaccinate them at their post?"

"I'm trying to come up with something, and all you do is say no. We have to come up with something and fast." Joseph studied the wall. Desai crossed her arms over her chest, and Hollis stared at the ground.

"Wait," Desai said, leaning forward. "I did a study when I was in medical school on a potent neurotoxin called tetrodotoxin. Are you familiar?"

A small smile spread on Joseph's lips. "Yes, go on."

"Tetrodotoxin or TTX is named after the order of highly derived ray-finned fish that carry it. Oddly enough, it's not a chemical created by the fish but a symbiotic bacteria. It's a sodium channel blocker. If too much is ingested, you become paralyzed and die."

"Yes, of course," Dr. Hollis said. "Everyone knows this. It will kill you."

Desai gave him a mean look. "We studied the effects of combining it with other drugs for alternative uses. In one limited test, we were able to modify the neurotoxin to ensure body could still function but outwardly seem dead."

Joseph followed her train of thought. "And if they appear dead, we can remove them from the cell."

"Exactly, given we were experimenting at the time," Desai said. "If you give me a while, I think I can replicate the test. We should have plenty of the toxin in one of the labs."

"But that only gets us out of the cell room."

Joseph turned to Hollis. "Where are bodies taken after a person dies?"

"The body bags are shipped out to a general crematory outside the facility. The risk of fire is too great to have one inside the mountain. In the event that we are 'buttoned-up,' and the blast doors are closed, we place them in a temperature-controlled storeroom near the docks."

"Do you have access to this storeroom?"

"It's not my section, but it's close to the storage facilities where we bring in and take out supplies or shipments."

"So if we got a pile of not-dead, dead bodies into the holding area, you can make sure they get on the right shipment out of here?"

"I will see. There are trucks that come in and out from all over."

"That's it. That's how we do it. They have to be dead." Joseph shared a grin with Desai.

Hollis frowned. "If the dosing is wrong, we could kill them."

"I will ensure the dosing is correct," Desai said.

"What chance do they have? They're already slated for execution," Joseph said.

Hollis sighed. "This is very risky."

"It must be done. Tomorrow, we inject them, fake their deaths, and ship them out. Easy."

Hollis peered at Joseph's desk drawer. "All this talk is making me hungry. Do you have anything to eat?"

Joseph pulled a mini bag of chips from his drawer and handed it to the perpetually starving man. "We need you to make sure a shipment of something is going out when Dr. Desai and I come up with the bodies."

"Let's see. There's a body disposal truck that comes every Thursday. It's supposed to come in the morning, but it's always late. They're incompetent at best."

Joseph nodded. "Hopefully, we'll get the B-squad of the security guards."

"Hopefully," Hollis said, between crunching bites.

STEELE
Camp Forge, IA

"Hi, Haley."

The little girl gave him a faint smile. A small tinge of pink had returned to her pale cheeks.

"Hi, Uncle Mark." She adjusted her head on her pillow so she could see him better. That forced a sad smile on his lips. Gwen had explained to the girl after they first arrived that he was an uncle. It helped explain in the child's mind that Mark was important in Gwen's life, therefore important in her life too, someone that could be trusted and depended upon.

"You feeling a bit better?"

She nodded her head but still gave him a pout indicating that she wasn't fully healed yet.

His words came softly. "You're doing all right, kiddo. Now get some rest. You want to know why?" He shared a knowing smile with Gwen.

"Because you know it's getting close to Christmas time now, and you know he's always watching."

Haley's eyes grew a fraction of a centimeter wider. "Santa?"

"That's right," Gwen said. She bent down to stroke Haley's cheek, her hand shifting to the young girl's forehead for a moment. "She feels better."

"And I heard he's got some presents for you," Mark added.

Haley's voice came out like a tiny mouse. "I can't wait."

"So get some rest so you're ready for Christmas."

Haley nodded with a smile-pout.

Gwen and Mark walked from the room, closing the door gently behind them. They stood in the hallway sharing a moment. He felt like he was practicing being a father. His hand fell to her abdomen. She was showing plenty now, enough for people to want to ask her about it. Her eyes sparkled at him. The baby moved inside her, and her smile deepened to joy. "Did you feel that?"

"Yes." He peered at her belly for a moment. "I can't believe we created this."

"I can," she said softly.

He kissed her for a moment and leaned back. "Thank you."

"For what?"

"For giving me hope that we can have life in all this darkness."

She cupped his face through his beard and locked lips with him again. "No, thank you."

They went down the stairs and into the parlor. Gwen snuggled on the couch near the fireplace with Becky and Lydia, and he took a seat behind his desk. He studied his map of southern Iowa. It was his only pastime. He was consumed by preparing their defense, and there was only one major factor keeping them alive: the Mississippi River. Even with an excellent physical barrier, there was so much ground to cover and so few people to do so.

The door opened and the chill of the outside came in. When the door didn't close for a moment, Steele rose to his feet. Scratching came through the doorway, followed by a grunt. John emerged in the foyer with an evergreen tree halfway through the door. He flashed Steele a sheepish grin. "Can't have Christmas without no tree."

Steele smiled, grabbing the tree by the trunk. "Let me help." Together they hefted the tree and carried it inside.

"Let's put it over yonder by the fireplace, why don't ya," John said. They ambled it near the fireplace.

"Oh John, it's wonderful." Lydia's hands went to her face and she covered her mouth. "Beck, can you run down to the basement and get the tree stand?"

"Sure thing, Gram." Becky smiled and left the room.

They stood the tree up, and John leaned back, admiring it. "Just because times are tough, don't mean we ain't gonna have a proper Christmas. We never once didn't have no tree, and we ain't about to start."

Tears came to Gwen's eyes. "Pa, it's so special."

Becky returned with the stand, and they set the tree upright in the corner. Lydia and Becky collected boxes of ornaments from the basement. Smiles were free and joyous as they hung ornaments. Each and every one represented a memory, taking everyone back to happier times.

Lydia and Gwen put on a pot for hot chocolate. Lydia had discovered a dusty box of the stuff in the back of their pantry and demanded they use it.

Steele stood alongside John. "This was a great surprise."

"Twas."

"I was thinking about surprising Gwen with something."

John regarded him for a moment. "Is that so?"

"It is." Opening his palm, he revealed a small square box. "I wanted to ask your blessing."

John raised a frail-speckled hand into the air to prevent him from continuing. "She's her own woman. If she has ya, I'll have ya too."

"I think she will," Steele said, with a smile.

"I think she will too." John put a hand on Steele's back and tried to shake him in happiness. "You are a big one." He wagged a finger at him. "I could pin a cow with one hand back in the day." His hand shook as he held it, forming a fist.

"No doubt in my mind you could."

"You'd be good to remember that, son." All of his words were in jest, more of an obligation between men. Customary words that men felt needed to be said despite the reality of modern times.

"I will."

The grandfather gulped back his emotions. "I watched that girl grow up. Took care of her." He stuck the corner of his tongue in his cheek.

"I'll take care of her. Hell, she takes care of me most the time."

The old man nodded fiercely, swallowing his emotions, a mixture of joy and change and a remembrance of the past. "Good. That one would bring in a lot of strays." He released his grandfatherly hold on Steele's neck and smiled at him.

"Hopefully, I'm the last one."

"You will be, son. She's a good one."

"And what are you two talking about?" Gwen asked as she came in the room with Lydia and Becky.

"Nothing, dear," John said.

Lydia eyed him with a knowing look. "You can't hide from me, Mr. Reynolds."

"Bah, I ain't got no time for your inquisition."

Lydia snorted. "You'll tell me, John. I'll get to the truth."

Steele gulped down the dryness of his parchment-like throat. He was more nervous now than when he'd faced a hundred infected. He was more nervous than when he'd fought and killed other men. Those things were second nature to him now, including watching men die. Even if he never got used to it, he knew it, he'd experienced it and could wrap his mind around it, but this. This was a whole new game. He walked over to the Christmas tree.

He bent down near a box of ornaments pretending to dig around inside. "Gwen," his voice croaked like a teenage boy. "Could you help me with this one?"

She smiled and stood, walking over to him. "You can't do it?"

He wrapped his hand around it and shook his head, it was the only general motor skill he could eke out in his nervousness. *Should I be this nervous? Is everyone this skittish before it happens? Can't back out now. The wheels are in motion.* He tried to swallow, but his tongue balled in his throat.

She knew he was in distress and half-smiled at him. "Are you okay?"

He nodded dumbly and let himself drop to a knee. She turned her head inquisitively at him. Lydia gasped.

Opening his mouth for a moment, he closed it quick and took a deep breath. "I can't tell you what this world may bring, but I will do anything for you and our child because you make this world worth living, and I can't live in it without you." He opened his hand revealing a simple gold ring. No princess-cut diamonds. No precious sapphires or rubies. Just a plain gold band that symbolized all he had to give.

Gwen's hands went to her mouth, a younger replica of Lydia doing the same. Becky covered hers with a single hand.

"This ain't flashy nor expensive." He gave a nervous laugh, holding out the ring.

"It doesn't need to be," she whispered.

With a knowing smile, he fixed his eyes on her. "Gwen Reynolds, will you marry me?"

Tears exploded from the corners of her eyes, chin bobbing. "Yes! I will marry you, Mark Steele."

He slipped the ring on her finger, and she helped him up. They embraced long and hard, both crying and kissing one another in a shaking union of two souls. "I knew I'd make an honest woman out of you."

She laughed, gripping his hands harder. "Stop it. You know I hate that."

"What? Being honest?"

She tilted her head to the side, and they let go. John hugged his granddaughter and shook Steele's hand vigorously. Lydia and Becky hugged everyone, and they all shared laughter and happiness and joy.

When everything settled down, John eyed Steele for a moment. "So when are we going to do the wedding?"

Steele shrugged his shoulders. "I hadn't thought about it much."

"Christmas Eve," Gwen said.

Steele raised his eyebrows at her. "That's only two days."

"Yes, Christmas Eve. We both know what dangers lurk out there, and I don't want to live another day not married to you."

"As good of a reason as any," Lydia said with a nod.

John smiled. "Aye, it is. That'll give me a couple days to round up a few pigs from the Carters."

"A damn fine plan. Tell him we'll pay whatever he asks. It's the Christmas spirit." The joy felt unusual in Steele when they'd grown used to so much turmoil and struggle. It was as if laughter and life were a foreign language that he was learning for the first time.

He laughed and shared a glance with Gwen before he turned to John.

"Would you care to be our officiant?"

John's smile deepened from ear to ear as he placed a hand over his heart. "It would be an honor."

MARGIE
North of Burlington, IA

Gripping her trembling body tight, she scrambled through the gray tree trunks. Her clothes stiffened as she ran, the water and the cold air threatening to freeze her literally in her tracks. The timber stopped before a white-covered field. Square structures rose up in the distance. Her feet were blocks of ice and she stumbled, numbness overtaking any sensation.

She trudged toward the buildings, the promise of humanity growing with every step. Ignoring the footsteps in the snow, she knew this refuge was her only hope. In a disoriented struggle, she collapsed on the front porch of a new-looking farmhouse. She brought her fist up in a single knock and fell into a ball.

***

She forced her eyes open. She could feel the various parts of her body and she was warm. *I'll never leave this place*, she thought. Snuggling deeper into the comforter, she went back to sleep.

"She's awake. I saw her move. Get mom," came a voice from her room.

A minute later a woman with maple syrup-colored hair and glasses appeared in front of her. "How are you feeling?" Her voice was had a nasally twang to it.

"Warm," she managed to say.

"You weren't when we found you or more like you found us. Where'd you come from?"

"I was on a boat going to Clinton."

"Clinton? This is no weather to be on the water." She paused. "Or in it."

Margie sat up and moved to a seated position covering her breasts with her hands. The woman bent near the bed.

"Your clothes are still drying. I figured you could borrow some of mine. We're about the same size." The woman placed a set of clothes on the bed and turned away while Margie dressed.

Margie hurried to cover herself, throwing a shirt over upper body. "What's your name?"

"Beth." A young teenage girl stood near the door. "That's Grace. My husband is Dennis, and our boys are Nicholas and Austin. Who are you?"

"My name is Margie." Mother of none. Wife of a corpse. Lover of a murder victim. She slipped on wool socks. "Thank you. Where are we?"

Cocking her head, Beth's curls jumped. "You don't know where we are? Where you from?"

"Michigan."

"Figures. We're in Kingston, Iowa. Why were you in the river?"

"Men ambushed us."

"Ambushed?"

"A traitorous biker gang. We were all militia forces under Captain Steele."

"You part of the group down in Burlington?"

"Yes, do you know them?"

"We know *of* them. We're hesitant to send our boys down for training when we need them here." Her eyes searched Margie for understanding why she kept her family out of harm's way.

"I must warn them. Can you take me?"

A man appeared in the doorway. He was over six feet and had thick arms that she bet used to be lined with muscle, but age had added a layer of fat over them. He had a blond mustache. "She's awake."

"Yes, dear, been talking about an ambush. She needs to get down to Burlington."

"Is that so?" he rubbed his mustache with concern. "An ambush? Don't sound good. By who?"

"Traitors. My entire team is dead."

"Shit." He sighed through his mustache.

Beth gave him a disappointed look. "Honey, please."

He pushed his mustache up with his lower lip. "Sorry. All right. I was trying to avoid heading down there, but I suppose it's time for us to see what all the fuss is about." He yelled over his shoulder. "Austin and Nick, get the horses ready. We're headed down to Burlington."

"Do you have any guns?" Margie asked. She read the woman and then the man.

"Guns?" he tilted his head. "Hell, we got plenty of guns."

"I need a gun."

"What kind? We got ARs, shotguns, .308s, a shit ton of handguns."

"Language," Beth chided with a disapproving look.

"Sorry, sweetheart."

"I'd prefer a 30-06 hunting rifle, but whatever bolt-action you got."

He smiled. "I think we can cover you."

***

Red Clare stood with her hands on her hips, a cigarette hanging from her lips. Her gang surrounded them in a menacing mass of women. They pointed guns at Margie and Dennis along with his sons.

Dennis held his hands in the air. "Shit, Margie, I thought they were the good guys."

Margie kept her arms high, praying to God she was right. "They are."

"They aren't taking too kindly to us."

"They will."

Red Clare took a few steps closer and coughed a wheezy laugh. "I thought you were all dead?"

"Not all of us."

"War Child said you turned on them on the river."

Margie raised her chin an inch. "It was the other way around. He ambushed us. Killed the soldiers and my crew."

"Don't surprise me. Never trust a War Machine. Ain't that right, ladies?" Red Clare said.

Chuckles and smiles came from the ladies, and they lowered their weapons. "Come on in before you freeze a tit." She waved them into the warehouse. Dennis's face flushed scarlet. "This is the militia? These women?"

"Yes, come on."

She swung off her horse and walked her mount toward the warehouse. Her ride hesitated near the door, its oval black eyes skittish. Tugging the reins, she attempted to maneuver the scared beast through the door. Her companions stayed atop their animals staring at her. She pulled the reins harder, trying to lead the wary horse into the building.

Peering over her horse, she said. "You'll freeze to death if you stay outside."

Dennis shook his head. "This don't seem right. If there's trouble, we're leaving." The men dismounted.

As Margie managed to goad the animal inside, she said to herself. "If there's trouble, we'll die."

They entered the warehouse tying the reins of their horses on a support beam inside.

"Why don't you warm up near the fire? I've got to talk to Red Clare."

Dennis nodded and his eyes shifted uncomfortably at the female bikers. But he did as she suggested and led his boys near the fire.

Margie marched for Red Clare's commandeered office, closing the door behind her. "May I?"

"Course."

The chair puffed dust as Margie plopped into it.

A cigarette burned in Red Clare's mouth and she sucked on it, flaring the orange tip, releasing tiny gray tendrils. "So you're telling me War Child is a big old liar?" Leather scraped as she took out her handgun and placed it on the desk. She rotated the pistol, pointing it in Margie's direction. Her hand rested nearby, fingers drumming on her desk.

It was hard to pry her eyes from the handgun, but she forced herself, connecting with Red Clare and clasping one hand tightly in the other. "Yes. His men slaughtered us on the river."

Surprise unfurled on Red Clare's face, fingers drumming. "How'd you escape?"

Margie made a fist with one of her hands as the other rubbed the top. "Tony shielded me from bullets with his body. I dove into the water." She exhaled forcefully.

Red Clare blew smoke out her nose and leaned forward, putting the cigarette out in an ashtray piled with butts. "What do you expect me to do about it? Turn the War Machines over to the cops?"

Her thumb dug into the meat of her other hand. "I expect you to do the right thing. He's betrayed Captain Steele, and we have to tell him before War Child can hatch whatever plan he's made."

The female biker president scratched her head. "War Child is a devious old fool, but I'm not getting my girls all shot up over a squabble between those two."

Red Clare's eyes were two orbs devoid of pity, and Margie wanted to wring her neck for it. "My people got all shot up for nothing. He's a traitor."

The other woman sat silently, her mouth settling into a tight pucker.

Pressing her thumb harder into the meat of her hand, Margie said, "My crew is a bunch of frozen corpses on a pontoon boat. All of them dead."

"I heard you the first time, sweetie." Her tone shut Margie's mouth. "Exactly what I'm trying to avoid for my girls. And I take care of my girls. It's your word against his, except he's got a whole crew at his back. Steele's got an army. There's no way War Child is going to go up against him by himself."

"What if he's not? What if there is someone helping him?"

"Honey, you ever hear about playing your odds?" Red Clare leaned back in her chair. Margie stared at her in silence, anger seeping from her eyes. This woman was supposed to be an ally, part of the greater good against the marching death.

"Why do you think all the bikers banded together to begin with? Why do you think we followed Thunder and then Steele? We had a lot better shot together than apart." With a creak, she bounced forward in her chair. "And when this is over, we will be stronger together once again. The boys can off each other to see who's got the bigger Johnson, but all the while my girls are safe, whole, and uninvolved." She paused. "Oh yeah, did I mention, not dead."

Margie peered down at her hands. *Would it always be the strong over the weak? Would someone not stand for what was just?* Her hands released from one another finding taut freedom. Her right hand found the handle of her knife and she drew it with speed and angry purpose. She pointed it at Red Clare, jabbing it close to her face. The biker didn't flinch.

"Honey, what is sticking me gonna get you? A moment to feel better. I'm just telling you how it is. Not how you want it to be."

Margie shook her head. "No. You make your choice here and now. You're going to help us or die. I don't care. Your people will kill me either way."

"Sister, you got a lot of nerve coming in here threatening me."

Margie eyed the woman shaking her head in disgust. "Not you too."

"I already told you. I do what's best for my club."

With a twirl of the blade, Margie flipped her knife and slammed it between Red Clare's fingers. Eyes bugged out of the biker's head. Margie lunged, grasping for the pistol.

"You bitch."

She stuck her index finger at the woman. "I don't give a shit anymore. Do the right thing."

Clare worked the blade back and forth out of the desk.

Margie cocked the gun, centering it on her face. "Do the right thing."

Red Clare's puckered mouth turned into a wrinkled smile. "You mean to miss?" She wheezed a cough that turned into hysterical laughter. Her breasts shook with laughter. She clutched her hand to her chest, struggling to breathe.

"You are much more of a cunt than you look," Red Clare said. She shook her head in amazement.

"Make your choice."

The biker president narrowed her eyes. "I see your point. I'll help ya and Steele, but under one condition."

Margie twisted her head, suspecting a trap. "What is it?"

With a slow hand, she grabbed her package of cigarettes and popped another in her mouth, bending to light it. Inhaling, she said. "You join my club."

Margie snorted. "Me join a biker club?"

"Those are my terms. Otherwise you'll have to pull the trigger and get gunned down outside." Her assassination of Red Clare would surely lead to Dennis and his boys' death. *What's a few more lives to my death tally?* But her heart wasn't in getting more innocent people killed.

Red Clare flipped the knife around and offered it to Margie.

"All right. I'll join your club, but after you help Captain Steele." She eyed the hilt as if it could bite.

"Deal it is." She smiled under her cigarette. "Go on."

Margie snatched her knife back, holstering it. "How do I know you'll stay true to your word?"

Red Clare inhaled smoke, and the cigarette flared orange. "Can't see how'd you know?"

"Swear to something."

Smoke drifted from her mouth in robust ringlets that hung in the air. "I'd swear to God, but I've seen men swear on that and kill a man a second later. Don't mean much."

"Your club, your sisters, your colors, swear on them," Margie spat.

"Fair enough. I swear on the Seven Sisters I'll uphold my word." She put a hand on her patch and nodded. "There."

A wrinkled hand stuck out, wavering, and Margie took it. Strongly gripping her palm, Red Clare pulled her close. "You never answered. Did you mean to miss?"

Margie held her gaze. "No."

A yellowing smile spread on Red Clare's lips. "That's my girl."

AHMED
Northern Missouri

The flames leapt like yellow sunflowers in a storm, fluttering from windows. The house blackened around the windows and doors as the fire fought to free itself from the confines of the structure.

Jim jumped from his horse, and Ahmed stumbled from the saddle behind. Both men sprinted for the house.

"Sadie!" Ahmed screamed.

He glanced at the open-eyed body of Kelly lying in the snow like she'd fell asleep while walking outside. Jim put his jacket up to his face, leaning inside the burning house.

"Barb!" he shouted. "Betty! Charley!"

The ceiling bellowed as it sunk inward and Ahmed gave it a worried eye. "Sadie!" Covering his face, he ducked through the doorway.

Inside, it was like an oven; the heat almost overwhelmed him. The fire swirled, a snowdrift filled with oranges and yellows.

"I'll check the bedrooms," Ahmed yelled. The ceiling sagged downward, struggling to maintain its form. Nodding, Jim dodged into the kitchen.

The roar of the inferno dominated any other sound in the house. A line of fire formed, blocking his path. Ahmed gathered his feet beneath him and jumped it, kicking his feet high, the lapping tongues of scalding heat slicing at him from below. Bounding to the end of the hall, he stuck a foot into a closed door. Fragments of wood burst, revealing a bedroom empty of people.

He turned around and kicked another door. A bed and nightstand and no people. "Sadie!" No one answered his call.

Behind him, the blaze expanded its quest for oxygen and fuel, growing taller and reaching chest level. He would never make that jump back to the front of the house. The flames spread along the ceiling in a spiderweb of orange and gold.

He fled for a bedroom. The windows were boarded with random two-by-fours and plywood forming a crisscross wooden barrier. They blackened beneath the fiery onslaught, charring and smoldering in response.

Ahmed planted a foot into the wood, and it bounced off like it was rubber. He kicked again and again, his boot beating his way through the boards to freedom as the fire came for him.

Light shone through the smashed holes. His hands blazed as he tore at burning pieces. Black smoke filled his lungs like a breathable evil forcing him to cough hysterically. He threw wood to the side, trying to breathe. Smoke inhalation would always bring you down before the fire. His lungs sputtered violently for reprieve from the black cloud.

He forced his body through the hole in the wood, squeezing into the window frame. The flames inching across the room licked at his feet and legs.

"Come on!" Fear drove him and the innate desire for survival. His shoulders free, he threw himself out the window. He toppled into the half-inch of accumulation and rolled from his back to his stomach over and over.

The snow watered and steamed as it embraced him, cooling his fiery body. He patted himself, crawling away from the building. His breath came out in fits and starts, his mind still in shock that he almost had burned alive for Sadie. Putting his hands into the white reprieve, they were met with frigid ecstasy, and he stood.

Walking around the other side of the house took him back to the other men.

"Ahmed," Jim said. Anger hung around the corners of his eyes. "I was hoping you'd found them."

Sucking in clean air greedily, Ahmed shook his head no. "I didn't."

"Bodies? Dogs?" Jim gulped. His face was coated in black soot.

"No bodies. No dogs."

Jim's chest heaved. "They have them. Fuck." He crouched down and wiped the hair from Kelly's neck. Her face was cool and pale and her eyes unblinking, glass marbles with blue centers.

Lee's voice carried from the timber nearby. "I found Barb."

Jim jumped upright. Lee held out a hand stopping anyone from coming closer. "She's gone, Jimmy."

"Traitors," Jim whispered. He stood facing his men. "They soiled the truce of the Grossman Farm."

"It could have been Macleod," Ahmed said softly.

"Could it? Sly is his fucking bitch. He had a hand in it." His eyes stared off into the distance. "This is a war of extermination, and we are on the losing end of it."

Lee placed an arm around Andy, holding the young man. "Where are we going to go? Foxworth house isn't too far."

"No. There's only one thing left. Finish them before they finish us." He blinked, the whites of his eyes reddened and distant. "You always knew it would come to this." Final absolution settled in his eyes. Ahmed could see it. He'd seen it in men since the outbreak, never before. But everyone he knew before wasn't facing life and death every day, kill or be killed situations. Victory or death. It was like being trapped into a singular purpose that would lead to death or mental burnout, a state of shell shock.

"If there aren't bodies, they have the others. That means they want to come to terms." Eyes drifted toward Ahmed. Every man had heard Macleod's speech. In all their eyes, he read the same thing: if we turn him over our troubles disappear. Even if it meant subservience to the likes of Macleod.

Ahmed gulped down his rising fear. This wasn't the first time men had thought about turning on him, an easy scapegoat for all the world's woes. But he knew if these men turned on him, he wouldn't survive. He was dependent upon their good faith. "I know what you're thinking." Ahmed leveled his chin. "Do what you have to do."

The Singleton party stared at him. Andy looked away. Jim's icy eyes bored him. "I won't be played and I ain't given you to dem. That's just one less gun.

No. We end this today." Jim looked at the ground for a moment. "Foxworth boys. Go home. I appreciate the sentiment. You're good folk, but this ain't your fight."

Paul stood firm. He was the oldest of the three brothers and in his late thirties. He had a lithe farmer's build and was taller than his two brothers, Brett and the youngest, not even eighteen, Ford. "We're in it now. Sly and that biker saw us. If they don't come for us now, it won't be long before they burn us out. Better to see it through."

Jim nodded. "Good boys." He gestured with a hand. "At least let Ford go back and let the lady folk know."

Brett Foxworth gave a short nod. "Boy, go back to Ma."

"I'm not running away."

"You ain't runnin'. I told you to do it." He shook the teenager. "You go and take care of Ma. Tell her to get west to Aunt Carol's. You hear? Aunt Carol's. I'll come for you when we's done settling the score."

"But, Brett. I can fight."

"No buts. You can fight. You're a brave lad. Go. Aunt Carol's."

Ford wiped his eyes and hopped atop his mount. He steered him away and heeled the horse hard. The horse and rider disappeared into the forest. Then there were six men all affiliated with the Singleton's clan. Cold men with rosy cheeks who'd been outside for too long but had no place to go other than their rival's homestead to warm themselves on the flames of their enemies' corpses. An action that meant a fight to death, and with such low numbers, Ahmed was sure their mission was a fool's errand.

Without a word, the men mounted their horses. Jim swatted his horse with the reins. Ahmed followed suit, whipping the leather back and forth on the beast's neck as its hooves beat the ground, speeding up until they were galloping.

Thunder rumbled in the air as the group pounded the hard, crisp snow-covered earth with hurried hooves. Each man kept his eyes on the indentation of the road, making peace with his god while knowing there wasn't much time left for peace.

STEELE
Camp Forge, IA

"They're not there?" Steele said into the microphone. The fire danced on the lightless Christmas tree. Red and green balls and silver bells and gold-sided ornaments reflected the flames. Homemade popsicle stick and macaroni keepsakes from Gwen and Becky's childhood and a crayon-drawn candle made by Haley the year before embodied a Christmas spirit that refused to die.

"Affirmative. Your troops have not arrived. Captain Heath has waited long enough. He's sending a single company north to discover what happened at Outpost Barron."

"I don't know why they haven't shown."

Steele held the radio mic to his head, tapping it. He hadn't relayed Thunder's betrayal to the colonel, feeling it was best left until he had decided what to do. The room was empty save for him, and it was odd to be having the conversations with Kinnick without his trusted lieutenant, Thunder, there to advise.

The radio rested silent for a moment. "Captain Heath will be looking forward to their arrival."

"As will I." He studied the map, looking at the river and talking to himself. "What happened, War Child?"

"Oh, and Captain Steele."

"Yes sir?"

"Have a merry Christmas."

A short grin formed on Steele's face. "Merry Christmas, sir."

"Enjoy it, okay? Try to forget this bullshit world and enjoy it." *What he's really saying is that this is going to be our last Christmas here on earth, so make peace with that and spend it the best you can.*

"I will, sir. You as well."

There was a bit of mirth shrouded in sadness in Kinnick's voice. "I will, Captain. I'd be lucky if we find a can of spam for us to feast upon."

Steele was acutely aware that he was going to be dining on roast pig. "You need to come our way, Colonel. We're roasting a pig."

Mirth filled Kinnick's voice. "Did you clear that with your commanding officer?"

"I'd have to ask him to clear it with my to-be wife."

Kinnick's chuckle came through the earpiece. "That is quite the occasion. Sorry to miss it."

"I'm sorry you'll miss it too."

They sat in silence on either end of the radios. Neither man knew what more to say. A somber reflection of their ongoing struggle settled upon them, keeping them quiet.

Kinnick's voice won over. "Keep us abreast of any developments."

"Yes, sir." Steele hung the microphone back on the side of his radio and flicked the power switch off. The battery life on the device would only last so long.

He eyed the fire crackling in the fireplace. War Child's unit could have befallen anything. Boat trouble. The infected. Jackson's men. Hell, literally any number of things could have caused their failure to arrive and Steele didn't have any idea.

"Something must have happened, or they are making a real slow go of it."

A knock on the door pulled him away from his thought. He stood and listened as Lydia answered. "Pastor."

Steele moved away from his desk and into the doorway off the foyer.

The tall wraith-like man, wearing a heavy black coat, filled the doorframe. His air and appearance gave one the impression of a slender Puritan judge ready to disseminate swift biblical justice. A long-fingered hand gracefully gestured. "May I, Mrs. Reynolds?"

Lydia gave a slight bow of her head. "Of course, Pastor."

He removed his outer garment and hung it on the coatrack next to the door.

"Pastor," Steele said, watching the man with distaste. "Come in."

Steele led the way inside the parlor and moved back around to his desk. He sat down and leaned back in his chair. "Why don't you take a seat by the fire and get warm?"

The pastor took his time finding a seat, meandering around the Christmas tree. He studied the decorations with a closemouthed smile.

"What a joyous sight in such troubled times!" He clasped his hands in front of him, sending a sharp little barb his way. "I didn't take you and the Reynolds for the religious type."

Steele kept his mouth tight. "We welcome the celebration of Christmas and the joy it brings to everyone."

Nodding, the pastor said, "I see. Christ's birth is a cause for joy and celebration."

"So are weddings," Steele said with a smile. "Gwen and I are getting married."

The pastor showed him some teeth now. "A very joyous time indeed. Go forth and populate the earth. We are blessed by the relative peace in this turmoil."

"Yes, we are. We can't stop living life because times are hard."

"Very true. Where's your bride-to-be? I must thank her for the medicine. Many of my people grow stronger every day because of her tenacity."

"She is with her grandfather picking out hogs and other food for the wedding feast."

"She will be glowing I'm sure." The pastor folded his hands together and rubbed them. "With all this talk of happiness, I hate to bring this up, but my reason for stopping was to discuss the fate of the Red Stripes."

Steele cleared his throat. "Go on."

The pastor's mouth stretched downward in a frown and his voice grew somber. "Over the past week, I've lost nine people to the flu, including four children." His lower jaw trembled. "Children." He averted his eyes for a moment toward the tree. "They were taken far before their time. And for what? Greed and wanton lust for life. Thunder and his men sat on that medicine for days until the *venerable* Ms. Tess discovered their treachery."

Steele eyed the distraught man. "I'm sorry for your losses. Many others are very ill. We almost lost Haley because of their deception."

The pastor's voice grew stronger. "Justice must be served. Innocents have perished because of Thunder's treason. I know I have been quick to pass judgment on those I've found guilty in the past." He folded his hands in front of his body like he was about to start a prayer. "I recognize there are other ways now and that God shows himself in many forms. But I urge you, these men are vile and have proven their untrustworthiness."

The Red Stripes' defection still soured his gut like he'd eaten a bad piece of meat. Every day the group of loyal men that surrounded him shrank, and they inched a bit closer to defeat. "Justice should be served." He paused, his gut churning. "What do you think is fair for the crimes?"

"You see, Mr. Steele. I am not in charge here. That decision does not fall on my shoulders."

"But I'm asking for your advice. What would you have me do?"

"In the past, I would have them burnt at the stake." The pastor's answer was flat and honest with no hint of duplicity. And Steele wholeheartedly believed the man.

"Admittedly, I have grown since then, but does this case not warrant an eye for an eye? In this camp alone, eighteen people have died and some of those were children. Some may still not pull through. This is a grievous act and I believe it warrants punishment of the most capital kind."

Sighing, Steele said, "This deserves punishment."

The pastor spread his fingers wide. "If we don't want to punish them with death, we could exile them into the wild like you did the soldiers. That way you can wash your hands of them and let God's elements do their work. A banishment if you will."

Steele stroked his beard. The flames danced in the fireplace. "Let me think on this. These men have been reliable in the past."

The pastor leaned forward. "I think you should move sooner rather than later. Your position looks weak by not punishing them. I've heard rumblings throughout the camp."

"Like your sermons in the fields?"

The thin-cheeked man tilted his head to the side as if Steele's words hurt him. "If you heard any negative speak, it was out of frustration not genuine malice. I sing your praises for your quick resolution of the matter." He dipped his head to Steele in a bit of acquiescence.

"My position is not weak, but it is weaker than it was. The fortifications are a great help in hardening our position against the dead or otherwise. We can fit hundreds if not thousands more inside the camp if we need to. Please try to quell any rumors of weakness. If we don't stand together, there is no chance for us."

"Of course." The pastor dipped his head again. "But what are you going to do?"

Steele got to his feet. "It's the holiday season. I'm getting married in a couple days. Let's decide their fate when tempers have calmed. Let them experience one more Christmas."

The pastor copied him, rising. "I understand your decision." He offered Steele his hand. His palm was damp, and a general coolness surrounded the man. A grin overtook his lips. "Merry Christmas, Mr. Steele. I look forward to your coming wedding and give my sincerest regards to your bride."

"And Merry Christmas to you." The fire crackled and popped, and the men released hands. "I will tell Gwen she has your warm regards."

"Please do."

ALVARADO
La Crosse, Wisconsin

"Rasmussen is going to take Riddle and the rest of the team across to Captain Butler's command."

Riddle shook his head with vehemence. He knew where she was heading with her orders already. "No, Major."

"This is going to be a running fight and you can't run. I will not debate this."

The sergeant's jaw set. "Then let me distract the bastards while you get planted."

Her eyes narrowed. "You're a stellar Marine, Sergeant. I'm not going to lose you to something stupid like a last stand."

"You can't carry all the explosives by yourself."

"There isn't much left without the front sled. I'll get as far south as we dare to go and head back to Butler's." She could feel the eyes of her fellow Marines upon her. There was admiration in them, respect, and a bit of fear.

"I will disobey your orders, ma'am." Riddle's nose flared at the end of his last word. His loyalty and dedication were admirable and exhausting at the same time.

"You will not. This is a single Marine mission. It will be me. I only need you to clear the way to the river. Then we will part." With fierce eyes, she dared any of them to suggest otherwise.

The Marine sergeant shook his head in disgust.

She ignored him. "Foster and Finch. You will be responsible for carrying Sergeant Riddle. Do not take him anywhere other than Captain Butler's base. The rest of you are to cover them while they move. Do you understand?"

"Yes, ma'am," Foster and Finch said in reluctant unison.

"We got your back, Major," said O'Bannon. The tall Marine looked down on her. His features had thawed in the relative warmth of the office but only a sliver.

"You will follow orders."

"We follow you, ma'am," said Johnson. The thick-bodied African-American Marine met her gaze steady, unafraid of her mission.

"Sergeant, I blame you for their brazen disregard of my orders."

"Ma'am, you should blame yourself. They follow you into the jaws of death out of respect, not disrespect."

"I will not risk the lives of Marines over another mile of river."

Riddle's wide jaw worked as he clenched it. "Major, by asking these men to not accompany you into the hornet's nest, you put their integrity as Marines on the line and those of the Marines that have gone before. Give them that honor."

She growled, shaking her head. They were stubborn and tough, and as much as their insubordination irked her, their tenacity gave her hope. Hope that could only be gained by having a squad of ornery Marines at your back. "You Marines are why I love the Corps. Like a pack of cornered dogs, you are going to follow me onto that ice no matter what I say. I can see it in your eyes." She stopped taking them in. She knew they weren't fearless.

All men and women knew the darkness of fear. But these Marines would fight, and that was the spark that burned in their eyes. A fire that overcame the cavernous depths of terror to confront death face-to-face.

"Affirmative. Finch and Foster are still on the hook for Riddle. I will not leave you to die for nothing." The muscles in her face quivered as if she were asking them to perform a task so alien they wouldn't know how to do it. The smallest of grins spread across her lips.

Finch pointed at her. "Did she just smile?"

Her Marines looked at one another in amazement.

Johnson shook his head, his voice rumbling. "No way. She was baring her teeth like a pit bull before they attack."

Rasmussen cough-laughed. "Like a badger or something."

Riddle matched her smile. "That was the first and last time any of you will see a smile out of the major. Remember where you were."

A small chuckle snuck from her throat. "You're correct, Sergeant." Expressing joy wasn't her strong suit. It hadn't been even when she was young. She'd been serious about her schoolwork and sports, always striving to reach the next level. Now she was freezing to death in Wisconsin with a handful of Marines, and she chose this place to make herself vulnerable to these men, no, these Marines. After so much death and adversity, what difference was a joyful crack in her persona going to make?

Her close-lipped grin faded. "When I said we'll be running, I wasn't kidding. At most, we will have a minute between blasts. If we time it right, we can be almost through before we attract even more attention from the dead. I will plant. The rest of you are pulling security. Understood?"

"Yes, Major," they said.

"We keep moving on this one. There'll not be time to clear the blast radius." She didn't want to say it, but she wanted her orders clear-cut. "If you fall, we move on."

Riddle's lips tightened knowing that his survival earlier was a calculation against the odds of completing the mission.

"Hello?" a voice whispered outside the room.

Guns pointed toward the door.

A soft knock sounded off the door. She nodded to Finch and sidestepped so that when the door was opened, she'd have an angle on shooting offset and not directly in the fatal funnel, dead center of the doorway.

The Marine twisted the doorknob and took a step back along the wall. Weapons were aimed in that direction, fingers resting silently on triggers.

"Don't shoot," the man called out. The African-American man in camouflage held up his hands.

She recognized him immediately. "Odom?"

"Reporting for duty."

"How?"

The Marine walked inside rubbing his hands together. His dark skin had a bluish tinge to it.

"Gave them the slip." Odom blew on his hands, nodding his head as if distracting and leading a horde of the dead was an easy feat.

"Welcome back, Lance Corporal. Give him a blanket."

Odom slapped hands with his fellow Marines but only briefly as he hunched over, trying to keep in his warmth. His body visibly shook. Foster unzipped a pack and pulled a foil blanket. It wouldn't do much, but at least they could offer him a chance to warm up. Exhausted, he took a seat next to Riddle.

"You all right, Sarge?"

"Bum leg. How'd you find us?"

"When the river blew, I was circling back down this bank. River ice broke even farther than we'd planted. Enough to make it unstable. If enough of them get on it, it'll go." He looked like a man wearing a crinkly tin spaceman poncho. "I followed the broken river until I got to the point where it wasn't. Saw the sled still out there. Figured you couldn't be far. Came in here."

Alvarado's gut jumped. "The sled's still out there? It wasn't blown?"

Odom nodded. "Yes, ma'am. It's about five feet from the edge of the ice, but it doesn't look stable. I wouldn't trust it."

A smile tinged on her lips again, but she held it in this time. She didn't want her reputation being spoiled for Odom or any other Marines in her command. If the rumor got out she was going soft, it would take years to pummel that mushy image back into the mean-spirited major she was today.

"Best news I've heard all day."

The best news she had all day was that an improvised sled of explosives teetered on the edge of the ice, and she was going to lead a handful of Marines in a running battle to retrieve and use them. Like any true Devil Dog, inwardly she beamed with morbid delight.

THE PASTOR
Camp Forge, IA

The pastor trudged carefully across the crisp white ground, his stride taking him far with each step. "Imbecile," he said to himself. "He is unfit to lead these people. His mercy will be the end of him."

He followed a worn path of brown frozen mud. He circled through cabins, the musky wood-fire smoke dominating the air. Pushing on a door, he entered his cabin. Most of his disciples waited for him. They all shared his domicile, always wanting to be closer to him to share in his holiness by proximity.

In an instant, Peter was by his side, taking his coat. "Father, how was your meeting?" He hung the garment near the fireplace.

The pastor stood in front of the fire for a moment, warming his long fingers. "It's just as I thought. The man is weak. Even with the planted evidence, he is still indecisive about the Red Stripes' fate."

"Father, we've gotten the signal."

The pastor smiled, watching the flames dance. "Ahead of schedule. Well done."

"Why don't we move on him now?" Luke asked.

The pastor turned around, putting his back to the warmth.

Luke licked his lips, salivating at the thought.

"Patience, young Luke." The long-haired man had always been rash and violent, an unpredictable follower at best, but savage men had their purposes if corralled properly. "We put nothing to chance. The timing must be perfect and the surprise ultimate."

"Yes, Father," Luke bowed his head.

The pastor tapped his chin as he thought. "Mr. Steele is getting married. I believe this to be the sign that we've been waiting for."

"At his wedding?" Peter asked. Discontent shown in his eyes. "There will be much innocent blood spent."

"No, no," the pastor said with a shake of his head. He eyed his lieutenant for a moment. *Is he lacking in faith?* Peter lowered his eyes, knowing his place. "As God's instruments, he would not have us interfere with their matrimony, but they will surely be drinking all night long on Christmas Eve." He regarded his followers. "A most foul sacrilege when time would be better spent on holy reflection."

Matthew ducked his head. "Amen."

Peter mumbled an, "Amen."

The fire leapt in his eyes, engulfing a burning farmhouse, the crackling and surrender of wood to the flame chimed in his ears, and he could taste the ash in his mouth. He blinked, his eyes coming back to his world inside the cabin.

All eyes were upon him. Eager eyes. Eyes willing to drink in whatever potion he gave or follow wherever he may lead. There would be no deviation or contradiction from them. They were loyal to the core. He need not inspire because God led him, and therefore, his men would follow him without asking. Faith was a powerful tool.

"Steele has it all wrong. He's grasping for any way to keep his people together when the answer has been clear the entire time. He needs God but refuses him in the same breath. It's the only thing that will triumph over the dead. Not guns or tanks or bombs, but God and faith." He made sure to finish his sentence with eyes on Peter. His big lieutenant dipped his head under his gaze.

His disciples nodded their heads in assertion. The answers were clear and easy in all their eyes.

"This camp was built on a weak structure for no foundation can be set without faith in God to keep it strong."

He stroked the head of his carpenter's hammer, feeling the roughness of the rusted surface. "So we must knock this hollow structure from underneath him and build anew an edifice founded on God's love and his power."

"Yes, Father. We shall rise," Luke proclaimed.

"The Red Stripes are imprisoned. Steele's forces are spread out and weak. They will be hungover and tired the day after the wedding." He unfurled his arms wide over his people. "We shall be victorious."

"Should we commit such violence on Christmas?" Peter asked.

Voicing your dissent? "Do you disagree?"

"No, Father. I only wish the Lord's will be done."

Or are you denying God's will?

"We have no place for doubt." He stepped forward and placed a finger underneath Peter's chin, raising it. "This is God's will."

Hard eyes stared at him. "Yes, Father."

"It will be the birth of a new order just as we celebrate the nativity of our Lord. God's Kingdom will be built upon their flesh and blood, and they will embrace God in death. We shall see to this."

GWEN
Camp Forge, IA

A man coughed a crackling wet hack in the crowd. The savory smell of roasting pig and campfire dominated Camp Forge. Rough, dry hands held her white gloved ones. She peered up into his eyes, drinking in his steel blue orbs that were wide with glee. A smile spread beneath his groomed beard. Becky had gone to town on it the night prior, brushing and chopping and picking at the poor man to ensure he was somewhat presentable for today's event.

His hair was brushed to the side, covering the scar and parting his hair along the top of his skull. The bones in his cheeks stuck out farther than she ever remembered, but there was joy in his eyes and sadness almost as if he'd foreseen all their deaths and knew that this moment here and now would never last.

Her grandfather cleared his throat. "We've gathered here today to celebrate one of life's greatest moments, the union of two souls as one." Despite the cold winter air, he wore a fine camel-colored sport coat that was too large for him. What few strands of hair he had atop his head were brushed to the side.

Mark grinned at her. She beamed back. Her insides glowed and her heart soared. She had waited for this day. It was hard to imagine it would be like this, here while surrounded by all these misplaced people. But one thing was real: this man here with her now.

"Marriage is many things, but its foundation is built on love and in trust, to know in your hearts that you want only the best for each other. It takes dedication to stay open to one another, to learn and grow even when it is difficult to do so." Her grandfather turned toward Mark.

"Do you have the ring?"

"I do," he said.

"Not yet, son," Pa said.

The people in attendance let out a chuckle. Smiling, Mark nodded. He took one of her grandmother's rings from his pocket. It was a simple design. A gold band with three humble diamonds along the top.

She held out her hand and found herself shaking not with fear but with excitement.

Her grandfather peered down at his notes. "Do you promise to love Gwen and respect her, to share your life and your dreams, to build with her a home that is a place of love, happiness, commitment, and growth?"

Mark's voice boomed. "I do."

"Do you promise to cherish and protect her?"

"I do."

"You may place the ring on her finger."

The small metal circle slipped over her knuckles all the way to the base of her finger next to the engagement ring.

She took out his ring.

"Now, Gwen, my girl, do you promise to love Mark and respect him, to share your life and your dreams, to build with him a home that is a place of love, happiness, commitment, and growth?"

"I do."

"Do you promise to cherish and protect him?"

"I do."

"You may place the ring on his hand." She slid the ring on his finger, and she could see the emotion rising in his chest.

"Before I pronounce you man and wife, let me remind you of these things. Love is not a wall; it is a bridge. Love does not confine; it sets you free. It leads as a pathway, winding to places unknown and mysterious. With love to light the way, you can meet any challenge together."

Becky and her grandmother sobbed softly from the front row. Seated nearby were Jake and Haley. He didn't look pleased, but he didn't look upset either, more of a general disappointment.

"I now pronounce you husband and wife. Mark and Gwen, you may kiss."

Everything was happening so fast. Her day was a blur, and this was one of the only days she wanted to crawl along. She felt his hand land on her hip and the other rest on her side. Her baby bump separated them, but it only made him lean in farther. His mustache and beard prickled her lips, and with a kiss that she could never forget, they became one before a camp of refugees and soldiers.

Uproarious clapping filled the air, and for a moment, she had forgotten the hundreds of people that had come to watch their wedding at the center of the base. Pa clapped Mark on the back.

"Atta boy, son." Pa held up his hand. "I just have a final word." He short-coughed and situated his paper near his face so he could read it better.

"This is a difficult world in which you go forth but do so with the knowledge that with this marriage rests the hopes and blessing of all these people." His voice cracked. "You give us hope that love may yet save us from despair." The old farmer smiled. "We got three pigs cooking and ready to be served in the barn over there. Merry Christmas, everyone."

Jerry Jessup started in on his fiddle, and Nowlton Gebert followed him by strumming a tune on his banjo. Gwen felt her hand be taken by Mark, and he led her into the throng of friends.

Harriet was there with Char and Freddy. The little boy hugged Gwen while Steele shook hands with Frank from the Iron Drakes. The people swarmed them with an almost forgotten happiness, smiles upon their faces. The DeVaults brought enough milk to drown them all. The Fogertys gifted them loaves of crusty brown bread for the feast. Tess hugged Mark then slugged him in the shoulder and wagging her finger at him while Gregor bear-hugged Gwen off her feet. Even the Chosen were among them. Down the line, hundreds of well-wishers came, but it was those that weren't there that chipped away at her soul.

"May your marriage be blessed," the pastor said to her. He patted her hand in his.

"Congratulations," Peter said, but his words did not match his sullen demeanor.

Luke gave her a nasty grin. "Many blessings have been bestowed to you. Enjoy them."

"Thank you," Gwen said, a fraction of confusion spreading on her face. She didn't expect the Chosen to be so friendly, but they were off-putting nonetheless.

For every person that passed by, it was painfully obvious all that were missing. While she held joy from her marriage, she also experienced deep sadness at the same time. She realized that the more people she knew, the more people that she knew were going to die. Someday they would be gone, every single one. Probably even sooner given the current state of the world.

She embraced and tried to understand that her sorrow wasn't going to go away and she would carry it with her throughout the rest of her life, long or short. Sadness at the loss of Steele's mother. The loss of Lucia and Lindsay. The loss of Kevin and Ahmed. The unknown whereabouts of her parents. Max and Bengy. Jarl and Ben. Her list went on as she hugged these people and received their love. She knew that they too would end up just like the others, gone and dead, missing from the living, vanished into memories.

She glanced at Mark for a moment. He smiled on the outside and clapped backs and shook hands and gave hugs, but his eyes still held a bit of anguish. She understood him, but she also accepted that this was a part of life. Joy and sadness in tandem and the acceptance that there would never be a time when they wouldn't balance each other.

The crowd flooded into the barn to eat, and Jake came to her. He came from the other side that Steele was on as to avoid contact with the man. She didn't know if it was fear or disappointment or some kind of shame of not being the man she'd chosen.

He hugged her. "Good ceremony. Not a dry eye in the place."

Gwen wiped a tear from hers. "Nope. Why don't you grab some food?"

"Suppose I will, Mom and Dad are already in there." He looked inside the open-doored barn as if he was trying to figure out the best way to say something.

"You know," he started.

She put a hand on his chest. He looked down at it for a moment.

"No. Not today."

He pursed his lips. "All right, Gwen." He looked away again and then back at her. His eyes pierced hers with a thousand unsaid words. "Time for that food. Merry Christmas."

"Merry Christmas, Jake." She watched a man that she had loved walk away and into the barn.

"Did you let him down easy?"

"Yeah, I think so." She felt a hand on her hip.

"Nobody is going to take you away from me. Not now. Not never." He nuzzled his cold nose into her cheek and kissed her. "Why did we wait so long?"

She gave him a playful gaze. "You never asked."

He nodded his head in mock realization. "I guess you're right. Probably should have asked earlier."

"Probably before this." She rubbed her belly. They had added pieces of white fabric on the sides of her grandmother's wedding gown in an attempt to create space for Baby Steele.

"Yeah, we got that cart before the horse."

They walked to the edge of the barn. The sounds of people eating and drinking along with the revelry created a loud din. Jessup's fiddle slowed to the beat of "We Three Kings." Gwen stopped and listened as he played, remembering the words.

She eyed the people as the somber tune flowed from his instrument mesmerizing her.

"What's the matter?" Mark said, squeezing her hand.

The words from the myrrh verse played in her head: Breathes a life of gathering gloom.

"Nothing, love."

He smiled. "Let's grab some food. I'm starving."

Hank came up and handed Mark a beer after popping the top. He slugged it back. "Damn, that's good." He glanced at her and took her hand. "Come on."

But it was the final words that stuck in her mind as if they were on repeat: Sorrowing, sighing, bleeding, dying. Sorrowing, sighing, bleeding, dying. Sorrowing, sighing, bleeding, dying.

She gulped back her fears and they walked inside.

JOSEPH
Cheyenne Mountain Complex, CO

Joseph nodded to the guards. He put his ID card to the top right corner of the proximity scanner, and it flashed lights, granting him access. He entered the cell room. The same two soldiers sat hunched over their single table playing cards.

"Greer, you're cheating."

Greer slapped his cards down on the table. "I ain't cheating. You're just a terrible player."

The other guard whined. "I always win at solitaire."

"'Cause you're prolly doin' it wrong."

Joseph cleared his throat. The two men looked at him. "I'm here to check the sick prisoner."

"You're late." Greer stabbed a finger at his partner. "No cheatin'." And he grabbed his submachine gun off the table.

Gulping, Joseph steadied himself. *I'm cool. I'm cool. I'm a fancy doctor with tons of science things to do.* "I'm busy making the vaccine. You know the one that will save your life if you're bit."

Greer cocked his head. "Figures they would make you waste your time with this lot."

Joseph shrugged his shoulders. "Government bureaucracy at its finest."

A smile cracked Greer's thin lips. "You can say that again." He flicked on his flashlight and they walked to the hole in the ground leading to the prisoners below. He lazily adjusted the ladder, letting it drop below with a crunch.

"They been quiet today. Guess they were hungry."

"They must have been." Joseph grabbed the ladder.

Greer stuck out a hand. "Wait."

Joseph blinked. "Yes?"

"I can't let you down there without looking in your bag."

"Of course, I forgot."

Greer laughed under his breath. "Don't want you bringing any weapons in."

Joseph removed his pack from his shoulder and handed it over to the soldier. "I understand your concern."

The guard opened the bag and jammed his hand inside, using his flashlight to illuminate the insides. He dug around forcefully, flinging contents like a monkey trying to use advanced tools.

Glass clanked and Joseph cringed. "Please, be careful. Those vials are fragile."

Greer slowed his rummaging. "Looks safe enough." He thrust the bag back in Joseph's hand. "Holler if they get frisky."

Joseph shouldered his pack and climbed down into the cave-like cell. He clicked on his flashlight, revealing the faces of over twenty prisoners.

"Byrnes?" Joseph said.

"Yes." The slender colonel stood shielding his eyes from the light.

Joseph hurried to him. Setting his bag on the ground, he glanced up at the man. "We don't have much time. We're getting you out today."

"How?" Byrnes breathed, his face a dour with the weight of weariness cloaking him.

Joseph crouched removing a vial and needle. He stuck the needle into the vial and filled the syringe. "Modified tetrodotoxin, courtesy of Dr. Desai."

Byrnes's scowl deepened. "TTX is extremely deadly."

A sigh escaped Joseph's throat, trying to calm his jumping jack insides. "You're correct." The two men eyed each other for a moment. "There's no other way. Desai says the dosage will work."

"I have enough for five of you." He spun his flashlight from side to side, and the tired beaten faces of the prisoners gazed back. He bent down, preparing more syringes. "The rest will be quarantined, and as we inject them, we will remove them from the complex."

"The longer this goes on the more likely we are to fail." Byrnes clasped his wrist with one hand, contemplating the situation.

Another syringe was prepped, and he set it next to the others. "Choose wisely. You either have a chance to live, or you will be executed. Your terms or theirs. Pick."

Byrnes eyeballed the needles, judging his morbid options for himself and the other prisoners. Two men and two women joined him. "They will execute all of us. They promised us that. But you have a choice now."

Each of the four people nodded.

"We'll do it," whispered a woman with a bun drooping off the top of her head. Age lined her face, and a permanent angry crease lined the center of her forehead. She wore a camouflaged blue and gray navy combat uniform.

Folding the sleeve of his soiled uniform, Byrnes nodded. "Good, Ava. It's decided."

Greer's voice echoed through the hole like a malevolent creator from above. "How they looking, doc?"

"Very sick. Give me another minute."

"Er, what's wrong with them?"

The slender colonel's lips tightened, and he gave him a slight nod. The needle poked into the bluish vein in his arm, and Joseph injected his fellow doctor. He set the needle back in his bag and picked up the next one.

The voice from above came again. "Doctor?"

Joseph made sure his voice carried. "It's just as I feared." He waved the next person closer. "Looks airborne." He rubbed a tiny alcohol wipe on the woman's arm.

"Do it," she said. "It's better than dying in a hole."

Joseph injected her and moved on to the next prisoner.

The faint curses of the guard from above trickled down in the underground cell. But Joseph was already on to the last prisoner. He whispered softly. "Better sit down." The others laid down on the cool rocky ground.

Quickly, he counted those that wanted to escape and only four had chosen to be left behind. It would take three separate trips to gather all the injected bodies. Joseph repacked his supplies and slipped a surgical mask over his face.

He walked to the ladder peering upward. "This doesn't look good." A flashlight beamed down on him like he was about to be abducted by a UFO, forcing him to shield his eyes. "The disease has spread like wildfire through them. I don't suspect most to make it much longer." Joseph eyed the fading prisoners. "Not much longer down here anyway."

"Dead?" Greer said. The light scanned away for a moment. "Fuck."

"I would say this whole area is contaminated."

"Contaminated?"

Rung after rung, Joseph climbed out of the hole. He dusted himself off and Greer took a step back in fear. "Most will die within an hour or two."

Greer wiped his face. "Must be why they've been so quiet." He turned toward his partner. "Jay, get over here."

The other guard sauntered to where they stood as if any extra effort would cause him extreme discomfort. He had a broad nose and blocky brow. "What is it?"

"Doctor here says they're sick and gonna die."

"So what? They're gonna die either way. What's the difference if they die down there?"

"Shouldn't we call it up?"

"Nah, let the next shift deal with it."

"Help," came a voice from the hole. "He's dead."

"I'll call my team down to retrieve the body. We'll need the HAZMAT suits for these ones. Real contagious disease. Stuff horror movies are made out of."

Greer took a step back. "Jesus. Do whatever you have to do."

Joseph gave him a quick scrutinizing look. "We're going to have to test you both for symptoms."

Jay shook his head. "They don't pay us enough for this shit."

"I'd really stay out of the way here. Even with medicine, I'm not sure many of those people will survive."

"You don't think we got it, do you?" Greer's eyes rounded in fear.

"We won't know for a few days. I'll need you to collect your stool samples daily and keep track of your temperature. If it goes up more than .2 degrees, I'll need you to come in."

Greer looked at Jay. "I was sweating last night. Woke up this morning, and my sheets were soaked."

"Not a good sign," Joseph said, shaking his head.

A pounding came on the door. Jay left to answer it. "Yeah, let 'em in. There's some sort of outbreak. No, not Zulus, but a few of them died."

A blue HAZMAT suit crinkled as Dr. Desai walked through the doorway.

"Doctor," Joseph said.

"Doctor," Desai replied with a nod.

"They're over here." He led her with the rolling stretcher to the hole in the ground. He waved at the guards. "We'll need your help getting the body up."

"Are you sure? Aren't they infectious?" Greer hesitantly held his ground away from the hole.

"I can't lift them without help." He removed latex gloves from this pocket and tossed them at the soldier. "Put those on."

Joseph climbed back inside the cell. Byrnes was lying on the ground like a corpse. For all intents and purposes, he was. His lips had a bluish hue fitting his normally dour state. His breathing was so light and his heartbeat so scarce that it would be difficult to detect even with medical devices.

"Help me," Joseph said to the prisoners. Two men picked up Byrnes and walked him over to the ladder. A rope was tossed down, and they tied it around Byrnes's body.

"All right, pull him up."

The guards grunted and heaved the body upwards. The colonel's head slumped forward as they hauled him out, a limp piece of meat.

"There's more," Joseph shouted.

A head poked in the hole. "What do you mean more?"

"These people are dead too." He gave Greer a dirty look. "I told you. You needed to take better care of them."

"Bullshit." Greer climbed into the cave covering his mouth with his shoulder and trained his MP5 on the prisoners. "Everyone on the wall." The captives moved with sullen reserve to the wall and stood aside. "Hands on it." Grimy hands rested on the rough surface. Four bodies lay unmoving on the rocky ground.

"You better put on a mask if you are going to be down here."

"I don't have a mask. There's no way these ones are dead too." He shined a flashlight, illuminating Ava in her naval uniform.

"I told you they were sick."

A prisoner coughed near the wall. Greer aimed his light in that direction. "Shut up." He went back to the nearest body and gave her a tap with his boot. Her leg shook, the foot coming to a rest. "Get up."

The woman didn't move.

"I told you they're dead." Joseph crouched next to the body and stuck his fingers into Ava's neck. "No pulse."

Greer gave her another kick, still covering his mouth. This time he directed the kick at the center of her thigh, a common pressure point that would give her severe pain if struck. Her body rocked. He kicked her again even harder. Her head lolled to a resting place.

"I'm telling you. In my expert medical opinion, she is dead, and you shouldn't be down here."

Greer took a step backward. He trained his submachine gun on the prisoners. "One move and I'll finish you all off. Nothing fishy." He skipped up the ladder rungs.

Joseph put his arms under Ava's armpits and dragged her over to the hole. They tossed him the rope, and he tied it around her body. He wouldn't know if the injection worked or not for a few hours when the toxins wore off. Then it was only a matter if they woke up or stayed dead. He repeated this process with the other bodies. "I'll be back later to pick up the others."

He followed the last hanging corpse through the hole. The two guards rolled out body bags and placed them inside. Then the guards piled the bodies atop one another on the rolling stretcher. When they were done, they stepped away. Their arms covered their mouths as they tried not to breathe in the invisible particles of disease circulating in the air.

Joseph pointed at them. "Remember what I told you. You must report your symptoms to me tomorrow. Keep all your stools."

Dumbly, the two soldiers bobbed their heads.

"Come, Dr. Desai. We must get these bodies out for processing. Then we will come back and grab any we couldn't fit."

They wheeled the stretcher out the door. The guards on the outside gawked at the pile of body bags.

"What the fuck happened?" one said.

"Airborne methicillin-resistant Staphylococcus aureus. Nasty, nasty business."

"Goddamn. Get that shit out of here."

"Wait," said the other guard.

"Who is it? Sergeant is gonna want to know when they ain't down there."

"You said yesterday. No names."

"Oh fuck."

"Feel free to take a look." Joseph opened a palm over the bodies. The body bags were indiscriminate and unmarked.

The guards stared at the bodies in disgust. One reached a hand for Byrnes's bag.

"I'd . . . "Joseph started. He held out a hand.

The guard glanced at him. "What?"

"I'd use gloves. This is a deadly strain. Sticks to everything."

His shorter partner leaned back into the wall. "Come on. Let them leave. We don't want to catch that shit."

The other guard eyed them. "All right." He waved them off. "I should have stayed on the outside."

Pushing the stretcher down the tunnel, the wheels ground and dug into the rocky uneven floor. Desai grunted as she pushed alongside him.

Her voice came at a whisper. "Do you think they bought it?"

"They aren't following, are they?"

Desai looked behind her. "No."

"Hurry. Let's get them to the docks."

TESS
Camp Forge, IA

She soaked her crumbling brown bread into the meat juices left on her plate by a generous portion of crispy roasted pork flank. Gregor belched loudly and lifted a beer at Hank. They clanged cans.

"Cheers!"

"Merry Christmas, brother."

Hoisting their beers back toward the ceiling, they shouted. "And a happy New Year!" They pressed beverages to their lips and greedily guzzled them down their gullets.

She ripped a piece of pork with her fingers and tore off a chunk of bread, shoving them both into her mouth.

Trent picked his teeth with his fingernail and stared across the table at her. "Best eatin' we had since Sable."

She swallowed her food. "Best eatin' I had since the outbreak. But nothing beats a midnight Beefy Taco run."

He gave her a grin and pulled out a can of chewing tobacco. He slapped the tin between his fingers and used a finger to pry it open.

"Come on, man. We're at the dinner table."

He smiled at her. "Lucky for me, we aren't the ones getting hitched." He shoved a wad of chew into his goateed mouth.

She raised her eyebrows at him and knocked back a glass of whiskey. The man was transforming into a more handsome devil by the hour, but his tobacco habit turned her surge of attraction down a notch. A few more drinks and she wouldn't care what he did or didn't do, just that he was a living, breathing man. With urges and needs that matched hers even if he wasn't Pagan or Steele, he was still a man. He licked the chew on his lip back into his mouth, and scooped up a beer can, and spit into it.

The fiddle and the banjo were almost drowned out by the clamor of people. The pastor had left early in the night, paying his respects to both Mark and Gwen. His Chosen followers retired in clusters generally devoid of any real celebration.

Tess tossed back shots with Trent. Shotgunned beers with Gregor. Sang carols with Harriet at the top of her lungs and ate more food with Larry when she was feeling the alcohol too much.

As the night went on, the well-wishers from Hacklebarney drifted home on horses and sleighs. Even the Sable Pointers went back to their barn for bed. The soldiers from Ludlow's command ate and drank as much as anyone. The music continued, but eventually, only the diehard drinkers and restless souls were left.

Trent's eyes drooped from the effects of alcohol. His speech came out in slurs. "Hey, you wanna get out of here?"

She was feeling it too, but she held her liquor with the best imbibers. She grabbed his face by the scruffy cheeks and drew him in close. She kissed his lips. He tasted like beer and his tongue lingered too long in her mouth like it had found a home and fell asleep. She drunkenly shoved him away. He blinked, attempting to keep from toppling over.

The words should have felt silly, but she whispered them with the maximum level of seduction. "How about you head back to the barn?" She hiccupped with a smile. "Warm that pile of hay up a bit. I'll be over in a few minutes."

He gave her a mock salute, his words slurring. "Yes, ma'am." He teetered as he made for the barn doors, now closed to keep in the heat.

She threw back a shot of whiskey, looking around at the other poor souls who couldn't find solace in the bottom of a bottle. She picked up a fifth of whiskey and swaggered over to the leftover pig. She piled all manner of meat on a big plate. She waved at the banjo player as she walked toward the door. He gave her a drunken once-over as if considering her as a viable option.

"Go home to your wife, Nowlton."

"Trying to avoid another kid."

She laughed and leaned into the barn doors, letting them slide open.

The night was dark and cold. Snow flurries trickled down from the sky like dizzy white dandelion seed parachutes. The soft warm glow of a dying fire leaked out of the Reynolds farmhouse. Light gray smoke billowed from cabin chimneys.

A half-filled bottle of whiskey sat on a table near the door. She dipped back in and snatched it. She raised it in the air to the men still lingering in the barn reception. "Good night, you heathens."

Her boots crushed into packed snow. She wavered a bit as she trod down the beaten snowy track toward her barn. She swaggered as she walked, her hips moving back and forth. The faint moan of the dead seeped over the water, a collection of mournful voices, unknowing why they called and only that fresh victims awaited them over the river.

She stopped. She couldn't see them in the night, but she knew they were there. Crowding, searching, waiting for their opportunity to kill everyone still living. She yelled across the water. "Good night, douchebags!" She hefted the liquor high in the air. The liquid sloshed around inside its glass container. She turned the container bottoms up and let the fiery liquid burn down her chest and wiped her mouth on a coarse sleeve.

She zigged and zagged until she reached a barn. Two men, nearly frozen to death, were standing guard outside. Scarf-wrapped faces turned her way as she neared.

"Hey," she said.

"Tess," came a muffled voice from the closest man. His name was Jon or Wes or something. He'd kept to himself since joining around Spring Lake. Nice enough guy, just nothing remarkably distinctive about him.

"I need you to let me in there." Her words came out a little more slurred than she'd expected.

"I'm sorry. Captain Steele said no one is to go in or out."

She raised her eyebrows. "I am acting on his behalf."

"He said no one."

"'Cept me. Open it up, Jon, or I'll clock ya."

"It's Wes."

"I don't care who ya are. I'll only be a minute."

His eyes darted back and forth, trying to see if anyone would notice. "One minute, Tess."

"One minute."

Wes and his partner counted to three and hoisted a heavy wood beam, setting it to the side.

Tess pulled on one of the sliding doors and grunted as it rolled open. A couple of bikers glanced at her. Most were asleep. A heavyset bearded man stood slowly.

"You can close it behind me," she said to Wes.

"What if something happens?"

"It won't."

Wes shoved the door closed. More of the Red Stripes got to their feet.

Thunder's voice cut the darkness. "What do you want, you treacherous little cunt?"

"Now that's no way to treat an old friend."

Fists appeared at his side.

"I didn't come here to fight. I came here to make peace."

"Peace? You fucking got us arrested."

Tess slung her pack off her back.

"Let's fucking brain her," came a voice from the crowd.

"We know how that ends. The guards come in and shoot everyone, and if they don't, you know Steele will. I brought some food. Bread, pork, and for you." She threw the half-filled bottle in the air and Thunder caught it. "Some booze."

A grin appeared beneath his shadowed gray beard. He unscrewed the cap and took a swig. "Tastes good."

"You want to break us out of here too?"

"Nah, what you did was rotten."

Thunder took another swill down. "It was planted. We didn't even know it was there."

She eyed him for a moment. The Red Stripes dug into their food with the loud smacking of lips of hungry men.

"We didn't do it. Why would I lie?"

"Why does anyone lie? Cause they got caught. Merry Christmas, Thunder."

"Merry Christmas. Suppose this means I'll see you on the other side."

She smirked. "What other side." She hauled hard on the door. Both Wes and his partner shouldered their guns as she stepped out.

"Jesus. It's just me."

"We didn't know. You were in there for longer than a minute."

"Eat a dick, Wes. I was giving them food. It's Christmas for God's sake."

He lowered his rifle, complaining beneath his breath. They rolled the doors back into place and set the heavy wood beam overtop.

"It's been fun, but this lady has to burn off a little steam." She walked down the line of barns all the way to the one holding the Sable Pointers.

She crept through the sleeping bodies of her people. The fire burned low near the center of the barn, only a lick of flame daring to dart out of the pit. Her footsteps creaked across the wood. She reached her corner and swept away her tarp that acted as a door to her small piece of worn wood-planked floor.

Trent's body lay in her makeshift bed of blankets and sleeping bags. He was topless and his skin was pale in the dark, a field of fresh snow. She tiptoed closer to him. "If you think for a second you're gonna pass out on me, you got a long night ahead of you."

He didn't stir, only kept his backwoods serenity. She stripped off her firearm shoulder harness, letting it drop to the floor. Drunken fingers fumbled around the button of her pants and she kicked them off into a heap in the corner. She crawled into the mass of blankets and ran a hand down his chest and abs all the way to his crotch. He was not ready for her. She fondled him for a moment, and her hand was met with limpness. His skin was cool to the touch.

"Come on, dude. You couldn't wait a few minutes for this top-notch shit?" Her drunken disappointment was zapped by sudden concern. *Had this lackwit good old boy drank himself into alcohol poisoning? Fucking lightweight.*

"Trent?" she whispered. She took her hand away from his member and grabbed his cheeks. Bristly whiskers jabbed her hand. His head was limp and heavy. She leaned her face close to his. "Drink too much?" His blank and glassy eyes stared at her, no life behind them.

"Trent?" she said louder, alarm rising in her voice. The floor betrayed something lurking in the shadows. She peered into the corner. It was darker than it should have been, even in the night. Rolling out of the blankets, she lunged for her gun. Fingernails scratched the coarse plank, bending and chipping, as she grasped for where it used to be.

A black bag went over her head and pulled tight over her mouth. Her hands went to her neck and something thumped off the top of her head. She squeezed her eyes open and closed but could see nothing, heightening her struggle. Her feet kicked out, searching for anything to strike. Iron-like hands gripped around her ankles. The hard object banged off her skull again and her vision went black as the night.

THE PASTOR
Camp Forge, IA

"On this blessed morn, may Christ guide our hand and our aim as we strike down the corrupt and the wicked in his name. Amen." The pastor dipped his head in reverence to the Lord. A quiet chorus of amens echoed from his men.

The fire died to embers behind him. His men had been prepared since the wedding feast the night before. They had been prohibited from drinking. All weapons were close, and as the last revelers went to bed or passed out, his men gathered in the waxing light. They had met for prayer in his cabin as they readied their souls for battle.

The door opened and cool air rushed inside. The flames wavered behind him with the entrance of more oxygen. Luke and Peter dragged in a hooded form, but he already knew who it was: the most wretched of the unbelievers but also the one who would discover the Red Stripes' supposed transgression.

"She's out," Luke said. He ripped off her hood. Her face slumped to the side and her mouth drooped with a gag wound tightly around her head. "Slipped her one of these to make sure she don't complain." He shook a bottle of pills.

"Good work. The War Machines will finish her preparations for purification."

With the chaos of planning the wedding feast, men and women frequently came and went in the camp. It hadn't been hard to sneak in some of the War Machines dressed in regular clothes and disperse them throughout his ranks inside the base. The men were talented in all means of violence and strengthened his forces for their attack.

Her eyes cracked and she mumbled a soft, "Fuck you." Her head rolled from side to side, and she settled to keeping her chin to her chest as if it were preventing her from spinning and staring through the tops of her eyebrows. "You'll never get away with this."

Luke dug a hand into her short hair and yanked her head exposing her neck. A knife glimmered in his hand, and he held its point to her throat.

Peter put a hand on Luke's. "No."

The pastor eyed his second in command with surprise. His disciples stared each other down in malice. Luke licked dry lips. "Got a crush?"

"No." He squeezed Luke's wrist, his knuckles turning white.

"He's right, Luke." The pastor lifted a graceful hand to stop him. "She still has an important part to play."

"I won't do nothing for you shitbags," she whispered.

The pastor raised his chin like a commanding parent. "You will do as I command." He walked to her leaning in. "Your act will be the biggest betrayal of them all because you will have led him to his demise."

Her head wobbled as she shook it. "No."

He forced her chin upward with a skeletal finger. "You did. You convinced him to arrest his most powerful ally for nothing."

"No, Thunder's medicine."

"You mean *my* medicine." His eyes glanced at his disciple over her shoulder. "Brother Luke has many talents. It wasn't hard for him to sneak in and hide it when they were out working, but you see, none of it would have mattered if you weren't suspicious. I know you, Tess, like the Lord knows you. You are untrusting at best. I knew that you would go looking for evidence, so I gave you what you wanted to find. I never thought it would be this easy to have you turn on each other, but your lack of faith made it extraordinarily easy."

Her eyes blinked, glassy with fogginess. "No." Spit dribbled from her lips.

"Yes. You've done this. You've brought about his fall."

Her head rolled upright. "Go to hell."

"I have confidence that God will accept his most humble servant with open arms on eagle's wings."

An echo of amens perforated the cabin, resounding from wall to wall.

"Prepare her. Luke and Peter stay. I need you." With a flick of his wrist, they dragged her away.

"Is everyone ready?"

Peter's curled head bobbed. "Yes, Father."

"On the signal, what is our sequence of attack?"

"Luke will kill the guards by the gate and open them for the rest of the War Machines. While he does that, Matthew will execute the Red Stripes and quickly move to the Sable Pointers."

"Remember, they will be cowed with the loss of their leaders and fighters. Only kill those that resist."

"What of the soldiers?" Luke asked.

"They are weaponless, but gun them down before they can cause trouble."

Luke bowed his head. "Yes, Father."

"I want Steele alive if possible, dead just as good, but if he can be taken, I want him. His soul is in dire need of cleansing."

"Yes, Father," the men said in tandem.

"All is in order. With the dawn comes victory. Pray with me until we are ready."

All his men bowed their heads, and he smiled, looking out among the tops of their skulls. "We will have a great triumph on this most holy of days. The blessed birth of a new world."

ALVARADO
La Crosse, WI

Major Alvarado peered through the half-inch gap of the heavy sliding warehouse door. She kept her eye close to the crack, trying to catch a glimpse of the sled. If it was gone, she would be leading men to their deaths. *God, hold that sled in place. Your Marines need it*, she prayed.

Something passed near the crack. Instinctually she jerked her head away from it, her heart skipping a beat. Being close to an enemy never got any easier. The grind of hard rotted flesh on metal scratched along as the infected marched toward the river.

Her Marines clustered behind her silently prepared to strike hard and fast. Even Sergeant Riddle in his makeshift wooden-framed stretcher on the concrete floor looked ready to fight. The Marines had crafted a litter out of the warehouse pallets to make it easier for them to haul the wounded sergeant. If needed, it could be pulled behind one man while the other fought. It would be painful for Riddle but less painful then being eaten alive, watching the infected tear chunks of flesh and muscle from his body.

She whispered, "When we open this door, we move fast and silent. Only go hot if necessary. Make time for Finch and Foster to cross. Then we move for the sled. Affirm?"

Heads bobbed in her direction. Gear had been traded between the men. Foster and Finch gave most of their extra ammunition to the men staying with Alvarado. It was a hard ask for Marines, but they did so willingly, knowing their brothers needed it more. Carrying the wounded could be the best way to survive or end up a walking corpse.

"On my mark." She ground her teeth in anticipation.

On either side of Riddle, Finch and Foster hoisted him airborne between them.

"Jesus, Riddle, what have you been eating?" Foster said.

Riddle grunted as they adjusted their hands. He held his M27 across his body. It would be difficult for him to hit anything while getting jostled around, but if it came down to it, she knew he would be slinging rounds.

We are all in for a treacherous run. Hope their PT is up to snuff. Three…two… one… In a deep voice she sounded off, "Move."

Rasmussen lowered a shoulder and rolled the door open wide enough for two people abreast to pass through. The sky was a bland gray, the sun unable to provide much of anything to the frozen earth below. The destroyed surface of the frozen river propelled stray mini icebergs into a growing pile on the still solid ice.

A Zulu stumbled past the door, clothing tattered and loose, unaware how close living flesh resided. It was followed by others with corrupted gray skin, hair hanging in clumpy soiled strings.

The Marines charged with surprising speed. She wouldn't attribute it to fear but rather fervor to accomplish the mission, the fast necessity that kept a soldier moving in combat when a position wasn't safe.

O'Bannon was the first Marine through. He went straight for the solid surface that hadn't been shattered by the explosives. Zulus splashed in the water where the weakened ice had broken beneath their weight. He clubbed a Zulu with the stock of his weapon. A damp thwack sounded, and the infected fell like tree limbs sinking into the snow, tree limbs that leaked almost black blood from fractured craniums.

Alvarado was the last one through. She cross-checked an infected with a crack as it rounded the corner, punching its thin nose back into its brain. Their snowshoes scraped over the frozen white while the dead were hampered with every step.

They ran over the ice that creaked beneath them in complaint about each excessive pound of American Marine on its surface. The man in front of her slipped, and she grabbed him to keep him steady. He caught himself, and they continued their sprint.

Her breath came in fits and gasps as they closed in on the sled, the freezing air zapping her lungs like electromagnetic pulses. The Marines brought themselves to an abrupt halt almost forty feet from the explosives.

The ice was darker here, and it was clearly unlike the packed together white ice they'd been destroying and dying on. Cracks splintered the ice like new tributaries, threatening to break apart any minute. The Marines set a quick perimeter, guns facing all around.

She hustled between them.

"What's the problem?" she shouted.

"Ice is cracking," Johnson said. The big man stood the farthest from the weakened surface, knowing that he of all people was in the most danger of falling through.

Finch and Foster continued to sprint over the ice to the other side, Riddle bouncing between them.

The answer was an easy one despite the challenge of the task. Alvarado stripped off her weapons and gear, letting them drop.

Odom's head swiveled between her and the dead. "They're closing in!"

"Permission to go hot?" Rasmussen gave her a quick eye before facing the encroaching dead.

Her frame became lighter and her body grew colder as the frigid air gained access to formerly protected skin with each layer she removed. "Go hot."

She studied the minefield of delicate, fractured, and entirely unstable dammed ice. Gingerly, she took one of her feet and tested it. Beneath her, the river soughed and was overtaken by the rippling clap of gunfire behind her. *One foot over the other. Nice and light. As light as a feather.* Each step was a tiptoe over the soccer field of her youth.

Nervously she trudged forward, thinking light thoughts. Feathers, clouds, and pillows crowded her mind, and they felt awkward there. Her eyes narrowed as she focused on the sled and the ice ahead of her. Back and forth her gaze went as she walked.

When the cracking of ice became audible over the gunfire, she stopped. Holding her breath, she lifted her foot. In front of her the jagged surface snapped and crackled, fresh new contours forming like the fault lines of an earthquake. They stretched for her and she sidestepped as fast as her feet could move to the side as the ice disappeared beneath her. She spread her feet wide on the solid surface, not daring to breathe.

She gasped for air, realizing she'd been holding her breath as she evaded the collapse. At her new angle, she hurried toward the explosive-filled sled.

Moans drummed her ears, which should have been a warning, but she ignored them. The only important thing was to keep the explosives from sinking into the freezing depths of the Mississippi River.

Bodies in the water splashed near the broken edges adding to the chaos. Pushing every distraction down deep into her belly, she carefully unclipped her snowshoes and let herself down to the uneven surface. She embraced the solid coldness like a reluctant child would a grizzly bear. The frigidness emanated into her body, chilling her core so cold she almost couldn't feel it. Using her hands to pull and her feet to push off errant piled ice, she crawled over the sandpaper surface, inching closer to her goal. Throwing an arm out, she dragged herself the last few feet to the sled.

She tried to keep her feet wide and her weight spread out along the fragile surface. She stretched as far as her little frame dared, clawing chunks of frozen white. The gunfire behind her picked up in tempo. They didn't have time to spare. They needed to run, plant, and run then repeat.

The rigged sled teetered on the river's solid edge. The rope and harness were strewn over the cool surface almost within reach, mocking her. As gently as she could, she nudged with her toes like a ballerina performing her first pointe technique, inching herself a little closer. The ice groaned like a sleeping titan as if her weight were a ton instead of a paltry one hundred and twenty.

Her gloved fingertips scratched the harness, gaining her only a dusting of white. Her arm and shoulder ached as she forced them to stretch longer than they should, her muscles struggling to obey. Her fingers wiggled their way through the rope like she was tickling the loop until they had the tiniest of holds on the fabric. She whipped her digits so it secured around her wrist.

She reversed, hooking her boot tips into the solid chunks and palming herself backward. She tugged the sled, and it scraped along like a resistant mule. The sled tipped and turned as it circumvented wedges of frozen river with the grace of a rhino in heat.

"Come on." Slowly she reversed toward her men.

Gunshots blared behind her, then a heinous moan filled her ears, and she twisted her neck.

A shadowy form bore over her. It reached a hand in the shape of a claw in her direction. Its hair had crystalized to its skull, making it almost glint in the masked sunlight. Its skin was a deep dark gray like dirty water in a mop bucket, and its lips were purplish black. The ice rippled beneath the Zulu, and it ignored the danger of the thin weakened platform beneath it.

She rolled on her side as everything beneath the fiend disintegrated. The dead shot downward into the river, arms flailing. She didn't cry when its icy hand hit her foot like a hammer. The full weight of the dead dragged her down, forcing her ankle further than it was meant to go. *I'm okay.*

Frozen fingers grasped her. She kicked at the creature with her other boot. The pain turned into shock as the ice around her gave way with a jump. Her heart leapt in fear, and within a fraction of a second, she splashed into the freezing waters of the Mississippi River.

The jolt of the polar water to her system was immediate. It was the sharpest punch to her gut she'd ever felt, knocking all the air from her lungs. She thought her heart might burst through her rib cage as her lungs screamed for air.

The water saturated her clothes greedily, not even giving her a second to think. Her remaining layers suctioned to her body, adding immediate weight. As she plummeted underneath, the sled traveled along, the ice still wrapped around her wrist. If she didn't reverse her plunge, the sled would fall in after her, expediting her arrival at the bottom of the river. Her muscles seized in the freezing water and locked into position, but she tore at the surface in frantic desperation. Kicking her boots like the worst flippers, her limbs turned into ice blocks under the frigid waters assault. Willing herself upward, first her hands then her face broke through the surface.

Sucking in precious air, she placed her elbows on the edge of the broken ice. Her first instinct was to crawl out as fast as she could. That instinct had killed many a person who'd fallen through unstable ice.

Her mouth formed into an O as she steadied herself. Letting her legs kick, she acclimated to the cold. She inhaled air through her nose and out her mouth trying to calm her system that could easily go into a hypothermic panic at any moment.

Her body begged to escape the water, but if she hurried and attempted to haphazardly pull herself out, the ice would crack and she'd fall back in. She would repeat this process over and over until she had wasted all her energy and then the cold water would accept her beneath its surface. Her escape had to be calculated and careful.

"Come on," she breathed. Stretching her arms wide, she flutter-kicked fiercely. She didn't pull herself out much with her hands, only letting them guide her on to structurally sound ice. This process took almost twenty seconds of scooting and kicking before she was completely free of the water.

"Oh, God." Her lips quivered. Her lungs barely seemed able to take in any air. She crawled over the ice toward her Marines, tugging the sled in exhausted fits and starts.

"Major!" Rasmussen cried. He grabbed her hand, lugging her near the group. The dead in close proximity had set their eyes on them, but her Marines had the sled.

"One snuck by," she said, her voice quivering. "Dragged me down."

"Jesus fucking Christ," Rasmussen said.

The cold air was desperately attempting to freeze her in place. "Not his fault, Marine." Her voice firmed. "We have to keep moving. Hand me one."

He placed a rigged explosive in her hand. Her fingers were cramped into a frozen C-shape. She willed them to work, sending icy pain through her limbs. She shook as she set it between chunks of white. Making sure it was in a proper spot, she forced herself upright, still hunched with the cold.

Her voice came out fierce and unstoppable. "Forward, Marines!"

AHMED
Northern Missouri

The wind lashed them as they rode through backcountry roads flanked by abandoned fields of discarded crops. Yellow stalks of grass and grain were layered in a thin sheet of white snow. The sound of hooves beating the hard earth rung out rhythmically for miles.

"If we kill the horses before we get there then we'll have to walk," he hollered at Jim.

Jim didn't say a word, only begrudgingly conceded, bringing his horse to a walk. Icy breath fogged from the animals.

"You can ride quicker to your death this way," Lee said quietly. He patted the flanks of his mount. "Maybe someone will survive the day if it's only the horses. Poor beasts deserve better."

They walked and rode like this for several walk-gallop durations. Ahmed's face was chilled through, and even though he wore a scarf wrapped tightly around his head, the skin around his eyes was stiff from the battering wind. His mind was numb to the violence they were sure to engage in.

"We're close," Jim said over his shoulder. "I know this treacherous country well."

Ahmed drove his horse closer to Jim's. "How do you want to do this? I'd rather not die today if possible." *Wasn't that always the plan?*

Their leader kept his eyes straight ahead as if considering a real plan would deter him from his purpose. "Ride in, give them hell, burn the place."

305

"Simple."

Glancing at Ahmed, he said, "You got a better idea?"

"Perhaps a little tact?"

Jim snorted. "What do you know?"

"Enough to not ride into gunfire." They sat in silence for a moment. "Is there a way we can approach to surprise them?"

A finger pointed, indicating the target home in the distance. "It's that farmhouse on the edge of the road up there."

The farmhouse looked to have been there for over a century. The back portion was all brick, and the front of the home looked to be an add-on from the early 20th century. A porch rounded the sides, enveloping almost the entirety of the addition. Slender pillars of white supported the overhang above the porch, providing porch sitters with shade.

The group stopped, inspecting their mountain that needed to be scaled and conquered.

"Maybe a few of us should go around back?"

Brisk air exited Jim's nose as he stared at the house. The men could practically see the anger rising in his blood. "Let's make them pay!"

"Wait," Ahmed said. But there was no waiting.

A second passed and Jim circled his horse and shouted. "Ya!" Urging his horse onward, the band of men followed. They galloped down the driveway toward two heavy-duty pickups parked facing out. Shotguns and rifles slid from saddles.

Jim jumped down and brazenly charged the front door. The rest of the men spread out in a loose line, taking cover behind trucks and trees. Ahmed scrambled from his horse, crouching down. *Damn fool. No plan. No surprise.*

Taking a stance a few feet off the porch, Jim fired his shotgun into the air. *Boom!* He racked the gun, expelling a shell, and stood waiting for his ancient familial enemy to emerge. "Sly, come out!" He shoved the stock of the gun to his shoulder and leveled it at the door.

A mixture of snow and dirt erupted at Ahmed's feet. He rolled to the side taking cover and scanned the second-floor windows for enemies. One was open about four inches.

A man's voice drifted from the window. "Get on out of here, Jimmy! Nobody has to get hurt!"

Ahmed aimed in on the window and squeezed a shot off. The wood framing burst and splinters flew. The shooter took cover inside.

"Fight us like a man. Come on out here!" Jim held his shotgun up in the air. "Hell, I'll fight you fisticuffs if you want. You just come out and get some."

Seconds dripped into the steadily building tension, pressing down upon each man, adding more pressure to fight. Ahmed kept checking the corners of the house to make sure Sly's men weren't sneaking out the back to flank and ambush them. Unlike his band, they had to be planning something.

The door cracked open. A hand waved a white kitchen towel pathetically out the door. Jim lowered his weapon. "Well, come on out then."

"Promise you won't shoot 'til you hear me out."

Jim shook his head. "Ah hell, I'll be honest with ya. We won't shoot right away. We got honor, more than we can say for your ilk."

Sly continued to shake the symbol of surrender as he stepped onto the porch. Ahmed glanced at the second-story windows again and then back to the side of the house. Nothing moved.

"We don't have to do this, Jimmy."

"Bullshit, you killed them and took Sadie and the kids."

The leader of the Baileys gazed away bitterly, shaking his head. "It wasn't us."

Lips turned into a snarl on Jim's face. "Bullshit." He pointed his shotgun at Sly's chest. A slug from that distance would put a huge hole in his chest. The man's demeanor was almost entirely devoid of fear under the threat of certain death. His peace with God must have been made long ago.

"Put the gun away. We don't have her."

Squinting an eye, Jim lined up his bead sight, deciding where to shoot his rival. "Where she at then?"

"They got her." Sadness spread on Sly's aging features. "They took her."

"Who?" Spit flew from Jim's mouth.

"The Wolf Riders."

"I don't believe you. You always wanted her."

"Yah, Rog always liked her, but they took her."

The shotgun dipped a fraction of an inch. "You're lyin'?"

Sly exhaled and put his hand on the door. "Bring 'em out." He waved inside.

Two young kids cautiously stepped out of the house, and Sly huddled them in front of his body.

"Betty! Charley!" Jim lowered his gun and gestured for them to advance. "Come here."

Thick hands held the children by their shoulders. "Wait a minute."

"Sly, you touch a hair on their heads, and I will fucking kill you."

"Jesus, man, you know why I have them right? The Wolf Riders dumped them on us after they took Sadie. They said they didn't care what happened to 'em, but through the grace of God didn't want to just let them die. Downright amazing if you ask me. They're kids, for Chrissake."

A determined anger clouded Jim's eye, and he hefted his shotgun again. "Let them go. They don't need to see a man without a head."

"You ain't hearing me, boy. By God, you never listen. This ain't our doing. I don't want this anymore than you do."

"Send 'em over then. Give us some *good* faith."

"I'll send em over, but who's gonna take care of them after we shoot each other to pieces?"

"I will. They'll be fine with their family."

"They won't have one if we shoot each other dead."

"You let them go now, or I promise this gets ugly."

Sly shook his head no. "You would shoot that thing so close to your kin?"

"If it means ending this, yes!" Carefully, Jim lined his shotgun at Sly's head.

Ahmed rushed toward them. "Wait!"

All eyes zeroed on him. He set his gun down on the ground and held up both his hands high into the air. "Stop!"

Walking forward, he tried to speak calmly. "Jim, just wait."

The Singleton captain peered at him over his shoulder. "You don't understand, Brownie."

"Don't you see? Sly isn't the enemy. Macleod and the Wolf Riders are. They have Sadie. They burned Lee's house down, killed Kelly and Barb."

"Those pricks murdered Dad and Kyle."

Ahmed held a calming hand out. "And you murdered his cousins. Blood for blood. It's settled."

"It'll be settled when they're worm food."

Sly called over. "Jimmy, you ain't hearin' me. I don't have her."

"You work for 'em. You're to blame."

The Bailey man's eyes were tired, even battered like he hadn't slept in a week, the lines of his face seeming to deepen. "I don't want to."

"I'll send you along then!"

Ahmed stepped in front of Jim's barrel.

He shooed him with the gun. "Get out of the way."

"I won't sit by while you shoot the man that knows where Sadie is."

Jim blinked several times. "Every Singleton knows that every Bailey is a lying sack of shit. He's prolly got her inside chained up or something."

Sly peered from around Ahmed. "I don't, you stupid redneck. Every Bailey knows that a Singleton will cheat them out of their shoes given the chance."

"I'll shoot you out of those shoes. Then take 'em."

Ahmed raised his hand and let it fall on Jim's shotgun. The barrel was cool to touch even after the gunshot blast minutes before. The temperature seemed to be dropping by the minute.

"He knows where Sadie is. He's got the kids." Ahmed's brow furrowed. "Please. Let's hear him out. It's clear he hates the Wolf Riders."

Sly nodded. "I do hate 'em. They're bastards, forcing us to work for 'em. We been supplying them with food and ammunition."

Jim lowered his gun a fraction. "They got you working for them?"

"Slavery more like. Just take, don't give no protection like they said. We're still on our own in that regard. Jimmy, there must be forty of 'em. They took Jes too."

"They took Jes?" Pain creased over Jim's face. "God damn."

"Said it was to keep us honest." Sly shook his head in anger. "I haven't seen her in weeks. I got no . . ." His voice sputtered and gave way to emotion.

"This whole world is taken, all my kin. My babies." He sniffed hard, running the back of his hand across his nose.

Jim let his gun rest, pointed it toward the ground. "I'm sorry. I know we don't have no love lost for one another, but Jes is good girl. That ain't right." He studied Bailey man for a moment. "Can I see the kids?"

Sly tightened his lips and nodded fierce. He nudged the children from behind. "Go ahead." They ran down the steps, wrapping tiny arms around Jim's legs. He patted their heads fondly, pulling them tight. His exterior softened. "They hurt you?"

"No, they be nice," Betty squeaked.

"Fed us cookies!" Charley said, as if they'd given him he greatest Christmas present in the world.

Jim crouched down. "Tell me about the bad men that came to Uncle Lee's house."

"Motorcycle men, Uncle Jim."

"Big black dogs on their clothes."

Jim ruffled their hair. "I'm glad you's all right. Why don't you run back with Uncle Lee?"

The kids trotted over to their wild-haired older distant cousin.

Audibly Jim exhaled, sharing a glance with Ahmed.

"The Wolf Riders are the enemy here. I know Sly's done you wrong in the past, but this is worse." Ahmed shook his head. "There are a lot of dead coming this way. We can't afford this fight." Ahmed pointed at Sly. "None of us can afford to be fighting each other. Not now."

Jim's mouth clamped shut and he wiped a hand over his head letting his fingers run through his hair. "Jesus. This is bad. Jes too?"

Sly stood at the top of the porch and nodded gravely.

Jim stared at him. "Can we come in? And talk about this? We don't have anywhere left to go."

The idea of bringing six armed men into his home reflected on Sly's chiseled face. Armed men that had come there to kill him. He nodded stiffly. "Get those children out of the cold." He waved them on, and the Singleton men walked up the stairs. Sly held the door open. "Hurry up now, letting all the warm air out."

The two family leaders met eye to eye.

"Come on in, Jimmy."

"All right, Sly. I will." He stood quietly, judging if Sly meant what he was saying or if he was hiding men with guns in the next room. "Thanks for apologizing the other day."

"You know I didn't mean it."

Jim smiled. "That's why I turned that jerk-off down on his offer." He planted a finger in the center of Sly's chest. "Didn't come from the heart."

"I mean it when I say you're welcome here."

Jim gave him a tired smile. "I appreciate that."

STEELE
Camp Forge, IA

The glow of the fire and candles in the dim morning light warmed the parlor. Steele draped an arm around Gwen, his new wife and mother of his child. He pressed his nose into the top of her head. Her hair held a faint scent of rich floral lilac. He closed his eyes for a moment, breathing her in, pulling her tighter into his body.

He whispered, "I love you."

She studied him with affection from below. "I love you."

"Gosh, quit it, you two," Haley said. She stared at them from beneath the Christmas tree. "Can we open presents yet?"

"Not until after we eat," Becky said. She aimlessly thumbed through the same magazine for the thousandth time.

"Come on, Mom, just one?"

The sisters shared a glance together until Gwen said, "Why not?"

Becky tossed her magazine down, holding a finger in there. "One. And don't be expecting anything anyway."

"I won't, Mom." She tore into a package wrapped in what was probably the last of the wrapping paper.

John smiled at Steele. "Can I get ya a warmup?"

"Thanks," Steele said, holding out his cup.

John took it and disappeared into the kitchen.

"Smells great, Lydia," Steele said over his shoulder.

"My newest grandson-in-law is quite the schmooze," Lydia called back.

John came back in and handed Steele a piping hot watery coffee. It was practically decaf at this point but at least it was some semblance of normalcy.

"Oh, man," Haley said in dismay. She held up two gray wool socks. They dropped to her lap in defeat. "Clothes again."

John stifled a shared laugh with Steele.

"Grandma made those," her mother said. "So be thankful."

Haley's face twisted in disappointment. "More clothes. I just want my iPad to work."

Becky wagged a warning finger at her. "Well, it ain't. Be thankful that you got anything."

Lydia came into the parlor. "How do you like them, sweetie?"

Haley rolled her eyes, and Becky swatted at her with a flat palm. "What do you say?"

Haley's voice came out as a mumble. "Thank you, Grandma."

Lydia grinned. "You're welcome, sweetie. We won't have you losing a toe this winter. Food's almost ready." She disappeared back into the kitchen.

"I'm going to help her," Becky said with a warning glance at Haley. "No more presents until after breakfast."

Haley stared dispirited into the fire.

Steele knew a fix. "Say, John. You didn't happen to hear anything last night?"

John crinkled his brow. "I thought I might a heard something outside."

"Me too. Jingle bells or maybe a hoof or two."

Haley's eyes lit up with wonderment. "Santa?"

Steele narrowed his eyes. "I mean, who else really could it be?" He stood and walked over behind the tree. He pulled out a package and held it close to his face, under thorough inspection. "Says right here: To Haley, Love, Santa." He looked back at Haley and shared a glance with Gwen. "Says Santa, so he had to have come." He handed the present to Haley. "Shhhh. Mom won't mind."

"Yup!" Haley ripped into the package flinging paper to the floor. She shook the oblong box. "It's heavy. I can't open it."

"Here, let me see," Steele said. He reached out for the box and took it from her. He slung out a knife that was clipped on his pants pocket and sliced the clear plastic tape on the end of the box and removed the weapon.

"Whoa!" Haley exclaimed. Steele handed her the empty firearm. Her eyes lit up.

John giggled at Haley's excitement, clapping his hands together. "I think I used to have one just like it."

A genuine smile crossed Steele's lips. The muscles in his face were beginning to fatigue from all the smiling. It was John's old BB gun cleaned and repackaged. He gave a questioning glance at Gwen. "I thought it would be a way to start marksman training."

Gwen nodded, a tear appearing in her eye. "I know."

He took the gun back from her. "I got my first one when I was only a little older than you. It shoots BBs. You might even be able to kill a squirrel with it."

"No way!" Haley exclaimed.

"Yup."

"Now there are strict rules with these. Never point it at anyone. You can only use it with an adult around. We don't play with it inside. If you show me that you can do this safely, then maybe we can start training with one of the big guns. Is it a deal?"

"Umm, yeah," Haley said. She took the BB gun back and hugged it. "So cool. Can we shoot it?"

"I'll set up a target after breakfast, and we can try it out."

"Awesome! I can't wait. Mommy, Santa got me a gun!"

Becky shouted from the kitchen. "I heard. I wonder if Santa thought you were a few years older than you are."

Haley wobbled her head back and forth. "Too late now. It's mine!" She brandished the weapon in both hands in the air.

He shared a look with Gwen. "She's going to have to learn sooner than later."

"I know, but it was always supposed to be a fun thing. Not a necessity."

"That's the way it is."

He hopped back on the couch and embraced Gwen, gripping her hands. "The first day of our new life."

She smiled at him. "I'm cherishing every minute of it."

TESS
Camp Forge, IA

Timid light shone on the other side of her eyelids as they lifted slowly into her head. Feeling as though they weighed a thousand pounds, her lids fell closed again, like steel curtains too heavy to keep open. Her body felt like she had been packed into a coffin then stuffed with cotton. Her limbs, numb and cold, tingled all over with pins and needles.

"Traitors," she mumbled. "Must tell Steele." She squeezed her eyes closed and tried to right her ship. Her head spun with a wicked buzz.

She tested her hands, flexing her fingers. Rough binding kept them in place near her waist. Shallow breathing came forced as if she had to remind herself to inhale and exhale on a regular basis.

Pushing herself upright, she shook her head. She lay in the corner of an empty spinning cabin. Bags, blankets, and trash littered the floor, but no people.

She tucked a knee underneath her and shakily stood, falling back into the cabin wall. Woozy, she rolled her shoulders stumbling forward. *What is wrong with me?* "Fuck."

Toppling into the door, she swung it open. The doorframe steadied her, giving her a moment to skim the rest of the camp. A fresh dusting of snow settled upon the cabins, barns, and farmhouse held within the protective walls of Camp Forge. Lazy flakes swirled in the morning light. It was a picturesque Christmas landscape, or at least would be if they weren't in the middle of the apocalypse.

The camp was quiet. Men and women would normally be moving about in the early morning collecting both water and wood for the start of their day, but no one was near the water pump. In fact, not a thing stirred in the camp.

She charged out into the bitter snow. *Must warn Steele. Traitors in the dark.* Her elbow propped her upright along the exterior of the cabin. *I can't think.*

When the log sides disappeared and only empty space met her arm, she stumbled and fell. White ground rushed to meet her face. *Crunch!* The crisp coolness melted into her face and hands. Breathing hard, she forced herself back up.

Armed men stood shadowed behind a cabin. They viewed her in silent indifference. Their faces were covered and dark. Their eyes cruel. They were men prepared to get a dirty job done and didn't care who got in the way.

"No!" Fumbling, she ran for the farmhouse. Her chest was heavy and tight. She felt her torso with numb fingers. A package was strapped around her, wires running from it. She blinked weighted eyelids. Her mind felt stuffed with cotton. *Must warn Steele.* Her feet broke through the snow as she stumbled forward. Snowflakes spun through the air like a tossed about snow globe.

She blinked at the two bodies sitting outside the Red Stripes' barn. They were slumped, heads hanging as if they had fallen asleep. A mass of men lined the side of Major Ludlow's troops' barn. Guns held in their hands, they watched her in eerie silence. Not one uttered a word.

Her voice belonged to a frog. "Help!" No one picked up a hand to help her onward. She rushed toward the Reynolds' white-and-black shuttered farmhouse.

Step by foggy step she trudged upward, each stair attempting to reach out and trip her. The cold air burnt her lungs with every breath. Collapsing to her knees on the porch, she bent forward and slammed her fists into the door. *We have a chance.*

STEELE
Camp Forge, IA

Three loud thumps resounded off the farmhouse door.

John stood from his parlor chair and tucked in the loose parts of his checkered green and red shirt. "How's that food coming, Lydia?" Dutch and Rocky barked and yipped near the door. "Quiet, you two."

"Just about ready. Eggs and bacon and plenty of it."

John meandered toward the door. "Little early for guests."

"Well, let them inside. We don't want anyone else getting sick," Lydia called from the kitchen.

He glanced over at Steele and Gwen with a broad smile. "But it's Christmas."

The dogs continued to bark. "Get back, you fools," he hollered at the animals.

Steele sat forward in his chair. "Haley, grab that box there." He pointed out a small package that contained pellets for her BB gun. "It's over there on the other side of the tree."

"I should really help Gram," Gwen said.

"Nonsense, love. Relax. It's our honeymoon."

Her eyebrows rose high on her face. "Honeymoon in Iowa?"

"We could take a trip down to Missouri?"

"Never thought I would say that this is exactly where I want to spend my honeymoon."

The clicks of nails on the hard wood floors escaped as the two labs ran back down the hall, fleeing the wrath of their master.

Steele called toward the kitchen, "Sure smells good, Lydia. Glad I didn't know you sooner or I would have been as large as a barn."

"We got plenty for you, big boy." Joy filled her voice at preparing to fix food for everyone.

"And big girl," Steele poked at Gwen.

She shook her head. "You're on thin ice."

"Already? We're only just married."

"It'll be the last day if you don't get that tomahawk out of my hip."

He adjusted the handle away from her. "Is that a tomahawk or are you happy to see me?"

She gave him an unamused smile. "Why do you wear those all the time? Can't we have one day off?"

"No, we can't."

Haley held up a red box. "This one?" Pellets clanged together inside.

"Yup. Bring it over."

There was a gasp from the foyer making the hair on Steele's neck stand on end. Gwen tried to look around him.

Alarm saturated John's voice. "Tess, dear God, what happened?"

Steele stood, his hand drifting for his firearm.

A white light embraced him, washing over everything like an ocean wave of heat. He only had a moment as the sound deafened him and sent him floating into the air a blind man.

JOSEPH
Cheyenne Mountain Complex, CO

"What happened?" The masked guard stuck a finger at one of the body bags, his eyes reading the situation with suspicion.

"Level 2 disease outbreak. AMRSA."

"AMRSA?"

"Airborne methicillin-resistant Staphylococcus aureus." The guard's eyes grew larger with each additional scientific word.

"Turn them Zulu?

"No, but." Joseph leaned closer and they leaned away from him. "If it were me, I'd rather turn Zulu than die like that."

"What's it do?"

"Suffocates you from the inside until you drown yourself. Horrible to watch."

The guard's hand stayed away from the zipper and clutched his M4 harder. Joseph scrunched up his nose. "It's been snowing outside. Been so long since I seen light. Real light. Let me tell you, it gets dark down there."

Shaking his head, the soldier goaded him. "Stop talking. Get those out of here."

Joseph nodded. "Sorry, I understand. Where do we normally take the highly contagious bodies for outside disposal?"

The guard motioned further down the loading docks. "There's a room on the side there."

Joseph started to push the stretcher. "Thank you." A small ounce of relief filled his insides with every step away from them.

With a little more distance between them, one of the sentries had a sudden burst of bravery. "Say, where's the normal guy who does this?"

Joseph brought himself to a halt. Sweat dripped along his skin. It had been a nightmare through every layer of the complex that they traversed. The soldiers, civilians, and everyone seemed to see them, but nobody had wanted too much to do with people pushing stacked body bags in HAZMAT suits and surgical masks.

"You tell me? You think I want to be pushing around a bunch of highly infectious corpses?"

The soldier blinked. He studied his clipboard for a moment. "All right. It's gonna be a few days though. They aren't making that run every Thursday and Saturday. Just Saturday's now."

Joseph's eyes grew in diameter. "What do you mean?"

"I mean just that. Once a week for body disposal. What's it matter anyway? As long as they ain't moving, I could care less."

"Got it." Joseph shook his head. His voice became a little gruffer. "They don't tell us shit down there."

The guard glanced up at him and he smiled with his eyes. "You and me both."

The loading docks were about two hundred yards through a curved dome entrance into the base of the mountain. Everything was off-loaded into a giant chamber that resembled a cave, but a cave that had been rounded out, no hanging stalactites or growing stalagmites.

All goods were inspected there before being carted farther into the interior of the complex. Everything went through a hulking X-ray scanner. *Shit. TSA has got better looking things than that*, he thought. Large boxy openings for semi-trailers lined the warehouse so goods could easily be unloaded. He passed soldiers unloading crates of ammunition from the back of a trailer.

Joseph steered his stretcher along the elevated platform. Hollis assured him as long as the base didn't "button up" due to a more heightened security threat, the mountain base would continue to receive supplies from the outside. He stopped near a plain gray warehouse door. He tested the handle. It was locked.

"I'll get that for you," came a familiar voice. Dr. Hollis ambled over, his white doctor's coat flaring at the sides. He put his ID card to the scanner and the door clicked open.

"Everything okay?" he whispered.

Joseph shoved the stretcher inside and flicked on a light. Four body bags lined the back wall. He turned on Hollis, speaking too loud. "There's no disposal today."

"I'll help you," Hollis said. He grabbed the plastic-covered feet of the first bag. "I know that now. They updated the scheduling. Nobody consulted me."

"What are we going to do? They can't stay in here for days. Someone will find them."

Hollis paled. "I don't know."

They set the body down on the ground. Joseph crouched next to the body bag and unzipped the zipper down the center. Byrnes's face was that of a man in a deep sleep and had the look of a deeply depressed brooding vampire, his cheeks gaunt and his face set in a permanent disapproving frown. Joseph stood and went for the next one.

They organized the bodies in a row with the others opening the bags of everyone yet living.

Hollis eyed them with worry. "I'll check on them in an hour."

"What are we going to do? Eventually they are going to figure it out."

Hollis grabbed Joseph's sleeve. "They think they're dead. There's no reason for them to come looking. We are fine. We must go on with the plan."

***

Joseph pushed the last stretcher of body-bagged prisoners down the loading dock. The wheel on his stretcher squeaked and twisted about forty-five degrees to the side in annoying intervals causing the stretcher to stick on the floor and turn errantly to the right. Then he would have to push harder until the dumb thing rotated back around. Thirty seconds later, he was steering the cart back on track. He almost lost a body in front of an officer when the wheel completely stuck, refusing to rotate at all, and he had to rock the stretcher to propel it back into motion.

He'd long ago pitted out his white doctor's coat, sweat saturating through his clothes. Dr. Desai was worse. They'd been lugging bodies for what seemed like hours, and she'd been in her HAZMAT suit all day long. Damp black curls stuck to her forehead, her skin glistening with perspiration.

Dr. Hollis's round shape hovered near the edge of the loading dock. His excuse had been to check vaccine crates for shipping within the Golden Triangle, ensuring they were properly packaged and stored. Joseph didn't know how long he could keep the ruse up of needing to be in the loading area. The guards had already rotated a shift since they'd started hauling out the bodies.

He directed the gurney into the storage room. Thirteen bags lay along the wall. Both he and Desai got on either end of a bag, hoisting it off the others.

"This one's heavy," Desai grunted. She strained under the weight.

"Soon they'll start to wake up."

They set the body down as gently as they could, repeating the process for each prisoner.

"If I got the dosing right," Desai said.

Joseph reached for her. Their eyes locked together. "You did."

A grim smile passed her lips. "I did."

A deep voice startled them both. "What happened down there?" A soldier in ACUs leered at them.

"You should stay back," Dr. Desai said, holding out a hand.

The guard didn't seem fazed by her warning, only more intrigued with the reason why he, the gatekeeper of his domain would not need to stick his nose into someone else's business. "Why?"

"Infected," Joseph said.

"I haven't heard any news of an outbreak." His hand reached up to his radio at his collar. "Sarge, can you confirm an outbreak inside the complex?" He took a step inside. "Toby." He waved to his partner and a second later his radio sounded off, "Affirm, Berger."

Joseph walked toward him trying to drive him back out. "We already went over this with the last guys, it's not the Primus Necrovirus but an airborne MRSA. Very deadly. Very contagious. Just being in this room puts you at risk."

The soldier had a chiseled jaw and a small mouth that looked like it loved to give short strict orders. He studied Joseph, eyes shifting over his shoulder. "Why the fuck is that thing moving then?" Berger stuck out an arm that felt like iron and shoved Joseph to the side. His weapon reported in the small room. A line of impacts puffed the back wall leading down to the body's head. The form collapsed back into the bag.

Joseph sucked in his breath and held before he whispered. "Oh, God."

The soldier stepped aggressively toward the bags, his weapon trained on them. "We should put bullets in the rest of them to be sure." He turned back to Joseph. "You sure about them not being Zulus? 'Cause that infected piece of shit was moving."

Joseph held up a nervous hand. "I can assure you. These are not infected with Primus Necrovirus." He ducked his head. "Please! Do not shoot them."

"We need them intact for testing," Desai shouted from outside the door.

"Fuck that," Berger said. His eyes grew wider. "They're moving." He pointed his carbine at the next body bag. *Bang.* The gunshot echoed from wall to wall reverberating on itself in the small room. The bag rippled with impact from his round. Joseph almost puked at the spray of gore splattering the wall.

Another soldier charged into the room. "What the fuck is going on?"

"These fucking bodies are moving." Berger, wide-eyed, stared at Joseph. "What's going on?"

Joseph held out a hand. "They're not infected."

Toby crouched down getting his face closer to the body. With his finger, he forced open an eyelid. "His eyes look normal." He glanced back at Joseph. "It doesn't look Zulu."

Berger turned his gun on Joseph. "They aren't dead, are they? And they ain't Zulu."

Joseph put up both his hands. *Have to run with my lie.* "You don't understand. This is a very deadly disease. You shouldn't be here without precautionary measures."

One of the prisoners sat up. Her voice came out slurred. "Don't shoot." Both guards pointed their guns at her.

"They're talking now?"

"I know her. She's one of those, those conspirators." Toby turned back to Joseph.

A second later, Toby rocketed into the air like he'd been hit by a train, his head whiplashing as he was launched off his feet. His head smacked the wall, and his body went limp. He collapsed on the row of bodies with a plastic crunch.

Berger gawked at his comrade strewn sideways over the bodies, and Joseph lunged for his gun. The guard reacted fast and body checked Joseph with his carbine. The hard metal of the weapon took the wind out of him, and his back smacked the solid surface with a slap.

Desai grabbed the guard around the neck and Hollis charged them, his hands clenched with the ferocity of a crazed silverback gorilla. His fists pummeled Berger's face once, twice, three times until the soldier was knocked unconscious with blood pouring from his nose.

"We don't have time," Hollis breathed, his neck stretching with each labored breath. He gave them a tired grin. "I told you I was a fabulous prop in the scrum." He rolled to the side and used the wall to help himself up. "We have to leave now. Grab their ID cards."

Joseph removed the ID and a radio from Berger's vest. "Docks, status? We heard gunfire, over."

"All clear, nothing to report."

"Berger, what happened?"

"Uhh," Joseph said before he clicked the button. He shoved the other soldier over and read his name tag. "Toby fired his gun by mistake. Everyone's fine."

"Send him the fuck over here. Jesus Christ. You know how many fucking reports I gotta do for this kind of shit?"

"He's going to the bathroom." Joseph tossed the radio on the ground.

Prisoners were waking up and holding their heads.

Byrnes wiped his forehead. "God, that's a headache." Joseph bent down and removed the carbines from the soldiers. He handed one to Byrnes.

"You're going to need this. They know we're trying to escape."

"The guards saw one of the bags moving and thought they were infected," Desai said hurried.

Byrnes frown deepened. "Do we have a vehicle?"

"There's a van over here," Hollis said. "It's the best I can do."

Hollis peered out the door and walked out of the room. "It's over there." He pointed. "I'll run interference."

The prisoners wrapped arms around one another in their groggy state, those that were more coherent carrying the others. Joseph led them across the docks to a white van parked near the wall. Hollis locked the door of the makeshift morgue and followed.

They slid the van door open. "Hurry," Joseph said. The prisoners crawled in. "We have to hurry."

Desai crawled out of her HAZMAT suit. "What are we doing?"

"We're getting out of here. Get in."

"How will we produce the vaccine?"

"We will figure out a way, but they will kill us or worse."

Her dark eyes scrunched in worry, but she nodded and climbed inside.

Joseph crawled into the driver's seat and turned the engine on.

"Hollis," Joseph low-shouted out of the window trying to inconspicuous.

The heavyset doctor began walking toward them and stopped. He turned. Soldiers marched within fifteen feet, their weapons pointed at him.

"We should go," Byrnes said from the passenger seat.

Joseph threw the van into drive but kept his foot on the brake.

A soldier lunged for Hollis, trying to apprehend him, but Hollis managed to get a hand on the weapon. The men struggled back and forth on the loading dock.

"We should go," Byrnes repeated. "There's nothing we can do for him."

Joseph twisted the wheel and drove down the cave corridor.

THE PASTOR
Camp Forge, IA

Orange fire burst from the farmhouse doorway, engulfing Tess's form like a singular flame from a dragon's mouth. She was standing one moment and simply disappeared into an inferno the next. Vanished and evaporated, she was turned into the nothingness of a brisk fiery breeze by the extreme heat and the holocaustal flames. The natural beauty of the entire thing took his breath away.

Shockwaves rippled forth, and the earth shook beneath him. It was an earthquake brought on by man's destructive ingenuity to destroy his enemies. The sound raptured, washing over the camp announcing the commencement of their takeover. He knew God looked down upon them and smiled.

"May God take your troubled soul, Tess." Debris rocketed into the air like fireworks of wood and siding. A door sailed airborne, flipping end over end. It finished its full rotation as it broke upon the second story of the barn across the yard. The orange explosion was topped off by opaque black smoke that billowed into the air, following close behind the fireball. His ears rang with the songs of angels.

His followers crouched next to the side of a nearby cabin. Debris rained from the sky. He turned to Peter, both of their shoulders pressed against the logs. "And so it begins. God wills it."

The Chosen brothers and sisters nearby eyed him, awaiting their chance to strike the enemy. Peter stared expectantly, ready to go to work.

"You may go, son. Vanquish our enemies. Raise the Kingdom of God on your shoulders."

Peter stood for a moment, hesitation in his step, then bowed his head. "A pleasure, Father."

Does this man still fear Steele? His servant's hesitation would mean nothing this day for their victory would be overwhelming.

Peter seemed to realize his weakness. Raising his voice to a shout, he shook his AK-47 high in the air. "Death to the unbelievers."

The pastor pointed to Matthew and his followers with his carpenter's hammer. He waved them forward. The handsome man gave him a white-toothed grin and charged into the open, surrounding the Red Stripes' barn. They kicked over the slain guards on their way by. A cluster of his men lifted the heavy beam to their shoulders and tossed it on the ground.

Distant gunfire tapped his eardrum. That would be Luke killing the guards by the gate and seeing that the War Machines had an easy time gaining entry into the compound.

Hungover men in camouflage ran from the other two barns. The bewildered men staggered as rounds exploded into their guts. Peter slowed to a walk, shooting some in the back. Their feet kicked up as they collapsed in red snow.

His boots crunched as he continued his march through the center of the camp, a feeling of euphoric impunity cloaking him. His mind buzzed with endorphins at the fall of their corrupt overlords. He felt like Moses freeing his people from their Egyptian slave masters.

Matthew's men sprayed rounds into the barn holding the Red Stripes. Gunfire erupted from the Sable Pointers' barn. The Chosen were met with screams for mercy from their enemies.

A Sable Pointer staggered and fell face-first, body penetrated by bullets. *We knew some would fight.* His men surrounded the barn, moving with godly purpose. His followers were clear of mind and went to their deaths willingly while his enemies were hungover and exhausted from their lewd debauchery excuse of a wedding.

Brothers Thomas and Anthony ran to him, hastily bowing their heads.

"Father, the Iron Drakes are pinned in their cabins but are putting up a fight. We've lost a few of our men already."

"Use the tools that God has given you. Burn them with God's fire, and do not let them escape. If they do not emerge, they'll be purified with his holy flames or our righteous bullets."

Thomas bowed his head. "Your will shall be done." The men ran off in the direction of the cabins.

He watched in glee as the two men holding the barn door of the Sable Pointers were mowed down into a twisted pile of arms and legs, their insides blown from their bodies. The others pushed inside, trying to escape. The doors swung closed, sealing them off.

Farther on his right, a cluster of soldiers sprinted for the river like they were making a prison break. Many were gunned down as they climbed the log and earthen wall, the wall they'd built to protect expediting their demise.

The pastor continued his walk through the death camp. He made it to the wreckage of the farmhouse. The heart of his enemies' lair. The house burned in yellow and orange flames that reached for heavens in praise. The back half of the house still stood but was alight. Time would bring it down. Pieces of blackened wood were strewn over the ground. He bent down and picked up a soot-covered silver bell. It tinkled as he held it. "Merry Christmas indeed." He placed it in his pocket.

Rough men in leather jackets with gears patches on them jogged into the camp. War Child marched front and center to the pastor. A nasty sneer spread across his lips beneath his tightly trimmed white beard. "Looks like you took care of most of them." Nonchalantly, he flipped open a pack of cigarettes and tossed one into his mouth. He flicked a lighter. He inhaled while nodding. "The bomb planted on Tess did the trick. Saw the explosion from a mile away."

Black smoke encircled the base. "It went according to plan. We've purified many souls this day." He searched the sky for his god. "May their souls suffer for an eternity. My followers tell me the Iron Drakes are putting up a stiff resistance."

"Ah, my boy Frank putting up a fight? Let me see if I can talk some sense into him. If not, I'm not really sorry about putting them in the ground." War Child turned to his club. "Come on, Machines. The old Iron Drakes need a talkin' to." He waved his men onward toward the cabins.

"This day truly is blessed." The smoke dissipated into the air, and the pastor raised his hands high.

AHMED
Bailey Homestead, MO

The Singleton men sat in a crude semicircle of chairs and couches, cradling their guns between their legs. The Bailey farmhouse had a spacious living room with a broad wood-burning fireplace in the center. A cluster of Bailey supporters and Bailey family stood on one side, arms folded unmoved across chests. It was a circle of mistrust, but a circle that wasn't currently shooting each other into pieces.

"I just don't see how we can stand up to them. There must be over forty of 'em, and they have our girls hostage." Sly shook his head thinking. "Macleod made it very clear that if we even looked at his club the wrong way, he would skin her alive. I can't lose another child to this world." He folded his arms over his chest and peered at Jim. "And I know he'd do the same to your Sadie." He paused a second. "He's got us by the balls and can geld us anytime he feels like it."

Even if the two families could come together on this, the predicament was overbearing. "Do you know where they've set up their base?" Ahmed asked.

Sly eyed him for a moment and realized he didn't know him. "You're that Arab boy from the meeting. Where'd you come from?" Mistrust crept into his eyes.

"I used to work with Macleod until he killed my friends and betrayed us."

"Not surprising knowing that prick job. Gina overheard some of his gang talking about a mine and quarry. Can't be only one around here. The old MacDonald Limestone Mine."

Lee spoke, his arm wrapped around Gina. She was still shaken by all the events but had been spared and dumped with the children to the Bailey homestead, having been deemed too old and angry for captivity at the club's expense. "Only one way in and one way out of there. They would see us coming a mile away and gut the girls before we even had a chance to rescue them."

"How do we get inside?" Sly said open-ended to the men.

"If we can ambush a group of them, take their clothes and bikes, we can sneak in. Then it's at least a rush to save them," Ahmed said.

Sly shook his head. "Too risky."

Jim's face was growing flush with irritation. "We can't just sit back and leave those girls to their whims."

"There has to be another angle we can take?" Ahmed said. He gestured at Sly. "You could turn Jim over as a prisoner."

"A lot of trust there, Ahmed," Jim said with a warning glare.

"He'd prolly just shoot him on the spot." Sly scratched his stubbly face while he thought.

Lee brought to mind a younger Albert Einstein getting shocked with a new theory. "I been there. We used to screw off in the mine after they closed it down. Elevator worked back then, but that was like thirty some years ago."

"Can we use it?" Ahmed asked.

Sly's look turned thoughtful. "He's right. I been there too. Back in the day."

"If we can get the engine going, it might work."

Ahmed shared a glance with Jim. "If we can sneak inside, we wouldn't need to rush the entrance."

"I like that," Sly said.

Brett Foxworth shook his curly-haired head. "Surely they would hear us coming."

"Then we will need a diversion." Ahmed grew in confidence. They were finally getting somewhere. "What if we draw them out? Set up a fake ambush so they call for help. Then we send men down the elevator to rescue the girls."

"Could work," Jim said.

"Roadblock them close to the hideout. Make it easy to call for help. Then we hightail it on out of there. They got those motorcycles; it'll be hard to give them the slip. Best we got is a truck." Sly rubbed his chin in thought.

"Go where a motorcycle can't," Ahmed said.

Lee spoke up. "I've lived here a long time and I know these roads like the back of my hand. Andy and I can lose 'em."

Ahmed faced Jim. "You and me to the elevator?"

Jim's icy eyes sparkled like a frosty sunny morning. "Yeah, that sounds like the plan."

"And me. I can show you how to work it," Sly said. "The rest of y'all are going to go with Lee. You're going to ambush the Wolf Riders and then you're gonna disappear except for Lee. Lee's gonna ride them all over the county."

"What happens after that?" Andy said.

All of the older men regarded Lee's son with questioning eyes. "What do you mean?" Sly said.

"I mean. After we get Sadie and Jes, then what? They'll be looking for us. For revenge." He cast his eyes down as if he were afraid of speaking too much to men he clearly respected.

"Once the girls are safe, we go to war. This is our turf." Sly looked at Jim, gauging his reception. "We had our differences, but I'll be damned if we give it up to some outsider running us through the ringer. What do you say?"

All the men eyed Jim. If there was no deal, then they may as well go back to killing each other or paying Macleod tribute.

Jim licked his lips, staring at Sly. "I hated you my entire life, and as much as I hate to say it, you're right. That bastard can't come in here and enslave us. I'm sorry I didn't figure it out sooner."

A sharp breath escaped Sly. "I regret what's been done in the past. I can't take it back, but we can make right going forward." He stood and stepped in front of Jim. For a moment, the room grew tense, like an unseen stress yoking every single man and weighing down on their necks and shoulders. He stuck out his hand to Jim. Deadpanned eyes zoned past Sly's extended peace offering, another brawl waiting to embroil the two families once again.

"Take it," Ahmed nodded at Jim's hand. "Change this course now. Do it for Sadie and those kids. Without peace, there is no future."

Jim flattened his lips and nodded. "Let's join as partners." He got to his feet and cupped Sly's hand.

Sly smiled. "Peace for war."

Jim put a hand on the back of Sly's arm. "Peace for war."

The men grinned. Each one gripped harder for more control over the other. Jim waved Ahmed up. "Never would have gotten here without Ahmed." His ice-pick eyes pierced Ahmed's dark brown ones. "Not sure where you came from, but you done good."

"Sadie's kept me here."

Sly's grin turned a bit devilish. "You takin' a liking to her?"

"I'm sure Jim doesn't want to hear about it, but I have. There's just something special about her."

"Ahmed, I think it's pretty clear, but if you hurt her, I'll kill ya."

"I have no doubt in my mind, my friend," Ahmed said with a grin.

STEELE
Camp Forge, IA

His eyelashes beat away flecks of dust and dirt. Blackened sky crushed upon him, a river of billowing darkness. He squeezed his eyes closed, granules of dirt irritating them. He triple blinked. A high-pitched constant ring screeched in his ears, deafening him. He brought a shaky hand that he was unsure was his up to his ear. Warm liquid seeped from them. Opening his jaw, he rotated it in pain. He pressed his eyes tightly together again and rolled on his shoulder with a violent cough.

A charcoal odor mixed with blood and burnt flesh took over his nose. He felt like he'd been trampled by a herd of horses. Fierce coughing overtook him, his lungs responding in seared pain. He tried to suck in air but only could inhale the smoke. He spit on the ground. Everything around him was unrecognizable.

The faint tap of gunfire made his heart jump faster. He looked up; the Christmas tree burned next to him. *I'm in the parlor.* The needles were ember-tipped and fraying black as they were eaten alive by flames. The ornaments melted down, shrinking and folding in on themselves.

A form lay near him on its side. "Gwen?" He crawled on his hands and knees toward her. His entire body shook like it'd been struck with a frying pan. He took her shoulder and gently rolled her over to her back. Her mouth hung open and her eyes rolled into the back of her head.

"Oh, god," he breathed. "Oh, god. Gwen, baby." He ran his hands over

335

her body searching for anything out of place. She seemed intact. There wasn't much blood on her, nothing that required immediate attention. He put a hand to her neck, pushing hard into her artery. He felt nothing, adjusted his fingers, and did it again. A faint beat of her heart tapped away through her veins.

The side wall was succumbing to the flames. He turned his woozy head, following the blaze and finding the entirety of the foyer and front porch had simply transformed into rubble. The white outside melted nearby, the debris from the house peppering the snow.

He stretched his jaw, attempting to equalize the pressure in his ears and unclog them. *I must get oriented.* Two men stepped lightly through the wreckage. *They've come to help.* He almost called out, *"Here we are. Help us,"* but something in his gut stayed his tongue. His mind was an opaque fog, but he held back.

No names came to mind as he studied them. His eyes blinked furiously trying to place them. They held guns to their shoulders. Men hunting for enemies, not coming to help the injured. His left hand fell upon his holstered M9A1 Beretta 9mm. He drew it deftly and aimed, wavering for a second, pressing the trigger evenly. The closest man flinched. He sank to his knees. A second later, Steele let two rounds go into the chest of the man behind him. He crumpled backward into the smoldering rubble.

Struggling to gain his feet beneath him, he managed to get upright. He had to focus to steady himself. Wavering, he bent back down. "Come on, baby," he said to Gwen's form. A little girl's wailing caught his attention away.

He followed the cries to the other side of the room. The room now opened into the kitchen. Little Haley beat her mother's chest with a hand. "Mommy, please." She sobbed and tears streaked her cheeks.

His voice came out hoarse. "Haley." He bent down touching her shoulder. She gawked at him with blackened cheeks and broke down into open-mouthed hysterical bawling where she couldn't breathe because every ounce of energy was emitting fear and pain. She hugged him. He scooped her up with his other arm, glancing down at Becky. "We'll come back for her." He ran back to Gwen and holstered his weapon. He crouched to the floor, placing her as gingerly as he could on his other shoulder. Driving with his legs, he hefted the two into the air. His body screamed at him, but he ignored its protest, shoving it deep inside.

Unsteady, he forced his quivering legs to obey, and he moved through a smoke-filled hallway toward the back of the house. He went into John and Lydia's bedroom. Dutch and Rocky danced around him, tails down and ears back. Dutch let out an excited bark.

He set Gwen on the bed and took his tomahawk out. He snapped the head of the light ax into the glass, breaking the window. Running the tomahawk around the frame, he knocked away any remaining shards.

"My arm hurts," Haley whined at him. Her fingers curled into a ball, and she held her arm out at him.

"Shhh, sweetie. You have to be quiet now." She tried to suck in a breath but struggled between the smoke and her terror.

He crouched down in front of her. "You're going to be okay. I'm going to set you down outside. I want you to run for those cabins right there and hide. I'll come and get you in a minute. Do you understand?"

Her lips trembled, but she nodded. He hoisted her through the window, setting her on the ground. She stared up at him for a moment. Her eyes filled with tears, eyes reminiscent of Gwen's but darker. She could have been his daughter, and he was setting her outside in the middle of a war.

He lifted his chin in an authoritative manner. "Run now, girl." She blinked and ran for the cabins, her little feet kicking up snow like baby powder. He turned back inside. Smoke flowed down the hallway and pooled into the room. He heaved Gwen's unconscious form and laid her outside in the cold snow. *She'll be safe. She'll be safe*, he reminded himself over and over. As fast as he could, he followed by hefting the two dogs outside. They laid by Gwen, ears perked, nuzzling her with muzzles.

He ran back down the hall, using the wall to support him. Turning into the blown-out kitchen, he gave it a once over. Lydia sat with her back shoved against her cabinets. Arms were thrown to the sides like she was waiting for a hug.

Steele rushed to her and checked her pulse. She had none. Her eyes stared back at him, open and unfeeling. "Goddammit." He wiped his hand over her soft lids, forever closing her eyes. He stood half-crouched, peering through the wreckage. There was a gunfight kicking off near the barns. The tap-taps and pop, pop, pops, rattled back and forth. More cautious men inspected the farmhouse wreckage outside.

There was no sign of John. He threw Becky into a fireman's carry. The ceiling above him dipped inward, dropping wood and lapping flames.

He took a step back and jumped the collapsed ceiling for the hallway. The heat from the growing inferno nipped at his heels, and he sprinted for the bedroom. He kicked the door closed behind him and rushed to the window. Smoke seeped through the cracks between the door and the floor.

He lifted Becky through the window and laid her by Gwen. Gwen blinked, raising herself onto her elbows. She coughed and placed a hand protectively on her lower stomach. "Oh, god!" The dogs licked her face and she shoved them. "Get away."

Steele jumped down and crouched next to her. "You're going to be okay." His eyes darted up. Men in leather with gears as patches marched through the cabins. They hadn't put eyes on them yet.

"What happened?" Gwen said.

"Somebody set off a bomb."

"A bomb?"

"Haley? Where's Haley?" Gwen's eyes frantically searched the camp. A booming crash reverberated from inside causing Steele to duck. "Where's Pa and Gram?"

"Gwen." She turned to him, confusion in her eyes. The look of fear and sadness on her face was something he could never stand to see again. He forced that down with the rest. "We have to keep moving."

She shook her head in little spurts. "No. No. Not without them."

He stroked her cheek. "They're gone. Help me with Becky."

Gwen sucked in air through her mouth. "I'm going to be sick."

"Later. We must move." He picked up Becky in his arms and ran for a cabin with Gwen. He pushed in the door. Gwen followed him inside, and he set Becky down as she closed the door.

"Gwenna," Haley exclaimed.

"Yes, baby," Gwen said. The little girl ran and jumped in her arms, causing Gwen to grimace. "Not too hard, sweetie." She smoothed her hair repeatedly as she held her. She eyed Steele. "What is going on?"

Men shouting and the pops of gunshots shook the air from the next cabin over. Gwen's eyes widened and narrowed. Steele eyed her, taking a deep breath. He removed his Beretta checking the magazine. Thirteen rounds. He slipped the magazine back into place. They locked eyes, the realization of what was to come was understood.

"They must not take us alive," Gwen whispered.

He nodded slowly. "They won't." The implications of his words hardened his insides.

ALVARADO
Northern Mississippi River

They'd lost Johnson to a Zulu a quarter mile back. By the time the dwindling squad of Marines had turned guns in his direction, he'd been bitten several times. The Marine had laid prone on the ice, shaking as the virus dominated his system.

Alvarado finished him off before they ran. No formalities. No salutes. Just a mercy bullet to make sure the beefy Marine didn't get back up again. Each death stung her, but she had to ignore the angry fire in her gut in order to keep going. Any moment spent dwelling on their deaths would be her last.

A fire smoldered down to embers in her belly, but despite the numbness of it all, the death and cold were still there. Sixty seconds after she'd shot him, it didn't matter. The C4 detonated, throwing pieces of ice and infected into the air like God had decided he'd had it with that part of the river and flicked it with a giant finger.

Her jaw chattered fiercely as they stumbled in exhaustion to the next section. She knew her core body temperature was dipping dangerously low. Her motor functions were rapidly decreasing, and only the desperate fight forward kept her from succumbing to hypothermia.

Each time they stopped, more dead closed in from every direction, except from the destroyed ice, where the frigid water encroached on the Marines. With every stop, they used more and more bullets. It was an unsustainable mission. Eventually, they'd hit a breaking point.

"Last mag!" Rasmussen fired two successive single round shots.

"Me too," yelled Odom. He let an empty magazine fall to the ice.

She slapped the timer on the C4 and set it down. "We got three more then we go home." The home part of her words sounded hollow even for her, but they had to keep it together or they would die quick painful deaths.

"Warm food. Walls," O'Bannon breathed.

"Sounds like the Ritz," Odom responded.

O'Bannon cracked a smile. "Better."

They jogged away from the explosives with heavy feet. The dead were slower, but eventually they would catch the Marines. The laws of physics demanded it. More dead congregated ahead of them. The Marines were not tireless; Zulus were. It was simple. They were playing in overtime, and while every second counted, ultimately it would be the end and they would lose.

Sixty seconds ticked by as they scrambled over the uneven ice. The only blessing bestowed upon them was that their sled was lighter than before. A huge boom rewarded their efforts, and the Marines kept their heads down as ice spilled from the sky around them.

She ducked as she hauled the sled with O'Bannon. The tall man leaned into his harness, his body almost diagonal in effort. Infected closed ranks for them ahead, an uncoordinated yet effective effort. Dark grotesque shapes of misery and death contrasted against the pureness of the ice.

"Ditch the sled. We'll carry the rest." She threw the harness off her, sucking in air. Her insides were already frozen in miniature crystals, each breath she took intensifying the pain.

She and O'Bannon scooped the equipment into their arms and ran over uneven ice. When she fell, she laid there for a moment, enjoying the rest from her freezing cold exertion. Footsteps crunched the frozen surface. O'Bannon's face hovered near hers. His eyes were wide with fight. "Ma'am. We ain't finished." He hauled her upright. She didn't respond. All she could do was nod her head, too tired and cold to say a word.

They ran for the remaining Marines standing in a small semicircle. She planted the next charge, listening to them expend what few rounds they had left in futile defiance.

"I'm out!" Odom shouted.

Rasmussen glared back at her. "Me too."

"Need more time."

The Marines closed ranks as to not be taken from behind, pressing in on one another. Almost shoulder to shoulder, they stood like the remains of a Roman legion ready to give their lives. M4s turned into clubs, knives were drawn, and E-tools were brandished. The dead moaned. Their prey was finally not evading them. They had given up from the long chase and now the dead closed in for the final kills.

"Rarr," Rasmussen yelled. He swung his M4 like a baseball bat, slugging an infected in the side of the skull. "We gotta hurry," he breathed, waiting for his next victim. The mass of infected drove in closer, flesh hanging from bones, tattered clothes covering dark gray skin, bony fingers ready to remove entrails for feasting.

With a quivering finger, she flicked on the timer. Sixty seconds.

"Move, Marines!" she commanded at the top of her lungs. She would have loved to surge forward like a bull rushing the dead around them, but it was more like a snail pushing a rock. Hands clawed at her and she shoved them off. She gripped a Zulu by the neck. It was impossible to tell if it was a man or woman at this point, only an androgynous killing machine. Its mouth chomped its teeth at her.

Odom's M4 carbine whipped around, crumpling the back of its skull. His voice came out exhausted. "You owe me one."

Her mouth shook out her every word, her muscles trying to keep her alive. "We're even." She tried to run ahead but was driven back into their small group. Guns swung wildly at the dead, and the Marines beat them to a stalemate with tooth-and-nail fighting. But they were losing. They would die on the ice. Holding the last explosive to her chest like it was her babe, she kicked an infected in the gut, sending it to the ground.

Odom called out, his voice higher in fear. He'd been dragged down to the ice. She thrust one away from him, but another tore through his pants. He screamed as it shredded his leg. Decrepit hands reached for her. Rasmussen charged the dead surrounding Odom, spiking one with his knife and jabbing another through the eye.

"There's too many!" His voice cut off as a Zulu hooked his jaw. He knifed one and another took its place. He went down when the gore-stained fingers separated his lower mandible from his face.

Chaos took them. Every time she would bring one down or shove one back, another was tugging her the other way. She didn't know which way the next threat would come from, they were everywhere. Moans surrounded her like quicksand.

"Major!" screamed O'Bannon. She turned back. He was the last Marine standing with her. Brave and mean, he was still in the fight.

He locked eyes with her and nodded. She knew. He knew. Better to take them with you than leave them existing on the field of battle. She flipped the switch and set the explosive behind her.

"Semper Fi, motherfuckers!" O'Bannon yelled. He jogged forward in a final charge to clear a pathway through the infected. His gun brandished left and right as he wielded it like a medieval bludgeon.

"Semper Fi!" she called back with every ounce of energy still inside her. Unslinging her M4A1, she held it like a baseball bat. She charged into the swath of slain corpses behind O'Bannon. He'd made progress destroying three, four, five, six Zulus, one after the other. She jabbed her M4A1 into a Zulu face and brushed off the icy fingers that clutched at her neck. For a brief second, she thought they might make it to the frozen Minnesota shoreline.

But the dead were many and relentless. They collapsed around O'Bannon. He raised his carbine for another swing, but he was too slow. His muscles weren't firing like they should. Marines were flesh and blood, not machines. As much as she wished he could go on killing forever, he couldn't.

Even as she swung her M4A1 into the back of a Zulu's skull, splashes of warm crimson blood were already melting the ice around him. Zulus fell upon his dying corpse, feasting on his defiant remains with no salute or victory chant for their valiant enemy, only heartless consumption.

It was an opportunity to make it a little farther. She ran away from them. Her squad was dead, the last bomb planted, and the mission would be complete. To die with her Marines would be an honor. Her insides felt like a cool ice-cream headache. She was tired of running. She was tired of losing.

She was tired of seeing her Marines fall to the dead. She wanted to call the shot of how she went out. Caught from behind as she ran or facing the enemy like any God-fearing Marine should? Her body shaking and her lips blue, she slowed down and stopped. Her breath burst from her chest like a cold-smoke locomotive.

With infected moans, the Zulus glowed with the prospect of adding her to the ranks of her dead Marines.

She spun on the dead. Clusters of Zulus, like pigs to a trough, surrounded the remains of her boys. It was easy to see along the white icy river. Masses of infected human scum devouring the bodies of her tough, loyal, fallen Marines. Odom stood back up, unsteady. Her heart didn't even skip a beat to the cruel jest because now he was one of them. Cold, dead, and now, her enemy.

The freezing cold made her shake. She shouted as loud as she could. "Fucking Wisconsin!" Her weapon in hand, her voice carried even louder. "Who the hell would want to live in this wasteland?"

Flashes of her childhood in L.A., sun beating down on the concrete jungle she called home, playing soccer in a dirt field, and the single-story duplex of her childhood. It almost didn't feel like her memory, but like something she'd seen in a movie and adopted as her own.

Her teeth chattered and clicked as her muscles tried to keep her alive. She knew it was all a losing battle. The dead or the cold would take her. She struggled to blink her eyes. Crystalized water had frozen her black lashes in frigid clumps. Her hair numbed her skull like a crusting white helmet. She clutched her M4A1 as if it would give her life-giving warmth.

"God is with me." She'd known that her entire life. "God bless the Corps." The thought pushed the smallest prickle of heat in her gut. "For God and the Corps." A small smile forced its way over her stiff lips. She took a step in their direction. It was only a few feet before they were close enough to kill, but the movement empowered her. She was in control of her destiny, not the white-eyed devils ahead of her.

She knew her hand broke when she rammed it into an infected head, but everything was a painful blur. Grappling with another dead, she tossed him over her hip. Spinning, she jabbed her gun into another neck and kicked in the knee of another. A hand clutched for her hair, digging into her scalp. She cried out as the strands broke off in its grasp and forced the barrel of her carbine into the Zulu's neck, using it to impale the disgusting rotting human.

The barrel stopped when it was deep enough to catch her front sight. She heaved, tossing it to the ground. More came for her. She would give them what they wanted: a bitter fight.

She chopped at arms, snapping brittle bones. Stomping, she crushed the side of a Zulu's skull. The graying shapes closed, and there was no more space to move, only a jumble of bodies. More grasped her neck as they tried to control her, and their weight bore her down to the ice. A jagged hunk of ice rammed her side as they piled on top. She didn't think about it as she fought from her back.

She grabbed the creature by its neck in return. Its teeth chattered in anticipation closing in on the tip of her nose; her teeth shook.

A sound like the earth breaking engulfed her. She held onto her foe as they were taken airborne. It still tried to bite her as they became weightless bodies unbound by gravity. Her fingers dug even harder into the thing's neck. She was a pit bull, never letting go.

STEELE
Camp Forge, IA

Gwen sat on the floor. Her legs laid to the side and Haley hung onto her, gripping her tightly, terrified of everything happening around them. Her sooty face was streaked with tears, and blood was drying out of her ears and nose. She squeezed Haley into her chest as if her body could prevent the violence from reaching her.

In his good hand, he held his Beretta and in the other his tomahawk. It felt light in his hand as if it were a bladed extension of his body. He wound his light ax in circles with quick flicks of his wrist, each circle ramping him up for the close combat brutality he was about to unleash on his enemies.

A fist pounded on the door and tightened him up. Gwen stared defiantly toward the impending intruders.

A gruff voice shouted, "Open the fucking door!"

Dutch and Rocky started to bark, crowding the door, fur standing along their backs.

Haley audibly sobbed into Gwen's breast, and Gwen reinforced her hold on the girl. "Shhh, baby." Her voice barely breached the edge of Steele's mind. He verged on violently exploding like a penned animal willing to kill anything in its path.

"If you don't open this door, it's going to be bad," the voice said into it, muffling the sound.

The sole of the man's boot was louder than his fist, and the cabin shook beneath it. Rocky and Dutch frantically barked. *Thump. Thump.* The door caved, its wood splintering into jagged pieces. A hand forced the door inward.

A biker in a leather coat took a few steps into the cabin. Rocky jumped on him and he caught the dog, throwing him into the wall. Rocky yelped. His eyes fell on Gwen and a cruel smile touched his lips. "Well, what do we have here?" He scolded her as he walked in. "You should have opened up when we said." He was closely followed by three more men. Dutch stood between them, barking and baring teeth.

Steele stood still, letting another man step into the doorway. The lead biker strode closer to Gwen. "Ah, pretty one. This should be fun."

"Ain't that Steele's girl?"

The first biker turned back toward the others. "Even better."

Dutch continued to snarl.

"Shut that fucking dog up!" One of the men took aim at Dutch with his handgun.

The biker in the doorway took another step inside and glanced in Steele's direction. His eyes opened a fraction as his mind processed that another man stood waiting unannounced.

Steele was a blur of vengeance. His tomahawk caught the side of the biker's neck. It seared through his flesh and arteries as if it were alight with fire. He continued his strike by hooking the soon-to-be dead man by the back of his neck with the follow through.

With a quick movement, he tossed the man headfirst and dying into the log wall. Steele flashed into the doorway. The biker standing outside tensed, his eyes gaping. But action was always faster than reaction. Two quick shots into his upper chest put him on his ass like he'd slipped on ice. Steele rotated back, facing the other three men.

He whipped his tomahawk back across the front of his face and slashed the next man through the throat. The bald-headed biker's mouth frowned in surprise. He dropped his gun, hands fleeing for the gash.

Steele punched out his single hand, firing a round into the chin of the biker closest to Gwen, dimpling it. Steele continued to twist his body, and the biker closest to him pounced on his arm, ripping at his pistol with both hands. Keeping his arm near his body where he had the most power and strength, he utilized his core muscles to keep his gun close. With a roar, he drove his feet, backpedaling the biker into the wall.

The goateed man cried out as they slammed into the wood. He used both hands to beat Steele's hand into the rock of the fireplace. Once. Twice. The third hit sent shockwaves of pain shivering up into his shoulder, and he released the gun. It clattered on wood planks.

The biker ripped Steele's arm the other direction, and he had to go with the movement or risk destroying his shoulder joint. As Steele went the other direction, he lost his tomahawk, and he was whipped to the floor in a Judo-style toss. The planks jumped as his back made contact, and the man dove atop him, straddling him in the mounted position.

Rough hands wrapped around Steele's throat. The biker's grip tightened like a vise as he found his life-erasing hold. Steele chopped down with his forearms into the man's hands, but the man was in a frenzied rage, growling as he squeezed the life from him. He redoubled his efforts, bearing down on Steele, compounding the constriction of the soft tissue in his neck.

Dutch's growls lingered as background noise. Steele bucked and went for the man's ball sack, but his strikes were unable to generate any sort of power. The dog latched on the biker's back leg, tugging him off balance. Air flowed into Steele's throat, and he scrambled to free his legs. The biker hammer-punched Dutch's head, beating him repeatedly. The Labrador held on for multiple blows until he yelped in pain, releasing him.

Steele wrapped his legs around the biker's torso. The man leapt at him again, and this time, Steele forced a leg around the man's neck. He locked his feet around the biker, yanking the biker's arm across his own body, tightening his hold. The biker struggled in his grasp, feeling the strength breaking him.

His tomahawk handle appeared from the top of the biker's skull as if he'd had a sudden growth of metal. Blood spurted on the wall. Blinking rapidly, the biker realized he'd been killed. Streams of blood traveled down his head and reddened the lines of his face. His jaw dropped open a fraction, and he let out a disgusted groan. Steele shoved the man against the floorboards with a thud.

Gwen stood over them both. The man started to convulse in his final moments. His fingers curled and his mouth twitched. She eyeballed him, pure hatred raging on her face.

Steele collected his Beretta from the floor and holstered it. Gwen picked up a shotgun, and Steele shouldered an M4A1 on his back and slung another around his front. He dug through the dead man's pockets for extra magazines. Gwen joined him in his search.

They worked briskly and in silence, Haley watching them from the corner, surrounded by the dogs. Steele placed his boot in the dying biker's neck, and brain gore splashed as he ripped the tomahawk free. He linked it loosely back into his belt.

"We have to keep moving. There'll be more."

"I know," Gwen whispered.

Shots from a gun battle were popping off on the other side of the camp, sounding like a bunch of kids playing with firecrackers instead of people killing on another. "We're still in this fight." Gwen nodded fiercely. "We can't take her into this."

He eyed Gwen and the child. "I can't carry Becky and fight."

The woman stirred as if they'd called her name. Becky sat up. "What happened?" Registering that bodies littered the cabin, she became fearful. Her breath came in gasps. "Oh God. Oh, my God."

Both Steele and Gwen shushed her, and she calmed slightly. "Haley. Baby, come here." The little girl ran to her mother and jumped into her arms.

Steele sidestepped and eyed outside the door. "There's more coming. We need to move."

"What's happening?" Becky asked.

"We're under attack. We have to get out." He continued to eye the outside rebellion.

Gwen helped her to her feet. "We have to leave."

"What about Pa and Ma?"

Gwen shook her head. "Later."

"Oh, my God," Becky said to herself as Gwen led them behind Steele.

Gwen spoke quietly over Becky. "Get us to the horses and I'll get help."

He shook his head, his eyes scanning the chaos with grim outlook. "No, that's where most of them are. We have to get you out of here. Over the wall. Run for town." He eyeballed them, ensuring they understood. "Over the wall and to town. Not a word."

Becky and Haley nodded, eyes blinking back fearful tears. He turned to Gwen. "Not a word. You run."

She shook her head at him in tearful anger. He knew she would rather stay to fight. He wasn't stupid, but they had responsibilities and hers right now was to keep herself and their baby alive.

He sighted his M4A1 down the row of cabins, keeping it at an angle to see as much as he could before stepping out into potential danger. He quickly checked the other way. "Quiet. Let's move."

Not hesitating, he rushed out of the cabin. The first thing that struck him were the bodies in the snow. So many lay dead, bleeding out, and it stung worse because he knew they were his people and not the enemy. The biker he'd shot earlier had made it to the edge of another cabin before expiring, leaving a snail trail of scarlet in the snow.

Steele cut around the corner of a cabin. He knew the women were right behind. Fear would keep them close. People crunched through the snow. Steele knelt, holding a finger up to his lips. A gang of Chosen walked by, driving prisoners in front of them.

A slimy looking man directed the others. "Get them to the farmhouse." The group continued on, shoving the backs of the captured prisoners, unaware of Steele's party hidden in the shadows.

The logged exterior wall of Camp Forge lay ahead. Steele ran for it, his stance aggressive like he was hunting another man. He scanned down either side of the enclosure. After a sharp wave, the two women and little girl ran for him, the dogs tagging behind. He offered his hand to help them over.

"Hurry."

Becky nodded and shoved a wet boot in his hands. He hefted her over as she kicked and squirmed. He bent low and grabbed Haley. "Shhh." He handed her over to the waiting arms of her mother.

Gwen eyed him, her green eyes wet emeralds in a pale field of snow.

"Not today," he whispered.

She nodded her head. "I'll be back."

"I know you will." He interlaced his fingers and she placed a foot inside his hand. He heaved her up and over and she disappeared to the other side. One after the other he helped the dogs over.

He'd done the best he could. Revenge flitted on the outskirts of his mind as did, rescuing as many as he could from this betrayal.

He took his M4A1 back to his shoulder and moved with speed to the fires at the far end of the enclosure and away from the gunfire. He weaved through cabins toward where the Iron Drakes resided. Sorrowful cries of the living and the screams of the dying splashed together with the trumpets of gunfire, a lattice of suffering that ruled the camp.

As he closed in on allied biker cabins, he heard voices. He pressed his back against a cabin wall, shallowing his breathing.

He spied around the corner. It was a quick glance, one a hunted man would do to gain intelligence while evading capture. A brief look and then back to safety. His head popped around the corner.

War Child stood with almost twenty of his men. A group of captured Iron Drakes were in a line with their hands in the air. In front of them, he recognized Barney, having been shoved to his knees at the foot of the ancient biker president. War Child spread his arms wide. An orange glowing cigarette hung from the corner of his mouth. "Where's Frank?"

Barney grunted not daring to look away and spat. "Dead."

Smoke billowed from the side of War Child's mouth. "You saying that he'd rather burn alive inside that cabin than come out and talk with his old friend?" A smile turned up his wrinkled mouth.

Barney's eyes drifted over at a cabin. "He's dead."

Cocking his head to the side, the ancient biker raised his eyebrows. "Really?"

Barney stared at the ground. "Yeah."

War Child put the barrel of his handgun an inch from Barney's head and pulled the trigger. It looked like something punched out the back of Barney's skull and he slumped over on his side.

"Bring him to me alive or dead. And I want to see my old buddy Thunder."

His men scrambled in different directions. A trio of armed War Machines led the group of captured Iron Drakes down to the burning farmhouse. Steele ducked back behind his cabin.

"Frank could still be alive," he said to himself.

The snowfall rained harder from the black-filled sky on Christmas morning. It was a determined snowstorm, one that would have made Steele think twice about leaving the house. One that could end up with you in the ditch with only a snowplow to pull you out.

Steele stood and spun. He jogged down the other side of the cabins and cut down a row ahead of the captives. He rested his back next to the cabin. He tried to control his heavy breathing even as the crystalized mist escaped his mouth.

The front captor stepped into view, oblivious to his surroundings. Steele waited as more prisoners passed. He crept from the shadows and curled quickly near the edge of the cabin. His carbine banged and the casing pinged as it was released from the weapon. He capped the two guards in the back while the other Iron Drakes jumped the lead guard. The ambush was over quick like it had never happened, and the men ran for cover between the cabins.

Steele grabbed one of them by the scruff. "Where's Frank?"

The biker's eyes fully opened. "He escaped. I don't know."

Steele took off his other carbine and handed it to the biker, unslinging the weapon on his back for another biker. The heavy sound of a fifty-cal thundered in the distance. *Please don't be gunning down our people already.*

"Follow me," Steele said to the Iron Drakes. They ran down the row of cabins.

"Steele!" a man yelled. His gun instinctually veered toward the voice. Larry peeped out from a cabin, his eyes peering from side to side. He waved them inside. Steele and the bikers forced their way through the door. Larry and Gregor were there with guns along with a cluster of soldiers.

Almost forty people stood crammed inside waiting for rescue or death or both. They were a mass of huddled fear.

"We didn't know what to do. They had everyone pinned in the big barn." Larry averted his eyes in shame.

Steele reached out. "You did fine. Who is with us?"

"I don't know. So much gunfire. The Chosen surrounded the barn and started shooting everyone."

"They tried to gun us down in our barn," a soldier said. "The ones that ran for the river were shot in the back."

"Where's Major Ludlow?"

The soldier shook his head.

"I'm with you," came a voice from the back. A man shoved his way through the others. The bearded man had a bandana wrapped around his head.

"Thunder?" Steele said.

"They gunned down my crew in cold blood."

Steele blinked as he digested what the man told him. "You weren't in on this?"

Thunder's mouth tightened. "No. It was the pastor and that motherfucker War Child."

"They're collecting everyone near the farmhouse," said Gregor.

Steele spied out the door. "Then we break them free."

MARGIE
Camp Forge, IA

The Seven Sisters huddled around her in the back of the pickup. The small convoy of six trucks drove as fast as possible down the river road in the direction of Camp Forge. The unplowed roads were quickly becoming unnavigable with the rising snowstorm.

Margie eyeballed the women. She couldn't even tell they were women with the layers of warm clothes covering them. Each of them had guns. Margie's hunting rifle lay across her lap. The wind whistled over the cab of the truck.

They zipped into the humble town of Hacklebarney. The sheriff flagged them down, waving from outside his office.

He kept a hand atop his hat. "What the hell is going on?"

"Camp Forge is under attack," Margie yelled back at him.

"From what? That place has been fortified something proper."

"Mutiny."

"Mutiny?" Sheriff Donnellson shook his head in disgust. "I suppose the mayor will have us respond."

"She's in danger. Hurry." She slapped the top of the truck cabin and they took off again, wheels spinning in the snow. Just outside the town, a black cloud floated over the camp.

"Looks bad," Roxy said. The Seven Sister was old enough to be Margie's aunt and the relative of a junkyard dog. All she needed was a spiked collar and the two would be interchangeable. She covered her mouth with a scarf.

354

"It does."

The unplowed roads took their toll on the convoy, slowing them to a crawl. Nothing had touched the snow, and it had accumulated high enough to make the tires spin. The convoy's lead truck acted as a trailblazer for the rest, carving twin tire tracks.

The black cloud increased its ominous magnitude by the minute. It hovered over the makeshift militia base, a canopy of evil encircling the camp from above. The burning smoke contrasted sharply with the sleet-gray billowing clouds carrying the winter precipitation.

The trucks came to a halt. The side door opened, and Red Clare stepped out of the cab. "Nobody does nothing without me giving the signal. You hear me." She pointed back at her club. "Nobody." She stared at Margie.

"Look!" Margie pointed out to the trees.

Two forms ran for them. One held a child in her arms. They were followed by dogs. Their feet high-stepped the drifts, and they waved their arms, attempting to flag them down. "Help us!"

All eyes turned to watch them run. It was immediately apparent they were not equipped for being outside for very long. Long pajamas and barefoot.

"Jesus jump-jacking Christ," Red Clare muttered.

The people reached the road, terror in their eyes. "Please help us," breathed a woman. She put a hand to her side and grimaced, red cheeks puffing while she caught her breath.

"Gwen!" Margie screamed.

Gwen's eyes jumped her way. Her head tilted as if she wanted to sob. "Margie?"

Margie clambered down from the bed of the pickup, her feet piercing the snow for the women as she ran. Margie stripped off her jacket and wrapped it around Gwen. "She's pregnant," she said with a glance back at Red Clare. *If you are thinking about betraying us now, remember you are killing innocent women.*

She wrapped her arms around Gwen's shoulders trying to squeeze some warmth back into her body. "God, what happened?" she said, leading them to the trucks.

"Get 'em in here," Red Clare waved them into the cab. The two women and the child climbed inside, and the dogs were helped into the pickup bed. "Thaw 'em out."

Involuntarily shaking, Gwen rubbed her hands together. "They blew up our house. Gunfire. It was the War Machines and the Chosen. Some sort of coup." She warily glanced at Red Clare and then back to Margie. Realization settled on her face that a large group of bikers that wasn't supposed to be in the area was at the base's doorstep. "Why are you here?" Blood drained away from her once cold-infused rosy cheeks. She gulped and put a protective arm over Becky and Haley. She shook her head in slow ticks. "No, not you."

"We're here to help," Margie said hurriedly.

Suspicion still racked her features. "How did you know?"

"War Child ambushed us on the river and killed my crew and the soldiers."

Gwen wiped the gray soot on her face, running her hand through her messy hair. "Jesus."

"Is Captain Steele still alive?" Red Clare asked.

"Yes, the last I saw him."

The biker president threw a cigarette into her tight puckered lips and cupped her hands over the end so she could light it. She breathed in deeply. She eyed the two women warily and then Margie shaking her head.

"Don't worry, I ain't gonna backstab ya."

"You have to take me to Hacklebarney to rally them."

"We told the sheriff on our way through."

Gwen nodded, shivering as she embraced the heat of the truck. "Why are we waiting? Give me a gun."

Red Clare rolled the cigarette from one side of her mouth to the other. "Move on over, ladies. There's one under the seat, but let's see if we can't take these boys for a ride." She wrinkled her nose. "Maybe they'll just let us in." Red Clare regarded Margie with indifference. "Get on back. We have to move."

Margie ran around the side of the pickup bed and climbed in with the help of Roxy and Dana. She sunk down into the bed and clutched her rifle as the truck spun its wheels, fishtailing left and then right as it gained traction. They plowed forward.

Camp Forge came into sight, and violence was afoot. Camouflaged bodies lay facedown, accumulation collecting on their lifeless forms. The smoke they'd seen for miles fed darkness into the sky, but it was blacker here as they could see the source: the Reynolds' white farmhouse was ablaze.

Men stood near the gate. One ran inside as they approached. A group of over ten men leveled long guns at them. Their leader, a thick-bearded man, marched up to Red Clare's window.

She rolled it down. "Hey, now. No need to point guns. We're friendly." He lowered his rifle a bit.

"To who?"

"We met with the War Machines a few days ago."

The Chosen man averted his gun. "You're late. We're almost done." He turned back to his men. "They're with War Child." The men lowered their weapons.

Red Clare gave him a hearty belly laugh but resonated in her throat. "Well, we were cleaning up after your mess. Look what I found in the woods." She threw a thumb back at Gwen and her sister.

Margie tensed, lifting her rifle slightly, preparing in her mind to start shooting. Killing live people never settled well with her, but she was getting used to it. She was becoming someone she'd never fathomed possible months ago.

The bearded man grinned. "The pastor will be pleased. We thought the bomb would have wiped the entire clan out." He stretched his neck so he could see in the back of the cab easier. "Lucky one, aren't ya?"

"Go to hell," Gwen said.

The man smirked. "You'll be there soon enough."

Clare shushed Gwen's mouth with a smoke-tainted finger. "Quiet, you pretty cunt." She turned back to the Chosen guard. "Anybody left? You catch that Captain Steele yet?"

The man adjusted his feet in the cold. Big flurries settled on his beard, making him seem older as if sudden bouts of age had caught him.

"We got a few holdouts. The Iron Drakes caused some problems. Some soldiers and Sable Point folks. Pastor's collecting all the dissenters in the center of the camp for purification. We'll melt all the snow with a great fire." He nodded his divine inspired approval. "God wills it."

Red Clare sucked hard on her cigarette and it fizzled softly. "All right. I'll let you get back to it."

She rolled up her window and knocked on it, giving the women in the back of the pickup bed a thumbs-up. The truck drove inside the wooden-walled camp. Several cabins were on fire or smoldering in the embers of wreckage.

Bodies of the fallen littered the roadway. Chosen men and women rounded up prisoners, all of which were being led to the center of the base. The convoy rolled deeper inside the camp. The Seven Sisters in the bed of the last truck opened fire on the unsuspecting guards, spraying rounds into their backs. Muted yells came from surprised mouths, but they were cut short by gunshots.

The female bikers dismounted from the truck beds and took cover near the cabins. Margie swung her legs over the side and hopped into the snow with a scrunch. She ran for the nearest cabin and pounded on the door. "Open up. You're free."

A scarred face shoved a gun into hers. She gulped down her fear. He was covered head to foot in blackened soot like he'd crawled through a field of ash. "Steele?"

He yanked her inside. "Margie?"

A crowd of armed men with desperate eyes stood at his back. He hugged her for a second. "Where'd you?"

She exhaled quick. "No time. Seven Sisters are here. We have a clear path to escape." Steele pushed past her and opened the door peering outside in suspicion. "Red Clare? She's not in on it?"

"No, I made her swear it."

His look was razor sharp. "Swear it?"

"She just killed a bunch of Chosen. She's with us, waiting to help you escape."

"We're not escaping. We're freeing these people."

He shoved open the rest of the door and dipped through. He let out a gruff muted yell, his weapon half-raised to his shoulder. "Clare."

The biker president eyed him and Margie.

"Be truthful or you die," Steele said, his gun reaching his shoulder. The Seven Sisters turned, training their guns on him.

She waved them off. "Be careful where you point that. Your baby mama is in my car. I'm here to help, you lackwit."

He dropped his gun and eyed her again.

Red Clare's cigarette had burned down, but her lips cradled it like a mother does her infant. "War Child's got a tiny prick. I trust him less than a bike with a wobbly wheel."

Gunfire kicked off from the center of camp. She stared for a moment then motioned them onward. "Hurry. We're attracting attention."

"We can't. There are hundreds of people that will murdered."

"Honey, you need to get your priorities straight. Get the Iowans and regroup. Today is lost."

He shook his head. "No, today this ends."

AHMED
Northern Missouri

Three men walked their horses along the side of a rusted-out metal-walled building. The rust had streaked the exterior walls with a reddish-brown corrosion overtaking the faded white paint of a business from the past. The lettering was uneven in neglect and too faint to make out unless one already knew what it said.

Next to the mine elevator and warehouse, dead vines spiderwebbed along a white cinder block building only a story high. They'd come from the north, the opposite direction of the quarry entrance to the facility that zigged in multiple rings around the limestone quarry below, part of which was guarded and access controlled by the Wolf Riders. The elevator and warehouse overlooked the quarry from above.

Sly led his horse through an open utility entrance large enough for a dump truck. Jim and Ahmed followed. The interior of the warehouse was dark. Thick structural support pillars ran from the floor to the roof, and crisscrossing beams and trusses lined the ceiling. A profuse coating of white dust covered everything inside and Ahmed sneezed.

The other two men glared back at him, shaking their heads. After dismounting their horses, they wrapped the reins around a metal pole. White dirt piles rested undisturbed.

"Where's the elevator?" Ahmed asked.

Sly gestured with his chin. "Over there." They spoke quietly, not wanting to take a chance on an errant Wolf Rider coming upon them. They'd waited in the trees for over an hour for any signs of Wolf Riders or the dead before they'd approached.

Their feet puffed clouds of dust as they marched through. It was fine, closer in texture to flour than a larger granule sand. Next to the interior wall of the building, a machine stood silent. Hard grimy metal buckets stood unmoving, the machinery as lifeless as the dirt surrounding it.

Sly immediately went about inspecting the machine. A bucket creaked as he laid a hand on it. "I dunno. Been probably thirty, forty years."

"What's that?" Ahmed had expected some sort of cage-style open elevator that would take them deep into the bowels of the earth, not a series of buckets on a conveyor belt.

Sly gave him a curious look. "It's the elevator."

"You said that you used to ride it down as a kid. Those are buckets for rock."

Ducking his head to study a gear, Sly chuckled. "We'd put it in reverse and ride down in the buckets."

Ahmed felt his gut drop a bit. "No cage or anything?"

Jim pushed a bucket with his hand. It gave a rusty groan and came to a rest. "You're inside the bucket," he said, shrugging his shoulders.

The pails moved in line with the rest where they would tip their goods down a slide. It was hardly enough space to fit a man kneeling.

"You guys are crazy."

Sly ignored him. "You just have to stand in it and hold on to the one above it."

Ahmed shook his head. "I can see that."

Jim gave him a smirk. "Come on. It's for the girls."

"I know what it's for." Ahmed shook his head again. "There's no way this is going to run."

Sly gave him a mean glance. "My father used to work this mine, and he always said there ain't nothing better than these machines. Never let him down. American made." Bending close he blew, and dust burst off the control panel. He wiped his arm over the panel. "Might need a bit of tender loving care, but I'll get it going. We just gotta wait until those Wolf Riders take the bait." Studying the panel, he tapped a few buttons.

Ahmed mouthed to Jim, "He can't be serious."

Jim shrugged his shoulders again.

"Jimmy, get that diesel in the tank over yonder." Sly directed him with a free hand. Jim walked over with a gas can and unscrewed a cap before tipping the can high in the air.

"Ahmed, come over here. When those bikers start rolling, I'm gonna need you to manually pull the conveyor belt downward. Think about it like winding her up."

"All right." He neared the hole in the ground. It was four-foot wide and across like a square, the buckets resting in their final position like ancient machinery from a lost civilization left to rust out into oblivion.

Distant gunfire banged like small hometown fireworks, not the quality ones you purchased by driving across a state border to one with lax firework laws. They were the safe kind that you might let a little kid play with—bottle rockets and Roman candles—but the men knew the sounds for what they actually were: the beginning of an ambush.

"That's them," Ahmed said under his breath. They listened as the gunfire fireworks picked up. A tap-tap-tap followed by cap-cap-cap.

Jim jogged to the warehouse opening. The thunder of motorcycles rolled over the quarry like a coming storm. "There they go."

"How many of them are going?"

Jim stood on his tiptoes. "Can't see."

Glancing over his shoulder, Sly said, "Hope it's all the slimy bastards."

"Me too."

"Start winding."

Locking his hands on the lip of the closest mining bucket, Ahmed heaved. It held its ground, staying in place. He jumped, gripping the side of the bucket. He grunted as he strained, pulling his arms down using his body weight. Metal groaned under his effort, refusing to budge.

Sly flicked a switch and jabbed a button. "Keep pulling!"

Ahmed jumped down again, throwing with all his might. The bucket complied, inching downward and rotating a new bucket over the top. Rusted gear teeth groaned under the pressure as they slowly interlocked once again like an old man's joints after a century at rest. He threw down another rusty metal tub. Sly jabbed the button. The rock pail slid down farther.

"Come on!"

The motor fired alive, awakening a tarnished decaying giant of the past. The screech of metal on metal grating atop one another filled the warehouse. The buckets wound over the highest point and then flipped, swinging with hesitation back into rusty place.

Sly shouted over the din. "Hurry!"

He timed the passing pails. Grabbing one, he hopped inside before it disappeared into the shaft. It swayed beneath him. Ahmed handed him a rifle, and Sly crouched down for balance.

"See you at the bottom," Sly said with a smile. He vanished into the mine.

Jim came back over. "The gunfire's dying, we have to hurry."

With care, he stepped into another one of the buckets, gripping his shotgun. "Let's get those girls." He disappeared as if the ground opened its mouth and swallowed him whole.

More buckets swooped by, and he took a deep breath. "They went down. Just hop in and hold on they say." He watched the rusted buckets descend into the unknown. "They did this as kids? Allah be good."

His monumental death-defying move as a kid was sneaking out to the batting cages with his friends, not climbing old industrial mining equipment like he had a death wish. His father had brooded over him for days after they were caught. *Why do you waste so much time on such a trivial sport? You will never be good enough to play professionally. Focus on your studies. Focus on business. I need a son to help me in this industry, not waffle around playing sports. Games will get you nowhere, boy.* The disappointed look on his face had set Ahmed back for weeks, but he was addicted to the sport. The siren's call of the crack of the bat lured him back. It was like a drug that he could never get enough of.

Ignoring the advice of his father, he went to a small college for baseball instead of business, focusing on the mechanics of a swing as opposed to the macroeconomics of global trade, and none of those things mattered much now. The auto industry trade restrictions in the 80s against Japan meant nothing to him. And all things considered, he'd used a baseball bat more than economics, clubbing to death so many infected at this point that he'd lost track of how many skulls he'd smashed with it, probably as many as balls he'd hit playing baseball. His average in the league was a cool .350; his batting average in the apocalypse was almost perfect. It had to be. It didn't earn him a place at the table in the big leagues, but he knew every day living was like getting a lease on life. If you struck out, you died. If you got the hit, you're still in the living game.

He gripped the side of a bucket and climbed in. Baseball, business, battered brains, none of it mattered to him, not compared to a country girl from Missouri held hostage somewhere in the bowels of the earth beneath him. Those were the things that meant something. Humanity. Life. Companionship. Those were worth risking it all for.

The metal bucket moaned as it swayed back and forth. He knelt in the crammed bucket and gripped the side with white knuckles, attempting to keep his weight balanced. The vertical conveyor belt of buckets continued its work and lowered him below. Darkness swallowed Ahmed whole; not caring for his noble purpose or past deeds, it ate all it could.

He chanced a look downward. The blackness gave way to light far below. Square wood beams outlined the shaft. Roots and vines lined the sides, years of neglect allowing nature to begin its reclamation of man's penetrative incursion. The gears clinked and clanked as they lowered his bucket and lifted others upward, a continual trade-off of circular motorized motion.

The bottom came fast. The bucket tipped sideways near the ground, almost dumping him outright. Ahmed stumbled and put a hand on the wall. The first thing he noticed was the warmth of the mine compared to above. It must have been in the mid-50s, a considerable improvement from the open air outside.

The corridor was pitch black aside from light coming down the hallway.

Jim's voice came out quiet and harsh. "Ahmed." A shadow moved nearby. "We follow the lights."

They stalked slowly toward the light. Feet grated on the gravelly ground, and more than once, Ahmed felt his ankle twist and turn on the uneven rock. He clutched his pump-action shotgun close to his body, aiming it away from his compatriots. The ceiling weighed down upon them as if threatening to crush them beneath thousands of pounds of vengeful boulders and stones every moment. His shoulder ran over thick square beams as they moved cautiously down the corridor.

Two men passed through the intersection ahead. They were merely black shadows with light blasting around their outlines. Ahmed and his comrades stopped. He held his breath and trained his gun in their direction.

One of them spoke, "Somebody was shooting at them."

The other man laughed. "Stupid fucks. Macleod is going to kill the lot of them. Too much trouble from these yokels. Better to just find some new ones to do the heavy lifting for us."

"You know what that means?" said the other.

"Was that?"

"New women."

The other form nodded. "They were hollering their heads off earlier. Let's go check on them."

The men didn't look in their direction, carrying on. Ahmed exhaled. It wasn't that they couldn't kill the men. It was being found out before they could escape.

The quiet group rounded the corner, stalking the men. The light traveled down the passage from an opening to another room. "They went this way."

They buddied within six inches of one another, creeping to the entrance of a massive room. Ahmed leaned out and peered inside. A large industrial floodlight spotlighted a cavernous rock-walled room with over forty-foot ceilings. A generator's engine rumbled near the far wall, keeping the light going.

Boxes, bags, and crates of supplies were stockpiled all over the cavern, enough to supply forty plus men for months if not a year. They were marked as canned and dried food. Others were survival supplies like clothes and blankets, jugs of water, boxes of ammunition, and guns.

The number of guns was staggering. *Are they building their own army?* Water pooled in one corner from a crack in the rock, and a fire sizzled in the center. Tarps and tents were placed along the wall farthest away from the men.

The black wolf patches of the two bikers veered toward the tents. Two other men were near a fire.

Ahmed dipped back to the corridor.

Jim whispered, "Let's kill them." He looked ready to charge in and unleash hell on the unsuspecting bikers. The Wolf Riders would never assume men would come from the interior of the mine. All their guards would be near the mine quarry entrance roughly a hundred yards in the opposite direction they came from.

"We don't know how many more are still in here. If we can get in and out before they know we are here, it would be best."

Jim shook his head. "We send a message for when they get back."

Sly's eyes darted back and forth. "Ahmed's right. Go in quietly. But kill those nearby in silence."

"Two by the fire first," Jim said.

Ahmed found himself nodding. How easily men can get roped into violence. Exacting vengeance on this gang would be gratifying after all they'd done. He snuck into the cavern. The floodlights gave off an eerie glow that cast long shadows along the jagged rock walls.

His back bent, Ahmed weaved through the boxes of supplies. He knocked one, and it teetered on the precipice of the box below. His heart leapt and he stood still. A silent hand steadied it.

One of the bikers glanced over his shoulder and the infiltrators crouched silent. "You hear that?"

The other biker didn't even bother to look. "Can't hear nothin'."

"Thought I heard something."

"What? Are you afraid of the dark?"

"Shut the fuck up. I ain't scared of shit." He took a swing from a bottle.

Jim gave Ahmed a nod. Ahmed exhaled and slowly crept behind the Wolf Rider standing by the fire. The man held a bottle of tarnished yellow alcohol loose in one hand.

"Took a while to get used to the dark round here. But I know this mine like the back of my hand now. Thought Macleod was crazy for setting up shop here, but it's warm in the winter. Cool in the summer. Protection from anybody on the outside."

The other man stared at the flames, his eyes distant above his black beard. "Pork said he saw something in the mines. Something not human." He sat with his back to a crate, watching the fire crackle and burn.

The one closest to Ahmed took a drawn-out swig of his gold-colored alcohol. "I told ya not to talk to me like that." He pointed a finger, holding the bottle.

"Jesus, man. Don't be so uptight. Of course there ain't nothing down in the mine. It's been abandoned since the Civil War or something."

"That's good. 'Cause I ain't got no problem with the dark." He brandished a Desert Eagle .50 caliber pistol. "Nothing that this baby can't take down."

The seated biker glanced at the shadows as Ahmed moved behind the standing biker. The leather-clad man turned his head to the side and then his eyes squinted as Ahmed crashed the stock of his shotgun into the man's skull. The biker emitted a soft "uff" as he lost consciousness, his body slumping onto the fire.

Jim rammed a deer-skinning knife into the side of the other biker's neck. The blade caused a revolting crackle as it bit through vital veins and tissue that kept the man's brain supplied with ample amounts of blood. Jim brought him down roughly to the ground.

Sparks sprayed around the body of the biker as he started to burn. Ahmed clasped a hand around one of his arms and dragged him out of the flames. He beat him with his hands to put him out.

"Roody?" came a voice. The name echoed from wall to wall of the cavern and over the generator. A fat biker plodded over from the tents. His chin had chins and his head was almost shaved bald. Sly's form popped like a lemur, and he fired his rifle into the man's chest.

The fat biker didn't even have a chance to be surprised, but the gunshots were louder than sirens, alerting anyone inside the mine that they were under attack.

Ahmed jogged to the tents. A man emerged from one, shirtless. Ahmed pumped a slug into his chest, and he fell in reverse, taking the canvas with him. He racked the handle of the shotgun, prepping another shell for devastation. Chu-chink.

A biker scrambled along the wall as Jim fired shotgun blast after shotgun blast at him, the barrel of his weapon releasing fire and smoke with each shot. His third slug took the man in his hip, forcing him face-first into the rock face. He smeared blood down the uneven surface and wailed in frenzied pain.

Jim marched over to silence the man while the other men ran for the largest tent. A frightened girl was shoved out the tent entrance. Fear laced her eyes, and her hair was black and wavy. A leather-coated arm tightened dangerously around her throat. A snarling Wolf Rider stood behind her, using her as a body shield. He had long dirty hair hanging around his shoulders and pressed a chrome-plated handgun to the side of her head.

"Listen up, fuckers. Put those guns down or the girl gets it." His lips stayed snarled like those of a rabid wolf with a drooping mustache. "More than she's already gotten it."

"You drop it!" Sly shouted. "I'm gonna kill him. I'm gonna kill him."

"Daddy!" Jes cried.

Ahmed held his shotgun zeroed in on the biker. The biker twisted his body back and forth. "I said drop 'em. Guns on the ground." He started to step Jes toward the entrance to the cavern. "Make room, fuckstick." He stumbled as he angled her toward them, his back away from their guns.

"Sly. Let's put the guns down. Nobody has to get hurt," Ahmed said.

The biker peered over Jes's shoulder. "Yeah, Sly. Listen to him. He's smart."

Sly shook his head. "Can't."

Jes's eyes were like a doe's in the headlights. Her hands curled around the biker's arm. "Daddy, please."

"Shut the fuck up." The biker jerked her, dodging his head from side to side to make himself a harder target. "Sly, look at that precious face. Put the gun down."

"All right." Sly set his rifle on the rocky ground with a clank of metal on rock. "Just let her go."

With his chin, the biker gestured at Ahmed. "You too."

Ahmed slowly shifted the barrel of his gun in the direction of the ceiling. "Where's Sadie?"

The biker sneered, eyes darting down a side corridor. "That's the boss's cunt."

Ahmed let the shotgun settle on the cavern floor. *It was a good run.*

"You two are a pair of dipshits." He shoved the girl and she stumbled, running for her father. Sly wrapped his arms around her body and kissed the top of her head. "It's okay."

"Stupid fuckers." Lining up his sights, the biker canted his gun slightly to the side.

A firearm blasted from behind them. The right side of the biker's face and skull disintegrated, leaving a bloody carving where a part of his face used to be. His single eye blinked a few times before he collapsed.

Jim jogged to them. "Where's Sadie?"

"Somewhere else."

Both men instinctually ducked as gunfire burst from the door to the outside. Three-round bursts chipped away at the hard rock around them, spraying fragments. Bullets thudded up Sly's back. Thump-thump-thump. He arched and fell into Jes, taking them both to the cavern floor.

Jim ran over and rotated Sly to his back. Sly's chest heaved, gaping exit wounds fraying his chest. He tugged Jes gently free of her father. "Are you okay?"

"Daddy?" she said. She scrambled over the loose rocks to her bleeding father.

A wet cough came from Sly. His eyes were wide as he tried to breathe. "Go, love." He stopped, his chest heaving. "Take care of my girl." His hand grasped for Jim's. "Promise me."

Jim gritted his teeth and nodded, wrapping an arm around Jes. "I'll do it."

"Get her out of here," Ahmed yelled at Jim. Gunfire whizzed overhead. Wolf Riders were taking cover in the hallway to the quarry, periodically leaning in to lay down fire.

"Sadie's down there," Jim said, pointing.

Ahmed eyed the other hall. Faint light slung out of the tunnel, tempting them. "I'll get her."

"Do it." Jim took Jes by the arm, and they sprinted for the rock elevator.

Sly's chest went still. Ahmed exhaled building his courage. A biker hesitantly stepped inside the cavern, his gun scanning the room. *One. Two. Three.* Crouching, Ahmed fired at him as he ran for the passage to Sadie.

The biker jumped and scrambled back for the quarry entrance. Ahmed racked his pump and sent another slug toward the door, keeping the bikers pinned down until he reached the safety of a rock hallway. More gunfire banged away, muffled by the mine.

He took a moment to breathe and quickly reload, shoving shells inside his shotgun. He began to stalk along the corridor. With frequent checks to the rear, he made sure no one pursued him.

The rock hall opened into a smaller cavern room. A battery-operated lantern illuminated the room from atop a table, shrouding every corner with darkness. Boxes lay against the wall. A tent that could hold twelve or more stood to the other side. Wooden chairs and a table were cluttered with bullets, glasses, plates filled with half-eaten food.

"Sadie?" Ahmed half-shouted. He poured over the room, looking for any sign of her.

A fist blurred into the side of Ahmed's head, connecting with the orbital just below his eye. His vision immediately disoriented, his eyes fogging over like a cool summer mist.

He toppled onto the rocky floor, his weapon clattering on the ground.

A man mocked him with a high-pitched nasal voice. "Sadie."

On his hands and knees, Ahmed scrambled for the shotgun. He crawled until a searing pain lanced through his calf. "Argh!" Held in place by pain, he peered back. Macleod had pinned him to the floor with the handle of his long Bowie knife, the blade sticking out of Ahmed's calf. It was like he was stuck in a bear trap. Any movement forced the sharp metal further inside, solidifying his demise.

Ahmed grasped for the gun again, and Macleod laughed as he twisted the knife. The shooting pain made him scream out, his hands digging into the rock.

Macleod wrapped a hand around Ahmed's other leg and dragged him farther away from the firearm. Rocks scraped and dug into his skin as the man pulled him away from the firearm. His hands scratched for anything to retard his progress, fingernails chipping on rough unforgiving ground.

Grunting, Macleod said, "You know, Ahmed, I just had this gut feeling you hadn't died out there, but I had no idea that you were behind these shenanigans." He stopped and tightened his grip on the handle of his knife. He ripped it free with a reddish-pink flourish like a painter's finishing touch.

"God!" Ahmed yelled.

Macleod studied the bittersweet liquid running along his knife. "You're a little bitch you know that?" Macleod stood and gave Ahmed a swift kick to the side.

Ahmed grunted in pain, trying to get his legs under him.

"Oh, Steele this. Steele that. Jesus. You two must be queer for each other." He jumped down next to Ahmed, leaning his face close. "I promised Sly I'd cut off his balls and feed them to him."

Squeezing his hands around his wound, he spat, "He's dead."

Macleod turned his head. "Too bad. I would have liked to have watched him eat 'em." His eyes ogled Ahmed with crazy mirth. "So you're leading this little rebellion?"

Warm blood trickled along Ahmed's hands, searching for a way out of his body. He didn't say a word.

An evil smile sat on his lips and he raised an eyebrow at Ahmed. "I guess you'll have to do, huh?"

Ahmed squeezed his calf, trying to stem the bleeding. "We want the girls back."

Macleod stood and laughed, his goatee wiggling with glee off his chin. "All this for a little bit of poonani? Should have just asked. I mean, I still would have cut your head off, but no reason to bring my protectees into conflict with the club. It's so hard to find good help nowadays. But I assure you, Sadie is filling her role just fine." He called to the tent. "Sadie, come on out."

With a flip of a tent flap, Sadie came out. A long chain cuff secured her hands, and her feet were bound with the similar silver chains. She wouldn't have been able to run even if they had found her in time.

Her voice was all misery. "Ahmed."

"You two?" Macleod said in surprise. "I wouldn't have thought a girl like you would fall for a man like Ahmed. I mean, on the account of his foreignness. I'll have to admit it's very cute. Just like in every single movie nowadays, country girl falls in love with city foreigner. Difference in cultures. Disapproving families. Blah, blah, fast-forward to you two breeding out a bunch of little mocha-colored bastards. Probably the cutest little things ever to grace this earth." He shook his head in mock heartfelt emotion. "Damn, that's precious to think about. A real-life fantasy, but some things just make you think."

He flung his arms apart in dismay. "If only the world was different. Softer, gentler, free of all this bullshit surrounding us. Then you." He pointed his knife at Ahmed. "And you, Sadie." His knife wavered at her. "Could be a happy little couple." He made a mock sign of the cross. "I pronounce thee man and wife." A grin split his face, and when neither of his captives laughed, he sighed heavily. "But alas, we don't live in that world, do we. We don't live in that fictional fantasy land that they want you to think is a possibility. We live here and now, and this world isn't going to have such a happy ending, and there's no way she is going to want a ball-less man as a husband. Isn't that right?"

"Fuck you, Macleod," Ahmed spat.

"Oh yes, fuck me, right?"

Ahmed inched and inched away from Macleod while he continued his tirade.

Macleod caught on. "Now where are you going? I was just getting to the fun part."

The room echoed Sadie's voice. "Stop, Macleod!"

Macleod bent down, grabbing Ahmed by the angle and dragging him back in front of him. She ran at Macleod, reaching out with chained arms for him. He laughed and grabbed her by the throat. "Oh, ain't that sweet. You can help me hold him down while I remove his man parts or whatever fleshy patch is down there. I suspect he ain't packing much on account of how nice and quiet he is." He forced her down on top of Ahmed's chest, pinning them both with one of his knees. He tugged at Ahmed's belt with a free hand. "Let's see."

Ahmed's hand grasped for anything. His own blood stuck gravel to his palms. His fingernails scratched the rocky floor until they felt something. They wrapped eagerly around a sizable rock.

The rock was grainy and rough in his hand like a sandpaper-covered baseball, but it didn't matter at all to him. He swung his arm as hard as he could into the side of Macleod's head.

Macleod toppled off them, falling to his behind. He sat staring for a moment, wondering what happened. "Feisty." Dazed, he shook his head.

Ahmed kicked as he pushed himself upright on one leg. Macleod tried to stand and fell back to the seated position, his eyes filled with stars. Ahmed hobbled for the corner. He'd seen it when he walked in and knew it instantly as his own. He hefted the wooden bat. Tan wood, dents and chips taken out of it. Red gore stained the grain of the wood. Macleod managed to regain his unsteady feet.

Ahmed twirled the bat in circles, feeling its perfectly weighted balance in his hands. "Batter up."

Macleod slurred his words. "You wait a minute." He leveled his knife at Sadie. "You, young lady, will get yours later after I take care of Humid." He gripped the handle and charged Ahmed. "Rarrrr!"

Spreading his feet just over shoulder width apart, the gravel gave beneath his back foot before it came to a standstill. His front leg held almost no weight. He tensed as Macleod neared but let his hips be free and loose. Macleod's jab was slow and he missed, staggering by Ahmed. The bat snapped around as Ahmed twisted his hips to generate more power behind the swing. It caught Macleod on the spine and he screamed, dropping to his hands and knees.

"You don't have the balls," Macleod spit. "My men will be back from dealing with the rednecks soon enough. You're all dead. You're dead. She's dead. Dead."

Ahmed zeroed in on the side of Macleod's skull touching it with his bat. "That's where you're wrong. Smashing your head in is no different than hitting a baseball. In fact, it's easier. More like batting practice with the machine on slow pitch." Ahmed circled Macleod. "You know what's funny? My father always told me that baseball was a waste of time." His voice morphed into his father's, "'You'll never do anything learning a silly sport.' But you know what?"

"Wha?" Blood dribbled from Macleod's mouth in red saliva stretched stalactites. He tried to push himself off the ground, but his legs refused to obey.

"Love is the most important thing in the world, but baseball is pretty great too." Ahmed chuckled. "Baseball and love are all you need." The bat whipped around in a blur of man and wood. It was a swing for the fences, not a lead-off single, but a full swing taking every ounce of his body. The thirty-three inch, thirty-one ounce piece of wood was a violent extension of his arms.

It wasn't the perfect swing, much lower than in a game, but a man's head is roughly three times larger than a baseball. So much more surface to aim for. At this point, with all his at bats throughout his life, he couldn't miss even if his calf was a bloody mess, especially with the game on the line.

Thwack! The smack was stomach-churning and sounded as if he'd hit a watermelon in the place of this man. Macleod's eye popped out of his shattered cheekbone. Brain and bone revealed themselves in clumps of pink and white, now exposed to the world. Macleod's hands and feet gave out and he landed in a pool of his own fluids. Ahmed felt glorious. He'd hit a grand slam with the game on the line.

"That felt good," Ahmed said to Macleod's corpse. "Like a grand slam."

If Macleod wasn't dead, he would be soon enough. He wiped blood and gore from the bat and searched Macleod's pockets for the key to Sadie's chains. He unlocked Sadie's cuffs, and she wrapped her arms around him. He felt more than love from her at this moment. They were two pieces being reunified into one.

"Let's make a run for home."

STEELE
Camp Forge, IA

Even as the black smoke defiled the sky, the whiteness of winter engulfed the darkness with a heavy snowstorm. Steele hid in the shadows as two men walked toward the center of his base.

"Psst."

The Chosen man turned his way and squinted. Steele swung his tomahawk hard into the side of his head. The blade bit deep, wedging itself in his skull. Larry and Gregor cut the other man down with knives, covering his mouth as he tried to scream. Their blades worked vengefully fast as they pierced him over and over. Some may have thought it was murder as murder is unauthorized and unlawful. This was killing, an authorized extinguishing of enemy combatants. They dragged the bodies into the shadows of a cabin.

Steele's crowd of men and women weaved the pathways in the murkiness of the storm. His paltry force was all that hadn't been captured that early Christmas morning.

In the place where Steele had been married the day before sat hundreds of prisoners around the flagpole. Men, women, and children were huddled in a terrified mass. The flag whipped in the wind, almost obscured by the falling snow.

The pastor's followers stood around them in a circle. Elevated above all sat the pastor and War Child in chairs behind the charred ruins of John's old desk that had been pulled from the rubble of the farmhouse. They overlooked

375

their new constituents with the ownership of a slave master.

A pile of bodies grew next to the prisoners as the War Machines and Chosen tossed the dead into a giant heap.

Like he was getting to go speak at the pulpit, the pastor stood. "It's time to feed the flames of our Lord with the unclean souls of the unbelievers. Their warriors will die, but the others will have a choice. Stay and live among us in safety or join the others in the cleansing." He nodded to a group of men and they doused the pile of dead with gasoline. A great jagged blaze engulfed the lifeless, rising thirty feet then leaping to fifty feet in the air.

The pastor called out to them from his pulpit of death. "Feel the warmth of our savior." He turned to the biker president. "Behold the man that will protect us and deliver us from harm."

War Child joined the pastor. "Today was a necessary evil of the world we live in. It needed to be done to ensure our survival. We need your cooperation, and everything will be fine."

Steele leaned out from behind his cabin and took aim.

"No," a female said behind him.

He lowered his weapon. "Hurry."

Margie took his place, aiming her hunting rifle. She zeroed in through her optic eye, focusing. It wasn't a new optic but an older simple one, nothing fancy, probably handed down through generations of hunters. She adjusted her sight alignment a fraction of an inch higher than normal to accommodate the distance.

Steele spoke to the men and women at his back. "Get ready." Her finger depressed the trigger bit by bit.

"For Tony," she whispered. The trigger clicked, and her gun banged sending waves of boom over the crowd. People screamed and ducked low. War Child flinched and fell backward, toppling over his chair. He crawled for cover on his elbows.

The pastor stood, his eyes blazing in the flames. "Traitors!"

Steele's men charged into the open, running quick on the other men. The numbers ceased to matter with surprise. Steele ran around the smoldering wreckage of the farmhouse. The smell of burning bodies stung his nose, but he continued turning left and right as he gunned down the Chosen with impunity. The prisoners scattered in all directions in panic. People shrieked, scrambling for cover anywhere, turning the scene into one of utter chaos. It was almost impossible to tell anyone apart.

Sprinting, Steele circled around the edge of the farmhouse. He popped out near the pastor's makeshift desk pulpit. A piece of wood filled his vision and struck him across the nose. *Crack!* His head snapped back and he staggered. A man grabbed at his long gun, wrestling for control, knowing control meant life or death.

Steele's vision was disoriented, and he front kicked the man away from him. The man kept hold of his gun, and it went end over end into a drift, the weight driving it towards the ground.

The man barrel-rolled to the side and clambered to all fours. He stood, lifting his wooden flail into the air. His handsome face sneered at Steele, and he wiped his wavy blond hair away from his eyes. "God wills it!"

More gunfire kicked off from the other side of the compound. *That would be Red Clare attacking.* Steele ran his hand along the top of his belt searching for his secondary weapon. Snow kicked up as Matthew ran for Steele, swinging his flail over his head like a helicopter. Steele's hand found his tomahawk. There was no time. The feet between them disappeared as the man sprinted.

The tomahawk emerged in the air as a shield. The head of the light ax knocked the flail, sending it swinging away from his face. He followed through with a crossover strike into Matthew's nose.

The blond man staggered and whipped his weapon back around, striking Steele's ribs. He felt a stinging crack and couldn't tell through the pain whether it was the wood breaking or the bones in his body.

"Fuck!"

Matthew wiped his nose, rubbing the blood between his fingers. He blew red snot from his nostrils and raised his flail high over his head. The wooden handle swung in circles over his head. He rushed Steele with wild rage in his eyes. "For the Chosen!"

Steele held his tomahawk close, the rear point touching his chest. His legs were tense with a bend in his knees. Matthew charged, barreling forward in fury. As he got within a few feet, Steele lunged toward him, keeping his hawk close, shrinking the distance rather than stretching it apart.

He caught Matthew's arm as it swung downward, pulling it into his body. Almost instantly, he brought his hawk slashing across Matthew's chest and in quick succession made short cleaving strikes. One along the left side of his neck, and using the hook of his tomahawk, he sliced into the right side. Matthew's eyes widened, but Steele continued his deadly work with systematic extreme violence. Taking the blade of his hawk, he used it to force Matthew's arm past Steele's body. The flail disappeared into fresh powder. The Chosen lieutenant stumbled a foot and fell knee first into the snowy ground, holding the jagged remains of his throat.

For the first time in seconds, Steele remembered to breathe. Matthew tipped over on his side in a gurgling pool of his own blood. Steele walked forward, leaving Matthew to bleed out. The man didn't deserve anything better.

His ribcage bellowed in pain as he walked. Gunfire roared between the groups. He stopped as another man stepped in front of him.

He had long greasy black hair and a partially grown spotty beard. *Luke.*

"I'll make it quick if you step aside." Steele twirled his tomahawk, deciding where to strike first.

Everything about Luke was dirty down to the bloody dinged knife in his hand. He licked his lips and grinned, showing his scummy yellow teeth. "You know I was there when she died."

"Who?" Steele grunted. In his gut he knew already, and it made his muscles tense with angry blood.

"Your mother."

"Fuck you."

He circled Steele, waving the knife around as he paced. "She screamed and screamed." His voice grew mocking. "Oh, help me. Save me!" He stopped to watch Steele's reaction. "You'll scream when we put you in the fire. They all scream. Every last one." He stopped for a moment, tapping the blade on his forehead. "That's after I take my souvenir from your flesh. What do you think? An ear. A finger." He narrowed an eye. "Those won't do. I'll take your scalp. The whole ugly puckered thing. And I'll make that whore of yours watch." He turned his head to the side. "You know, maybe I'll take hers too. That'd be sweet. His and hers scalps."

Steele's vision settled into the red. He bounded forward and Luke tensed as he ran. Bringing the hawk down in an overhead cleaving strike, Luke parried his attack and sliced Steele's forearm. Then Luke swung long across Steele's chest. His blade bit Steele's flesh, cutting through clothes and skin alike. Steele retreated backward, ignoring the warm blood dribbling down his torso. Caution. *He knows how to use that blade.*

Steele spun his hawk in his hand and circled the vile man.

"You know who else screamed?" Eyebrows lifted on his skull. "Your girlfriend Tess when we got her." He laughed harsh notes. "We had her so drugged she didn't even know she carried a fucking bomb or what we did to her." He snorted more laughter, edging closer to Steele. "It was beautiful to watch." Increasing in volume, his voice turned into a shout. "God's glory." Maniacal laughter erupted from his throat.

Luke inched closer and tried for a slash along Steele's gut. Steele sprawled backward and hooked Luke's elbow, helping him on by. With a quick strike, he brought the tomahawk down into his enemy's Achilles tendon, and with a sickening slap, into his spine.

The Chosen disciple collapsed in the snow. He swung wildly with his knife, searching for flesh to split. Steele ripped his tomahawk out of his back, and it was Luke's turn to scream. In a flash of metal, he slammed the small axe into the man's knife hand and severed it from his body. The hand lay with its fingers curled around the hilt, gradually melting into the whiteness. Bittersweet liquid spurted from the stump, steaming the fresh powder.

Luke breathed hard into the cold ground. "I can't feel my legs. I can't feel my hand." He sucked in frantic air.

Steele turned away.

"Kill me!" He laughed then cried. "Kill me!"

Steele continued his march to the pulpit desk, ignoring Luke's pleas for mercy. Mercy was the last thing on his mind.

Gunfire blared from the gate, sounding like trumpets of angels. The pastor stood tall at his pulpit. His eyes darted fearfully toward the sounds of resistance as more armed men and women entered the compound. *Iowans. Slow to the fight, but here for the win.*

"You," Steele said. Every breath felt like fire in his lungs.

The pastor's mouth shook at the corners. "My disciples. My boys. You have martyred them straight to heaven."

"I sent them to hell, where they belong."

The pastor pointed at Steele. "Kill him, Peter."

Peter stepped near the pastor, training his AK-47 on him. Steele never thought he'd be getting gunned down by an AK in America. Perhaps abroad when he worked with the Division, but never here.

"Father." Peter's face twisted with indecision.

"Come, Peter." Steele gestured at the man with his light ax. "I believe we have some unfinished business."

The pastor's finger wavered over Steele's form in condemnation. "Kill him. He's the antichrist in his truest form."

Peter pressed the wood-stock to his shoulder and aimed at Steele, but his eyes were undecided. He didn't hold the resolute violence in his belly. He lacked the will.

"It's over. War Child is dead. Luke is dead. Matthew is dead. I have appealed to your reason time and time again, yet you still fall under this evil man's spell. The battle isn't between us. Our battle is against them." The tomahawk wavered as it incriminated the infected on the other side of the river. "Yet we kill each other for what? So your master can have power over everyone? What do you think Colonel Kinnick is going to do here when he finds his base taken over? He's going to order the destruction of it all, and we will have lost the true battle."

Peter continued to train his aim at Steele.

He waved him off. "Ah, fuck it. Do what you have to do."

Squinting an eye, Peter focused his aim.

The blood ran down Steele's arm and into his hand, the glue sticking his palm to his grip. The growing blizzard continued to blanket everything in a cold white.

The pastor hissed, "Finish this, Peter." He faced his most loyal disciple. "You are my rock. Do God's will and kill this man."

Wind blew flurries swirling about their faces. Cold men eyeballed one another, waiting for the end. And Peter blinked. His posture visibly relaxed as if the fight had gone from him. His eyes told a different story than violence.

Steele's fast twitch muscles were fatigued and worn yet still stiff in the freezing air. He swung his arm back, letting his front foot step forward. He whipped the tomahawk behind his ear and heaved. The haft of his hawk grazed his sticky fingers as he released the weapon.

The light melee weapon flew end over end, cutting through flurries with ferocity. The handle flipped around, chased by the head turning over, and led the way blade first until the momentum drove the other end of the tomahawk sailing. It rotated like this in the fog of close combat that always flowed slower in the fighter's eye. The tomahawk head sunk into the center of the pastor's chest with a thud.

Peter lowered his rifle. His mouth opened in shock. His inaction killed his master as much as Steele. The pastor stood tall for a moment before realization registered on his face. The handle quivered, embedded in his chest.

Long slender fingers ran down the shaft of the weapon as if it were a curious growth appearing out of the pastor's body. He stared at Steele, finally blinking. His gaunt face frowned in pain. His hands gripped the end of the tomahawk, and after a few pulls, tugged it free. Blood replaced the blade. He tossed the hawk on the ground in front of him and pointed at Steele.

"You. You wretched man."

Peter dropped his gun and wrapped his arms around the pastor as he collapsed to his knees. He leaned the old dying man back to the snowy earth.

Steele marched toward the two men. The gunfire slackened in its symphony of battle, the climax already come and gone. Peter held his master. The pastor's lips moved quietly as he prayed. Steele bent and picked up his blood-drenched tomahawk. He ran his hand down the drenched shaft and swung it to the side, flinging off gore.

Steele's voice was firm. "Step aside."

Peter leered at Steele with tear-filled eyes. "You killed him."

"No, we killed him."

Peter placed his head near the pastor's chest.

"Move aside."

Begrudgingly, Peter let the pastor's body, his lips still moving, rest in the snow. Steele stood over them, watching the old man die. The pastor seemed so weak and feeble in his current state, not imposing or commanding, only an elderly man on his deathbed.

"You have brought great sorrow to our people. You have butchered in the name of God, and now your wretched life has come to an end. No more. Not now. Not ever again."

Steele grasped the pastor by the hair. Flurries had settled atop him, whitening the aged man. "I condemn you to death for the murders of Tess, John, Lydia, and my mother." His fingers clutched the pastor's hair like a handle. "You've been found unfit for society." He squeezed and his arm tensed as he hauled the pastor off the ground. The pastor's neck stretched long, and Steele swung with all his might. "Rah!"

The blade cleaved halfway through the pastor's extended neck. What blood remained found an easier path to escape, squirting into the fresh powder. Wide eyes and trembling lips took over the pastor's face. Steele swung again harder with the rage of injustice. The blade broke through bones in his neck, fragmenting them. The pastor's mouth stayed ajar. Steele swung again a third time, cutting through the last of the muscle and tendon holding the man's head on his body. Steele held the long-faced head high in the air. Streams of crimson escaped from the pastor's jaggedly hewed neck, pooling in the snow.

Peter sobbed on the ground nearby. Townsmen and women from Hacklebarney led captured Chosen toward the center of the camp. Red Clare and Margie had the remains of the War Machines in a collective. A host of camouflaged soldiers held weapons in their hands, bug-eyed Major Ludlow at their front.

"This didn't have to be this way," Steele screamed at them. "We could have been united against this threat, and now we are broken. Never again. You are either for us or against us." He stared at them angrily. "If you are against us then you die." He took the pastor's head and tossed it through the air.

The head floated end over end until it landed on the mass of burning bodies. The mouth opened and closed one last time, eyes staring blankly. Its skin blackened around his ears, hair burning atop his head. The eyes shut and it was engulfed by the fiery inferno.

JOSEPH
Cheyenne Mountain Complex, CO

Joseph drove toward the tunnel light slowly so he wouldn't draw any unnecessary attention. A convoy of two-and-a-half ton green military trucks drove the opposite direction into the mountain base.

Byrnes eyed each one, cradling his M4 carbine with the unfamiliar nervousness of a man who hadn't handled a long gun in years, but his muscles held the memories somewhere inside.

The light grew brighter and brighter as they neared the outside, the dim winter sun needing little strength to penetrate the tunnel's darkness. White carpeted the ground, surprising Joseph. It didn't seem possible that months had passed since he'd reached the Cheyenne Mountain Complex. The brightness of the outdoors stung his eyes, causing him to squint, and he'd almost forgotten the beauty of the mountainous countryside.

Joseph whispered, "It's been so long."

Byrnes covered his eyes with the back of his hand. "I know." He busied himself straightening his uniform and wiping whatever dirt and grime that came from being captive inside a cave cell. He ran a hand through his hair atop his head leaving it straighter than a moment before.

"Everyone stay quiet," Byrnes said.

People shifted in the back and then lay still.

Joseph brought the van to a rolling halt at the guard post. An airman stepped out of a white guard shack. The cold had made his cheeks rosy and he wore a knit cap along with gloves. He walked over to the window rubbing his hands.

"IDs?"

Joseph held up his personal ID card. The guard skimmed it quick then eyed Byrnes.

"ID, sir?"

Byrnes fumbled with his ID card stolen from the soldier.

The sentry took it with a nod. "Give me second, gentlemen." He disappeared back into his tiny post, hardly enough for two men. He picked up a black phone and put it to his ear.

Joseph's voice came out quiet but harsh. "What are we going to do?"

Byrnes scrutinized the guard in his post, his eyes glinting with an uncharacteristic danger. The airman turned and studied them, speaking into the mouthpiece.

"I don't like the way he's looking at us," Joseph said.

Byrnes continued to study the airman, his hands on his gun. The airman hung up and walked back from the booth. He ducked his head looking inside.

"Where are you headed today?"

"We're headed to Peterson for a medical briefing."

The airman smiled and nodded. He motioned out at the mountain roads. "There's only a few main roads plowed. You'll want to avoid any others. Blizzards really got us bogged down. If you get stuck in this thing, it'll be awhile before anyone can get to you. Lower manpower than usual."

The phone in his booth started to ring. The sentry turned to look back. Joseph stifled his fear, watching the phone vibrate in the booth.

The guard took a step back and waved them onward. "Have a good day."

Joseph gassed it a little too much and the wheels spun. He glanced in the rearview mirror, and the guard stood in the middle of the road watching them depart. The thruways had been plowed and salted from the complex to the interior Golden Triangle.

They winded down the mountain roadway, picking up speed as they went. Humvees drove past them going the other way. Joseph eyed them in his mirror; each foot they went in the opposing direction eased his anxiety the tiniest fraction.

"Turn here," Byrnes ordered. Joseph hooked the van off the man roadway. The snowfall hadn't been addressed recently on the side street. The van's wheels skipped and slid until they found their place inside the track marks left by other trucks. The van weaved its way down the residential lane.

"Left," Byrnes said.

Joseph turned and they drove on.

Desai and the others sat up in the back.

"Did we make it?" she said softly.

"Long way to go," the colonel said. He pointed out their next turn. Joseph took that too. He thought his anxiety would subside with every turn and mile put between them and the mountain, but it didn't. Something deeper than self-preservation dug at his insides like a wicked mole. *Am I doing the right thing? The work is back the other way, not out here. Don't I have an obligation not just to my team but to mankind as a whole?*

It was a daunting thought, but he knew their work would save lives and give Americans a chance to fight back. The infected could still kill a vaccinated person, but infection rates would decrease dramatically. Despite their efforts, there wasn't enough produced. The nation needed so much more. One for every person left in this dying country. If he had his way, one for every single person left on the planet. It wasn't just something he wanted to do. It was something that he felt in the pit of his gut. The testing. The death. The sacrifice. The murder. Everything that had been done in the name of science to get them to this point.

Joseph switched his foot off the gas and let it depress the brake. The vehicle rolled then slid a few feet to a stop.

"What are you doing?" Byrnes said. Being so close to escape when death loomed, he twisted his face in anger. He spun in his seat, weighing the threat out the back of the van.

Desai hand jostled him for attention. "What are you doing?"

Joseph let his chin drop and slowly shook his head. "No." His glasses slipped on his nose and he adjusted them back into place.

"What do you mean no? We're in it. Thick," Byrnes said. "Doctor. Drive this van."

Joseph released his hold on the steering wheel, staring at the snow-laden housing development, almost a romantic winter scene aside from the whole end of the world bit. "No. I'm going back."

"By God, you're not. Drive this car. Now!"

His hands settled comfortably in his lap. "I can't. I have to go back."

"We don't have time for this." The dour man eyeballed Joseph. "Why?"

"We need more of the vaccine. People need this. They cannot replicate what we were doing. Without us, there is no vaccine."

"We will set up a new lab."

"All of our research and stockpiles are back there. That will take forever to replicate without our research. You know this, Byrnes. Someone has to go back."

"They should have thought about that before they started murdering us."

"I know. You go. This is something I have to do. I'm not a brave man, but someone needs to continue the production and hope that it gets to the people."

Byrnes sighed heavily. "I can't go back. I'm in too deep. The Sons and Daughters need me out here."

"I understand that, but this is my purpose. This is why I fight. That vaccine is our future. It could be the only thing between us and annihilation."

"Doesn't mean much under a dictatorship."

"That isn't my battle."

Byrnes put a hand on his arm. "I can't say what they'll do to you if you go back."

"Neither can I. It's a risk I'm willing to take."

"You won't get another chance to escape."

"I know. Good luck, friend." Joseph stuck out his hand and Byrnes took it.

"And to you. The Sons and Daughters will look for you when the time comes."

A grim smile formed on Joseph's lips. "I know you will."

He opened the door and cold blasted him. Byrnes hopped out and ran to the other side.

"Wait!"

The van door rolled open and Dr. Desai jumped into the layered powder. She closed the door and the van's wheels spun as it picked up traction throwing compressed snow into the air. It drove away, disappearing down another residential street.

He put an arm around her, and she held herself with her own arms. They struggled back to a main road, high-stepping over the tightly packed snow. Trucks and Humvees, even an MRAP, passed by them before anyone stopped.

They didn't bother to handcuff them, only led them to the backseat of a Humvee like scolded children caught running away from their parents. Joseph and Desai went willingly. Nothing needed to be spoken. They had aided and abetted the escape of thirteen political and military prisoners, surely something that could be punishable by indefinite imprisonment or even death. Who was he if he didn't try to produce more of the vaccine? His cause wasn't political or military or monetary. It was humanitarian. He wouldn't say he was above those things, but if he had to put himself at the mercy of a dictatorship to accomplish a worthy goal, then he would sacrifice himself for it.

They rode in silence. The winding mountain road twisted like a slithering snake back to the Cheyenne Mountain Complex. Trees stuck out of the mountain, the pines providing the only green in a field of chalky white. The tunnel entrance loomed ahead of them, a mountain giant opening its massive mouth to swallow them whole.

The Humvee slowed at the guard shack, and he waved them by. The mountain mouth engulfed them, and once again, they were shrouded in the darkness of the governmental complex's underbelly. The lights faded behind them as Dr. Desai studied Joseph with dark eyes. She offered her hand and gripped his. Their hold was tight on one another. He knew this was only the beginning of a long brutal struggle.

STEELE
Camp Forge, IA

He marched to the flagpole. The black-smoke-laced snowstorm shrouded the flag. Frozen fingers reeled the flag down the pole and ripped it off its metal brackets. Steele's blood and the pastor's blood stained the Stars and Stripes.

"You swear loyalty here and now. We do this together." In a fist, he held up the Stars and Stripes for all to see.

"I swear to you all here. I will defend your lives against all threats. I will do everything in my power to ensure that we survive the coming battles. I swear it on the symbol that we've all held dear and my loyalty to this cause."

He gripped his tomahawk, pointing it at Peter. "What say you? Can you commit to these people? Can you commit to fight for our lives?"

He commanded the man upright with the blade of his tomahawk.

"We swear to this flag to see this through to the end. United as a single people fighting for a single cause. No more Chosen. No more Sable Point. Just one people." He leveled his tomahawk at the rabble, letting it waver over individuals in the crowd. "You swear it here and now over everything else or meet your fate." Steele aimed his tomahawk at the broad-shouldered curly-haired man.

"You're first. Swear it or join your master."

Peter stood, his hands and clothes stained with the blood of his beloved leader. He brought himself level with Steele. His eyes darted downward. His voice came out as a whisper. "I swear it."

Steele used the head of his hawk to lift the beaten man's chin. "What do you swear?"

Peter spoke with more conviction. "I swear to protect the survival of these people."

"And to fight for us to the end?"

His blue eyes hardened. "And to fight for you until the end."

Steele let the blade of his tomahawk leave the man's neck.

"Bring me the next man."

Men shoved War Child before him. The elder biker president breathed hard, blood weeping from a wound in his shoulder. Nathan handed Steele a handgun in a worn leather shoulder harness. Steele slid it from the holster. It was a classic piece. The metal along the slide had been worn dull from being shoved in and out of a holster and the brown grip faded from sweat and wear.

"He had it on him."

Steele flipped the Colt .45 1911 to the other side, inspecting the weapon.

"This was Tess's." It wasn't a question, but a statement.

The War Machine president peered at him and sneered. "She wasn't going to need it where she was going."

Steele nodded in grim acceptance of his friend's death. Anger lurched in his gut. He battered it deep down inside him. "What do you have to say?"

The white-haired man sneered. "Should have put a bullet in your head a long time ago."

"Then I condemn you to death for the murder of Tess." He stopped for a moment, collecting himself and realizing he didn't even know her last name. He shoved her weapon back into its harness and handed it to Margie behind him. Using his tomahawk, he gestured to his men to hold the prisoner.

The biker spit on the bloodied brown slush in front of him.

Steele nodded to Nathan and Gregor. They pushed the man down to his knees.

"Do you have any last words?"

War Child's eyes searched the bedraggled people before him. His voice grew in volume. "He's too weak for this world. He doesn't have what it takes to see us through the coming storm."

Steele's mouth formed a mean flat line. "That all you got?"

"I'd do it again." The old biker nodded his head and bent his neck, whipping his ponytail out of the way.

Steele stared at the back of War Child's weathered neck. He positioned himself on his flank and gripped and readjusted his hand on his melee weapon handle. His eyes never left the slightly tan skin of War Child's exposed neck. The tomahawk moved in a blur.

The blade of his tomahawk head bit into the flesh and bone alike. It severed muscle and tendon, and the split in his skin instantly became crimson.

War Child slumped forward in the arms of his captors. He gurgled and groaned with the trauma to his spine, his jaw working, but only blood spewing forth. His body jerked, but his head hung limply, incapable of resistance. The tomahawk blurred through the air again. The blade sunk deeper into his neck like a red sapling. Steele tugged his weapon free and swung again. Gore flew with each swing. He lost count as he butchered the traitor, each swing severing more of War Child from his body.

The old biker's head thunked into the snow, rolling in the powdery layer. The flurries covered everything in fluff, as if the sky tried to mask the gruesome violence of mankind.

Steele bent down and grasped War Child's ponytail, hefting his head into the air. He lifted it high and tossed his head in the fire. The flames lapped his skin, blackening the edges first, using it as fuel to engulf the entire thing. Gregor and Nathan dragged the headless body back to the fire and heaved him in.

"Bring me the next one."

GWEN
Camp Forge, IA

One by one, Steele administered justice to the traitors. She watched in utter misery. Both of her grandparents were gone. John and Lydia Reynolds had been taken in the single bomb blast along with a woman who had become a friend, Tess. The blood spilt in the snow did nothing to quench the thirst of loss.

Worse, the temperature had dropped almost fifteen degrees over the course of the morning. The night would be worse as more people would be crammed together in the barns and cabins.

"Next," Steele said.

A man in riding leathers covered in patches was brought before him. She didn't know his name. His captors shoved the War Machine to his knees. Steele placed the blood-soaked American flag in the man's face. A flag that was stained with the blood of patriots and traitors alike.

"Do you swear on this flag to protect these people and unite for survival?"

The biker stared at the melted crimson slop in front of him where over a hundred men had already been executed as traitors. He stayed silent.

After the first few executions, Steele had instructed his men to get a charred bench from the farmhouse to lean the traitors over, exposing their head and neck. Gregor and Nathan pushed the biker's body over the bench, holding his arms back.

Steele held a wood axe now, having found his tomahawk a less than optimal tool for execution. "Your choice has been made. Any last words?" He stood on the prisoner's flank, both hands on the axe, watching the man.

The biker turned his head to the side. His words came out hurried and forced. "War Machines for life."

"So be it."

Steele stood back. Raising his arms, he swung down with controlled ferocity. The wet slap of the axe blade sinking into the man's flesh made her want to gag, and she turned away. She retreated through the open doors of the Sable Point barn.

Bullet holes peppered the sides of the barn like a giant woodpecker had gone mad and pecked hundreds of holes. The fire at the center of the barn had been remade. Shocked and miserable people sat around it. They were quiet but for the crying. A little blonde girl stood staring at the flames, her arms loosely holding a little boy.

Gwen wrapped her arms around Char's shoulders. She wheeled the girl and boy away from the grisly scene of apocalyptic justice before them. Gwen wiped Char's hair. "It's going to be okay."

Char pouted, angrily looking at her. "Do you know how many times Harriet said that? Do you know how many times my parents said that? Do you know where they are now? All of them?"

Gwen opened her mouth and closed it. "I do. They're dead." Harriet had been hit with a bullet when the Chosen men had raided the barn. Her body lay outside, hole in her chest, in a line of corpses with the rest. Hank was gone. Trent was gone. Tess was gone. So many lives snuffed out because of men's desire for power.

Char's lip quivered. "They all said it was going to be all right, and it got them killed. So quit saying shit that isn't true."

"You're right." Gwen bit her lip. "I won't bullshit. You're old enough. You've seen enough." She nodded. "I have no idea. We will probably die, but in order to keep living, you have to have hope that something you do will make a difference. So we fight." Gwen touched Char's face. "Fight for Freddy. Hope that tomorrow is better."

Char pulled her face away and Gwen released her. Becky and Haley sat nearby.

Haley stared at a burnt checkerboard and moved a piece. Her arm in a makeshift sling. Dutch and Rocky sat smushed around the girl, watching every person with interest. They mirrored the people around them in sadness.

"How is she doing?" Gwen asked softly. She knew the things these young people had seen in the last few hours would haunt them forever. The young were fragile. They didn't have the mechanisms in place to understand why death danced about them, stealing people left and right.

Becky glanced at her shaky cigarette in hand, tears in her eyes, her body still covered in ashy gray soot. Her mouth opened but closed instead around her cigarette, and she inhaled, lighting the tiny ember on the end of the white stick. Her voice came out like a whisper. "I'm not sure I'm ready to talk about it."

Gwen put her arms around Becky. Both women smelled like they'd rolled through a fire pit for two weeks straight. Gwen whispered to Becky. "I miss them so much already."

"Me too." She didn't know how long they sat head to head watching Haley play checkers against herself. Her tiny fingers slid pieces of melted and burnt red and black checkers back and forth.

The little girl looked back at them. "Where's grandpa?"

Gwen swallowed hard. "He's gone, sweetie." Her breath caught in her chest. "He's gonna be gone for a long time."

Haley's eyes didn't leave the game. "Why?"

"He had to go. Him and Grams." She reached across the board and wiped the young girl's dirty face. "But we'll see him again."

"I'll leave the board setup so we can play when he gets back."

Gwen gulped. "Just play, baby. You can set it back up when him and grandma get back."

Struggling to keep her breath inside without breaking down and crying all over again, Gwen studied the wood ceiling of the barn. Becky rested her head on Gwen's shoulder, and they sat in silence watching Haley play checkers.

AHMED
Missouri-Iowa border

"The People of Iowa Welcome You: Fields of Opportunities." Four miles back, the convoy of trucks and horses had passed a sign that said this. They hadn't seen any people or opportunities since entering the state except for the roadblock ahead of them near a casting metal factory. Dead littered the roadway. Exploded skulls and dead bodies were piled upon one another. The stench was fierce, even with the cold to keep it down.

A man's voice boomed through a bullhorn. "You've come close enough. State your purpose!"

Ahmed opened the door of the pickup and got out, holding his hands in the air. Moments later he was joined by Jim.

"Who the hell are these guys?"

"I dunno, militia? They don't look like military."

Jim skimmed the people behind them. They were the remains of the Singleton and Bailey families with a smattering of Stantons and Foxworths and a few Carlyles on the Bailey side. Almost a hundred people when they'd dug them out of their homes. After the families had tried one last time to go to war with one another over the death of the Bailey patriarch Sly, they'd come together. They'd unified over the words of Jes, Jim, and Sadie and under the vigilante justice of the captured Wolf Riders.

With the death of Macleod and the assault on the mine, most of the Wolf Riders fled the area. Those that stayed were captured and the Missourians

395

administered their own justice with a rope and oak tree under the watchful eye of Deputy Vance, who could do nothing except sanction the executions.

"Let's go talk to them." Ahmed pulled his bat out of the car, leaving his shotgun.

"No guns?" Jim asked.

"Nah, just gonna talk."

"What if they're bad?"

"Then we're at their mercy."

Jim narrowed his eyes and tucked a handgun into the small of his back. "You can be at their mercy. I'll be ready."

The two men strolled forward, Ahmed limping. They weaved around and stepped over the fallen bodies in the snow. An infected clawed the white powder, slowly crawling toward the roadblock. Ahmed put a boot on its back, holding it still.

Jim stopped, eyeing the infected. "You ever play golf?"

Ahmed gave it a golf-style swing thwacking the side of its skull inward. Its arms quit working and it laid still. "Nah, never had the patience."

The two men ranged closer to the barricade beneath the violent gaze of gun barrels until a voice called to them, bringing them to a halt. "That's far enough, you two." The speaker's head poked out over the barrier. A winter skull cap covered his head. "What do you want?"

Ahmed leaned on his bat to take the pressure off his damaged leg. "We're headed to Hacklebarney."

"What you want up there?"

The response to this would answer whether or not these men were allied forces or enemies. The answer would grant them a slightly longer life on the frozen earth or certain death facedown in the snow, no better than the infected Ahmed had destroyed moments before.

"I'm looking for somebody. More like a group."

"Who's that?"

Ahmed shared a look with Jim. Jim gave him a cocky grin, his hand resting on the side of his belt.

"I'm looking for a man, Mark Steele, or a Gwen Reynolds."

The head disappeared while the other men continued to point guns at them, and when it reappeared, Ahmed thought he saw the barrel of the gun trained on him. His heart skipped a beat. He tensed his muscles, flexing for action. *How many lives do I have? Can I survive this if they start shooting?* A man jogged off in the direction of the factory. Ahmed eyed him as he ran.

The head reappeared. "Sounds like you're looking for Camp Forge."

Ahmed squinted. "Camp Forge? What's that?"

"That's Captain Steele's base. This is Outpost Victory."

Ahmed mouthed the words. Captain Steele? Outpost Victory?

"He's got a base?"

"Yeah, he's our commanding officer."

"I'm sorry you must be thinking about somebody else. We will be on our way. Can we trust you to not put a bullet in our backs?"

"Sure."

Ahmed and Jim turned away. More men jogged back from the factory. One was decked out in a military-style vest with a long gun slung over his chest. He had another man in full military camouflage. Either he'd stolen it or was a remainder of some overrun unit.

Ahmed eyed them, quickening his pace.

"More are coming," Jim said, turning toward the running men.

"Get those trucks turned!" Ahmed pointed at the lead pickup in his group. People scrambled to obey him.

"Wait!" the man shouted.

The unlikely duo stopped. "I ain't running nowhere," Ahmed said.

Jim shrugged his shoulders. "You know me. Not much of a runner."

"Or a talker."

"Or a talker."

Yells carried from the gate and it rolled open. Ahmed turned around. The two camouflaged military men walked through. "Who are you?" They cautiously crossed the open road avoiding the bodies. Ahmed and Jim started walking back to the barricade.

"I am Ahmed, and this is Jim Singleton."

Both men appeared under stress ready to go hot at any moment. The taller of the two shouted back. "How do you know Captain Steele?"

"I was with him in D.C."

The two soldiers exchanged glances. "D.C.? Not Michigan?"

"Well, both. I've been with him since the beginning."

"Where in Michigan?" the older man asked.

"We were at Little Sable Point and then Pentwater."

"Your base was at a dam there?"

Ahmed shook his head confused. "No, it was a lighthouse."

The man nodded and smiled. "You do know him."

"That's what I said."

The man walked closer and stuck out a hand to Ahmed. "Van Fogerty. I am the militia commander of Outpost Victory. Sorry for the rude introduction. We've had some difficulties the past few days. Why don't you bring your people inside? It's warm and secure."

Ahmed exhaled, taking the man's hand. "Sounds like a good idea."

"We'll talk more inside."

"So this friend of yours is some sort of military leader?" Jim asked as they returned to their vehicle.

"Well, he was in charge but nothing formal."

"Those guys were talking about U.S. Military," Jim said excitedly. "Been a long time since we seen or heard from our boys."

"We heard a bit too much from them over the last few months."

"Really? We ain't heard shit."

"They weren't the nice kind of military."

"Hmm." Jim turned to the convoy waving his hand in a circle. "We're going inside."

***

"He defeated Colonel Jackson?" Ahmed asked.

Two soldiers, Van, Ahmed, Jim, and Sadie stood in a small conference room. Van nodded his head slowly. "These men here joined Steele from Jackson."

Over a month ago, these same men were trying to gun him down. The thought put an uneasy feeling in his gut. They appeared regular enough. Men roughly his age with enough dark circles around their eyes that Ahmed felt they knew each other well.

"We are under Colonel Kinnick in Operation Homefront."

Ahmed shook his head. "I can't believe this. Steele is in charge of the defense of southern Iowa."

"That's correct. He sent me and a hundred militia with military advisors to build up this outpost. There's a problem though."

"What's that?"

Van shared a glance with his military advisor. "We haven't heard anything in days."

"No communications?"

"Nothing on the radio or in person."

"Not just that."

The sergeant nodded. "We're starting to see hordes of Zulus coming through. Almost twenty times the regular number and they're coming from the north."

"Hordes?"

"Dead in the hundreds even thousands. They almost caught us the first night."

"No comms and lots of infected. That don't sound good," Jim said.

The sergeant nodded. "No, it doesn't."

Van spoke, "We've had contact with the colonel. He's lost comms with other units north."

"I'll lead a group north and reestablish communications with Camp Forge," Ahmed said.

Van traded looks with his sergeant. "I'm not sure that's a great idea. You'd be taking all those people into immediate danger."

"I must link with him and these people go with me."

Jim nodded. "We do."

Van ran a hand through his silver hair. "All right. I need you to take this radio. On the off chance that it's just his comms, this will get them back on track. But boys, if it was a bad comm, I would expect Steele to already be here or sending a boat down river."

"Does the river freeze?"

Van shook his head, his kind eyes worrying. "Not that I can ever remember."

"We will be moving north then to Camp Forge."

"Keep me posted on what's happening. I hate operating blind out here. Just feels like the walls are closing in."

"When doesn't it?"

Van laughed. "Give my best to my family. I'll be rotating out of here soon enough."

"I will."

"Safe travels."

Ahmed knew that his travels would be anything but safe, but neither was stealing back home. There was always the chance they could throw you out in the process, but that made the steal that much better.

He stared at Sadie for a moment. Her muddy-brown hair stuck out from under her winter hat, laying on her shoulders. She gave him a soft smile, a bit unsure but mostly caring along with a fraction of hope, and all of it was for him. He had everything he needed to survive this world. His bat, his girl, all he needed was home. "Let's steal home."

ALVARADO
La Crescent, MN

Her body was afire. Like she'd been plopped into a furnace and left to incinerate.

Flashes of the dead surrounding her Marines replayed over and over in a cinematic nightmare, ruling over her level of consciousness. Ice, wind, and snow swirled around the edges.

"River...frozen," she mumbled. Trying to sit up, she found herself trapped and unable to stand. She fought blindly, and the darkness stole her fight from her.

Her mind came and went as she traveled across planes of her existence. Faces of the Marines she'd left behind came and then faded into oblivion. They joined the Marines she'd left on the river. It was as if she dreamt a hundred dreams at the same time, each one overlapping with the last.

She awoke and blinked her eyes into focus. A broad-faced man with ears like bat wings leaned near her. His face was simple and his jaw thick, like a person she could trust to carry a couch or rip the arms off a burglar, but he was more than that. An ugly face that she immediately recognized.

"Captain Heath?" She closed her eyes and opened them again.

A wide smile split his lips, and it seemed unnatural for him. His voice rumbled, "Major Alvarado. Welcome back to the land of the living."

She gave a weak snort and managed to mutter the only thing in her foggy mind that her body screamed for, "Water."

"Yes, ma'am." He disappeared and reappeared holding a water bottle to her lips. She eagerly swallowed as fast as she could. The cool liquid flowed down her scratched and fiery throat.

"Should have known better than to doubt you," he said, taking the bottle back. "You were blue when we found you. Not just any shade, but navy blue. Thought you went squid on us."

"God, Captain. That bad?" Her head pounded and she pushed herself up.

"Stiff as a board too."

She glanced around the room. "Where am I?" Small desks and a green chalkboard hung on the far wall. Little cubbies for shoes and books lined the other wall.

"La Crescent Elementary, ma'am."

She sat up with her legs crossed for a moment. "What are you doing here, Captain? You are supposed to be in the south."

He handed her the water bottle.

She took the bottle. It crinkled having been refilled too many times. "Thank you."

He took a seat in a small chair that he made look even smaller with his mammoth frame. He scooted closer to her. "When we lost comms, I moved men north to find out the cause. I chose to lead the company."

"Tired of sitting in outpost?" she said with a smirk. This massive Marine would do anything to get into the fight. Her left hand was in a hard splint. She wiggled her fingers, and the swollen appendages fired back at her with bloated pain. Her body felt like she'd been to hell and back while being dragged behind a team of demon horses. Every single muscle in her felt torn, every bone bruised, and every ligament ripped.

"Ma'am, you know I'm not one to sit."

She grimaced as she pushed herself off the classroom floor. He offered her a hand. She shook her head no, forcing herself to her feet. For a moment, the cold made her self-aware that she only had a tank top covering her nakedness. Her skin prickled with the frigid onslaught. The situation wasn't normal with a subordinate no matter how much she liked the man.

Heath handed over her shirt and jacket. "It's cold in here."

"Thank you, Captain." She turned away and pulled the clothes on. The warmth was almost instantaneous. She looked over her shoulder. "Has word gotten to Colonel Kinnick about the dead crossing?"

Heath nodded. "I brought a backup comm. Your unit is reconnected to command." He watched her as she smoothed her combat uniform.

She raised an eyebrow at him. "Captain, you are staring." Her side was already darkening with the storm of a bruise.

"Ma'am, it's not that."

She didn't doubt the man, but she was still a woman. A woman with no kids or husband, she was married to the Corps, but in these times, she wouldn't put it past any man to sneak a peek at a woman if it was just to remember what they were fighting for. Even her best male Marines were still made of flesh and brawn. At their most basic biological level, they were still men. "What is it then?"

"It's what you did here."

She stood shakily, every muscle screaming defiance. "What have I done? Where's Captain Butler?"

"He's in the next room." He shook his head. "Major, you stopped them. You destroyed the ice. This section of the river is secure. I sent word to my Marines already to keep tabs on their sections of river. We have civilian militia assisting us in scouting potential ice jam points."

"Somebody would have figured it out once they came across farther south."

"I have no doubt that you're one of the only ones that could have done it after the fact."

"Nine Marines sacrificed their lives for that endeavor."

"It was only six. Two Marines and a wounded sergeant made it back. And it could have been hundreds. Hell, could have been thousands of civilians that died because of this ice bridge. It could have been the rest of the nation." He stopped speaking for a moment. "You and those men prevented that."

Her jaw tightened and a grim smile touched her lips. "I'm glad they survived." Her mind didn't stay on her Marines' survival for long. She had only bought time in a never-ending war. "Show me to Butler."

He held out a calming hand. "You should rest."

"You can rest when you're dead."

She marched out the door past him. Marines smiled at her as they walked by. "Majors" and "Ma'ams" were said as she passed.

The door was open to the room holding Butler, Wess, and Riddle. A shit-eating grin crossed Riddle's face, and the corner of her mouth lifted just a fraction. She was going to have to keep her emotions, joy or otherwise, in check.

"Mad Isabel the pit bull herself!"

"Sergeant. Your familiarity is uncalled for," Butler said with a scowl.

Riddle's smile hardly faded despite his commander's rebuke.

She held up a hand. "Captain. It's fine."

Butler didn't look convinced but did not object.

"Sergeant, I'm glad to see you in one piece."

He leaned against a chair. The medics had set his leg with a makeshift walking boot.

"I ain't running anywhere, but I ain't crawling neither."

"Good to see." She faced Butler. "What's our sitrep?"

Butler took in a deep breath. "Much better than it was. The ice bridge is broken here. Captain Heath's men are making sure any sections near them are staying broken apart." He shook his head. "A lot of dead got across. Caused plenty of chaos."

"Any number on that?"

"I'd say roughly ten thousand."

She shook her head. "Too many."

"Well, we aren't in the heavy population areas either. We were able to destroy some of them as they crossed, but others passed on by to the north and south of our position. The line is stabilizing here, but people in the interior might have a rude awakening."

"I understand. You've gotten word to the southern outposts?"

Butler walked over to the wall. A radio sat on top of a short and stout table made for elementary school students. "Our AN/PRC-158 was destroyed. We have this comm. We've gotten word to Captain Heath's outpost; however, they are reporting that Camp Forge has gone dark."

"Kinnick knows this?"

"He does, ma'am. He's saying to hold tight while they figure out what's happened."

"So we don't know if the line has held?"

"We know south of St. Louis is holding. Our breakthrough here is contained, but the southern Iowa AOR is nonresponsive."

"We were supposed to receive reserve units from them almost a week ago. Captain Steele communicated he sent units, but they haven't arrived."

Jesus Christ help us. "We can't catch a break."

Butler shook his head. "No, ma'am."

"Spring can't come soon enough." She stood for a minute, breathing in the dusty air. When you didn't have the numbers, the men, the supplies, or the support, you had to rely on guts to have a shot, and guts were the only difference between the dead and the living. She knew what needed to be done. "Heath, get your men ready."

Confusion spread on the large Marine's face. "Ma'am? We thought we'd stay and help in reestablishing Outpost Barron. Clear the surrounding area before we travel back."

"Butler can handle clearing the area on his own."

Butler kept his mouth flat. He wouldn't denounce himself as unready or inept. He was neither, but the man could use a spinal recharge to stiffen him up. She supposed that being on the frontline against the dead half of the nation would be enough to shake even the steadiest of soldiers.

"I'm going with Captain Heath back south. We will link with Steele's command and ensure his area of responsibility is secure. This is our line, and by God, we will hold it, not because we want to but because we have to. Those are our orders. So we hold on until the bitter end because we're Devil Dogs, and we don't know a damn thing otherwise." She eyed the Marines in the room. Helmets under arms. Weapons slung over chests. "Oorah, Marines?"

Their voices were filled with grim vigor. "Oorah, Major!"

"Good. Heath, we move as soon as you are ready."

"Yes, ma'am. I'll get them ready." He dipped his chin and walked out of the room.

"I'll brief you before we leave," she said to Butler.

He gave her a slight nod. "Yes, Major."

She walked across the hall to a sunlight filled classroom. She stopped at the window and stared out at the land before her. There were houses down the street. A dead swaggered its way near the building. A gunshot rang out. It collapsed into the packed powder falling face-first, sending up a cloud of dusty white into the air. *Every last one of those dead devils will be destroyed.* For she was a pit bull. She would never let go, never give up, and she would win this war.

GWEN
Camp Forge, IA

A sense of nothingness absorbed the time. Tears fell from eyes. Gwen held Becky, and they took turns rocking Haley when she grew tired of her game. The barn was mostly quiet except for the soft crackle of a fire and sobs of mourning. The barn doors slid open and voices grew louder.

She turned around, looking over her shoulder. He walked inside the barn and people shied away from him, murmuring to one another. An M4 was slung along to his side, and he carried a wood axe in his hand. For a moment, he reminded her of the brute Puck. She stood, brushing her clothes to rid herself of the thought.

With bold steps, he made his way to her. He was horrific to behold. Stained in blood, he could pass for an exhausted Ares, God of War. She cupped his soiled beard in her hands, finding his almost frozen cheeks. His hands fell upon her stomach, the fire in his eyes lessening as he watched her belly.

"It's done. They're loyal or dead." His head shook a bit. "I didn't want this. By God." He closed his eyes for a second. His voice came out shaky at first but then got steadier. "We had to. There's no room for error. We either fight together for a chance or we die."

She caressed his cheeks. "I know, baby." His forehead bent down and rested against hers. "Please tell me you're okay." His hands stroked her stomach. His voice came out surprisingly soft. "The baby?"

407

She tensed her jaw and forcefully closed her eyes. "I don't know. Dr. Miller said that as far as he could tell it's okay, but only time will tell if something happened."

He nodded and licked his lips. "I. Um. I broke some ribs, and I'm going to need some stitches."

She released him. "Jesus. Why didn't you say something earlier?"

"It's not bad." He looked wearily at the ground. "The alternatives were much worse."

"I can do it. Sit over here."

She sat him near Becky, and he hugged her and Haley. He gingerly removed his arms through his shirt, stripping to his bare chest. Gwen grabbed a first-aid kit and sat next to him. His side was already beginning to look like a stormy horizon on a summer day.

"How did this happen?"

"Matthew with his wooden flail."

She brought her hand up to the slice across his chest, navigating through the coarse dark brown hair sticking in the wound. She used her fingers to spread the slash.

He sucked in air. "Mmm. That feels good."

She took out a needle specially made for stitching and surgical thread.

"No locals, so it's going to hurt."

"I know."

She stuck the needle into his skin just below the wound and brought the needle through the laceration and pricked it back through. Drawing the thread back out, she concentrated as she tied the thread into a knot. She could feel his chest tensing beneath her. "Try not to tense."

"It's hard not to." He grimaced. "I'm sorry for what happened." He gazed at her as she worked, his eyes still a little distant. "I should have seen it coming."

"It's not your fault." She gave him a slight dip of her chin and focused on her work. She would not lose him, not after everything they'd been through. She would keep him alive and her child safe. *Please be okay*, she prayed, continuing her repair on the man she loved.

"Ah, Mayor?" Gerald said. He took off his cap and watched her. He looked like he'd been butchering pigs without an apron. Most of the Iowans had stayed to help with what they could, and that boiled down to salvaging shelters and the collection of corpses.

"Yeah," she glanced at him.

"I'm sorry for your loss."

She bent her head down, tying another knot. The fact that her grandparents were gone still didn't feel real. Everything felt fake and hazy like she was viewing it from afar. "Thank you."

"John was a good man, and Lydia a fine woman. We're sure going to miss them."

"Thank you. I am too." The words were foreign in her mouth.

"There's something I think you and Captain Steele should see."

"We'll find you when I'm done patching him up."

Gerald's face crinkled as if he thought better of it. "Maybe now would be better. I just don't want anything sneaking up on us."

"What is it?" Steele asked.

"Infected. Outside."

"Motherfucker," he swore. He snatched up his shirt and jacket, putting both on and stood.

"How many?"

"About twenty."

Steele gingerly slung his M4 over his shoulder and across his body. Gwen felt for her handgun on her hip. Dug out of the rubble of her grandparents' home, it would stay on her hip now and forever.

They charged outside into the smoldering wreckage of Camp Forge to the wails of women and the cries of men mourning the dead and gone.

Their feet dug into the fresh powder coating the blood, soot, and debris from the battle in a soft white. The air was bitterly cold, dropping far below zero degrees. Her breath crystalized in front of her.

Jake stood manning one of the four square sandbag machine gun nests sitting above the walls. He shaded his face from the incoming storm.

Mark climbed the short ladder while Gwen followed, carefully maneuvering the rungs. When she reached the top, the wind howled around them, sounding like a dozen packs of wolves circling their prey. Snow swirled as it was thrown into the air by frigid winds.

Gaping mouths of blackened teeth growled endless streams of moans in her direction. Hands with chipped and broken nails raked the bark-less wooden logs of the fortifications. A few wore camouflage and still had the pinkish skin of recently killed men, but most were dark and gray, full of rot and ruin.

"That's more than we've seen in a long time."

"More than I've ever seen," Jake said. He pointed the machine gun in their general direction.

"The gunfight and smoke must have drawn them in from the surrounding area. Can you grab a couple guys from Hacklebarney with some long spears or sticks and finish them?"

"No bullets?" Jake asked.

"Save the bullets. Brain 'em the old fashion way."

"I'll take care of it."

Jake's eyes found her, worry stretching on his simple face. "You guys okay?"

Mark reached for him, squeezing his arm. "We'll be okay."

Jake acknowledged him and then eyed her. "I'm sorry."

"It'll be fine." Gwen tried to catch her breath. Her stomach felt like she was falling but would never reach the bottom.

"You've given us a minute to breathe."

Jake nodded his head. "Today's been an ugly day. I suspect the worst day ever seen in these parts." His voice indicated more than the deaths bothered him.

Mark inspected the wooden walls with an eye of scrutiny. "It looks slick. Nobody falls."

A field reached down from the farm to the Mississippi River. The blizzard and gusting winds made the normally easy view of the river a cloud of blowing white.

Jake waved at Gerald below. "Grab Nowlton and brain these from on top the wall."

"Aight." Gerald trudged off in the swelling storm.

Gwen cocked her head to the side. The blizzard was always moving, but there was something additional moving inside the fury of whiteness. She brought her hand to her brow, shading her eyes from the stinging wind and snow flurries. She blinked, squinting her eyes and trying to focus on the movement again.

The wind's moan was subdued and deep across the growing darkness of the day's end. It came from afar and echoed over the dead just beneath them.

"What is it?" Mark asked. He studied her from her periphery.

"I thought I saw something out there."

Mark took another glance. Snow laced his beard, settling as if it'd found a permanent home. His arm found its way around her. "Let's go back inside. Jake and the guys can take care of this. I don't want you coming down with something."

She separated herself from him. "No, wait."

Peering hard, she looked for anything out of the ordinary. A light gray shape surrounded by white moved little by little as if it were a buoy bobbing through a colorless sea. She studied it. It took the shape of a person.

"Somebody's out there." She pointed.

Mark settled his M4 to his shoulder, using his optic to scan the terrain. He lowered his gun, staring at her. "Where?"

Her hand wavered. "There!"

He placed his eye near the optic. "Yeah, I see it. Could be one of ours coming back."

Lighter shapes formed in the blizzard around the first until the field was filled with the outlines of people. Her heart leapt. "Oh no." She grabbed a handful of Mark's sleeve. "Look!"

The gun snapped back to his shoulder scanning the land. An unholy discord of moans joined the howls of the wind, increasing in volume. The shapes turned into a wall of frozen flesh. A gray and frigid slow-moving wall of death.

He let his carbine lower. Sharp air currents buffeted them without mercy, whistling fiercely overhead. She held her breath waiting for his assessment but already knew the answer.

His voice came just above a whisper against the power of the storm. "They're across."

A Message from the Author

Whew! That was an intense ending. Thanks for reading! I hope you enjoyed this installment of The End Time Saga. As you may have gathered, there is another book in the series coming your way, *The Standing*, Book 6 of The End Time Saga. This is scheduled to be the final installment of the series and the grand finale. I just can't wait to get the next novel in your hands! Looking for the rest of **The End Time Saga**?

Vist http://www.amazon.com/gp/product/B07RWF7DSW

The Greene Army Newsletter: Want exclusive updates on new work, contests, patches, artwork, and events where you can meet up with Daniel? An elite few will get a chance to join **Greene's Recon Team**: a crack unit of talented readers ready and able to review advance copies of his books anytime, anywhere with killer precision. Sign up for spam-free Greene Army Newsletter today!

Visit http://www.danielgreenebooks.com/?page_id=7741

Reviews: If you have the time, please consider writing a review. Reviews are important tools that I use to hone my craft. If you do take the time to write a review, I would like to thank you personally for your feedback and support. Don't be afraid to reach out. I love meeting new readers!

You can find me anywhere below.

Facebook Fan Club: *The Greene Army - Daniel Greene Fan Club*
Facebook: *Daniel Greene Books*
Instagram: *Daniel Greene Instagram*
Website: *DanielGreeneBooks.com*
Email: *DanielGreeneBooks@gmail.com*

A special thanks to all those who've contributed to the creation of this novel. A novel is a huge feat and would remain as a file cluttering my desktop without the contributions of so many wonderfully supportive people. This includes my dedicated Alpha Readers, Greene's Recon Team, Greene Army, my editor Lisa, my cover artist Tim, Polgarus formatters, and especially my readers. Without readers, this is an unheard/unread tale. I can't wait to share more stories with you in the future.

About the Author

Daniel Greene is the award-winning author of the growing apocalyptic thriller series The End Time Saga and the historical fiction Northern Wolf series. He is an avid traveler and physical fitness enthusiast with a deep passion for history. He is inspired by the works of George R.R. Martin, Steven Pressfield, Bernard Cornwell, and George Romero. Although a Midwesterner for life, he's lived long enough in Virginia to call it home.

Books by Daniel Greene

The End Time Saga
End Time
The Breaking
The Rising
The Departing
The Holding
The Standing (Coming Soon)

The Gun (Origin Short Story)

Northern Wolf Series
Northern Wolf
Northern Hunt
Northern Blood

Made in the USA
Coppell, TX
24 January 2021